Sebastian wrapped one hand around the bedpost and looked at her with hooded, unreadable eyes. "I wish to speak to you about this engagement of ours. I have had enough of this foolishness."

Dismay swept through her. "You wish to end it so soon, sir?" Prudence floundered for a logical, rational reason that would forestall the inevitable. "What about our investigation?"

"Forget the damned investigation. I am beginning to think that if the matter were put to the test, I would finish a poor second to your interest in conducting investigations."

"I did not mean to imply that you are not also quite interesting, my lord," Prudence said desperately. "Indeed, I have never met a more decidedly *interesting* man."

"*Enough*." He released the bedpost and came toward her with an air of grim intent.

"Sebastian? What are you about?"

"Why don't you apply your intellect to that question, Miss Merryweather? I'm certain you will very quickly arrive at the answer."

He caught hold of her and swung her up into his arms before she realized what he intended. . . .

DANGEROUS

Amanda Quick is a bestselling, award-winning author of contemporary and historical romantic fiction. There are over 20 million copies of her books in print. She feels that the romance novel is a vital and compelling element in the world of women's fiction and adds that something about historical romance, in particular, defines the very word 'romance'. Amanda Quick lives in the North-west of America with her husband, Frank.

DANGEROUS

Amanda Quick

ORION

An Orion paperback
First published in Great Britain in 1995 by Orion,
a division of Orion Books Ltd
Orion House, 5 Upper St Martin's Lane, London WC2H 9EA

Reissued 1996

A CIP catalogue record for this book is available
from the British Library.

Printed and bound in Great Britain by
Clays Ltd, St Ives plc

One

It was the darkest hour of the night, nearly three o'clock in the morning, and the chilling fog clung to the city like a ghost. Prudence Merryweather reluctantly concluded that it was an uncomfortably suitable time and setting in which to pay a call on the man known as the Fallen Angel.

She shivered in spite of her bold resolve as the hackney drew to a halt in front of the mist-shrouded door of the town house. The new gas lamps that had been installed in this part of town were useless against the thick mist. An eerie silence gripped the cold, dark street. The only sounds were the rattle of the carriage and the thud of the horses' hooves on the pavement.

Prudence briefly considered ordering the coachman to turn the hackney around and drive her straight home. But she banished the thought as quickly as it had come. She knew she must not falter now. Her brother's life was at stake.

She summoned up her courage, adjusted her spectacles more firmly in place, and stepped down from the cab. She tugged the hood of her aging gray wool cloak down to shield her face as she started determinedly up the steps of the town house. Behind her the hackney began to roll forward down the street.

Prudence stopped and whirled around in alarm. "Where do you think you're going, my good man? I said I would give you an extra few coins to wait for me. I'll only be a few minutes."

"Don't fret yerself none, miss. I was just adjustin' the reins, is all." The coachman was a featureless dark blob in his heavily caped greatcoat and a hat that was pulled down low over his ears. His voice was slurred from the gin he had been drinking all evening to ward off the bitter chill. "I told ye, I'd wait for ye."

Prudence relaxed slightly. "See that you're still here when I return. Otherwise I shall be quite stranded when I finish my business."

"Business, huh? Is that what ye call it?" The coachman sniggered as he tipped his gin bottle and poured the contents down his throat. "Pretty fancy piece o' business, if you ask me. Mayhap yer gentleman friend will want ye to warm his bed for the rest o' the night. Bloody damn cold this evenin'."

Prudence scowled at him but decided there was nothing to be gained from engaging in an argument with a drunken coachman at this late hour. She did not have the time for such nonsense.

She gathered the enveloping cloak more tightly about her and hurried on up the steps to the front door of the town house. The upstairs windows were unlit. Perhaps the notorious owner of the house was already abed.

From all accounts that would be an unusual state of affairs. It was said that the legendary Earl of Angelstone seldom went to bed before dawn. The Fallen Angel had not earned his formidable reputation by keeping reasonable hours. Everyone knew the devil preferred the cover of night.

Prudence hesitated before raising her gloved hand to knock on the door. She was well aware that what she was about to do carried a certain risk. She was country bred and new to London, but she was not so naive as to think it was normal for ladies to pay calls on gentlemen at any hour, let alone at three in the morning.

Prudence rapped sharply on the door.

It seemed to take forever until a disgruntled-looking, half-dressed butler opened the door. He was a balding, heavy jawed man who put Prudence in mind of a large, ferocious hound. The candle he held in one hand revealed first annoyance and then growing disgust on his bleak features. He took in the sight of Prudence's cloaked and hooded figure with severely disapproving eyes.

"Yes, miss?"

Prudence took a deep breath. "I have come to call upon his lordship."

"Have you, indeed?" The butler's lip curled into a sneer that would have suited Cerberus, the three-headed dog that was said to guard the entrance to Hades. "I regret to inform you that his lordship is not at home."

"He most certainly is." Prudence knew she must be firm if she was to get past the Fallen Angel's hellhound. "I checked with my sources before making my decision to call upon him. Please inform him immediately that he has a visitor."

"And who should I say is calling?" the butler asked in sepulchral tones.

"A lady."

"Not bloody likely. No *lady* would be here at this hour. Take yourself off, you obnoxious little baggage. His lordship doesn't consort with your sort. If he's in the mood for a bit o' muslin he can look a good deal higher than a strumpet fresh off the streets."

Prudence went hot beneath the insults. This was clearly going to be even more awkward than she had anticipated. She set her teeth. "Be so good as to inform his lordship that a party who has an interest in his forthcoming duel wishes to see him."

The butler stared at her in astonishment. "And what,

pray tell, would a woman of your sort know about his lordship's personal affairs?"

"A great deal more than you do, apparently. If you don't tell Angelstone that he has a caller, I vow you will live to regret it. I assure you that your position in this household depends upon your informing him I am here."

The butler did not appear to be entirely convinced by the threat, but he was starting to waver. "Wait here."

He slammed the door, leaving Prudence standing on the step. The icy fingers of the fog crept close and wrapped themselves around her. She huddled deeper into her cloak. This was turning out to be one of the most miserable evenings she had spent in her entire life. Things had been so much simpler in the country.

The door opened again a moment later. The butler looked down his nose at Prudence and grudgingly indicated she should enter.

"His lordship will see you in the library."

"I should think so." Prudence stepped quickly over the threshold, grateful to escape the clutches of the fog, even if it meant walking into the very jaws of hell.

The butler opened the library door and held it for her. Prudence swept past him into a dark, shadowed room that was lit only by a small blaze on the hearth. The door closed behind her just as she realized there was no sign of Angelstone.

"My lord?" Prudence came to an abrupt halt and peered intently into the gloom. "Sir? Are you here?"

"Good evening, Miss Merryweather. I trust you will forgive my butler's rudeness." Sebastian, Earl of Angelstone, rose slowly from the depths of a huge wing chair that faced the hearth. He had a large black cat tucked under one arm. "You must understand your visit is somewhat unexpected. Especially considering the circumstances and the hour."

"Yes, my lord. I am aware of that." Prudence caught her breath at the sight of him. She had danced with Sebastian earlier that evening, but that was only the first time she had met the Fallen Angel. She realized now it would take more than one or two encounters before she adjusted to the impact he made on her senses.

Angelstone was anything but angelic in either appearance or temperament. It was said in the drawing rooms of the *ton* that he bore a strong resemblance to the Lord of the Underworld. It was true that it would take a formidable imagination to envision him with a pair of wings and a halo.

The firelight flickering behind Sebastian seemed a little too atmospheric tonight. The glow of the flames threw his fierce, saturnine features into harsh relief. His black hair was cut short. His curious, amber eyes blazed with a cold, penetrating intelligence. His body was hard and lean. Prudence knew from her experience with him on the dance floor that Sebastian moved with a lazy, dangerous masculine grace.

He was clearly dressed for the privacy of his own home, not for receiving visitors. His white cravat hung loose around his neck and his ruffled shirt was unfastened far enough to reveal the crisp black hair on his chest. His buff-colored breeches hugged the sinewy lines of his thighs. He had not yet removed his black, mirror-polished Hessians.

Prudence knew very little about style. It was a matter of extremely limited interest to her. But she realized that there was an innate masculine elegance about Sebastian that had little to do with his attire. It was a part of him, just as it was a part of the cat he held.

The only jewelry Sebastian wore was a gold ring on one of his long-fingered hands. It gleamed with a dull sheen as he slowly stroked the cat. Prudence stared at the ring. Earlier, when she had danced with him, she had noted that there was an elaborate letter *F* engraved on it. She had assumed it stood for *Fleetwood,* the earl's family name.

For a moment she could not seem to tear her gaze away from Sebastian's hand as he petted the cat. When she finally managed to meet his eyes again, she saw that he was smiling slightly.

She was startled at the frisson of sensual awareness that rushed through her. She told herself she was simply not accustomed to seeing a man in dishabille. Unfortunately, she'd had the same reaction earlier this evening when Sebastian had been properly attired for the ball.

The man had an enthralling effect on her, Prudence acknowledged. She wondered fleetingly if he was real. Even as she stood there staring at him, Sebastian began to dissolve like a specter into a gray fog.

For a few seconds she was so startled to see him turn into an apparition before her very eyes that she could not think clearly. Then she realized what the problem was.

"I beg your pardon, my lord." Prudence hastily removed her spectacles and wiped off the cloudy mist that had begun to obscure her vision. "It is so very cold outside, you know. When I stepped into this warm room it caused a vapor to form on the lenses. It is one of the annoying problems one faces when one wears spectacles."

Sebastian elevated a black brow. "My sympathies, Miss Merryweather."

"Yes, well, thank you. Not much that can be done about it. One gets used to it." Prudence replaced her spectacles on her nose. She frowned at Sebastian. "I expect you're wondering why I'm here at this rather late hour."

"The question did cross my mind." His gaze skimmed over her old cloak, which had parted slightly to reveal the prim, unfashionable fawn-colored ball gown underneath. Amusement danced briefly in his eyes before it was replaced by a speculative look. "You came alone?"

"Yes, of course." She looked at him in surprise.

"Some people would say that was rather unwise."

"I had to see you alone. I am here on a very private matter."

"I see. Pray be seated."

"Thank you." Prudence smiled a little uncertainly as she perched on the other large chair that faced the fire. She reminded herself that she had liked Angelstone on sight earlier this evening, even though her friend Hester, Lady Pembroke, had been horrified when he'd forced the introduction.

Surely he was not as bad as everyone insisted he was, Prudence told herself as she watched Sebastian settle back into his chair. Her instincts about people were generally very reliable. There had only been that one unfortunate occasion three years ago when she had found herself sadly mistaken about a man.

"This is a trifle awkward, my lord."

"Yes." Sebastian stretched his booted feet out toward the fire and went back to slowly stroking the cat. "It is also a trifle dangerous."

"Nonsense. I have a pistol in my reticule and the coachman who brought me here has agreed to wait for me. I assure you, I shall be quite safe."

"A pistol?" He eyed her with some amusement. "You are a most unusual woman, Miss Merryweather. Did you think you would need the pistol to protect yourself from me?"

"Good heavens, no, my lord." Prudence was genuinely shocked. "You're a gentleman, sir."

"Am I?"

"Of course you are. Pray do not tease me, my lord. I brought the pistol along as protection against footpads. I understand they are very prevalent here in Town."

"Yes. They are."

The cat crouched on Sebastian's lap and gazed at Prudence with an unwinking gaze. It struck her that the beast's eyes were almost the exact same shade of gold as those of its master. She was momentarily distracted by that observation.

"Does your cat have a name, sir?" she asked suddenly.

"Yes."

"What is it?"

The faint smile briefly edged Sebastian's mouth again. "Lucifer."

"Oh." Prudence cleared her throat discreetly. "Yes, well, as I was saying, I am not at all unusual, merely a very ordinary woman who is, unfortunately, new to the ways of Town life."

"I disagree, Miss Merryweather. You are the most unusual woman I have ever met."

"I find that extremely difficult to believe," she said tartly. "Now, then, I seem to have been the cause of some trouble between you and my brother this evening and I wish to put a stop to it at once."

"Trouble?" Sebastian's amber gaze narrowed in speculation. "I am not aware of any trouble between myself and Trevor Merryweather."

"Do not try to fob me off by pretending ignorance of the situation, my lord." Prudence clasped her gloved hands tightly in her lap. "Word has reached me that you and Trevor are to engage in a duel at dawn. I will not have it."

"How do you intend to stop it?" Sebastian watched her with lazy interest.

"As to that, I have researched the subject of duels during the past few hours and have come up with a solution."

"Have you, indeed?"

"Yes. An apology will end this piece of idiocy. As soon as I realized what had to be done, I immediately tracked down Trevor at the Atkinses' soiree and spoke to him first. Unfortunately, he proved to be ridiculously stubborn about the whole thing, even though I could tell he was terrified of what is going to happen at dawn. He is very young, you know."

"Not too young to offer a challenge, apparently."

Prudence shook her head. "He kept saying he had to go through with it because my honor as well as his own is at stake. *My honor.* Can you imagine?"

"That is generally the case in such affairs. Duels would be

unbearably dull for all concerned if there wasn't the issue of a woman's honor involved."

"What rubbish. Allow me to tell you, my lord, that if you actually believe that, you have no more common sense than my brother."

"An unnerving thought."

Prudence ignored the sarcasm. "It's utter nonsense to think that I have been insulted simply because you spoke to me and asked me to dance with you. I was not insulted in the least. I told Trevor as much."

"Thank you."

"The thing is," Prudence said earnestly, "Trevor has felt very protective of me since the death of our parents. He feels that as the man in the family he has certain obligations. He means well, but sometimes he gets carried away with the notion of looking after me. It is ridiculous for him to call you out over such an inconsequential event."

"I'm not entirely certain it was an inconsequential event." Sebastian's elegant fingers moved thoughtfully on the cat. "You and I did have a rather extended conversation at the ball."

"About matters of mutual intellectual interest, nothing more," Prudence said quickly.

"And we did dance the waltz."

"So did a great many other people. Lady Pembroke tells me it is all the rage. Everyone is dancing the waltz these days. Really, Trevor's challenge is beyond belief."

"Not in the eyes of some people."

Prudence bit her lip. "Well, since he has issued the challenge and since I cannot talk him into apologizing to you so that the duel may be properly called off, there is only one solution."

Sebastian's golden eyes met hers. "I am extremely curious to hear your solution, Miss Merryweather."

"It is really quite simple." Prudence gave him a hopeful smile. "You must apologize to him."

Sebastian's hand went very still on the cat. His ebony lashes veiled his gaze. "I beg your pardon?"

"You heard me. You must apologize to him." Prudence leaned forward. "It is the only way, my lord. Trevor is barely twenty, you know. He is nervous and I believe he knows he is in over his head, but he is much too young and too hot-headed to admit that this situation has gotten out of hand."

"Your brother may not feel that it has gotten out of hand. He may be entirely convinced that challenging me was the only proper response under the circumstances."

"Ridiculous. You must try to understand, my lord. Ever since Mama and Papa were killed in a carriage accident two years ago my brother has been attempting to shoulder his responsibilities as the head of the family."

"I see."

"He is at that dreadful age when young men feel things so very intensely. I expect you were young once yourself."

Sebastian gazed at her, clearly fascinated. "Now that you mention it, I believe I was. It was a very long time ago, of course."

Prudence flushed. "I did not mean to imply that you are old now, my lord."

"Thank you."

Prudence gave him an encouraging smile. "Heavens, you are probably not much above forty."

"Thirty-five."

Prudence blinked. "I beg your pardon?"

"I am thirty-five, Miss Merryweather. Not forty."

"Oh. I see." Prudence wondered if she had offended him. She sought to recover whatever ground she had lost. "Well, you certainly have the aspect of the sort of sound maturity one would expect in a much older man, sir."

"Kind of you to say so. Others have said that my face bears the marks of a blighted soul and too much hard living."

Prudence swallowed. "The thing is, my lord, I fear we

must rely on the wisdom and common sense that you have no doubt acquired during the past thirty-five years if we are to put an end to the foolishness of a twenty-year-old boy."

Sebastian studied her for a long moment. "You're serious, aren't you, Miss Merryweather? You actually expect me to apologize to your brother."

"I am quite serious. This is a matter of life and death, my lord. According to my sources, you are an extremely excellent shot." Prudence tightened her clasped hands. "I understand you practice regularly at Manton's and that this will not be your first duel."

"You appear to be remarkably well informed."

"I am very good at investigating things, my lord," Prudence said stiffly. "It is a hobby of mine, as I explained to you earlier this evening."

"So you did. But I was under the impression that your primary interest was the investigation of spectral phenomena."

Prudence glanced at the cat. "It is true that I have specialized in such matters, but I assure you my interests are actually quite wide-ranging. I enjoy finding answers to puzzling questions."

"Do you believe in ghosts, Miss Merryweather?"

"I myself am extremely skeptical on the subject," Prudence admitted. "But many people do believe in ghosts. They often think they have evidence of spectral phenomena. My hobby involves examining that evidence and attempting to find a logical explanation for it."

"I see." Sebastian gazed into the flames on the hearth. "It was because I had heard of your rather unusual hobby that I asked to be introduced to you."

Prudence smiled ruefully. "I am well aware of that, my lord. I realize I am accounted an Original here in Town. You are not the first gentleman who has sought an introduction simply because he was curious about my hobby. Do you have any notion of how irritating it is to be asked to dance merely because one is considered odd?"

"I believe I have some idea," Sebastian said, his tone curiously dry. "The *ton* is always intrigued by the unusual. It reacts like a small child with a new toy. And if it happens to break that toy, it will toss it aside and go on to another bright, glittering object."

"I understand." Prudence's heart sank. Had she actually hoped that he had found her a bit more interesting than a new toy? This was the Fallen Angel, after all. "You are telling me that you asked me to dance because I am the newest of the *ton*'s entertainments. You were merely amusing yourself."

"No." Sebastian watched her with hooded eyes. "I asked you to dance because you intrigued me, Miss Merryweather. It occurred to me that you and I might have some interests in common."

She stared at him in astonishment. "Really, my lord? Are you involved in investigations of spectral phenomena?"

"Not exactly."

"What, then?"

"I don't think it's important at the moment. There are more pressing matters concerning us, are there not?"

"Yes, of course. Your duel with my brother." Prudence pulled herself back to the business at hand. "Then you will apologize to Trevor? I know it will be dreadfully irritating to do so when he is the one in the wrong, but surely you can see that this duel must be stopped."

"It is not my habit to apologize, Miss Merryweather."

She moistened her dry lips. "The thing is, I cannot convince Trevor to do so."

"Then I fear your brother must face the consequences."

Prudence felt her hands go cold. "Sir, I must insist you act the part of a mature, responsible man. Trevor is as new to the ways of Town as I am. He did not know what he was doing when he challenged you."

"You're wrong, Miss Merryweather. Your brother knew precisely what he was doing. He knew who I was and he knew my reputation." Sebastian smiled faintly. "Why do you think he was so outraged over the fact that I asked you to dance?"

Prudence frowned. "I have learned a great deal about your reputation during the past three or four hours, my lord. It seems to me it has been blown out of all proportion to the facts."

Sebastian looked briefly startled. "Do you know the facts, Miss Merryweather?"

"Most of them." She ticked them off rapidly on one gloved hand. "Years ago your father defied his family to run off with an actress. The Fleetwoods were furious. Your parents were forced to leave the country because of the scandal. There were never any announcements of a wedding made, so everyone, including your relatives, assumed your father never actually married your mother."

"That sums up most of my relevant history."

"Not quite. When you returned to England two years ago, the *ton* took great delight in labeling you a bastard."

"So it did." Sebastian looked amused.

"It was very cruel of people to say such things. You were certainly not responsible for the circumstances of your birth."

"You are very understanding, Miss Merryweather."

"It is a matter of common sense. Why should a child be blamed for the actions of his parents? However, as it happens, you were not born out of wedlock at all."

"No."

Prudence eyed him thoughtfully. "For reasons of your own, probably because you found it amusing, you were content to let everyone go on thinking that you had been born on the wrong side of the blanket."

"Let us say I could not be bothered to correct the impression," Sebastian conceded.

"Until your uncle, the old earl, died last year. He had never married, so he left no son to inherit the title. Your father was next in line, but he unfortunately died four years ago and you were presumed to be a bastard. Thus, everyone thought that your cousin Jeremy, whose father also died some time ago, would become the next Earl of Angelstone."

Sebastian smiled and said nothing.

"But," Prudence said, "you confounded the entire social world by producing conclusive proof that your parents had, indeed, been legally married before you were born. You were the legitimate heir to the title. I am told your relatives have never forgiven you."

"A circumstance which does not particularly bother me."

"In addition, at the time you came into the title, you had already made a fortune of your own which cast the Angelstone inheritance into the shade," Prudence said. "That is something else that your relatives do not appreciate."

Sebastian inclined his head briefly. "I compliment you on your investigations, Miss Merryweather. You have learned a great deal about me in a relatively short span of time."

"There was no lack of people willing to gossip about you, my lord."

"There rarely is."

"Your reputation borders on the legendary."

"Perhaps with good reason," Sebastian observed softly.

"It is so formidable, in fact," Prudence continued smoothly, "that it could certainly withstand the few inconsequential remarks that might be made if you were to undertake an apology to my brother."

Sebastian's jaw tightened. Then his eyes gleamed with reluctant admiration. "A telling blow, Miss Merryweather. And very neatly executed, if I may say so."

"Thank you, my lord. I merely pointed out a small truth. You could apologize to my brother and come away with your extraordinary reputation still intact. Those who learn of your act of generosity toward Trevor will view it as a kindness on your part."

"I am not known for being kind, Miss Merryweather."

Prudence smiled encouragingly. "You will be, after word gets out that you refused to meet my brother. Everyone knows that you could have lodged a bullet in him, had you chosen to do so."

"It is an interesting and rather amusing perspective on the situation."

"I'm delighted you understand, my lord. I believe my little scheme will work very well. All you have to do is apologize to Trevor."

Sebastian reflected on that for a moment. "I must confess I do not quite see any clear benefit to myself in all of this."

"You will be spared the inconvenience of a duel at dawn," Prudence pointed out. "Surely that is a great benefit."

"As it happens, I am generally awake at dawn, anyway." Something cold flickered in Sebastian's eyes. "A duel would be no great inconvenience."

Prudence stared at him in shock. Then she thought she detected a devilish amusement in his amber eyes. "My lord, you are teasing me."

"Do you think so?"

"Yes, I do. Surely you can have no great desire to fight a duel with a young, inexperienced boy. You have nothing to prove. Promise me you will end this with an apology before blood is spilled."

"You are asking me to set aside the small matter of my own honor."

"I am asking you to be reasonable."

"Why should I bother to be reasonable?"

Prudence was nearing the end of her patience. "My lord, I must insist you cease acting like a cork-brained idiot. We both know you are too intelligent to want to engage in something as foolish as a duel."

"A cork-brained idiot?"

Prudence flushed. "I apologize, sir, but that is how your behavior appears to me. I expected better of you."

"I am desolate to know that I have not lived up to your expectations. But then, I rarely live up to anyone's expectations. I am surprised you did not learn that in the course of your investigation this evening."

"You enjoy confounding others," Prudence said. "I realize that you undoubtedly feel that you have just cause to carry on in such a manner. It is no doubt your way of getting some revenge on Society for the way it treated you before you assumed your title."

"That's a very magnanimous attitude on your part."

"However," Prudence said very deliberately, "I am asking you to rise above your inclinations in this instance and behave like the generous, responsible, kindhearted man I know you are capable of being."

Wicked laughter briefly lit Sebastian's eyes. "What in the name of the devil makes you think I'm capable of behaving in such a manner?"

Prudence was exasperated. "You are a well-read man with an inquiring mind, sir. I learned that much about you on the dance floor when we discussed my investigations into spectral phenomena. You asked perceptive questions and you displayed a keen intellect. I refuse to believe you cannot behave with some generosity of spirit."

Sebastian rubbed Lucifer's ears while he considered that suggestion. "I suppose it might be a novel experience."

"Just the thing to relieve your boredom." Prudence hesitated and then added gently, "I understand you suffer from ennui."

"Who told you that?"

"Almost everyone," she admitted. "Is it true?"

Sebastian leaned his head against the back of the chair

and gazed at the fire in front of him. His mouth curved without any real humor. "I don't know," he said quietly.

Prudence stared at him. "You don't know what you are feeling?"

He slanted her a strange look. "Much of the time I am not certain that I feel anything at all, Miss Merryweather."

"I experienced a similar sensation for a while after my parents were killed," Prudence said softly.

"Did you?"

"Yes. But I had my brother, Trevor. And Lady Pembroke was very kind. We were all able to comfort each other. My spirits eventually revived."

"That I can well believe." Sebastian's tone was laced with mockery. "You are definitely not without spirit, Miss Merryweather. But the matter of whether or not I suffer from ennui is neither here nor there. Let us return to the subject at hand."

"Yes, of course." She gave him an anxious little smile. "I'm aware that I am asking you to do me a great favor, my lord."

"Very true. Apologies are extremely foreign to my nature. And so is the business of granting favors."

"I'm sure you'll survive the experience."

"That remains to be seen," Sebastian said. "I should perhaps remind you that when one grants a favor, one expects to be able to collect payment in return at some future time."

A fresh flash of alarm went through Prudence. She eyed him warily. "What, exactly, are you suggesting, my lord?"

"Merely that in return for my doing you this favor tonight, you will agree to do one for me should I ever request it."

Prudence held herself very still. "What sort of favor would you expect in return for sparing my brother's life?"

"Who knows? One cannot see into the future, Miss Merryweather. I have no notion now of what sort of boon I might someday require of you."

"I see." She drew her brows together in concern. "But you expect to collect this favor from me at some point?"

Sebastian smiled slowly. His eyes and those of his cat reflected the firelight. "Yes, Miss Merryweather. Someday I shall most definitely collect what is owed to me. Do we have a bargain?"

A dangerous silence settled on the shadowed library. It was broken only by the crackle of the flames on the hearth. Prudence could not look away from Sebastian's steady, unreadable gaze.

She would have to take the chance that her intuition about this man was correct. He might be dangerous, but she did not believe he was evil.

"Very well, my lord," Prudence said quietly. "I will agree to this bargain."

Sebastian studied her for a long while, as if seeking to see beneath the surface, just as she had sought to penetrate his secrets. "I do believe you are a woman who keeps her bargains, Miss Merryweather."

Prudence scowled. "Of course I am."

"You need not be offended. Genuine honor is a rare enough commodity in either men or women."

"If you say so. Does this mean you will apologize to my brother?"

"Yes. I shall see to it that the duel is called off."

Relief poured through her. "Thank you, my lord. I am so very grateful. It is really very good of you to do this."

"Enough, Miss Merryweather. I do not need your thanks. We have struck a bargain, you and I. You will repay me soon enough." Sebastian set the cat down on the carpet.

Lucifer blinked at Prudence in irritation, as if he blamed her for being disturbed from his comfortable position. Then he flicked his tail and strolled off to settle himself onto a red and gold silk pillow.

Sebastian uncoiled from his chair and reached down to

take hold of both of Prudence's hands. He pulled her to her feet.

"My lord?"

He did not reply, but his eyes were banked flames as he drew her close. He bent his head and brought his mouth down on hers.

Sebastian's kiss was a deliberate, calculated statement of sensual intent. Prudence had never received such a kiss in her entire life, yet some part of her recognized it instantly for what it was. A shocking thrill went through her all the way to her toes as she realized that in some indefinable manner, Sebastian was claiming her for his own.

Prudence was stunned.

She trembled. She could hardly breathe. A fierce excitement shimmered within her. Her entire body was suddenly alive with a new, pulsing energy.

The whole thing was over before Prudence could even begin to adjust to the sensual onslaught. She gasped when Sebastian raised his head.

"Now that we have sealed our bargain, Miss Merryweather, it is time you went home."

"Oh, yes. Yes, of course." Prudence struggled to adjust the hood of her cloak with shaking fingers. She told herself she must be as nonchalant as he was. She was five and twenty, not a green girl. "No one will have missed me, however. Lady Pembroke's household is extremely well run and I left distinct instructions when I retired to my bedchamber that I was not to be disturbed."

"How did you get out of the house?"

"Through the kitchens. It was a bit difficult to find a carriage, but I managed. The coachman said he would wait."

"The hackney in which you arrived has already been sent on its way."

Prudence looked up sharply. "It has?"

"Do not concern yourself. I shall see you home, Miss Merryweather."

"That's really quite unnecessary," she said quickly.

"I have already ordered my carriage brought around."

"I see." She could not think of anything else to say.

Sebastian guided Prudence out of the library, into the hall where the hound-faced butler was waiting.

"My coat, Flowers." Sebastian smiled his strange, humorless smile. "By the by, it appears I do not have an appointment at dawn, after all. Please see that breakfast is served at the usual hour."

"Yes, my lord." Flowers cast Prudence a startled, questioning glance as he assisted Sebastian into a black greatcoat. But like the well-trained servant that he was, he said nothing. He opened the front door without another word.

A black carriage horsed with two black stallions waited in the fog. Sebastian handed Prudence up into the cab. Then he climbed in and sat down across from her. The coach lamps cast a fiery glow across his stark, forbidding features. In that moment Prudence had no difficulty understanding why the gossips had given him the title of the Fallen Angel.

"I appreciate your escort, my lord, but this really isn't necessary." Prudence wrapped her old cloak more securely about her as the coach started down the dark street.

"Ah, but it is necessary, Miss Merryweather. You and I are bound by a bargain now. And until I have collected the favor that you owe me, it is in my own best interests to keep you safe." He smiled again. "Have you not heard that the devil looks after his own?"

$\mathcal{T}wo$

$\mathcal{S}$ebastian *waited silently in* the shadows as Prudence opened the back door of Lady Pembroke's elegant town house. He smiled to himself as she paused briefly and lifted a hand in farewell. The lady might not appreciate being labeled an Original, but she most definitely qualified as one.

He had never met anyone like Miss Prudence Merryweather. She was certainly the only other person he had ever encountered whose intellectual curiosity had led her into a hobby that was as unusual as his own.

A most fascinating creature. And now she owed him a favor. Sebastian preferred having people in his debt. It gave him an advantage.

He turned and walked slowly back toward the waiting carriage. In the distance the vehicle's lamps were dim beacons that were barely able to pierce the heavy fog.

Sebastian hated the fog, yet he knew it might be his natural element. *Or his ultimate fate.*

His boot heels rang with a hollow echo on the sidewalk. Cold tendrils of mist ebbed and flowed around him, threatening to trap him forever in an endless gray void. He knew what waited for him in that vast emptiness. It would be a place where there was no sensation at all, not even the feeling of unrelenting cold.

On occasion lately he thought he had caught glimpses of that emptiness waiting behind the icy barrier he had created to protect himself.

He had recognized it as the same gray nothingness that had been waiting for him four years ago at dawn in the mountains of Saragstan.

A small, scraping sound emanating from a nearby alley brought Sebastian's attention instantly back to the present. He paused, listening carefully. His fingers curled around the pistol in his pocket. His instinct for survival was still strong, he noted wryly, in spite of the strange mood that plagued him more and more of late.

The soft, scurrying noise faded quickly. A rat or perhaps a cat, Sebastian thought. He walked on toward the waiting carriage.

It was a dangerous night to be abroad. But then, all nights were times of great risk.

Miss Prudence Merryweather had braved the danger and the darkness to see him, Sebastian reflected. He smiled faintly. She was, indeed, made of sturdy stuff.

Sebastian opened the door of his carriage himself. "To my club," he said to the coachman.

"Aye, m'lord."

The carriage rolled forward. Sebastian leaned back against the cushions, gazed out into the fog, and contemplated Prudence.

She was more than brave; she was headstrong. A decidedly difficult trait in a female. He suspected that not many men could deal with her. She was too intelligent, too fearless, too bold, and too curious for the majority of males. She was also full of lively spirit and a staunch, rather naive faith in the basic goodness of others.

The fact that Prudence was twenty-five and still unmarried was a strong indication that the men she had encountered thus far had either failed to comprehend the subtle feminine challenge she offered or chosen to ignore it. The men must have been blind, Sebastian decided.

Either that or they had been put off by the spectacles which Prudence wore like a battle shield. Sebastian gazed out at the darkened streets and thought about the eyes behind the spectacles. Fantastic eyes. Deep, clear pools of an indescribable shade of green. Intelligent eyes. The eyes of an honest woman, a woman of deep, unshakable integrity. Such eyes made her very much a novelty in Sebastian's world.

There was, he realized, an earnest, thoroughly wholesome quality about Prudence that he found inexplicably enthralling. He thirsted for a taste of her refreshing, invigorating goodness even as he mocked it.

Sitting there in his library lecturing him about his responsibilities, she had made him feel every heavy ounce of the darkness that weighed down his soul. Prudence was a creature of the sunlight and she made him very conscious of the fact that he was a man who dwelt in the deepest shadows of the night.

They were opposites, yet he had wanted her from the moment he was introduced to her. It made no sense. Sebastian wondered why he found himself so captivated by Prudence. For captivated he was.

She was pretty enough, he supposed, although not a great beauty. What physical attributes she possessed, however, were effectively concealed by the effects of what appeared to be a total absence of a sense of style.

Sebastian had been amused by the fawn-colored gown she had worn earlier that evening. The pale brown shade had been distinctly unflattering on Prudence. It had failed to bring out the brilliance of her emerald eyes and it had dulled her honey-colored hair. The demure cut of the high neckline and the brown roses that decorated the skirts had marked the gown as having been sewn up in the country. No fashionable London modiste would have dressed a client in such a countrified style.

Prudence had evidently found her fan to be a nuisance. Instead of wielding it in the fine art of flirtation, it had dangled uselessly from her wrist. Her spectacles had, of course, only added to the spectacularly unstylish effect she had managed to achieve.

But Sebastian had seen beneath the surface of Prudence's outlandish facade. His father had been an explorer, a skilled observer of the customs of distant peoples and of the terrain of foreign lands. He had taken his family with him on his travels and he had trained Sebastian well in the science and art of observation.

It is in the details that one sees the truth, Jonathan Fleetwood had often explained to his son. *Learn to look for them.*

Tonight Sebastian had seen that Prudence's hair was richly threaded with gold. He had observed that she had a generous, laughing mouth and an amusing little nose. There was a firm, assertive quality to her catlike chin that he found intriguing. And he had looked deep into the bottomless green pools of her eyes.

He knew that compared to the great beauties of the *ton* her looks could only be called passable. She was not a diamond of the first water, yet she had been the only woman he had been aware of in that ballroom tonight.

Sebastian allowed his thoughts to drift to the rest of Prudence, mentally skimming a hand over her as if he were about to undress her and take her to bed. She was slender, but gracefully rounded in all the right places. He had seen enough of her in her modest ball gown to know that her breasts would be shaped like small, ripe, exotic fruit, perfectly suited to his palm and to his mouth. The scent of her, a mixture of fresh flowers and natural womanly fragrance, still lingered in the carriage, filling his head.

He would kiss her again soon. If he had any decency he would resist the impulse, but no one expected decency from the Fallen Angel. Just as well. He was not certain how much he possessed, himself.

What he had in abundance was a deepening sense of the gray, formless cold that threatened to engulf him from the inside out. The only way to forget about it for even a short while was to occupy himself with his amusing little hobby. He must take it up again, and soon.

First, however, there was the matter of Prudence's brother.

The carriage came to a halt at the front door of the club Sebastian favored. He had memberships at most of the best establishments, but this was the one where he always felt most comfortable. Probably because it was not one of his cousin's preferred haunts.

He got out, went up the steps, and into the warmth of the well-appointed masculine retreat. Several heads turned as he walked into the card room. A ripple of interest passed through the large crowd gathered about the gaming tables. Sebastian knew that gossip of the impending duel had probably reached every club in St. James.

A tall, thin blond man detached himself from a game of whist and strolled across the room to join Sebastian.

Sebastian watched him closely and was quietly relieved to see that Garrick Sutton's gaze was clear again tonight. Sutton appeared to be overcoming his practice of losing himself in strong spirits, a habit he had brought back with him from the war.

"What's this, Angelstone? I thought you were spending the rest of the night at home preparing yourself for your dawn appointment."

"I've changed my mind, Sutton. There will be no dawn engagement. I want you, as one of my seconds, to convey my most abject apologies to Mr. Trevor Merryweather."

Garrick's mouth fell open in dumbfounded amazement. Sebastian smiled. It was worth apologizing to young Merryweather just to see the amusing effect it would have on everyone.

Garrick was one of a very small handful of people Sebastian called friend. Sebastian included Garrick in the select group because he was one of the few people who had accepted Sebastian without reservation two years ago.

After a lifetime spent abroad, Sebastian had at last been obliged to come to England. His ever-expanding business investments had made it necessary to establish his headquarters in London, the very center of the social world that had once turned its back on his parents.

His financial power had brought him in contact with any number of people who were anxious to claim friendship. But he knew that behind his back they called him the Fleetwood bastard. They had gossiped with relish about his father's scandalous affair with an actress all those years ago. They had talked of how the title would eventually go to Sebastian's cousin, Jeremy, because of Jonathan Fleetwood's unsavory and irresponsible connection with a cheap lightskirt.

During that time Garrick had been one of the few people who did not want anything from Sebastian except friendship. He had also been one of the few who had no interest in the old scandal or in the legitimacy of Sebastian's birth.

Garrick had been carrying deep, invisible scars from the war. He had felt an instinctive bond with Sebastian, who, he must have sensed, carried scars of his own. Neither man spoke much of the past. It was not necessary.

"Are you serious?" Garrick demanded. "The Merryweather boy challenged you over a mere trifle. You did nothing except dance with his sister."

"I am aware of that," Sebastian said quietly.

"Are you telling me you're going to let him get away with that?"

"I have it on excellent authority the young man is hotheaded and not very wise in the ways of the world."

Garrick snorted. "Then you may as well teach him his first lessons."

"I am inclined to leave that task to someone else."

"I don't understand this." Garrick grabbed a bottle of

port and dashed some of the contents into a glass. "Not like you to let an upstart young pup get away with this kind of thing. What's going on, Angelstone?"

"I've changed my mind, that's all. There's nothing more to it than that. Tell Mr. Merryweather that I have no interest in meeting him at dawn."

Garrick eyed the port he had just poured as if surprised to find it in his hand. He carefully put the glass down again without tasting the contents. He looked at Sebastian. "I know damn well you aren't afraid to meet him. You're bound to best him in the encounter. The boy has no experience in this sort of thing."

Sebastian smiled thinly. "Which makes the whole event something of a bore, don't you think?"

Garrick's brows rose. "No doubt. But what's going to happen the next time you elect to dance with the Original? And I know there will be a next time, Angelstone. I saw the look in your eye tonight when you spotted her in the crowd. Haven't seen you react that way to a female before."

"If Merryweather sees fit to issue another challenge—"

"Which he will, especially when he sees how quickly you apologized after this one."

"Then I shall simply convey another apology," Sebastian concluded easily.

Garrick's blue eyes widened. "Damnation, man. You'd give him a second apology?"

"And another after that, if necessary. I have discovered to my astonishment what appears to be an inexhaustible supply of gentlemanly remorse, Sutton. I do believe I can continue to apologize as long as Merryweather can continue to issue a challenge."

"Good God." Understanding dawned in Garrick's eyes. He started to grin. "In other words, you're going to amuse yourself with his sister as long as you please and Merryweather will be helpless to force a duel because you will simply apologize every time he issues a challenge."

"That's the plan."

"Incredible." Garrick shook his head in admiration. "No one will believe for a single instant that you're actually afraid to meet the boy, of course. Your reputation is too well known. People will say you are merely amusing yourself again. Merryweather will become a laughingstock."

"Perhaps. That's not my problem."

"The club betting books will fill up with wagers on when you'll finally get tired of the game and put a bullet in him," Garrick said.

"What goes down on the betting books is not my concern, either." Sebastian helped himself to a small swallow of Garrick's untouched port. "In the meantime you'll see that my apologies are conveyed to my worthy opponent?"

"If you insist. This is a first for you, though, Angelstone. And not in your usual style."

"Who knows? Perhaps I'm changing my ways. It's just barely possible that I am becoming more responsible as I advance into my mature years."

Garrick eyed him with some concern. "You're in a strange mood tonight, my friend. Mayhap it's time you indulged yourself again in your little hobby. It's been a while since the last occasion, I believe."

"Perhaps you're right. Then again, perhaps I'm in a strange mood because it's been a rather strange night."

"And getting stranger," Garrick muttered. His gaze shifted to a point behind Sebastian's left shoulder. "Your cousin just walked into the room. Odd. He rarely visits this particular club."

"Only because he knows I can frequently be found here."

"Precisely. So what, one might ask, is Fleetwood doing here tonight?"

"That's easy enough to guess." Sebastian set down his glass. "He has no doubt come to wish me luck on the field of honor."

"Not bloody likely." Garrick frowned. "The opposite, no

doubt. Fleetwood would not weep any tears if someone were to put a bullet in you, Angelstone, and everyone knows it. As far as he's concerned, you usurped the title, and he's never forgiven you. He and his overbearing mama both assumed for years that he was next in line."

Sebastian shrugged. "As did everyone else in the family."

Garrick fell silent as Jeremy Fleetwood came up behind Sebastian.

"Angelstone." Jeremy's voice held the raw, brittle tone of a young man who knows he is facing an older, more powerful male. It was a tone balanced between fear and bravado.

Sebastian ignored the interested hush that fell over the crowd at the nearest gaming tables. He knew everyone in the room was straining to hear the confrontation without appearing to do so. The entire *ton* was aware of the icy feud between Sebastian and his relatives.

It was highly unusual for either side to even speak to the other. The fact that young Fleetwood was here in Sebastian's favorite club and had actually addressed his cousin by name would no doubt fascinate the gossips every bit as much as the rumor of a duel.

"Was there something you wanted, Fleetwood?" Sebastian turned slowly to face Jeremy. "Aside from my title, that is? Or have you come to wish me good fortune on the morrow?"

Jeremy's handsome face flushed. His eyes were a much darker shade than Sebastian's, brown rather than gold. His hair was lighter in color, a deep mahogany rather than midnight black. Nevertheless, Sebastian knew the family resemblance between himself and his cousin was unmistakable. He also knew that obvious fact irritated the rest of the Fleetwoods. They would have preferred him to have resembled his fair-haired mother.

"You bastard." Jeremy doubled a hand into a fist. "One of these days someone is going to put a bullet through your cold heart and it will serve you right."

"Thank you." Sebastian inclined his head politely. "Always nice to know one's family is behind one in a time of crisis."

"It's true, then?" Jeremy demanded, appalled. "You're going to subject the family reputation to another round of scandal by engaging in a duel with some country yokel?"

"You'll be happy to learn that the rumors of a duel are false."

"I don't believe it."

"It's the truth, cousin." Sebastian smiled. "Tell your doting mama to cancel her order for mourning clothes. I imagine she has already selected something appropriate in black on the off chance that her fondest wish might come true on the morrow. Unfortunately for her, I intend to live yet another day."

Jeremy scowled. "I heard that the brother of the Merryweather chit challenged you."

"Did you? Amazing how gossip flows through the *ton*, isn't it? A pity that so much of it is false."

"Damn it, man, what are you up to this time?"

"Nothing that need concern you, Fleetwood."

"You're an arrogant bastard, cousin."

"Arrogant I may be, but I am most definitely not a bastard." Sebastian smiled again. "And that, dear cousin, makes all the difference, doesn't it?"

Jeremy's mouth worked, but in the end he seemed to be unable to find words. He spun around on one well-shod foot and stalked out of the room.

The buzz of conversation resumed at the card tables. Sebastian turned back to pour himself another glass of port. He stopped when he saw the thoughtful expression in Garrick's eyes.

"Don't worry, my friend," Sebastian said. "Fleetwood and I have an understanding. Long ago we both made a pact to detest each other."

Garrick's gaze remained on the door. "I believe he truly hates you."

"Not entirely his fault, I suppose. His mother has taught him to do so from the cradle. She never forgave my father for running off with my mother and thereby soiling the family name for all eternity. When I came into the title last year instead of her precious Jeremy, she nearly keeled over with apoplexy."

"I am well aware of your family history. Be careful, Angelstone. I swear there was murder in Fleetwood's expression just now."

"Calm yourself, Sutton. Your imagination is running riot."

"I'm not so certain. I have the distinct impression that if Jeremy Fleetwood could find a way to do you in without making himself look guilty in the process, he wouldn't hesitate a minute." Garrick smiled suddenly. "There's a solution to your dilemma, you know."

"And that is?"

"Do your duty by your title, man. Get yourself a wife and then get yourself an heir as quickly as possible. Once the title is secure for another generation on your side of the family, the Fleetwoods will cease praying for your demise. If you have an heir, there would no longer be any point in hoping you'll kick the bucket."

"I congratulate you on your pragmatic approach to the situation," Sebastian said. "Perhaps I shall give your notion some consideration."

Garrick gave him a sharp, inquiring look. "What's this? Don't tell me you've finally decided to be sensible."

"I have been told that at my age a man should begin to demonstrate the qualities of wisdom and responsibility, Sutton."

Garrick shook his head again. "You truly are in an odd mood tonight."

"Yes. Perhaps you'd better convey my apologies to young Merryweather before I change my mind."

Sebastian ignored the gossip that swept through the *ton* the following afternoon as the haut monde learned of his apology to Trevor Merryweather. Instead of making himself available to the curious in his club or retreating to the privacy of his library, he took himself off to keep an appointment at a certain coffeehouse near the docks.

Whistlecroft's message had reached Sebastian just as he had sat down to a leisurely late breakfast. The note had been short and to the point. Whistlecroft's messages generally were brief, as the Bow Street Runner did not read or write with any great skill.

> SIR,
> *There be a matter of interest I wish to discuss with you. If it be agreeable with you, I suggest the usual place at three.*
>
> Yrs.
> W.

At three o'clock Sebastian walked into the coffeehouse and found Whistlecroft waiting for him in his customary booth. The Runner raised his mug in greeting. Sebastian went forward to join him.

Whistlecroft was a heavyset man with a florid, bewhiskered face and shrewd little eyes. The purple veins in his nose bespoke a fondness for gin and he seemed to have a perpetual cold during the winter months. He always wore a grimy scarf around his neck and snuffled a great deal.

"Good afternoon, yer lordship. I see ye got my message."

"I trust this matter will prove more amusing than the last, Whistlecroft." Sebastian sat down in the booth across from the Runner. "I am in the mood for something a bit more challenging."

"Yer too good at this sort o' thing, that's yer problem." Whistlecroft grinned, displaying several gaps in his teeth. "Well, I got a new one that should interest ye. Same arrangement as before? I collect the reward from the suitably grateful party what hired me?"

"The reward and the credit, Whistlecroft. Neither are of any use to me."

"Must be nice to be rich," Whistlecroft said with a sigh. "And have a fancy title into the bargain. Don't mind tellin' ye, I still don't understand why ye take such an interest in these little affairs."

Sebastian signaled for coffee. "I've explained that before, Whistlecroft. You provide me with an amusing hobby. Every man needs a hobby, don't you agree?"

"I wouldn't know about that, yer lordship. Ain't never had time for no hobby. Too busy trying to keep food on the table for me and mine."

Sebastian smiled coolly. "I trust you and yours are eating somewhat better since we began our partnership."

Whistlecroft chuckled. "That we are, m'lord. That we are. My wife's getting plump and the five little ones is all filling out nicely. We moved into a little house just last week. Real pleasant, it is."

"Excellent. Then let me hear what you have for me this time."

Whistlecroft hunched forward and lowered his voice. "A little matter o' blackmail and a nice bit o' jewelry, m'lord. I think ye'll find it amusing enough."

Three

"What do I know of Angelstone?" Hester, Lady Pembroke, paused with her teacup halfway to her mouth and looked at Prudence. "Only that he is not on speaking terms with his relatives and that he has an exceedingly dangerous reputation. All of which makes him extremely interesting, of course. Why do you ask?"

Prudence smiled. Hester was an awesomely built woman of indeterminate years, whose size was exceeded only by her generous heart and her lively interest in the affairs of the *ton*. As she had once explained to Prudence, she had long been deprived of her natural place in the social world due to the mysterious disappearance of the famed Pembroke jewels a generation earlier. One could not move in the best circles of the *ton* without money, regardless of one's pedigree.

Now that she had money, Hester was happily indulging herself in all the pleasures of society that had previously been denied to her. She had concluded that she had an innate sense of style and when the *Morning Post* reported that gowns of lavender and violet hues were the most fashionable this season, Hester had redone her wardrobe accordingly. Today her stout frame was encased in a heavily flounced and ruffled lavender gown trimmed with pink lace.

Hester was an old friend of Prudence's family. She and

her late husband had lived in an ancient, tumbledown manor house that was located not far from the Merryweather farm. The Pembroke ghost, which was almost as famous as the missing Pembroke jewels, had provided Prudence with her first real experience in the investigation of spectral phenomena.

"I'm asking about Angelstone because Trevor has taken this ridiculous notion into his head that I must be very careful around the earl," Prudence explained. "He seems to think the man is out to seduce me. Utter nonsense, of course, but Trevor is very agitated about it."

"As well he should be, I suppose. The earl is, as I said, most interesting, but there is no indication that he is casting about for a wife as yet. Therefore, we must assume that when he pays attention to a young lady, he has other things on his mind."

"He might simply wish to converse with her about matters of mutual intellectual interest," Prudence suggested hopefully.

"Not likely." Hester put down her teacup, her expression thoughtful. "One of the reasons Angelstone is so completely fascinating is precisely because he flouts Society's rules. Treats the Social World with contempt, for the most part, just as it once treated his parents."

"But you said he's invited to all the best balls and soirees."

"Certainly. There is nothing Society thrives on more than being treated with contempt by a titled gentleman who has money to burn and more than a hint of danger about him."

"I see. How very odd."

"Not at all. Only recall how Society has doted on Byron. Angelstone is very shrewd. He knows how to stay just this side of the boundary of what is acceptable. And since he assumed the title, every hostess in Town vies to lure him with an invitation to one of her affairs."

"He is certainly an interesting man," Prudence said.

"Yes, indeed." Hester turned thoughtful. "And one of the most interesting things about him is why he has not used the power he acquired along with the title to crush his relatives."

Prudence frowned. "Crush them?"

"It would be easy enough for him to do. He controls a fortune, after all. And he has great social power. Everyone assumes the reason he has not gotten his relatives banished from Society is simply that it amuses him to play cat-and-mouse games with them."

"I cannot believe he would deliberately hurt his family. I rather liked him," Prudence ventured.

"I'm sure he can be charming when he chooses. And he was no doubt more than charming when he asked you to dance with him. The thing is, Prue, Trevor is absolutely correct to be concerned about any connection between you and the earl. Angelstone is said to amuse himself in some rather odd ways. He might find it entertaining to ruin this Season's most interesting Original."

Prudence bit her lip. "Come, now, madam. I am five-and-twenty, after all. A bit past the age of ruination."

"Not yet, my dear. Not yet. And if there is anything Society loves more than a Fallen Angel, it's a good, juicy scandal. You are the talk of the Town at the moment. Every eye is upon you. If your name is linked to Angelstone's, there will be no end to the gossip."

Prudence took another sip of tea. "The only reason I'm the center of attention is because of that business with the Pembroke family treasure."

"Of course, my dear." Hester beamed with delight and gave an affectionate pat to the diamond pendant around her throat. It had been part of the cache Prudence had discovered. "Everyone knows you found my jewels when you investigated the Pembroke ghost. The *ton* is quite enthralled with the tale."

Prudence wrinkled her nose. "Too bad I did not locate

the Pembroke family ghost while I was at it. Encountering evidence of genuine spectral phenomena would have been far more interesting than discovering a bunch of jewels."

"But not nearly as useful, Prue. Not nearly as useful. You have changed my life, my dear, and I do not know how I can ever repay you."

"You know very well you have more than repaid me by bringing Trevor and me to London for a visit. Since the death of our parents, Trevor has been extremely restless in the country. Here in Town he is gaining experience in the ways of the world and he is having a wonderful time."

"It was the very least I could do to thank you," Hester said. "I know how concerned you were about Trevor. But I would love to do so much more for you, my dear." She frowned at Prudence's demure, unfashionable muslin frock. "I do wish you would allow me to buy you a new wardrobe."

"Now, Hester, we have been through this before. I am not about to allow you to buy me a trunkful of gowns that I will never be able to wear when I go home to Dorset. It would be a complete waste."

Hester sighed. "The thing is, Prue, now that you have the attention of the *ton*, it seems only proper that you should dress in the first stare of fashion. I cannot comprehend why you do not take more of an interest in your clothes. You would look lovely in lavender."

The door of the drawing room opened before Prudence could think of a suitable reply.

"Good afternoon, ladies."

Prudence looked up as Trevor made his entrance into the room with the swaggering, elaborately casual style he had painstakingly learned from his newfound friends.

Everything Trevor did lately was done with that peculiar style. It was getting a bit wearing, Prudence decided.

Her younger brother had turned overnight into a young blood of the *ton*. From the top of his intricately tied cravat to his padded coat, striped waistcoat, and snug pantaloons,

Trevor was the very glass of fashion. He had taken to carrying a cane and had an enormous number of decorative seals dangling from the fob of his watch.

As irritating as some of his new mannerisms could be on occasion, Prudence was nevertheless very fond of Trevor. She told herself he was merely a high-spirited young man who would do very well once he had settled down a bit and matured.

Her younger brother was also a fine-looking young man, she thought proudly. He had no real need of the padding in his jacket. His hair was the same honey-colored shade as hers was. Trevor had inherited their mother's excellent blue eyes, rather than their father's green ones. He had no need of spectacles, although he had experimented briefly with a monocle last week. He had dropped the affectation when he discovered it was too difficult to keep the glass in place.

Prudence worried sometimes that Trevor would not want to return to the quiet life of a country squire after having been introduced to the pleasures of Town.

And, if she were honest with herself, Prudence thought, she had to admit that Trevor was not the only one who might be a bit bored in the country now. She had found life in London far more exciting and more intriguing than she had expected.

It was not the endless round of balls and soirees that fascinated her, but the endless array of bookshops, museums, and the like. Here in Town she could research spectral phenomena far more thoroughly than she could at home. She also stood a much greater chance of encountering people who would need her special investigation skills.

"Hello, Trevor," Prudence said.

"Good afternoon." Hester picked up the pot. "Will you have tea?"

"With pleasure." Trevor came forward eagerly. "Wait until I tell you my news."

"We are all ears, dear," Hester murmured.

"You are not going to believe this." Trevor preened as he accepted the cup and saucer. "But I, Trevor Merryweather, wrung an apology out of the devil himself, by God."

Hester blinked. "Did you really?"

"I certainly did." Trevor turned proudly to Prudence. "Angelstone won't bother you again, Prue. You may depend upon it. Made the bastard apologize for insulting you. Whole world knows it, too. He had one of his seconds convey his apologies to me right there in my club where all my friends could hear him."

Prudence glared at Trevor as he sprawled in one of Hester's delicate satinwood chairs. "For the last time, Trevor, I was not insulted by Angelstone. He behaved himself quite properly. There was absolutely nothing about his manner on the dance floor that gave offense."

"Man's got a reputation." Trevor helped himself to a small cake off the tea tray. "You wouldn't know about it, of course. Not the sort of thing a lady should know about. Point is, he certainly ain't the type you want hanging about. Everybody agrees he don't have anything respectable in mind when he starts paying attention to a female."

"For goodness' sake," Prue said. "Name me one female Angelstone is said to have ruined. Just one."

Trevor scowled. "Good lord. Surely you don't expect me to discuss that sort of gossip with you."

"Yes, I do. If I'm being warned off, I want to know precisely why. Who was his last innocent victim?"

"If he ain't had a victim this Season it's only because respectable families are keeping their daughters out of his reach."

"I want a name," Prue said evenly.

Trevor glowered at her and then appealed to Hester for support. "I've a hunch you're more conversant with that sort of tale than I am. Give Prue a name. Perhaps it will convince her she's playing with fire when she accepts a dance with Angelstone."

"A name?" Hester tapped her chin with her forefinger and studied the ceiling for a moment. "Well, his name was linked with that of Lady Charlesworthy at one time, I understand, but that was last Season and the lady is a rather notorious widow in her own right. I'm not sure she counts as an innocent victim, if you see what I mean. In any event, I'm told that affair ended some time ago."

"What happened?" Prudence asked, deeply curious in spite of herself.

"The *on dit* is that Lady Charlesworthy made the mistake of trying to incite the Fallen Angel's jealousy," Hester said. "She gave her favors to another. There are rumors that a duel was fought."

Trevor frowned. "A duel?"

Hester nodded. "Apparently Angelstone wounded his opponent, but did not kill him. They say the Fallen Angel left the dueling field and went straight to the lady's house. The story has it he went upstairs to her bedchamber and awakened her personally just to tell her that their affair was over."

Prudence shivered. She could well imagine that Angelstone would have been made coldly furious by Lady Charlesworthy's tactics. "You're quite right, Hester. Lady Charlesworthy does not count as an innocent victim. It was very unkind of her to try to make Angelstone jealous."

"Unkind?" Hester gave Prudence an amused glance. "I expect the poor lady was desperate for some indications of warmth from Angelstone. They say he is made of ice."

"Nonsense. Back to the matter of a name. We're looking for genuine, innocent victims here," Prudence said. "Can you think of even one young woman who was ruined by Angelstone?"

Hester raised a brow. "Actually, no. I can't. Now that I think of it, from what I hear, Angelstone tends to pass over the fledglings in favor of the more worldly sort of female."

Trevor was irate. "The man's got a reputation, I tell you. Everyone knows it."

"Not for ruining innocent young women, apparently," Prudence said. "So you will in future kindly refrain from interfering in my social affairs, do you comprehend me, Trevor?"

"Now, see here," Trevor shot back, "I'm your brother. Got a responsibility toward you."

"I am perfectly capable of taking care of myself."

"Don't be so certain of that. Truth is, you don't know that much about men, Prue. You ain't a good judge of 'em. Keep in mind what happened three years ago."

Hester clapped loudly for attention. "Enough, my dears. If you wish to wrangle, you may do so someplace other than my drawing room. We have other business to attend to."

"What other business?" Prudence asked, more than willing to change the topic.

Hester chuckled. "Why, the little matter of deciding which invitations we shall be accepting this week. Prudence, my dear, you are very much in demand. We shall have a busy time of it, I fear." Hester reached for a silver tray littered with cards. "Now, then, let's go through this little lot. Can you believe that all of these arrived just today? I don't think we can possibly manage to squeeze in everything."

"You make the selections," Prudence said. "I don't really care which parties we attend. They all seem the same, somehow. The rooms are too crowded and too hot and there is so much noise it is difficult to converse."

"One must make sacrifices when one is moving in Society." Hester picked up a card. "Ah, yes, we shall most definitely put in an appearance at the Thornbridges' ball. The new Lady Thornbridge is causing talk."

Trevor swallowed his cake, looking interested. "How's that?"

Hester gave him a knowing smile. "She's quite a bit younger than her lord. And very beautiful. Word has it Thornbridge is mad with jealousy these days. Should be interesting to see if there will be a scene or two at their ball."

"It sounds rather unpleasant to me," Prudence observed. "Who wants to see a jealous husband make a fool of himself over a young wife?"

"Most of the *ton*, my dear," Prudence assured her cheerfully.

The door of the drawing room opened again at that juncture. Hester's butler, chosen for his imposing air, appeared in the opening.

"A Mrs. Leacock to see you, madam."

"How lovely," Hester said. "Show her in, Crandall."

A birdlike woman with silvery white hair, dressed in an expensive mourning gown of black crepe, was ushered into the drawing room.

"How kind of you to call, Lydia," Hester said. "Do sit down. You know my dear friends Trevor and Prudence Merryweather?"

"Yes, of course." Mrs. Leacock's bright little eyes darted nervously from Hester to Prudence. "Actually, this is not precisely a social call, Hester. I have come to consult with Miss Merryweather."

"Have you, indeed?" Hester picked up the teapot. "Don't tell us you have a ghost you want investigated?"

Mrs. Leacock alighted on a silk-cushioned chair. "I am not certain. But something rather odd has been happening of late in the west wing of my house. The incidents have begun to affect my nerves and I fear for the consequences. My doctor has warned me that I have a weak heart."

Prudence was immediately intrigued. "This sounds far more interesting than choosing which parties we shall attend. Do tell me everything about these incidents, Mrs. Leacock. I would be happy to investigate."

"I should be forever grateful, Miss Merryweather." Mrs. Leacock's cup rattled in its saucer. "I fear I really am getting rather desperate. I have never before believed in ghosts, but lately I have begun to wonder."

"Let me get my notebook," Prudence said eagerly.

· · ·

Mrs. Leacock left an hour later, looking vastly relieved at having engaged a professional investigator. Prudence was delighted with the prospect of a puzzle to solve.

"If you will excuse me, Hester, I am going straight upstairs to read a new book I purchased this morning. It is all about the usefulness of electricity machines in detecting vaporous substances in the atmosphere. Perhaps I shall learn a technique I can apply to my new case."

Trevor looked briefly interested. "My friend Matthew Hornsby has an electricity machine. Made it himself."

"Does he?" Prudence asked with great interest.

"Yes, but I doubt that you'll need it." Trevor made a face. "Your new case is composed of nothing more than the imaginings of a nervous old woman."

"I'm not at all certain of that." Prudence went to the door. "It sounds to me as though there have indeed been some disturbances that require an explanation."

Hester looked up. "Are you saying you believe Lydia might actually have a ghost in her house?"

"I shall let you know my thoughts on the matter after I have had an opportunity to study my notes. In the meantime I want both of you to give me your word that you will say nothing of this to anyone."

"I shall not say a thing, my dear," Hester assured her.

Trevor grimaced as he got to his feet. "You needn't worry about me spreading the news of your case. Damned embarrassing having a sister who investigates spectral phenomena. Wish you'd give it up, Prue."

"I have no intention of giving up my hobby." Prudence went out into the hall.

"Prue, wait, I would like a word with you." Trevor hurried after her.

Prudence waited for him on the bottom step of the staircase. "Don't try to talk me out of this, Trevor. I am very bored with parties and soirees. If we are to stay in London until the end of the Season, as you wish to do, I must find something interesting to occupy my time."

"No, no, it's not about your silly investigation." Trevor glanced around to make certain none of the servants were within hearing distance. Then he leaned forward.

"Since you somehow learned of the duel I had scheduled with Angelstone, I don't mind telling you a rather interesting fact I have learned about the infamous Fallen Angel."

"What's that?" Prudence asked warily.

"He may have a ferocious reputation, but the man's a bloody damn coward."

Prudence was shocked. "Trevor, how can you say that?"

"Perfectly true." Trevor nodded once in satisfaction. "Man's an out-and-out coward."

"That's not true."

"He's the one who called off the duel, you know. Apologized rather than meet me on the field of honor this morning."

Prudence was infuriated by Trevor's interpretation of events. "If you want my opinion, Angelstone showed the sort of mature, responsible behavior one would expect in a well-bred gentleman. If you truly believe he's a coward, then you are a fool, Trevor."

"Now, Prue, calm yourself. Truth is, the man's a coward and that's a fact. By this evening, the entire social world will know it."

"Rubbish. Utter rubbish." Prudence picked up her skirts and dashed up the carpeted stairs.

Angelstone had kept his word. He had spared Trevor's life. Prudence prayed that the Fallen Angel would not put too high a price on the damage she had apparently done to his formidable reputation.

Four days later on the night of the Thornbridge ball, Prudence decided she had had enough. She was thoroughly annoyed with Sebastian and she let him know it the moment he sought her out in the crowd.

"My lord, you are making a laughingstock out of my brother."

Sebastian, dark and predatory-looking in his black and white evening clothes, managed to make every other man in the room look like a fop. He seemed unsurprised and unmoved by Prudence's accusation. His mouth curved in the familiar humorless smile.

"At least he is a live laughingstock rather than a dead one," he said. "Isn't that what you wanted, Miss Merryweather?"

She glowered at him through her spectacles. He was being deliberately difficult. "No, it is not what I wanted. Not precisely, that is."

Sebastian's brow rose inquiringly. "You would rather I had accepted one or two of the numerous challenges I have received from him in the past few days?"

"Certainly not. You know perfectly well that the last thing I wanted was a duel between the two of you. That was the very thing that I wished to avoid."

"You have gotten your wish." Sebastian's amber eyes gleamed. "I have kept my end of the bargain. Why are you berating me, Miss Merryweather?"

Prudence felt herself turning pink at the reminder of the deal they had struck in his library. "You know perfectly well I expected you to handle this entire matter in a more subtle manner, my lord. I did not think you would turn it into a joke."

The realization of exactly how Sebastian was dealing with her brother's outrage had finally come to Prudence earlier that afternoon. Hester, torn between amusement and affection for Trevor, had outlined the latest gossip to Prudence only a few hours ago.

"It is common knowledge that Trevor is issuing a challenge every time he learns that Angelstone had talked to you or danced with you," Hester had explained over tea.

"Oh, no." Prudence had gazed at her friend in shock. "Why on earth can't Trevor learn to keep his mouth closed?"

Hester had shrugged. "He's very young, my dear. And quite determined to protect you. In any event, Angelstone has made a game of the entire affair. He promptly sends a flowery apology each time Trevor calls him out."

"And Trevor accepts it?"

"There is nothing else the boy can do. Angelstone's reputation is not harmed in the least because no one would dream of suspecting him of cowardice. His reputation is far too formidable. There isn't a soul who believes he is actually afraid to meet Trevor."

Prudence had brightened slightly. "I suppose everyone realizes Angelstone is showing compassion and a mature nature by refusing to meet my brother."

"Not quite, my dear," Hester had said. "The assumption is that Angelstone is refraining from putting a bullet in poor Trevor because he is reluctant to cause you distress."

"I don't understand."

Hester sighed. "It's perfectly obvious, Prue. Everyone believes Angelstone is indulging you for the moment because they believe you are marked as the Fallen Angel's next victim."

"Nonsense." But Prudence had been acutely conscious of the shock of excitement that had shimmered through her. It was madness to entertain the notion that Angelstone might have anything other than an amused, intellectual interest in her. Nevertheless, she could not put the memory of his kiss out of her head.

Tonight she was determined to confront him on the subject of the way in which he was treating Trevor. She intended to be quite firm.

Sebastian now contemplated Prudence's resolute expression. "If you will recall the terms of our bargain, Miss Merryweather, you will remember that you did not specify exactly how I was to avoid future duels with your brother."

"It did not occur to me that Trevor would make a fool of himself by continuing to challenge you. He was so anxious after he called you out the first time that I assumed he would be grateful to have escaped unscathed. I hoped that he would take pains to avoid a future encounter."

"Forgive me for saying so, Miss Merryweather, but I fear you don't know much about the workings of the male brain."

"Not about the workings of the *immature* male brain," she said. "I'll grant you that much. And it seems to me, sir, that your approach to dealing with my brother is no more mature than his is in dealing with you. I won't have you amusing yourself at my brother's expense."

"Is that right?"

"Yes. And while we're on the subject, I would also like to inform you that I will not allow you to amuse yourself with me, either." She felt herself turn pink, but she held her ground. "Just in case you have taken a notion to do so."

"How will you stop me?" Sebastian asked with grave interest.

"If need be, I shall put a stop to this nonsense once and for all by declining your invitations to dance." She lifted her chin in challenge. "Perhaps I shall cease speaking to you altogether."

"Come, now, Miss Merryweather. Don't make threats you will be unable to carry out. You know that you would soon be as bored as I am at these affairs if you were to cut me dead."

"I'm certain I could find one or two other interesting people with whom I would enjoy conversing," she said. But her words were spoken out of sheer bravado and she suspected he knew it.

It was Sebastian who made the endless round of soirees and balls bearable. It had gotten to the point where Prudence actually looked forward to going out in the evenings now because she knew he would turn up at one or more of the parties she was attending.

Sebastian's eyes glittered with a knowing expression. He took her hand and led her out onto the dance floor. "Look around you, Miss Merryweather. There is no one else here tonight who shares your interests. No one else with whom you can discuss techniques of investigation. As far as the *ton* is concerned, you are merely a new and quaintly amusing toy."

She searched his face. "I rather suspect that is all I am to you, too, my lord."

Sebastian swept her into the waltz. "Unlike many others here tonight, I know how to take care of my toys. I do not take pleasure in breaking them and then discarding them."

Prudence caught her breath. "What is that supposed to mean, sir?"

"It means you are safe enough with me, Prue," he said softly. "And so is your annoying young pup of a brother."

Not knowing how to take the first part of that vow, Prudence seized on the latter. "Then you will cease tormenting Trevor?"

"Never fear. Sooner or later he'll figure out that when I want something, I do not let anything get in my way. Eventually he will desist. Now, then, I have been thinking about our last conversation and I have another question for you."

Prudence eyed him uncertainly. "What is that?"

"You said you found the Pembroke jewels beneath a wooden floorboard while looking for signs of spectral phenomena. I doubt that you tore up every board in the house looking for a ghost."

"No, of course not," she agreed.

"Then how did you know which boards to remove?"

"Oh, that was easy, my lord," she said. "I rapped."

"Rapped?"

Prudence chuckled. "With a cane. The legend of the Pembroke jewels was connected to the Pembroke ghost, you see. I knew that if I could find the jewels, I might be able to prove or disprove the tales of the ghost."

"So you went looking for the jewels in hopes of finding the ghost. Naturally you reasoned that the jewels, if they were still hidden somewhere in the house, would have to be in a concealed safe of some sort."

"And a safe hidden in the floorboards or the walls would likely produce a hollow sound when I rapped on the wood above it," Prudence concluded happily.

"Very logical." There was genuine admiration in Sebastian's gaze.

"I went through the entire house with a stout cane and rapped on every wall and every floor. When I discovered a place that sounded hollow, I instructed that the boards be removed. The jewels were hidden in a secret opening beneath one of them. Lady Pembroke's grandfather had forgotten to pass the secret of his hiding place down to his descendants, so the jewels had been lost."

"Very clever." Sebastian looked down at her with cool approval. "I'm impressed."

Prudence's flush deepened at the praise. "I am happy for

Lady Pembroke, of course, but I must admit it was rather disappointing not to find some evidence of spectral phenomena."

Sebastian's smile was ironic. "I'm certain Lady Pembroke would far rather have the jewels than the Pembroke ghost."

"That's what she says."

"How did you become interested in such an unusual hobby?" Sebastian asked.

"The influence of my parents, I suppose." Prudence smiled reminiscently. "They were both devoted to the subject of natural philosophy. My father studied meteorological phenomena. My mother made extensive observations on the species of animals and birds that lived in the vicinity of our farm."

Sebastian watched her intently. "And they taught you how to make observations?"

"Yes. And how to conduct a logical investigation to discover the answer to a question. They were very expert at that sort of thing." Prudence smiled proudly. "Both of them had papers published in the journals of several important scientific societies."

"My father had portions of some of his journals published," Sebastian said slowly.

"Really? What sort of studies did he carry out?"

"He kept extensive records of his travels and explorations. Many of them were of interest to scientific societies."

"How exciting." Prudence was fascinated. "I collect you were allowed to accompany him on his travels?"

Sebastian smiled briefly. "When I was growing up my father took all of us—my mother, myself, and my little brother—with him nearly everywhere he went. Mother had the knack of being able to make a home in the middle of a desert or on an island in the South Seas."

"What happened when you grew older?"

"My mother and brother continued to travel with my father. But I went off on my own. I looked for interesting

investment opportunities in foreign ports. I did some observations of terrain for the military during the war. That sort
of thing."

"I envy you the sights you must have seen and things you
must have learned," Prudence said.

"It's true that I learned a great deal about the world."
Sebastian's eyes were as hard, brilliant, and cold as faceted
gems. "But the price of my education was too high."

"I don't understand," Prudence whispered.

"Four years ago my parents and my brother were killed
by a great fall of rock while they were traveling through a
mountain pass in a godforsaken corner of the East called
Saragstan."

Prudence came to a halt on the dance floor. "How terrible for you, my lord. I know how you must have felt. I
remember all too well my feelings at the moment I received
word my parents had been killed in the carriage accident."

Sebastian did not seem to hear her. His gaze was turned
inward as he led her off the floor. Prudence sensed that he
was focusing on some distant landscape that only he could
see. He came to a halt near the French doors and stood
looking out into the night.

"I was to meet up with them in a small town at the foot
of the mountains. I had business dealings there. The local
weavers produce a very fine cloth which I purchase and have
shipped to England and America. My parents and my
brother never arrived."

"I am so very sorry, my lord." Prudence sought for
words of comfort. "Such tragic accidents are very difficult to
endure."

Sebastian veiled his eyes briefly with his long, dark lashes.
When he raised them again and glanced sideways at Prudence she knew he was once more in the present. "You misunderstand. My parents and my brother did not die in an
accident."

Prudence stared at him. "What are you saying?"

"The fall of rock which killed them was deliberately caused by bandits who preyed upon travelers in the mountains. I did not know that the bandits were a problem in the region when I sent word to my father to meet me in that damned town."

"Dear God." Prudence's eyes widened as she realized what he was saying. "Surely you do not blame yourself, my lord?"

"I don't know." He leaned one shoulder against the doorframe and continued to gaze out into the darkness. "The fact is they would all be alive today if I had not asked them to join me there in Saragstan."

She touched his sleeve. "You must not assume the responsibility for what happened. You did not destroy your family. The bandits did that. Were they ever caught and punished?"

"Yes." Sebastian looked down at her. "They were punished." His mouth curved in his chilling smile. "Now, Miss Merryweather, I suggest we change the subject. I would rather not discuss such unpleasant matters with you."

"I quite understand, my lord," Prudence said seriously. "I do not think it is a good thing to dwell too much on the past. It is the present and the future that are important. Don't you agree?"

"I have no idea." Sebastian acted as though the question bored him. "I'll leave such philosophical decisions up to you."

The devil was up to mischief tonight. Prudence was certain of it an hour later when Sebastian took his leave of her and started toward the door.

During the past few days she had come to feel that she had gotten to know this enigmatic man quite well. There was a sense of recognition deep inside her. She did not fully understand it, but she knew it was there.

She thought she could see past the cool facade he showed

to the world. She believed she could even read the small signs that indicated the subtle changes in his dark moods.

Tonight, Prudence decided, there was an air of keen alertness about him, a sense of barely suppressed anticipation like that of a predator on the hunt. It worried her. Sebastian had been in the same strange mood for the past three nights.

She watched him make his way through the glittering room. He would soon be lost from sight in the throng of guests that filled the Thornbridge house.

This was not the first time this week that she had watched him quietly disappear from a crowded ballroom. He had vanished from three different ballrooms last night, two others the previous night, and two more the night before that. On each occasion he had reappeared a short while later acting as if he had never been gone. No one but Prudence seemed to have noticed. After all, the rooms were so crowded that it was nothing to lose sight of a person for a while.

But Prudence was very aware of Sebastian's presence whenever he was around and she sensed his disappearances instantly.

Anyone who noted his progress tonight would assume he was leaving. It was past midnight, after all, and Sebastian had already spent more than an hour at the Thornbridge ball. The earl was well known for his propensity to become easily bored.

Prudence had begun to suspect that Sebastian's restless nature had led him to amuse himself in some rather unfortunate ways. She knew he liked puzzles and she could not forget that he had shown a keen interest in her search for the Pembroke jewels. Indeed, his questions about her investigation had been extremely specific in nature.

Prudence put the two facts together and came to the uneasy conclusion that Sebastian might have developed a penchant for opening closed doors and prowling through locked safes in crowded houses merely because it amused him to do so. Perhaps he enjoyed the thrill of discovering hidden jewels even though he was richer than most of his hosts.

Sebastian surely wouldn't steal whatever valuables he chanced to find, Prudence assured herself. But he might very well revel in the dangerous business of searching for them.

The game he was playing involved far too much risk. He needed to be stopped before he got himself into trouble.

She took a last swallow of her punch and put down her glass with a firm resolve. Tonight she was going to find out just what sort of unholy business the Fallen Angel was engaging in when he disappeared from a crowded ball. When she discovered the exact nature of his amusements, she was going to give him a stern lecture. Boredom was not an excuse for engaging in mischief.

It was a simple task to slip through the crowd in Sebastian's wake. The people who noticed her nodded pleasantly, no doubt assuming she was on her way upstairs to one of the withdrawing rooms provided for the ladies.

Prudence smiled and chatted briefly with one or two of Hester's acquaintances, all the while edging toward the hall where Sebastian had vanished.

Several minutes later she found herself alone in an empty corridor. She glanced quickly around, picked up her mustard-colored muslin skirts, and hurried toward the back stairs.

When she reached the staircase, she paused again to check that none of the household staff was in the vicinity. None of the Thornbridges' handsomely liveried servants were in sight. At this hour they would all be occupied in the kitchens or circulating through the crowds with trays of punch and champagne.

Prudence gazed uneasily up into the darkness at the top of the stairs. Perhaps she was wrong in thinking Sebastian had come this way. She'd only had that last brief glimpse of him disappearing down this hall.

She started up the stairs, her soft dancing slippers silent on the wooden treads. When she reached the second floor, she hesitated again, trying to get her bearings. Two hall sconces were lit, but for the most part this section of the mansion was in shadow.

A small sighing sound from the far end of the darkened hall caught Prudence's attention. Someone had just closed a bedchamber door very quietly.

She went down the carpeted corridor until she reached the door. As she stood gazing at it, uncertain of her next move, a thin line of candlelight appeared at the bottom. Someone was inside.

Prudence's fingers trembled as she gripped the doorknob. If she was wrong in thinking Sebastian had entered the bedchamber, her next move could prove extremely embarrassing. She readied two or three logical excuses as she cautiously opened the door.

The glow of light she had seen a moment earlier disappeared instantly as she stepped into the room. The chamber was in complete darkness.

Prudence stood in the doorway for a few seconds, letting her eyes adjust to the lack of light. When she could just make out the bulky shape of a huge, canopied bed, she closed the door gently behind her.

"Sebastian?" she whispered. "Where are you? I know you're in here."

There was an almost soundless movement behind her. A man's hand clamped over her mouth. Prudence froze in fright as she found herself pinned against a large, hard body. Then she started to struggle furiously. Her teeth sank into the palm that covered her mouth.

"Bloody hell," Sebastian muttered in her ear. "I should have known it would be you. Give me your word you won't raise your voice above a whisper and I'll let you go. Nod your head if you understand."

Prudence nodded frantically. Sebastian released her,

gripped her by the shoulders, and spun her around to face him. She could see almost nothing of his features in the darkness, but the tone of his voice and the manner in which his fingers dug into her shoulders told her he was furious.

"What the devil do you think you're doing up here?" he asked.

"Following you."

"You little fool." He gave her a small, exasperated shake. "Do you think this is some sort of game?"

Prudence braced herself. "No, but you apparently do. What is all this sneaking about, sir? You're clearly up to some mischief. You should be ashamed of yourself. What sort of behavior is this for a man of your background and title?"

"Just what I needed. A lecture on my behavior."

Too late, Prudence had a sudden, dreadful thought, one she had not previously considered. It very nearly robbed her of her breath. "You're not planning to meet someone up here, by any chance, my lord?"

"No, I am damn well not planning to meet someone. I've got business up here, if you must know."

Prudence wondered at the sense of relief that shot through her. "What sort of business?"

"It involves a necklace, not that it's any of your concern."

"I was afraid of that." Prudence wished she could see his face more clearly. "Sir, I refuse to believe that you have resorted to stealing necklaces in order to amuse yourself. You cannot have grown that bored with life in Town."

"Damn it, I am no thief." He sounded genuinely affronted.

"Of course not. I didn't think so. But you are a man who enjoys puzzles, aren't you? Tell me precisely what you're doing in this bedchamber."

"I told you, I was looking for a necklace. I'm not going to stand here explaining myself to you, however. We've got to get out of here before someone comes along. There's no telling how many people saw you come up here."

"No one saw me," she assured him.

"How would you know? You're hardly an expert at this sort of thing."

"And you are?"

"I've had a bit more experience at it than you." He grasped her arm and started to open the door. The squeak of a floorboard out in the hall stopped him. "Damnation."

"What is it?" Prudence whispered. "What's wrong?"

"Someone's coming down the hall. We can't go out there now."

"What if he comes in here?"

"Then there will be hell to pay. And it will be all your fault, Prue. A fact which I will not soon forget." Sebastian tugged her across the room toward the massive mahogany wardrobe.

"Where are we going?"

"We're going to get you out of sight." He opened one of the wardrobe doors. "Get inside. Hurry."

"Angelstone, wait. I don't think this is such a good idea. There are so many clothes in here. Women's clothes. Good lord, this must be Lady Thornbridge's bedchamber."

"Get in there. Now, for God's sake." He seized her around the waist as if she were a sack of potatoes and tossed her into the wardrobe.

"Good heavens." Prudence nearly suffocated amid a pile of expensive silks, satins, and muslins. She flailed about wildly, trying to regain her balance.

"Move over," Sebastian muttered. His hands cupped her derriere as he attempted to shove her farther into the depths of the wardrobe.

"There's no room." Intensely aware of his hands on her bottom, Prudence pushed frantically at the clothing in an effort to shift some of it aside. But the wardrobe was stuffed with expensive garments. "Why don't you hide under the bed?"

"Hell. Maybe you're right." Sebastian released her and backed out of the wardrobe.

He closed the mahogany door, leaving Prudence in tomblike darkness. At that instant the bedchamber door was flung open with a resounding crash.

Prudence did not need Lord Thornbridge's outraged roar to know that Sebastian had not had a chance to get beneath the big bed.

"Angelstone. You? Why, you blackhearted son of a bitch, I never thought to find you here, man. I was certain t'was someone else she would be meeting tonight. Devil take it, I thought . . . I believed . . . that is to say, I was told . . . How dare you, sir?"

"Good evening, Thornbridge." Sebastian's voice was amazingly cool. Incredibly, it was even laced with his customary cynical amusement. He sounded as if he had just encountered Thornbridge in his club rather than in Lady Thornbridge's bedchamber.

"I'll see you dead and in hell for this, Angelstone. Don't think I won't."

"Calm yourself, Thornbridge. I am not here for an assignation with your lady."

"What other reason could you possibly have for being here in her bedchamber? Don't you think I know she's disappeared from the ballroom? She's on her way up here to meet you, isn't she?"

"No."

"Don't try to deny it, you bastard," Thornbridge raged. "You're here to seduce my wife. Right here in my own house, by God. Have you no shame at all, man? No sense of decency or honor?"

"I have no notion of the whereabouts of Lady Thornbridge, sir. But I can assure you, I have no intention of meeting up with her here. See for yourself, she's nowhere in the vicinity."

"I suppose you've got a reasonable explanation for being in her bedchamber?" Thornbridge asked in disbelief.

"I was looking for the new water closet I'd heard you'd had installed."

"Do not think to fob me off with that banbury tale." Thornbridge was clearly infuriated. "The water closet is under the back staircase, exactly where it is in most respectable houses."

"My mistake, sir," Sebastian said politely. "I evidently got somewhat disoriented when I left the ballroom. I could have sworn one of the servants said it was on this floor. I believe I may have had a bit too much of your excellent champagne tonight, Thornbridge."

"You're not going to get away with this, Angelstone." Thornbridge's voice shook with the intensity of his emotion. "I don't care how good a marksman you are."

"If you're going to call me out, Thornbridge, I suggest you save your breath. In case you haven't heard, I've given up that sort of thing."

"You think I'll accept one of your mocking apologies?" Thornbridge's voice rose to a high, desperate pitch. "I'm not some stupid country squire to be taunted the way you're taunting young Merryweather."

"Thornbridge, listen to me for a minute. I can explain everything."

"I don't give a damn about your explanations. And you can save yourself the trouble of having your seconds convey your apologies. I have no intention of meeting you on the field of honor."

"Then what do you intend to do?" Sebastian asked quietly.

"What do you think I'm going to do? I am going to put a bullet in you right here and now, you bloody devil. Right where it will do the most good. You may bid farewell to your ballocks, sir. They will be of little use to you after tonight. We'll see how well you rut with other men's wives in future."

"For God's sake," Sebastian said. "Put the pistol down, man. I swear I have no designs on your lady wife. My attentions are directed elsewhere these days."

Prudence froze. She realized from the way the conversation was going that Thornbridge had a pistol. He was working himself up into a state that would enable him to pull the trigger.

"Don't expect me to believe you're genuinely interested in the Merryweather chit," Thornbridge stormed. "You're hardly the type to be amused for long by an oddity such as her. You're using that poor young woman, aren't you?"

"Thornbridge, will you kindly listen to me for a moment?"

"You're making a show of courting her, but what you're really doing is using her to distract attention while you pursue your true goal. You're using the Merryweather female as a blind while you dally with my wife."

"I have no interest in Lady Thornbridge," Sebastian said. He sounded as if he had abruptly lost his patience. "I give you my word, Thornbridge, I am not here in this bedchamber to await your wife."

"There's no other possible explanation," Thornbridge declared. "She's so beautiful. God knows that every man who looks at her desires her. You think you can just take what you want, don't you, Angelstone? Bloody damn arrogant bastard."

"Thornbridge, I urge you to try to contain yourself. You're losing control."

Prudence knew she dared not wait another minute. It was obvious Sebastian was not going to be able to talk Thornbridge out of his rage. It was time to repay the debt that she owed to the Fallen Angel.

She took a deep breath and pushed open the wardrobe door.

"I beg your pardon, my lords," Prudence said crisply as

the door swung open. "I believe it's time we put an end to this foolishness before someone gets hurt."

"What the devil?" Thornbridge swung toward her. In the light of the candle he had brought with him she could see the shock on his heavily jowled face. The pistol in his fist wavered precariously. "Miss Merryweather, by heaven. What are you doing here?"

"You must forgive Miss Merryweather, Thornbridge." Sebastian took a single step forward and deftly removed the pistol from Thornbridge's fingers. "She is still fresh from the country and has not yet learned the fine art of making a well-timed entrance."

Thornbridge ignored him. His astonished gaze was fixed on Prudence. His anger was rapidly turning to confusion. "What is going on here?"

Prudence blushed under the accusing stare, but she gave the baffled man a reassuring smile. "Isn't it obvious, my lord? Angelstone and I sought out a private place in which to discuss certain matters involving spectral phenomena and I fear we wandered in here by mistake."

"Spectral phenomena?" Thornbridge looked more mystified than ever. He also began to look doubtful.

Sebastian quirked a brow. "She has also not yet learned to tell a social lie. Not that there are many tales that could explain our presence in here. I believe we shall have to go with the truth on this occasion."

Thornbridge glowered at him. "The truth being that you brought this innocent young woman up here to seduce her. Isn't that correct, Angelstone?"

"Not precisely," Sebastian said.

"He had no such intentions," Prudence said briskly.

Thornbridge continued to scowl at Sebastian. "You should be ashamed of yourself, sir."

"You're not the first one to point that out to me to-night."

"My lord, you don't understand." Prudence jumped

down from the wardrobe. "Angelstone did not bring me up here with the intention of seducing me."

Thornbridge gave her a pitying look. "My poor dear Miss Merryweather. This business will well nigh break Lady Pembroke's kind heart. You are so pathetically naive."

Sebastian folded his arms and leaned against the wardrobe. He gazed meditatively at Prudence. "Naive is not quite the right word for Miss Merryweather. Harebrained might be a better one. Reckless. Ungovernable. Imprudent. Yes, I can think of a variety of terms that suit Miss Merryweather far better than naive."

She pushed her spectacles higher on her nose and glared at him. "That is unfair, my lord. I am attempting to explain this extremely upsetting situation to Lord Thornbridge. He has every right to know how we come to be in his wife's bedroom."

"By all means," Sebastian replied, his golden eyes brilliant with devilish laughter. "Explain it to him."

Annoyance flared in her as she realized he was not going to help her out at all. Damn the man, he was amusing himself again, this time at her expense. Considering the fact that they were in this situation because of his actions and that she was merely attempting to save his wretched neck, the least he could do was assist her in the task. Prudence turned back to Thornbridge.

"The thing is, my lord, this is all a terrible misunderstanding," she said earnestly.

Thornbridge cut her off with a flick of his hand. Now that he was no longer obliged to play the outraged husband, he had apparently decided to assume another role, that of the outraged host. He drew himself up and gave Sebastian a narrow-eyed look.

"Do not trouble yourself, Miss Merryweather. The facts speak for themselves. You are alone up here in a bedchamber with one of the most notorious men of the *ton*. No further explanations are necessary."

Prudence hesitated as she began to sense the new direction in which this was all going. She cautiously cleared her throat. "Sir, I believe you are under a very serious misapprehension."

Thornbridge paid her no heed. He was still glowering self-righteously at Sebastian. "Well, sir? Do you intend to do the proper thing by this young woman?"

Still standing with one shoulder propped against the wardrobe, Sebastian inclined his head with mocking gallantry. "As it happens, Thornbridge, Miss Merryweather and I are in this bedchamber because we were seeking some privacy in which to discuss our future. I have decided it is time I married. For her part, Miss Merryweather has wisely concluded that she is not likely to get a better offer due to her advanced years. We have therefore reached an agreement."

"Angelstone," Prudence got out in a strangled voice.

Sebastian did not even hesitate. "Allow me to present my fiancée, sir. Miss Merryweather and I are engaged."

Five

I am sorry to have to say this, my lord, but the disaster in which we find ourselves is entirely your fault," Prudence announced as Sebastian turned the sleek black phaeton into the crowded park.

"You are far too generous, my dear." Sebastian guided the two beautifully matched black horses into the stream of traffic. "I believe we can give you most of the credit for last night's proceedings."

Prudence retreated beneath the brim of her plain chip straw bonnet. She twitched her slate-colored bombazine skirts over her sturdy half boots and sought for a way to defend herself. "I was only trying to help."

"Were you, indeed?"

"If you had allowed me to make the explanations to Lord Thornbridge, everything would have been satisfactorily resolved." Prudence gazed straight ahead, acutely aware of the stares she and Sebastian were receiving from passing carriages.

It had been like this since last night when Thornbridge had accompanied them back to the ballroom and announced the news of the Fallen Angel's engagement.

The Thornbridges' guests had been first stunned and

then titillated and finally deeply intrigued. This was far and away the most entertaining event of the Season. The notion of the Fallen Angel marrying the amusing Original was obviously more than most members of the *ton* could bring themselves to believe.

Society's reaction was nothing compared to that of Hester and Trevor. They had been shocked speechless. Sebastian had warned Prudence not to attempt to explain the situation to either of them, as it would only make things more complicated. Prudence was forced to agree with him on that score.

Surprisingly, it was Hester who had recovered first from the stunning announcement. Once she had digested the news, her eyes had turned oddly speculative.

"Not quite what I expected," Hester had mused. "But then, the Fallen Angel rarely does what one expects. And it follows that he would choose someone out of the ordinary for his future countess."

"He's playing another one of his bloody games," Trevor had snarled.

"I'm not so certain of that," Hester had said. "An engagement is an honorable commitment. Whatever else one can say about Angelstone, he has never been known to break his word. In any event, there's nothing to be done about it now. Prue is engaged to the Fallen Angel and that's a simple fact. We shall have to go on as if everything were quite normal."

The engagement was definitely not a normal event as far as polite society was concerned. All of London was agog. Sebastian had decreed the drive in the park this afternoon, saying it was better to make a bold show than to try to hide from the unwanted attention. Prudence was not entirely certain that his reasoning was correct.

"Pray, do not take offense, Prue," he now said. "The truth is that your explanations to Thornbridge were doing more harm than good."

Prudence glared at him. "I do not see how they could have done any more harm than your ridiculous explanations, my lord. And I do not recall giving you leave to call me by my first name."

Sebastian's mouth curved faintly. "I didn't think you would mind. We are engaged, after all."

"Not by my doing."

"No?" Sebastian's black brow arched mockingly. "What did you think was going to happen when you leaped out of that wardrobe?"

Prudence clutched her large, practical reticule very tightly. "I was attempting to save your life, sir. In case you had not noticed, you were in a somewhat untenable position at the time."

"Yes, I was, wasn't I?" Sebastian looked unconcerned about the matter. "But you jumped to my rescue and I was saved."

"I am glad you appreciate that much, at least." She was stung by his amused sarcasm. "Under the terms of the bargain we made, I was in your debt. I was merely attempting to discharge my obligation to you."

"Ah, yes, our bargain."

"I thought I could repay you by saving you from Lord Thornbridge."

"I see."

Prudence subsided back into the guilt-ridden gloom she had been nursing since last night. "I collect you must be very angry, my lord."

Sebastian shrugged. "Not particularly."

Baffled, Prudence slanted him a sidelong glance. "Why ever not?"

"I don't think that our engagement will be a problem."

Prudence brightened. "You have a plan for dealing with our predicament?"

"I suppose one could say that I have."

Prudence gazed at him in growing respect and relief.

"My lord, that is excellent news. What, precisely, do you intend to do?"

Sebastian smiled at her, but his gaze was unreadable. "It's a very simple plan, my dear. I intend to enjoy to the fullest the benefits of being an engaged man."

Prudence's mouth fell open. "I beg your pardon?"

"You heard me." Sebastian inclined his head with chilling civility to an elderly lady in a passing carriage who was staring at the black phaeton. The woman looked away quickly.

"You intend to let our engagement stand?" Prudence demanded in disbelief. "Why on earth would you want to do that?"

"I don't see that we have much choice in the matter, do you? If we announce to the world that our engagement is a hoax, your reputation will be in shreds."

"That would not matter a great deal, my lord. I shall simply retire to the country somewhat ahead of schedule. Society will soon forget about me."

"What about me, Prue?" Sebastian asked gently. "The *ton* will not forget my role in all this very quickly, I assure you. Thornbridge, for one, will undoubtedly decide that his initial suspicions concerning my presence in his wife's bedchamber were correct. He will very likely come after me again with his pistol."

Prudence caught her lower lip between her teeth and peered at Sebastian. "Do you really believe he would do that?"

"I would say it is highly probable."

"I had not thought about that. What are we going to do, my lord?"

"Finish the Season as an engaged couple," Sebastian said calmly. "When June arrives, you may return to Dorset and I shall continue on about my affairs. The gossips will gradually lose interest."

"I take your point," Prudence said, thinking it through carefully. "Sometime during the summer I shall quietly announce that I am crying off. By fall everyone will have forgotten about the matter."

"Very likely."

"Yes, it just might work." Prudence frowned in thought. "It means that for the next two and a half months we shall both be obliged to carry out the pretense of being engaged."

"Do you think you can act the part of a happily engaged lady that long, Prue?"

"I don't know," she said honestly. "I have never tried my hand at amateur theatrics."

"I am certain that with a little practice, you will soon get the hang of it."

"Do you think so?" Prudence tilted her head to one side and gave him a shrewd glance. "What about you, my lord?"

Sebastian's mouth curved faintly. "There is no need to concern yourself, my dear. I assure you that I can handle my role. A talent for playacting is in my blood."

"Yes, that's right, it is, is it not? You are extremely fortunate that your mother was an accomplished actress." Prudence sighed. "I am really very sorry about all this."

"Look on the bright side," Sebastian suggested. "Perhaps now your pest of a brother will stop issuing a challenge every time I dance with you."

"There is that, I suppose." Prudence cleared her throat discreetly. "There is just one small point concerning last night's events that I wish to have clarified before we go forward with this pretense of an engagement."

Sebastian smiled. "Allow me to guess what that small point is. You probably want to know precisely what I was doing in Lady Thornbridge's bedchamber."

"Yes, as a matter of fact, I would like an explanation. I do not believe for one moment that you had an assignation with her. I have observed you closely of late, my lord, and last night was not the first time that I've seen you mysteriously disappear for a while from a ballroom. As far as I could determine, you were not meeting anyone on those occasions."

Sebastian glanced at her with an expression of cool admiration. "You've been very observant. But I cannot say I'm surprised. You are a most amazing female."

"I am not at all certain that is a compliment. Now, are you going to tell me what was going on last night?"

Sebastian's amber eyes gleamed briefly as he considered the question. "Did you really believe I had become a cracksman?"

Prudence narrowed her gaze behind the lenses of her spectacles. "It occurred to me, my lord, that in a misguided attempt to alleviate your ennui, you might have resorted to a somewhat unfortunate hobby."

"In other words, you thought I might have turned into a jewel thief. I am crushed to learn that you hold me in such low esteem."

"Well, I wasn't altogether certain that was what you were about," Prudence said quickly. "After all, it is not as if you need the money. Everyone says you are as rich as Croesus. So what were you doing in Lady Thornbridge's bedchamber?"

"You were partially correct in your initial assumption. As I tried to tell you, I was looking for a necklace. A very particular necklace."

"What?" Prudence gazed at him in astonishment. "I do not believe it."

"It's quite true. The necklace did not belong to Lady Thornbridge, however."

Prudence was immediately intrigued. "Whose necklace was it?"

"It belongs to a certain lady of the *ton* who gave it to Lady Thornbridge."

"Why did she give it to her?" Prudence asked.

"She had hoped to purchase Lady Thornbridge's silence," Sebastian said softly.

"Her silence?" Prudence leaped to the obvious conclusion. "Lady Thornbridge was blackmailing this woman?"

"Precisely. When Lady Thornbridge demanded another piece of jewelry in exchange for further silence, however, the victim realized there would be no end to the demands. She decided to see if anything could be done to stop Lady Thornbridge."

Prudence frowned. "The victim came to you about this matter?"

"No, she consulted a Bow Street Runner named Whistlecroft. Whistlecroft decided to contact me. He and I have worked out an arrangement, you see. He has instructions to bring some of his more interesting cases to me."

Prudence was enthralled now. "And he came to you with this case?"

"Yes."

"How exciting," Prudence breathed. "Did you find the necklace last night?"

Sebastian's arrogant smile contained more than a trace of smug satisfaction. "Yes, as it happens, I did."

"Where is it? What have you done with it?"

"It was returned to its rightful owner this morning. Whistlecroft handled that end of the business. I prefer to remain anonymous in such matters. No one else except you, Whistlecroft, and a friend of mine named Garrick Sutton knows about my little hobby."

"I see. I can understand why you wish to keep your hobby a secret. But what about Lady Thornbridge? Won't she make good on her blackmail threats once she realizes her victim is no longer cooperating?"

"I doubt it."

"Why not?"

"Because before I was so rudely interrupted by you and

Thornbridge, I had time to leave a note in Lady Thornbridge's safe, in place of the necklace. She will discover it soon enough."

"A note?" Prudence asked. "What did it say?"

"Merely that an anonymous party was aware that Lady Thornbridge's pedigree was not quite what Society and Lord Thornbridge believed it to be. To put it bluntly, Prue, Lady Thornbridge came from the gutters and she would be ruined in Society if that fact were ever revealed."

"The gutters?"

"She is an exceedingly clever, ambitious little creature who has fought her way up in the world. I do not fault her in the least for creating a respectable facade that has fooled the *ton* and landed her a wealthy husband."

Prudence chuckled. "In other words, she worked hard for what she's got and you respect her for it, but you cannot countenance her falling back into her old ways, is that it?"

"Not when she chooses a victim who has also fought her way out of the stews and into Society. Lady Thornbridge has everything she wants now, so there is no need to resort to blackmailing another lady of the *ton* who has a background similar to her own."

"Quite right." Prudence nodded briskly in agreement. "You told her that in your note?"

"Yes."

"But how did you learn Lady Thornbridge's secrets?" Prudence asked.

"I have my methods of investigation, just as you have yours."

Prudence recalled his recent disappearances from various ballrooms. "Your methods must be clever, indeed, my lord. Lady Thornbridge has succeeded in fooling the entire *ton*, yet you found her out. Brilliant, Angelstone. Absolutely brilliant."

"I had a feeling you would appreciate my efforts."

"I most certainly do." Prudence laughed in delight. "You handled the whole thing very well, my lord."

"Thank you."

"But won't Lady Thornbridge guess that it was you who left her the note?"

"I doubt it. Even if Thornbridge tells her that it was her bedchamber in which he discovered us, she probably won't connect me to the note she'll eventually find in her safe."

"Why not?"

"For one thing, it may be several days before she discovers the note. She won't have any way of knowing when it was left. For another, even if she does think about the fact that I was found in her bedchamber, she'll recall that you were with me," Sebastian said.

Prudence tilted her head to one side and studied him from under the brim of her bonnet. "I don't understand."

"Like everyone else, she'll think that we disappeared upstairs so that I could seduce you in the first available bedchamber I found."

"*My lord.*" Prudence was shocked, in spite of herself. She could feel her cheeks turning violently pink.

"A charming picture, is it not?"

"I suppose that is what everyone is thinking today," Prudence said morosely.

"No doubt."

Prudence was silent for a moment as she contemplated what Sebastian had just told her. "This information explains everything, of course. You have found yourself a most interesting, if rather dangerous hobby, my lord."

"I enjoy it from time to time," Sebastian admitted.

"It is not unlike my own little hobby."

"I am aware of that." Sebastian flicked the reins lightly over the horses' rumps. "It gives us something in common, don't you think?"

"Yes. Yes, it does." Prudence turned to him, bubbling

over with sudden enthusiasm. "Sir, it occurs to me that we could combine our interests."

Sebastian slanted her a wary glance. "What the devil are you talking about?"

"I do not see why we could not conduct investigations together, my lord. Between the two of us, we would make an excellent team."

"The way we did last night?" Sebastian asked bluntly. "May I remind you that I very nearly got shot by a jealous husband because of your helpful assistance?"

"That is very unfair, my lord. What would you have done without me?"

"Hidden in the wardrobe myself and avoided Thornbridge," Sebastian said succinctly. "He would never have seen me."

"Oh." Prudence sought for a successful counterargument with which to demolish his reasoning but could find none. She decided to try a different tactic. "I urge you to think of how very interesting it would be for us to work together, sir. Only consider the fascinating conversations we shall have."

"I have considered that. Why do you think I told you about Lady Thornbridge's blackmailing scheme? I did not say I was opposed to discussing my cases with you."

Prudence's hopes rose again. "Then you do think we might work together?"

"On a consulting basis only," Sebastian said evenly. "I am willing to discuss my cases with you, but I will not allow you to accompany me on my investigations. I want no more scenes such as the one that transpired last night."

"I don't see why not," Prudence retorted. "The damage has already been done. We are already trapped in this farce of an engagement for the remainder of the Season. What else could possibly go wrong?"

Sebastian's mouth tightened in a grim line. "There is always a certain risk involved in my investigations. I do not want you confronting any more pistols."

Prudence's eyes widened. "Does that sort of thing happen often in the course of your investigations?"

"Of course not. But I am not going to take any chances. As I said, I shall discuss my cases with you, but that is as far as it goes." He gave her an indulgent look. "After all, my dear, your expertise is in the field of spectral phenomena, not in the investigation of blackmailers and other such criminals."

"But I feel certain many of my methods would apply equally well to the investigation of criminal activities as they do to the investigation of spectral phenomena," Prudence assured him earnestly.

"Trust me, my dear, there is a world of difference between the two types of investigations."

Prudence glowered at him. "How would you know?"

"It's obvious." Sebastian's gloved hands moved almost imperceptibly on the reins. The horses quickened their pace to a trot.

"My lord, I must say, you are being extremely stubborn about this. As we are going to be obliged to spend a great deal of time in each other's company for the next two and a half months, I do not see why we should not spend that time assisting each other in our various investigations."

"The answer is no, Prue, and that is final."

There was no mistaking the ring of inflexible steel in Sebastian's words. Prudence lifted her chin. "Very well, my lord. If you choose to be arrogant and thick-skulled about the matter, there is little I can do."

He smiled in approval. "I'm glad you aren't the sort of female who whines when she doesn't get her own way. I find that sort of thing extremely tiresome."

"Whine? Me? Not at all, my lord." Prudence tried to imitate his cool smile. "I would not want to bore you. In any event, I expect I shall be busy enough with my own investigations."

Sebastian inclined his head politely. "I shall look forward to hearing about them."

Prudence did not care for the slightly condescending tone she thought she detected in his voice. "Perhaps I will be able to give you a full report on my latest investigation as early as tomorrow morning."

"That soon?" Sebastian glanced at her. "Have you found a client here in Town?"

"A friend of Lady Pembroke's has brought me a most fascinating case." Prudence leaned closer. "Are you acquainted with Mrs. Leacock?"

Sebastian reflected briefly. "I've heard of her. Her husband recently died and left her his fortune, as I recall."

"Yes, well, she has recently been having a great deal of trouble with a ghost in the west wing of her home. I had hoped to be able to test out some of my latest theories by using an electricity machine to trap this particular ghost, but I fear that would be a waste of time on this case."

"How are you going to catch your ghost?"

Prudence gave him a superior sort of smile. "Lady Pembroke and I are going to stay the night with her. Tonight I shall sleep in Mrs. Leacock's bedchamber in the west wing."

Sebastian slanted her a curious glance. "You're going to trade places with Mrs. Leacock?"

"Correct. But we are not going to tell anyone about the switch."

He was amused. "Why not? Do you think the ghost will care?"

"As a matter of fact," Prudence said, "I think he just might care a great deal."

Sebastian eyed her sharply. "He?"

"I have concluded my initial inquiries. There are several interesting factors about this particular case of spectral phenomena," Prudence confided. "The first is that the apparition did not begin appearing until very recently."

"How recently?"

"The incidents began occurring shortly after Mr. Leacock's death," Prudence said. "Mrs. Leacock had never before encountered the ghost in the west wing. Nor had anyone else. There were no rumors of the house being haunted until now."

"The woman has just suffered the loss of her husband," Sebastian reminded her. "She is probably having nightmares."

"I'm not entirely convinced of that. You see, the second interesting feature of this case is that Mrs. Leacock has no children of her own. But according to Lady Pembroke, she does have three greedy nephews. And all three are aware that their aunt has recently been told by her doctor that she has a weak heart."

"Bloody hell." Sebastian stared at her. "Are you telling me you think that the nephews might be deliberately trying to terrify their aunt in hopes of causing her heart to fail?"

"I think it's quite possible. Tonight I intend to find out."

"By confronting the ghost?" Sebastian's jaw set in an implacable line. "I think not."

"You, my lord," Prudence said sweetly, "have nothing to say about it."

"The devil, I don't. I'm your fiancé now, Prue."

"In name only."

"Nevertheless," he said between his teeth, "you will listen to me."

"I have been listening to you, my lord." Prudence smiled serenely. "And you have made it very clear that we are to conduct our investigations separately. As I understand it, you do not wish us to work together as a team. Or did I mistake your meaning?"

"Don't throw my words back in my face, you little baggage. You know damn well what I meant."

Prudence gave him a lofty smile. "I heard you very

clearly, my lord. We are allowed to discuss our cases with each other, but we are not to assist each other in the actual investigations. Don't worry, I shall tell you all about my discoveries tomorrow."

Sebastian's eyes glittered. "Prue, you have a great deal to learn about being an engaged woman."

"Do you think so, my lord? How odd. And here I thought I was adapting rather nicely to my new role."

"Prue, I will not allow you—"

"*Prudence.* By God, it is you. I didn't believe it."

Prudence flinched at the sound of the familiar masculine voice. She had not heard it in nearly three years, but she was hardly likely to forget it. She turned her head and looked straight into the soft gray eyes of the man who had taught her that her intuition was not infallible.

"Good afternoon, Lord Underbrink," she said quietly as the newcomer guided his handsome gray stallion closer to the phaeton.

Prudence took a deep breath and forced herself to examine Edward, Lord Underbrink, with polite detachment. To her surprise and overwhelming relief she felt nothing except a sense of deep chagrin at the memory of her own gullibility. What a little fool she had been three years ago to think that Underbrink was serious when he made his proposal of marriage.

There had never been any question of the heir to the Underbrink title marrying the daughter of a country squire. Edward had merely been amusing himself that summer.

He had not changed much in three years, Prudence reflected. His hair was still as fair as she remembered, his eyes still as open and guileless. His pleasant features were still quite appealing, although she thought she detected some signs of plumpness developing around his jawline. He was dressed in a well-cut coat that was the exact same shade of pearl gray as his expensive mount.

"This is astonishing," Underbrink said. "I just got back into Town yesterday. I learned that you were here for the Season last night, but I could hardly credit it." He glanced uneasily at Sebastian. "There were rumors of an engagement."

Sebastian flicked a brief, dismissing glance over Underbrink. "The rumors are true."

Edward's gaze jerked quickly back to Prudence. "I don't understand."

"In that case, Underbrink," Sebastian said softly, "I suggest you try reading the notices that will appear in tomorrow's morning papers. Perhaps that will make it clear to you."

Edward frowned. "Now, see here, Angelstone, Prudence and I are old friends. I have every right to be interested in her engagement. You cannot blame me for being surprised by this announcement."

Prudence saw the cold fire pooling in Sebastian's eyes. She did not know why he was acting as if he were annoyed by Edward, but she decided it would be best to head off a confrontation.

"How is Lady Underbrink these days?" Prudence asked brightly. She had never met the woman Edward had married, but it seemed safe enough to inquire after her.

A deep, angry flush stained Edward's cheeks. "She's well enough," he said brusquely. "Listen, Prue, I shall be at the Handleys' soiree this evening. Will you be there?"

"She will not be attending the Handleys' soiree," Sebastian said. "And in future, Underbrink, you will address my fiancée as Miss Merryweather. Is that very clear?"

Edward straightened quickly in his saddle. His flush deepened. "Of course."

"I'm glad to see you are capable of comprehending a few simple things. You will be the healthier for it." Sebastian urged his horses to a faster pace. "Now you must excuse us, Underbrink."

The black phaeton sped down the wide path, leaving Edward behind.

Prudence took a deep breath. She knew she ought to reproach Sebastian for his rudeness, but she could not bring herself to do so. She suddenly realized how tense she had been during the encounter.

She did not know what she had expected to feel upon seeing Lord Underbrink again, but the only emotion she was truly aware of was a sense of relief. *Relief that he had not married her after all.* It was difficult to recall that she had once thought herself in love with him.

Sebastian said nothing for a few minutes. He appeared to be concentrating entirely on his driving. Eventually he eased the horses back to a walk.

"How do you come to be acquainted with Underbrink?" he asked without any inflection in his voice.

Prudence adjusted her spectacles. "Three years ago he spent a great deal of the summer in Dorset. He was staying with friends who were neighbors of ours. We met on several occasions. Assemblies, card parties, that sort of thing."

"What happened?"

Prudence flashed him a quick glance and then returned her attention to the ears of his horses. "Not a great deal. At the end of the summer he returned to London to become engaged to the woman his family wished him to marry."

"Lucinda Montclair."

"Yes, I believe that was her name," Prudence said quietly. "Her father is said to be very rich."

"He is. Lucinda is also a very wealthy young woman in her own right."

"So I was given to understand," Prudence murmured.

"And an extremely jealous woman," Sebastian added. "Word is that Underbrink is henpecked. Apparently his wife keeps him on a very short leash. Did he seduce you during that summer in Dorset?"

Prudence nearly dropped her reticule. "Good heavens, my lord. What a thing to ask."

"It seems a reasonable enough question to me."

"It is a very unreasonable question," Prudence retorted. "But for your information, Lord Underbrink was a perfect gentleman at all times."

There was no need to explain that Edward had kissed her on several occasions. A lady was entitled to some privacy, after all. In any event, Edward's kisses now appeared distinctly uninspired compared to the searing kiss Sebastian had given her the night she had gone to his town house.

"So you and Underbrink were no more than friends three years ago?"

"Precisely," Prudence said tightly. "There was never anything of a serious nature between us. Lord Underbrink was merely amusing himself in the country that summer."

She must keep in mind that Underbrink was not the only one who sought to amuse himself in ways that could prove painful for others.

Shortly after midnight that night, Prudence put on a white muslin cap and climbed into the massive canopied bed that dominated Mrs. Leacock's bedchamber. She was wearing a serviceable woolen gown rather than a night rail and she had on her spectacles. She did not intend to sleep tonight.

She had to admit she was having a few second thoughts about her investigation. The west wing of the Leacock mansion seemed eerily quiet. There was no denying that it was a fine setting for a real ghost. Prudence could not even hear the normal street sounds of carriage wheels, nightmen, and drunken revelers because the bedchamber faced the vast, silent Leacock gardens.

The notion of spending the night in Mrs. Leacock's bedchamber had seemed an excellent one when Prudence first thought of it. If one or more of Mrs. Leacock's greedy nephews was up to some nefarious trick, this was the only way to catch him. Poor Mrs. Leacock had suffered enough.

Prudence leaned across the bed to open the drawer in the nightstand. She reached inside and touched the cold metal of the small pistol she had put there earlier.

Somewhat reassured, she leaned back against the pillows and gazed up at the heavy canopy overhead. It was going to be a very long night.

Not that she didn't have plenty to think about, she told herself. Her life had certainly taken an interesting turn of late. She still could not quite believe that she was engaged to Sebastian. The fact that the engagement was not going to last very long did nothing to diminish her excitement.

She must remember that her relationship with Sebastian was doomed to remain a friendship. He was, after all, an earl and he could certainly look much higher than herself when he finally got around to choosing a wife. He would do his duty by his title and family name, just as Edward had done three years ago.

But she also knew in her heart she was wildly attracted to the Fallen Angel. The sense of deep recognition that she experienced when she was with him was startling in its intensity. It was also infinitely more seductive than the far more shallow feelings she had experienced toward Edward.

It would take very little for her to fall in love with Sebastian, Prudence thought. In truth, she suspected she was already in love with him.

Prudence scowled and adjusted the heavy quilt. She must not indulge herself in foolish, hopeless, romantic dreams about Sebastian.

Instead she would content herself with savoring the pleasures of an intellectual connection to the only man she had ever met who understood and shared her interests.

If she were very fortunate, she thought, suddenly optimistic, such an intellectual connection might continue to exist even after she was obliged to return to Dorset. Perhaps she could correspond with him. He could keep her informed of his investigations. He might be interested in asking her advice on certain topics. She would tell him about her research into spectral phenomena.

Yes, a correspondence might very well be possible. At least until he acquired a wife. Prudence was instantly downcast. Sebastian was very likely to find himself a wife quite soon. He had a certain responsibility, after all.

A small muffled thud snapped Prudence out of her reverie. The soft noise sent a jolt of alarm through her. She sat up against the pillows, straining to listen.

The notion of confronting the ghost alone suddenly seemed somewhat more daunting than it had earlier. If she was correct in her suspicions concerning Mrs. Leacock's nephews, she might be in some danger. Prudence wished Sebastian were with her. He would be a very competent assistant in this phase of the investigation.

She peered into the darkness, watching for candlelight beneath the door that connected Mrs. Leacock's bedchamber to the next room. Mrs. Leacock had said that the ghost carried a candle.

Another muted thud made Prudence's pulse race more swiftly. She started to reach for the pistol in the drawer.

She froze when she caught sight of the dark shadow of a man standing on the ledge outside the window. Panic assailed her. Nothing had been said about the ghost entering from that direction.

The window opened abruptly. Cold air swept into the room.

Prudence found her voice. "Who goes there?" She wrenched open the drawer and grabbed the pistol.

The cloaked figure that had been looming outside on the ledge stepped into the room.

"Stop, whoever you are." Prudence pushed aside the covers and scrambled out of bed. She clutched the pistol with both hands.

"I pray you won't use that pistol, my dear," Sebastian said calmly. "Only think of the gossip that would ensue were you to shoot your fiancé a day after announcing your engagement."

Six

Allow me to compliment you on your enchanting nightclothes, my dear." Sebastian surveyed the plain woolen gown and muslin cap that Prudence was wearing. "I should have expected that your choice in such garments would be spectacularly original."

"What on earth do you think you're doing, sir?" Prudence slowly lowered the pistol. The moonlight streaming through the window glinted on her spectacles and revealed her strained expression. "You gave me a terrible start. I might have shot you."

"It was a near thing, was it not? My life does seem to be filled with adventure these days. First Thornbridge tries to shoot me and then my fiancée takes aim at my vitals. I am not certain how many of these encounters my nerves can tolerate."

She gave him an annoyed look. "I asked you a question, my lord."

"So you did." Sebastian glanced around the shadowed bedroom, taking in the dark, heavy furnishings and the massive bed. "The answer is that I came here tonight in order to give you the benefit of my expertise."

"And what is that supposed to mean, pray tell?"

He smiled slightly at the suspicious tone of her voice.

"Isn't it obvious?" He swung his greatcoat off his shoulders and tossed it over a chair. He was wearing only his shirt and breeches beneath it. He had decided a coat and cravat were not called for on such an occasion. "I'm here to help you investigate your newest case of spectral phenomena."

"I do not require your assistance, my lord. I thought we agreed this afternoon that we would not work together on our cases."

"As to that," Sebastian said easily, "I've reconsidered the matter."

"You have?" The pale light illuminated the hopeful look on her expressive face. "That is wonderful news."

"It's not as if I had a great deal of choice in the matter," Sebastian muttered under his breath.

"I beg your pardon?"

"Never mind." There would be time enough at some later date to explain precisely how their new partnership would work.

It was very simple, really. Sebastian fully intended to supervise Prudence's more adventurous investigations, but he had no intention of letting her risk her neck helping him with his own cases.

Prudence put the pistol on the end table. "How did you find me in this particular bedchamber?"

Sebastian shrugged. "I watched for the last light to be extinguished in this wing."

"Very clever of you." Prudence went to the window and looked down into the gardens. "Good heavens, it is a sheer drop. However did you climb up the wall?"

"I didn't. I entered the house through the kitchens and climbed the stairs to this floor. Then I opened a window in an empty room and discovered that very convenient ledge outside. It led me straight to this bedchamber."

"An excellent approach to the problem, my lord."

"It was nothing, really. A matter of simple logic and reason," Sebastian said modestly.

"Yes, of course, but I doubt that many people would have thought of that approach."

"Possibly not," he admitted, gratified by her admiration.

It occurred to Sebastian that although he had not given a damn about anyone's opinion since his parents and brother had died, lately he found himself increasingly hungry for Prudence's approval.

She was the only female he knew who was capable of appreciating his peculiar talents and interests. He wondered if she had any notion of how badly he wanted to bed her.

He watched her standing at the window and contemplated the possibility that he was going slightly mad. No woman had ever had such an effect on him. When he was with her the icy barrier inside him seemed much smaller and farther away. He could almost forget it and the emptiness that it concealed.

At that moment Prudence turned her head to look at him. The weak moonlight fell across her features, revealing her glowing smile. Desire swept through Sebastian in a great wave, leaving him shaken.

It had become painfully clear during the past few days that the sensual hunger Prudence had aroused in him that first night was no fleeting fancy.

It was equally clear and profoundly annoying to realize that Prudence's interest in him appeared to be inspired primarily by his hobby. He wondered again how much Underbrink had meant to her. He had been gnawing on that question ever since he had returned from the drive in the park that afternoon.

"Now that you are here, we ought to make some new plans." Prudence cast a thoughtful glance at the wardrobe. "We must discover a way to conceal you in case the apparition appears."

"You may forget the wardrobe," Sebastian said. "I have no intention of spending the rest of the night in it."

"Where will you hide, then? Under the bed?"

Sebastian swore softly. "I don't think it will be necessary for me to conceal myself until we have some indication that the ghost is about to make his appearance."

"But if the apparition proves to be one of Mrs. Leacock's nephews, we don't want to let him know you're here. We cannot light a candle and we must be very quiet."

Sebastian raised his brows. "I assure you, I can be extremely quiet. There is plenty of light from the moon, so we do not need a candle. For once there is no damned fog, although I suspect it will arrive again at dawn. Our only concern now is how to pass the time until our ghost chooses to appear."

She looked at him expectantly. "We probably should not converse. We might be overheard."

"I agree." Sebastian walked toward her.

"I suppose we could play a hand of whist," Prudence suggested. "Unfortunately, I do not happen to have any cards with me."

"Then we shall have to think of some other method of amusing ourselves." Sebastian caught her chin between thumb and forefinger. He gently raised her face so that he could see her eyes more clearly.

Prudence stood very still, as if the touch of his hand had stunned her into immobility. She looked up at him with a wide, searching gaze that held both curiosity and wariness.

"My lord?" she whispered breathlessly.

"There is something I wish to know, Prue."

Her lips parted slightly. The tip of her tongue touched the corner of her mouth. "What is that?"

"Do you think it possible that you can discover something more to recommend me than just my amusing little hobby?"

"Whatever do you mean?"

"Allow me to show you," he said softly.

Sebastian bent his head and brushed his mouth slowly

across her lips. She made a small, inarticulate little sound that utterly captivated him.

Deliberately he deepened the kiss and traced the fine line of her jaw with his thumb.

A delicate shiver went through Prudence. Sebastian felt it instantly. Relief and satisfaction poured through him. He could make her want him, he told himself.

Prudence moaned softly as he eased apart her lips. He felt her hands move first to his shoulders. Then her arms stole around his neck. She pressed herself closer.

Heat rose within him. He could hardly feel the cold at all now. It had been temporarily banished by the fire of his need for Prudence.

Prudence gasped when he temporarily freed her mouth to explore her soft neck. "Sebastian, I don't know if this is a sound notion."

"Trust me, Prue."

"I do trust you," she said quickly.

"Good." He slid his hand down her back, deliberately urging her closer until her soft breasts were crushed against his chest and the gentle curve of her mound pressed against his shaft. His body was already hard with arousal.

"Sebastian, you make me feel so very strange." Prudence gently touched the nape of his neck. The caress sent a thrill of anticipation through him. She stood on tiptoe and tangled her fingers in his hair. Then she began to return his kisses with untutored passion.

She had obviously not learned much from Underbrink, Sebastian thought with deep satisfaction.

His blood surged through his veins like heavy lightning. All thoughts of trapping a ghost fled. He could handle an apparition or two if one happened to appear tonight. In the meantime there were far more important matters.

He was going to make love to Prudence, who, whether she knew it or not, would soon be his wife.

"Sebastian?"

"It's all right, my sweet." He drew her toward the vast bed. "Everything will be all right."

"I cannot seem to think clearly when you are kissing me," she complained.

"Neither can I." Sebastian smiled. "Fortunately, there is no pressing need for clear thinking at a time like this." He gently removed her spectacles and set them on the nightstand.

She gazed anxiously at him, as if he had lifted a veil and left her completely exposed. An aching tenderness welled up within Sebastian.

"You are lovely," he whispered.

Her eyes widened in startled surprise. "Do you really think so?"

"Yes, I really think so." He took her earlobe between his teeth and bit gently. "And I want you very much."

"You want me?" She sounded dazed now, as if her exceedingly clever little brain had suddenly come up against a truly baffling dilemma. "I'm not certain I comprehend your meaning, my lord."

"You will comprehend it soon enough. God knows I cannot hide it much longer. You have no notion of your effect on me, do you?"

Her smile was tremulous. "If my effect on you is anything like yours on me, we are faced with a most unusual problem, sir. I am not at all certain what we should do next."

"As it happens, I know precisely what to do next."

Sebastian lowered his head and kissed her again. Her arms tightened around his neck. When he felt her lean into him in a silent signal of feminine surrender, he eased the toe of his boot between her slippered feet.

She drew in her breath but made no protest when he gently forced his thigh between her legs. The skirts of her gown rode upward as he lifted his knee and planted his foot on the bed behind her.

Prudence gave a tiny, muffled shriek when she abruptly

found herself straddling his thigh as if she were perched astride a horse.

"*Sebastian.* Good heavens." She clung to him in shock.

"Hush, my sweet. We must not make too much noise. We don't want to scare off the ghost." Sebastian groaned as he felt the intimate heat of her soft, warm femininity burning through his breeches.

Not just heat, he thought triumphantly, but a telltale dampness, too. He caught the faint, tantalizing scent of Prudence's growing arousal and very nearly lost his self-control.

"My lovely, Prue," he said in awed wonder. "Where have you been all these years?"

"In Dorset," she said very seriously.

Sebastian hid his smile in her hair. He slipped his hand up along her stocking-clad leg and touched the top of her bare silken thigh. She flinched in reaction. Then she breathed deeply.

"For some reason," Sebastian said, "I feel I know you very, very well. It is as if we were old friends, you and I. Or perhaps lovers."

"How very odd." Her voice was dreamy now, soft and warm and thick with desire. "I was thinking much the same thing just before you arrived. It is as if we have been intimate acquaintances for years, although we have known each other for only a very short time."

"We are going to know each other even more intimately before this night is done," Sebastian vowed.

He could wait no longer. She wanted him and he wanted her. They were engaged. It was suddenly all very simple and straightforward.

Sebastian eased his booted foot back down off the quilt, lowering Prudence slowly onto her toes. Before her feet had quite touched the floor, he was pushing her back onto the bed.

He drew in his breath at the sight of her lying there amid the rumpled white sheets. Her skirts foamed above her knees, revealing the garters that secured her practical cotton stockings. The curve of her calf was very elegant as it tapered down to her delicately shaped ankle. Above the garters her thighs were beautifully rounded.

Sebastian stared down at Prudence's legs and envisioned them wrapped around his waist. He heard himself make a hoarse, inarticulate sound deep in his throat.

"Is something wrong?" Prudence looked up at him in concern.

"No, nothing is wrong. Nothing has ever been this right." Sebastian ripped at the fastenings of his shirt. He heard the fine linen tear, but he paid no attention. All that mattered now was making love to Prudence.

He got the shirt open, but he did not take the time to shed it completely. He was too impatient to feel Prudence's fingers on his bare skin. He sat down on the edge of the bed and yanked off his boots.

"You seem in a great hurry, Sebastian."

"I am."

He lowered himself down beside Prue and gathered her into his arms.

"Touch me," he said. He caught her hand in his and guided it inside his open shirt. "I want to feel your hands on me."

"Yes. Yes, I would like that very much, too." Prudence gave a tiny, broken exclamation of pleasure as she skimmed her fingers across his bare chest. She grasped handfuls of the thick, curling hair she found there.

Sebastian sucked in his breath.

Prudence looked up at him. "I love the feel of you. There is so much strength and power in you. The first night I saw you, I thought you were the most wonderful creature I had ever seen."

He was stunned into temporary speechlessness by the sweet, honest desire in her moonlit eyes. There was no coyness in her, he thought. No artifice at all.

He thrust his thigh between her, bent his head, and kissed her throat. He finally found his voice. "You won't regret this, Prue. I swear it on my honor."

Her lips brushed across his shoulder. "I do not expect to regret anything that I do with you. How could I? It is all far too wonderful for words."

"Prue, you take my breath away." Sebastian pulled her close and started to unfasten the row of shell buttons that closed the back of her gown. The process seemed to take forever. So damned many buttons.

"Bloody hell," he muttered, fumbling with the last of the buttons. He was suddenly chagrined at his lack of self-control.

"Are you all right, Sebastian?"

"I'm fine." But that was not true, he thought as he slowly lowered the bodice of her gown and revealed her small, firm breasts. He was far from all right. His hands were shaking. He felt as if he were consumed by fever. His lower body was throbbing. His mind was dazed with the force of his need.

No, he was definitely not all right. But that was all right, too. He had not felt so completely *right* for longer than he cared to remember.

"Sebastian?"

He stared down at her exquisitely curved breasts. He really was going mad.

"God, but you are perfect, Prue." He bent his head and took one firm little nipple between his teeth.

"*Oh.*" Her fingers clenched in his hair and her slender body arched as if she had touched an electricity machine.

Her instant reaction to his caress drove Sebastian closer to the edge of his control. He reached down and pushed his hand up beneath the edge of her skirts.

He stroked her thighs until she trembled. Then he probed higher, seeking the moist heat he knew he would find waiting for him. Just for him. Only for him.

He found it.

"Sebastian." Prudence shuddered and tried to lock her legs against him. He sensed the movement was instinctive on her part, her natural reaction to a caress she had never before experienced.

"It's all right," he whispered encouragingly. "I want to feel all the secret places. I want to know you as intimately as a man can know a woman."

"Yes, but this is so strange." Her voice was muffled against his shirt.

"You are a lady who delights in investigating the strange and the unusual," he reminded her. He gently forced her thighs apart again and found the soft petals hidden in the even softer hair.

"Yes, I know, but . . . Oh. Good heavens. Oh, my God. Sebastian, what are you doing?"

She was as hot and wet as he had known she would be. Sebastian sank one finger deep into her slick, tight channel. The small passage tightened around him like a well-made glove. The sensation was indescribable. He feared he would humiliate himself by spilling his seed then and there.

"I did not know making love would feel like this," Prudence confided breathlessly.

Sebastian looked down into her wide-open eyes. "Neither did I."

Suddenly his own pounding desire was not nearly as important as his need to give Prudence her first real taste of passion. He wanted her to experience the thrill of release and to know that he had been responsible for that release. There would be plenty of time to satisfy himself later. They had all night.

Sebastian eased his finger out of her until he felt her clench in frustration. He found the sensitive bud with his thumb and slowly pushed his finger back into her wondrously warm passage.

Prudence made a tiny sound that was halfway between a

shriek and a moan. Sebastian covered her mouth with his own and deliberately repeated the caress between her legs.

She gave another muffled cry and clutched at the fabric of his shirt. Her knees clamped shut again, trapping his hand against her.

"You must relax a little." Sebastian dropped a series of soft, persuasive kisses across her breasts. "Open yourself. Yes, that's it, my sweet. Let me inside, Prue. Deep inside." He felt her hesitate and then slowly part her soft thighs again. "You are so warm," he whispered. "I want to feel your heat. I need to feel it."

He stroked into her again and again, gradually widening her until he thought he could slide a second finger into her. He started to do so.

Prudence's reaction was immediate and intense. She went rigid. Her mouth opened on a soft, silent scream and then she started to shiver. Sebastian felt the tiny ripples rush through her. The moment of her release was gratifying beyond anything he had ever experienced in his life.

He raised his head and watched Prudence's face as she gave herself up to her climax.

"Beautiful," he whispered.

And then she went limp against him. She mumbled something into his shirt that Sebastian could not understand. He smiled and reluctantly withdrew his hand from between her legs.

Now it was his turn.

He inhaled Prudence's scent as he started to unfasten his breeches. He was so fully aroused that he doubted he would be able to last for more than a few strokes at the most. Hell, he thought, he would be lucky to last long enough to get inside her.

The muffled clank of a chain broke the spell.

Sebastian felt as if someone had just doused him with a bucket of ice-cold water. He went absolutely still. He felt Prudence tense.

"The ghost," she whispered.

"Bloody hell." Sebastian shook his head in an attempt to clear away the cobwebs of passion. He fumbled with the opening of his breeches and managed to get it closed. "If this is an example of the sort of poor timing that damned specter exhibited when he was alive, it's no wonder someone murdered him."

The heavy clanking sound came again. It was closer now, reverberating through the walls. A low moan came from the other side of the connecting door.

"Lydia. Lydia, I have come for you."

"Bastard." Sebastian pushed himself up off the bed.

"What are you doing?" Prudence mouthed the words as she struggled to right her clothing.

"I'm going to take care of that ghost." Sebastian yanked the bedding up over her head. "Don't move. Don't make a sound."

He left her lying there, a large, interesting lump under the quilt, and quickly crossed the room to the window. He yanked the heavy drapes together, cutting off the moonlight. The room was plunged into stygian darkness.

"Lydia, where are you? Your time has come. I have waited a long, long while for you to join me in my grave."

Chains rumbled again on the floorboards in the other room. From his vantage point near the wardrobe, Sebastian watched the crack under the door. Candlelight appeared.

The door opened slowly and the clanking was suddenly much louder. A startling figure moved into the room with slow, ponderous steps.

Sebastian retreated deeper into the dark shadows cast by the big wardrobe and watched with interest as the apparition clanked toward the bed.

The candle revealed a hideously scarred face partially concealed by the hood of a cloak. There was a great, gaping wound in the specter's throat. One gloved hand held the candle. The other hand was hidden beneath the folds of the cloak. The chains appeared to be attached to the ghost's ankle.

The ghost moved inexorably toward the bed. *"Lydia. Lydia. Where are you, Lydia?"*

Sebastian took a step forward. But before he could reach the apparition, Prudence tossed aside the bedclothes and sat up. She had her pistol clutched in her hand.

"Stop right where you are or I shall put a bullet in you," she announced.

"What the bloody hell?" the ghost squawked. "You're not Aunt Lydia."

"I most certainly am not. And you're no ghost." Prudence scrambled off the bed, careful to keep the pistol pointed at the apparition. "And this sorry business has gone quite far enough." She fumbled with her glasses and managed to get them on her nose. "You should be ashamed of yourself."

"Christ, who the devil do you think you are? I'll teach you to interfere in my affairs."

The intruder withdrew his hand from beneath the folds of the cloak, revealing a long dagger. He raised the blade and started purposefully around the edge of the bed.

"Halt or I'll shoot." Prudence took a step back.

"Not bloody likely," the ghost said. "Ladies don't know how to use pistols."

Sebastian launched himself at the dagger-wielding ghost. He grabbed him by the shoulder, yanked the hood of the cloak down over the man's eyes from behind, and spun him around. The candle went flying.

"What in blazes?" The ghost struggled to throw aside the hood of the cloak which was effectively blinding him.

Sebastian gave him no chance to raise the hood. He could not risk having the ghost see him and recognize him. There would be far too much explaining to do.

Sebastian knocked the dagger aside with one hand. Then

he slammed a fist straight into the ghost's jaw, which was just barely visible beneath the hood.

The intruder reeled backward, struck his head against the bedpost, and crumpled, unconscious, to the floor.

"Well done, my lord," Prudence exclaimed as she hurried to pick the candle up before it could singe the carpet. "And just in the very nick of time. I do believe he actually intended to use that dagger on me."

Sebastian stood over his victim and stared at her. Rage at the risks Prudence had taken mingled with relief that she was safe.

"You little fool. Do you realize what could have happened?"

She blinked at him in surprise. "Well, it was a bit of a near thing, I'll grant you. I really did not want to have to shoot him, you see. I've never actually fired a pistol and my aim might have been a bit off."

"A bit of a near thing?" Sebastian repeated in outraged disbelief. He stepped around the fallen body of the ghost and loomed over Prudence. "He could have slit your throat with that dagger. He might have killed you, you fluff-brained little idiot."

She started to frown. "Really, Sebastian, there is no need to shout."

"I am not shouting. But I am seriously considering putting you over my knee and paddling you so hard you won't be able to sit a horse for a week. You nearly got yourself killed tonight."

"I had my pistol," she reminded him.

"Have you any notion of how hard it is to actually bring a man down with a small pistol like that? I have seen men keep going with two bullets in their guts. I have seen them go on to kill other men before they collapsed."

Prudence stared at him. "Where did you see that sort of thing, my lord?"

"Never mind." This was hardly the time to describe the

horrors of bandit hunting in the mountains of Saragstan. "But believe me when I say that a bullet does not always fell a man."

"Now, see here, Sebastian, this is my investigation and I was fully prepared to handle it. I did not ask for your assistance."

"No, you did not," he acknowledged through his teeth. "Instead you chose to risk your neck."

"What of it?" she flung back, equally outraged now. "'Tis my affair, not yours."

"It is most certainly my affair, Miss Merryweather. You happen to be engaged to me."

"Yes, well, that can be remedied soon enough."

"Damnation, woman."

The man on the floor groaned. Sebastian scowled down at him, annoyed at the interruption.

"Oh, dear, I believe he is going to awaken soon," Prudence said. She held the candle over the fallen ghost. "He appears to be wearing a mask."

"Give me that candle." Sebastian realized there were matters to be attended to before he could continue his chastisement of Prudence. He took a grip on his temper and on the candle which Prudence obediently handed to him.

He knelt down beside the unconscious man, groped for and found the edge of the mask. With a single motion he wrenched it off, revealing an unfamiliar face.

"Do you recognize him?" Prudence asked.

"No, but I would lay odds he is one of Mrs. Leacock's infamous nephews."

"Most likely." Prudence reached for the bell rope. "I shall summon assistance at once. Mrs. Leacock has several strong footmen in her employ. They can manage our ghost until the magistrate arrives. You had best be on your way, my lord."

"How do you intend to explain the fact that your damn ghost is unconscious?" he demanded.

Prudence thought a moment. "I shall say that he tripped and fell when he lunged at me. He hit his head against the bedpost and lost consciousness. Who can gainsay me?"

"I suppose that will work," Sebastian said reluctantly. "It has been my experience that people who suffer from being knocked unconscious rarely recall anything about what happened in the moments immediately before the incident. He'll likely believe that he did trip and fall, if that's what you tell him."

"Then that is precisely what I shall say. Now off with you, my lord."

He shot her a disgusted glance, knowing full well she was right. For her sake, he could not allow himself to be discovered by Mrs. Leacock and her staff. The rumpled condition of the bed, Prudence's disheveled appearance, and his state of undress would lead everyone to the obvious conclusion that he had been making love to his fiancée.

Being discovered like this with Prue would not be a complete disaster. Society would wink and turn a blind eye. After all, the pair had already declared their intention to wed. Nevertheless, there were some limits. Society expected romantic assignations to be conducted with some discretion. Being found together in this situation would virtually require a special license.

A special license. Sebastian paused at that interesting thought.

"Well, my lord? Hadn't you better hurry?" Prudence handed him his shirt. "Pray, do not forget your boots."

"You are quite correct, my dear." Sebastian smiled grimly. "I should be on my way. Your reputation is already hanging by a thread, is it not?"

"'Tis not my reputation which concerns me," she said tartly. "It is your own."

The woman never ceased to amaze him. "Mine? Why in God's name are you worried about my reputation?"

"You have the most to lose, do you not?" she asked softly.

"People already take great pleasure in viewing your reputation in the worst possible light. I have no wish to see you titillate the *ton* with an escapade such as this."

Sebastian was taken aback. No one had ever worried about his reputation before. It took him a moment to find a response. "I assure you, I do not give a damn for what Society thinks of me."

"Well, I do. Furthermore, I'm sure there is no need to point out that if we are found together in an awkward situation such as this, you will be obliged to marry me out of hand. I have already inconvenienced you enough, my lord. I would not wish you to be leg-shackled in a marriage you undoubtedly cannot want."

Sebastian cleared his throat. "Well, as to that, Prue, I've been thinking—"

"Hurry, I hear footsteps in the hall."

Sebastian frowned. He heard them, too. Mrs. Leacock's trusty footmen were hastening to obey the summons of the bell. He glanced at the alarmed expression on Prudence's face and swore silently. She definitely did not have the appearance of a lady who wanted badly to be married out of hand.

He would have to give her more time. He was not yet done with this crazed courtship, he thought.

Sebastian picked up his boots, slung his greatcoat over his shoulder, and went reluctantly to the window. He opened it and stepped out onto the ledge.

He paused there and looked back at Prudence. She looked so sweetly serious, her eyes anxious as she watched him leave. He remembered how she had trembled in his arms.

Next time she shivered like that, he vowed silently, he would be buried deep inside her.

"Good night, Prue."

"Good night, Sebastian." Her smile glowed in the candlelight. "And thank you for your assistance tonight. I look forward to helping you solve your next case. I knew we would make an excellent team."

Life with Prue, Sebastian reflected as he made his way along the window ledge, was going to be maddening, infuriating, and alarming by turns, but he was definitely not going to be bored.

Or cold.

Seven

*W*histlecroft *sneezed into a* dirty handkerchief, wiped his bulbous red nose, and leaned across the wooden table. He lowered his voice to a harsh, guttural whisper. "Have ye heard about Lord Ringcross breakin' his neck during the house party at Curling Castle?"

"I heard the news." Sebastian sat back in an effort to avoid Whistlecroft's obnoxious breath. "The tale was all over Town two days ago. The fool got drunk and fell from one of the tower rooms. What about it?"

Sebastian had not known Ringcross well, but he had not particularly liked what he had known about the man. Ringcross had had a reputation for favoring brothels that featured very young innocents of both sexes. Few people mourned his passing when word of his death circulated among the *ton*.

"Well, m'lord, as it happens, there's a gentleman who wants me to look into Ringcross's death." Whistlecroft hoisted his mug of ale and eyed Sebastian expectantly. "I thought the case might interest you."

"Why?"

"Why?" Whistlecroft's bushy brows quivered in surprise. "Because we may be discussin' a murder, sir, that's why. You ain't had an opportunity to investigate a murder for several months now. Usually we find ourselves dealin' with matters o' blackmail, stolen goods, and the odd bit of embezzlement."

"I'm well aware of that." Intriguing cases involving murder among the *ton* were rather rare. Members of polite society managed to get themselves killed readily enough, it was true. But the culprits were usually footpads, opposing duelists, or the occasional outraged husband. Such cases seldom presented an interesting puzzle for Sebastian.

"I believe you'll find this case very fascinatin', m'lord," Whistlecroft said persuasively. "A right puzzle it is."

"Who in blazes hired you to look into Ringcross's death? I cannot fathom why anyone would give a damn. The world is well rid of him."

Whistlecroft shrugged his massive shoulders and looked important. "Afraid, in this case, the identity of my client must remain confidential."

"Then you may find someone else to help you investigate." Sebastian made to rise from the booth.

Whistlecroft set down his mug in alarm. "Hold on there, m'lord. I need yer help on this one. There's a fat reward involved."

"Then investigate the matter yourself."

"Be reasonable," Whistlecroft whined. "If Ringcross was murdered, the deed was done by someone from your world, not some ordinary footpad from the stews. A Runner such as myself won't get far tryin' to investigate among the fancy. You know that as well as I do."

"The thing is, Whistlecroft, I don't particularly care about Ringcross's recent departure from this earth. In all likelihood it was an accident. But if it transpires that someone pushed him, it is a matter of no great moment to me. As far as I am concerned, the murderer did the world a favor."

"My client just wants to know what happened." Whistlecroft yanked out his filthy handkerchief and blew his nose again. "He's a bit anxious."

"Why should he be anxious?"

"Don't know." Whistlecroft leaned close again. "He wouldn't tell me. But if you ask me, he's scared the same thing might happen to him as happened to Ringcross."

That bit of information piqued Sebastian's interest. There was a puzzle here. Perhaps an interesting one. He kept his face expressionless as he contemplated Whistlecroft.

"I'll have to know the name of your client," Sebastian said. "I won't go into this blind. If you want my help, you're going to have to tell me who it is who wants Ringcross's death investigated."

Whistlecroft gnawed on his lower lip while he pondered the problem. Sebastian was not surprised when he shrugged again and took another swallow of gin. Whistlecroft was nothing if not pragmatic.

"Well, if ye must know, it's Lord Curling who wants to discover what happened in that tower room," Whistlecroft said.

"Curling? What's his interest in this?" Sebastian was acquainted with the baron, a dark, heavily built man in his late forties. Curling belonged to some of the same clubs that Sebastian frequented.

He was well known in some circles for the lavish entertaining he did at his country house. Curling Castle was less than an hour's ride from the city. During the Season Curling held house parties nearly every weekend. Sebastian frequently received invitations, but he had never bothered to accept. House parties generally bored him.

"Ringcross died at Curling's country house," Whistlecroft pointed out. "Mayhap Curling just wants to assure himself he ain't been entertainin' a murderer all Season."

Sebastian gazed thoughtfully at the street outside the window of the coffeehouse. "Or mayhap he knows more about the incident than he told you."

"It's possible." Whistlecroft finished off his gin. "All I care about is the reward. And all you care about is how interestin' the mystery is. Have we got a bargain, m'lord?"

"Yes," Sebastian said. "I believe we do."

He realized he was already looking forward to telling Prudence about his newest investigation. He had never had anyone to discuss his cases with in the past except Garrick. Garrick had been more amused by Sebastian's hobby than genuinely interested in it.

But Prudence would be enthralled by the notion of investigating a possible murder. Of course, there was a potential problem, Sebastian acknowledged ruefully. She would want to get involved in the investigation.

He would handle that issue when it arose, he thought as he walked out of the coffeehouse. There might be a way to let her assist him and at the same time keep her safely on the periphery of the case.

It would be amusing to work with Prue on the matter of Ringcross's death.

Half an hour later he walked through the door of his town house, took one look at the expression of gloom on Flowers's face, and smiled wryly.

"Something wrong, Flowers?"

"A Mr. Trevor Merryweather to see you, sir." Flowers accepted Sebastian's hat and gloves. "He insisted upon waiting until you got home. I put him in the library."

"As good a place as any, I suppose."

"Should I have had him thrown out, m'lord?"

"Of course not, Flowers. He is my future brother-in-law. We can hardly have him tossed out on his ear every time he shows up."

"Yes, m'lord. I was afraid that would be the case. He seems a rather difficult young man."

"He is attempting to protect his sister from me," Sebastian said. "Some would say that makes him a rather brave young man."

Flowers blinked his large, drooping eyes. "I take your point, m'lord. I had not thought of it in that light."

Sebastian walked quietly into the library. Lucifer rose from his position on top of the sofa, jumped lightly down onto the carpet, and trotted forward to greet him. Sebastian picked up the cat and glanced at his visitor.

Trevor was standing stiffly near the window. The outsized shoulders and extremely tight waist of his overpadded coat gave him an unfortunate insectlike silhouette. He whirled around when he realized someone had entered the room.

Sebastian stroked Lucifer and contemplated Trevor's painfully stylish appearance. The younger man's cravat was tied in an excruciatingly complicated manner that severely hindered the movement of his head. Sebastian wondered that Trevor did not choke on it. The collar of his elaborately ruffled shirt was so high it framed his chin. His trousers were elaborately pleated and his waistcoat was a startling shade of pink.

"Angelstone."

"Good afternoon, Merryweather." Holding Lucifer in one arm, Sebastian went across the room to the table that held the claret decanter. "Will you join me?"

"No." Trevor flushed. "Thank you. Sir, I have come to speak with you about my sister."

"Ah, yes. You no doubt wish to discuss settlements and that sort of thing. Do not concern yourself, Merryweather. I will take good care of your sister."

"Now, see here." Trevor squared his shoulders determinedly. "I have had enough of your mockery and sarcasm, my lord. You have gone too far."

"Not yet." Sebastian took a sip of claret and wistfully recalled what he had been doing just before the ghost's untimely interruption at the Leacock mansion. "But I have every hope of doing so quite soon."

Trevor turned crimson with anger. "We both know you are only amusing yourself with Prue. You have no intention of actually marrying her. I won't let you play your devilish games with her, Angelstone."

Sebastian put Lucifer back on the sofa. Then he walked around behind his desk and sat down. He propped his booted feet on the polished wooden surface, brushed a cat hair off his breeches, and eyed Trevor thoughtfully. "What makes you think I won't marry her?"

"Damn you, sir," Trevor exploded. "You know very well she is not your type."

"I disagree."

"You bastard," Trevor seethed. "I won't let you hurt her the way Underbrink did. I don't care what I have to do to stop you."

Sebastian studied his claret. "What, precisely, went on between your sister and Underbrink?"

"He asked her to marry him." Trevor's hands clenched into fists. "He never quite got around to asking my father for permission, of course, because he never actually intended to go through with it. But Prue thought he loved her. She thought he was going to marry her."

"Prue loved him?"

"She cared very much for him," Trevor muttered. "He courted her all summer. Danced with her at the local assemblies. Sent bouquets of flowers to the house. Read romantic poetry to her."

"And told her he wanted to marry her?"

"That's right. But he was lying. He knew all along that he was going to have to marry a great heiress in order to restore the Underbrink fortune. There was no question of him marrying Prue. We all discovered the truth when he went back to London."

Sebastian gazed into the claret. "Did your sister cry for him?"

"Yes, she cried." Trevor braced himself. "And I won't have her cry again because of a devil like you." He hurled himself forward without any warning.

Sebastian took his feet down off the desk and rose swiftly. The claret sloshed onto the floor as he got out of Trevor's path.

Trevor flew across the desk and crashed into the chair Sebastian had just vacated. He fetched up against the wall.

Sebastian set down his glass. "Merryweather, I assure you there is really no need for this sort of exertion."

Trevor got groggily to his feet and stumbled toward Sebastian. He swung wildly with his fists.

Sebastian ducked a blow, stuck out his foot, and allowed Trevor to trip over it.

"Damn you." Trevor sprawled facedown on the floor. He rolled painfully onto his side and struggled back to his feet.

"I'm going to marry her, Merryweather." Sebastian stepped back out of reach as Trevor attempted another punch. "You have my word of honor on it."

"What good is your word?" Trevor gasped. He staggered forward, hands extended toward Sebastian's throat.

"Your sister trusts me."

"Hah. What does she know about dealing with the devil?" Trevor threw himself into the fray once more.

Sebastian sidestepped the lunge. Trevor sailed straight past his target and hit the wall again. He turned, dazed but game.

Sebastian held up a hand. "Enough. If you go on like this you might do some serious damage to yourself. Prue would no doubt blame me for it."

"Damn your eyes, Angelstone, this is not another amusing little jest for you to enjoy. This is my sister we're talking about."

"I am aware of that," Sebastian said quietly. "What would it take to convince you that my intentions toward your sister are honorable?"

Trevor stared at him. "There's nothing you can say that will convince me. I don't trust you."

"Merryweather, let us be clear on one point. I would

rather not spend the rest of the Season wondering if you're going to leap out of the nearest alley and go straight for my throat. I will strike a bargain with you."

Trevor was instantly suspicious. "A bargain?"

"Give me the opportunity to prove that my intentions are honorable and I will see to it that you learn how to use your fists properly." Sebastian smiled slowly. "And perhaps a pistol as well."

Trevor scowled in confusion. "I don't understand."

"It's quite simple. I shall arrange for you to take instruction in boxing at Witt's Academy and I shall see to it that you are allowed to practice your shooting skills at Manton's."

Trevor narrowed his eyes. "I would never be accepted by Witt. He operates the most exclusive boxing academy in London. Only gentlemen from the highest ranks of the *ton* get instruction there."

"I can get you in," Sebastian said.

"I cannot afford a decent set of dueling pistols with which to practice at Manton's," Trevor persisted.

"I shall loan you mine."

Trevor gazed at him in growing uncertainty. "Why would you do that?"

Sebastian smiled faintly. "Two reasons. The first being that if I fail to marry your sister as promised and if you do elect to come after me because of it, we shall at least be able to engage in a fair fight. There is no amusement to be had from participating in an unequal contest."

"What's the second reason?"

"I once had a younger brother of my own. You remind me of him." Sebastian picked up the decanter and poured two more glasses of claret. He handed one to Trevor. "Do we have a bargain?"

Trevor looked down at the claret and then raised his eyes to meet Sebastian's. "Are you really going to marry Prue?"

"Yes."

"And you'll get me into Witt's boxing academy and Manton's gallery so that I can learn how to fight you properly if you fail to marry her?"

"Yes."

"I believe you actually mean it," Trevor said slowly.

"I mean every word."

Trevor took a swallow of the claret. "All right, then. And if you don't, I shall tear your head off your shoulders or put a bullet into you."

"Fair enough."

Trevor looked visibly relieved. "Well, that's that, then."

"I certainly hope so."

Trevor cleared his throat. "There's something I've been wanting to ask you, Angelstone."

"Yes?"

"If you really are determined to be my brother-in-law, would you mind very much doing me a great favor?"

Sebastian raised his brows. "What sort of favor?"

"Would you teach me how to tie a cravat the way you tie yours?"

Sebastian smiled. "I'll go one step further. After I have introduced you at Witt's and Manton's, I shall introduce you to my tailor."

"Nightingale? I say." Trevor was truly awed. "He is far more exclusive than Witt."

"With good reason." Sebastian eyed Trevor's pink waistcoat. "His craft is infinitely more important to a gentleman."

Prudence watched Drucilla Fleetwood bear down on her across the crowded ballroom. She braced herself for the encounter. It would have been difficult to miss Sebastian's aunt, even if someone had not already pointed her out.

Drucilla was an impressively stylish figure in her marigold silk gown. There were matching plumes in her fashionably dressed hair. The diamonds in her ears sparkled as brilliantly as the crystals in the chandeliers.

It was obvious Drucilla had been a beautiful woman in

her youth. She was still quite attractive, Prudence thought. It was unfortunate that her striking features were set in such unpleasant lines. Drucilla had the expression of a woman who has committed herself to an extremely distasteful task.

Hester had warned Prudence barely an hour ago that Drucilla was expected to put in an appearance at the Craigmore ball.

"The *on dit* is that she is not at all pleased to hear of Angelstone's engagement," Hester had explained. "She was rather hoping that some dreadful accident would befall the earl or that he would get himself conveniently killed in a duel before he got around to marrying. The last thing she wants to see him do is produce an heir and secure the line for that branch of the family."

Prudence had blushed furiously at the mention of an heir. "I'm sure it is none of her business. In any event, Angelstone and I will not be getting married for some time yet. There is certainly no rush. We intend to enjoy a very lengthy engagement."

Hester gave her an odd look. "Do you, indeed? I am surprised to hear that, my dear."

"Why?"

"Because I cannot conceive of Angelstone tolerating a long engagement. Having made his choice in brides, a man of his nature is bound to be impatient to get on with the business."

Prudence stared at her in astonishment. "Hester, are you by any chance anxious to marry me off?"

"To be perfectly blunt, my dear, now that the engagement has been announced, I feel it would be best to settle the matter as quickly as possible."

"You mean before Angelstone changes his mind?" Prudence had inquired dryly.

"Precisely. The man is dangerous. I have told you that. One cannot be entirely certain of his intentions. I will feel much more secure once you are wed."

"You are so eager to see me married to the Fallen Angel, then?"

Hester had looked thoughtful. "I believe you will be safe enough in his care. Angelstone will look after his own."

Hester's remarks were still fresh in Prudence's mind when Drucilla finally came to a halt in front of her quarry.

"Well, well, well." Drucilla looked her up and down and was clearly unimpressed by Prudence's pale gray gown. "So you are the clever little ghost hunter whom Mrs. Leacock has been telling us about?"

Prudence swallowed a sharp retort and managed a smile. The subject of Mrs. Leacock's ghost had been on everyone's lips that evening. Prudence had been hailed as a clever, extremely brave heroine by a very grateful Mrs. Leacock. Fortunately, as Sebastian had predicted, the ghost, who had indeed been one of Mrs. Leacock's nephews, had recalled nothing of how he had been rendered unconscious. As far as he was concerned, his downfall had been an unseen bump in the carpet that had caused him to trip.

"Good evening, madam," Prudence said politely. "I collect you are Mrs. Fleetwood?"

"Of course I am. And you are the Original who is engaged to Angelstone."

"Yes, madam, I have that honor."

"I suppose I should not be surprised that he has chosen such an odd creature to be his countess. The man has absolutely no respect for the noble title that has come his way by sheerest accident."

"I was under the impression the title came to him in the usual manner, madam. He was next in line for it."

"Bah." Frustrated rage burned in Drucilla's fine brown eyes. "He got it because of the most flukish of circumstances. In actual fact, it should never have gone to him at all."

"It is not fair to say that," Prudence said gently.

"It was bad enough that his irresponsible father ran off with that actress. Jonathan Fleetwood had no business marrying that little lightskirt. If he had not been so stupid, your future husband would have been born the bastard he has taken such pains to become."

Prudence was rapidly losing her patience. "I cannot allow you to insult my future husband's family, madam."

"I am part of his family, you silly chit. If I wish to insult his side of it, I shall do so."

"An interesting point of logic," Prudence acknowledged. "Nevertheless, I believe Angelstone's side of the family has borne enough insults, don't you?"

Drucilla's gaze was scathing. "It should be obvious that nothing I say could be as insulting to the family name as what he has done."

"What is that supposed to mean, madam?"

"Merely that it is entirely in keeping with Angelstone's character for him to have selected a completely unsuitable female as his countess. The thought of a little countrified nobody like you becoming the next Countess of Angelstone is insupportable."

There were several gasps and murmurs of excited dismay from those hovering around the pair. Prudence overheard them and realized that the scene with Drucilla was threatening to turn into a delicious morsel for the *ton* to chew on tomorrow morning over breakfast. Sebastian did not need the added notoriety.

Prudence determinedly brightened her smile as if Drucilla had just paid her a great compliment. "How kind of you to take the trouble to introduce yourself to me, madam. I have been rather curious about the rest of Angelstone's family."

"Have you, indeed?" Drucilla drew herself up and looked down her elegant nose. "The first thing you should know is that the title which Angelstone takes such delight in dragging through the mud at every opportunity should have been my son's. If there is any justice in this world, it will someday come to Jeremy."

"I was under the impression that the question of my husband's right to the title had been settled long ago."

"Rubbish." Drucilla's face turned a dull red. "I wish you joy in your marriage, Miss Merryweather. Perhaps you can produce a ghost or two on your wedding night with which to amuse your husband. You will certainly need to do something unusual to retain his interest for longer than a fortnight. Angelstone is very easily bored."

Drucilla had gone too far and the shocked reactions of those standing nearby indicated that everyone realized it. Prudence knew that when Sebastian heard of this exchange, he would be coldly furious. He was highly unlikely to allow the insult to his fiancée to go unpunished.

She looked into Drucilla's tormented eyes and suddenly felt very sorry for her. The poor woman was only too well aware that she had overstepped the line.

"I appreciate your concern about the family name," Prudence said quietly. "It is obvious you have worked hard to keep it as untarnished as possible under extremely difficult circumstances."

Drucilla stared at her. For a moment she appeared completely taken aback. "I have done my best," she said finally.

"I realize it has not been an easy task," Prudence said. "Please rest assured that I am very concerned about Angelstone's name and reputation, too. For the sake of the family, I shall exert every effort to see that scandal is avoided."

Drucilla's gaze flickered in outraged bewilderment. "What sort of game are you playing, Miss Merryweather?"

"I am not playing any games."

"Then we must wait to see what devilish game Angelstone is playing." Drucilla turned on her heel and walked off through the crowd.

A strong sense of misgiving went through Prudence as she watched her adversary's rigid back disappear into the throng.

"Well, now. I expect Angelstone will have something to say about this," a voice murmured behind Prudence.

She turned to see Garrick Sutton standing behind her. Sebastian had introduced her to him at the Bowdreys' soiree. He had made it clear he considered Garrick a friend. Prudence noticed that Garrick was one of the few people in the room this evening who was not holding a glass of champagne. She gave him a worried smile. •

"I would rather Angelstone did not hear of this little scene," she said.

Garrick's mouth curved wryly. "Not much chance of preventing him from learning about it, I'm afraid. Too many witnesses."

Prudence glanced uneasily around. "I suppose you're right. Well, I shall just have to speak to Angelstone before he does anything rash."

"What's this? You think you can talk him out of exacting a bit of revenge on the Fleetwood clan?"

"There is no need for him to avenge me," Prudence said. "That poor woman has obviously suffered a great deal over the years."

"That poor woman," Garrick said coolly, "was almost single-handedly responsible for seeing to it that the Fleetwoods never accepted Angelstone's mother."

"Nevertheless, Angelstone is the head of the family now. He can afford to be charitable toward the other members of the clan."

"Charitable?" Garrick grinned. "Are we talking about the same Lord Angelstone?"

"This is not a humorous situation, Mr. Sutton."

"No, it's not. But it should prove interesting. Take my advice and stay out of the matter, Miss Merryweather. Angelstone is well able to handle the Fleetwoods. He's been doing it for some time now."

"What do you think he will do about tonight's unfortunate scene?" Prudence asked. •

Garrick gave an unconcerned shrug. "Who knows? Angelstone controls much of the family's income. Perhaps he will cut off some of the Fleetwood portion."

"Oh, dear."

"Then again, he may simply content himself with getting Drucilla and her son barred from the best guest lists this Season. Or he might arrange to have his dear cousin kicked out of some of his clubs. No doubt Angelstone will think of some suitable vengeance. He is rather creative."

"He may think of some method of revenge, but I do not believe he will go through with it," Prudence said forcefully.

Garrick cocked an inquiring brow. "Who will stop him?"

"I shall see to it that he behaves sensibly and in a manner befitting the head of the family."

Garrick glanced at a point just beyond Prudence's shoulder. His smile was suddenly one of keen anticipation. "I cannot wait to see how you handle him, Miss Merryweather."

"And just who is she going to handle?" Sebastian asked with bland interest.

Prudence whirled about again and found Sebastian looming over her. He looked magnificent, as usual, in his evening attire. His white cravat was folded with stark simplicity and his well-cut coat revealed the breadth of his shoulders. His golden eyes gleamed as he looked at her.

"You, of course," Garrick said.

"I am delighted to hear it." Sebastian smiled at Prudence. "Come with me, my dear. We shall find ourselves something to eat at the buffet."

"I already had something to eat," Prudence said.

Sebastian took her arm. "Did you? Well, then, you may come along and watch me eat lobster canapés. I want to talk to you."

"Oh, I see." Prudence smiled. "As it happens, I am anxious to have a chat with you, also, my lord."

"Excellent." Sebastian inclined his head toward Garrick. "You will excuse us?"

"Of course." Garrick winked at Prudence. "The best of luck to you, Miss Merryweather."

Prudence frowned at him over her shoulder as Sebastian led her through the crowd.

"What was that all about?" Sebastian asked without any sign of concern.

"Nothing."

"Nothing at all?"

"A small, uh, domestic matter."

"Ah." Sebastian nodded at an acquaintance. "A family matter, then?"

"Well, yes, in a way."

"Whose family?" Sebastian asked evenly. "Yours or mine?"

"My lord, this is hardly the time to talk about it."

"Mine, then," he said. "I collect it must be about the scene my aunt conducted a few minutes before I arrived."

Prudence glowered at him as he drew her to a halt near a table full of hors d'oeuvres. "You already know about it?"

"My dear, you must understand that there will never be any lack of people anxious to keep me informed about such matters."

"No, I suppose not." Prudence slanted him a speculative glance. "You aren't going to do anything overly dramatic, are you? It was all extremely unimportant."

Sebastian surveyed the canapés. He finally selected one that was topped with an oyster. "You need not concern yourself, my dear. I will handle things."

Prudence did not trust the coldness in his eyes. "Sir, I must insist that you do not attempt to punish or humiliate your aunt in any way because of the conversation she and I had. She was very overset at the time."

"No doubt." Sebastian bit into the oyster.

"She has only recently learned of our engagement," Prudence explained. "The news has taken her somewhat by surprise."

"You mean it has alarmed her greatly." Sebastian picked up another canapé. "She is afraid I might actually produce an heir which would make it even more unlikely that her son will ever assume the title."

"I believe," Prudence said meaningfully, "that Mrs. Fleetwood is genuinely concerned about the good name of the family and the reputation attached to the title."

"She is certainly concerned about it, I'll grant you that."

"Not without some reason, perhaps," Prudence said grimly.

Sebastian stopped munching and swallowed. "What are you implying, Prue?"

"Merely that you have not gone out of your way to reassure her that the title is in safe hands."

"I would not go out of my way to assist my aunt across the street, let alone reassure her that I'll keep the title unblemished." Sebastian took Prudence's arm again and steered her toward the open French doors. "Enough of this nonsense, Prue. I have more important things to discuss."

Prudence looked up at him as he guided her out into the gardens. "My lord, I am not going to allow you to finish with this topic until I have your word that you will not retaliate against your aunt for what she said this evening."

"I have grown quite bored with that subject."

"That is too bad, sir, because I have not yet done with it."

Sebastian stopped beside a fountain and turned her toward him. "Damnation, Prue, why do you care what I do to Drucilla Fleetwood? She deserves to pay for insulting you and she will do so. That is the end of it."

"The insult was to me, not to you. I choose not to retaliate and I will not allow you to do so on my behalf. Do you comprehend me, my lord?"

"Any insult to you is an insult to me," he said softly.

"Sebastian, I mean it, I will not have you going about getting even for the most trifling slight." Prudence touched his face gently with her gloved fingertips. "You are the head of the family and you must act the part. If you choose to take vengeance against your poor aunt, you will only widen the rift that already exists between yourself and the rest of the Fleetwoods."

"Bloody hell, Prue—"

"Your title obligates you to be generous toward the members of your family. You owe them protection." Prudence smiled warmly. "But I'm certain you don't need me to tell you that. You are perfectly well aware of your duties and responsibilities to your family and I know you will act accordingly."

Sebastian eyed her grimly. "The last time you lectured me on my responsibilities, you made a bargain with me. When you tried to fulfill it, you wound up getting yourself engaged to me. What do I get this time if I decide to indulge myself in a fit of mature, responsible behavior?"

Prudence concentrated on adjusting her spectacles. "Really, Sebastian, there is no need to tease me about this. I am well aware that things did not turn out as planned last time."

"I assure you, Prue, I am bloody well not teasing."

She looked up at him warily. "You're not? You actually expect me to reward you for behaving as befits your rank?"

"Your notion of what befits my rank," he corrected smoothly. "And yes, I think it only fair I get something for my effort, don't you?"

She could not tell if he was serious, but she had the unpleasant suspicion that he was. As far as Sebastian was concerned, she had once again deprived him of his rightful prey. She sighed. "What sort of reward did you have in mind, sir?"

"I'll give the matter some thought and let you know." Sebastian's hand closed around her shoulders. He pulled her close, bent his head, and gave her a quick, hard, possessive kiss. When he raised his mouth from hers, his expression was one of brooding intensity. "I imagine I'll think of something that will compensate me."

Prudence shivered beneath the dark sensuality in his words. Two nights ago she had learned the meaning of passion and she knew she would forever associate the lesson with Sebastian. Now he was telling her without any subtlety that there would be more lessons. She did not know whether to be alarmed or overjoyed.

She was still confused by the emotions that had raged through her when Sebastian had touched her that night with such startling intimacy. She knew that with every passing day of this false engagement she was falling deeper in thrall to the Fallen Angel.

Her common sense warned her that it would be exceedingly dangerous to allow Sebastian to make love to her any more thoroughly than he already had. But Prudence was not at all certain she had the fortitude to stop him.

"You are being deliberately difficult, my lord," she accused.

"Yes, I know, but it amuses me." Sebastian rested one booted foot on the edge of the fountain and smiled. "Now, then, I have something far more interesting to discuss with you, my dear."

"What is that?"

"My Bow Street Runner acquaintance has brought me a rather intriguing case that requires investigation. I thought you might like to hear about it."

Prudence instantly forgot how annoyed she was with him. "Sebastian, how wonderful. Tell me all about it. I shall so enjoy assisting you."

"I am not asking for your assistance," he said carefully. "But I thought you might enjoy the opportunity of observing my methods."

"How am I to do that?" she demanded. She had absolutely no intention of being relegated to the role of observer, but she would explain that to him later.

"The curious death I am to investigate took place a few days ago at Curling Castle. You may have heard about it?"

Prudence frowned. "A man named Ringcross fell from a high window and broke his neck, I believe. He was said to have been quite drunk at the time and his death was presumed to be an unfortunate accident."

"Someone, namely Lord Curling, is not so certain, apparently."

"He has hired a Runner to look into the matter?"

"In strictest confidence. No one, including Curling, must know that I am to do the actual investigation. As far as he is concerned, Whistlecroft is making the inquiries."

"Yes, of course. I comprehend you wish to keep your hobby a secret. Perfectly understandable, given your position. Also, you would not be nearly so effective in your work if everyone knew what you were about, would you?"

"No."

"Sebastian, this is fascinating. What are we going to do first? I am so eager to learn your techniques and methods."

He gave her a look that might have been described as smug. "First, we shall visit the scene of Ringcross's death."

"A sensible notion." Prudence absently tapped her closed fan against her gloved palm. "That means we shall have to go to Curling Castle. How are we to do that without letting anyone know our goal, my lord?"

"Rather easily, as it happens. As usual, I have received yet another invitation to one of Curling's weekend house parties. This time I shall accept on the understanding that you will also be invited."

"Excellent. But will no one think it odd that I have suddenly been asked to one of Lord Curling's parties? I have certainly not been on his guest list previously."

"No one will think it at all odd." Sebastian was clearly amused at her naïveté. "Not when they realize that I have accepted an invitation as well. Indeed, they would find it strange if you were not at Curling Castle, too."

Prudence tipped her head to one side and studied him closely. "Am I missing something here, sir?"

Sebastian drew her closer so that her skirts brushed against his leg. "I take it you have not been to many tonnish house parties, my dear."

"No," she admitted. "Why?"

"I think you will comprehend the appeal of a large country house party once you have attended one."

Prudence could feel the muscular strength of his thigh. He still had his boot braced against the fountain so she was pressed lightly against the inside of his leg. The intimate position in which she found herself sent a thrill through her.

"I believe various games and pastimes are enjoyed by the guests at such parties," she said quickly in an attempt to sound knowledgeable on the subject of house parties.

"They certainly are. And the most interesting games and pastimes are played late at night when everyone has retired for the evening."

"I don't understand."

Sebastian's mouth curved slightly. "A large country house party provides almost unlimited opportunity for dalliances and liaisons of a romantic nature, my sweet."

Prudence widened her eyes. "Oh."

"In a large house such as Curling Castle there are literally dozens of bedrooms. And they are all conveniently situated quite close to each other."

Prudence felt herself turning very warm. "Good heavens. I had not thought of that aspect."

"Conducting an affair takes planning and care here in Town," Sebastian said. "But at a large house party such as the sort Curling gives, one has only to go across the hall to rendezvous with one's lover or"—he smiled—"one's fiancée."

Prudence lifted her chin and gave him a severe look. "I expect Lady Pembroke will insist on accompanying me."

"I expect she will." Sebastian was clearly not worried by the prospect of Prudence having a chaperone along. "My man of affairs will secure an invitation for her, too."

Eight

Sebastian put down his cue and glanced at the handful of other players gathered around Lord Curling's billiard table. "If you will excuse me, gentlemen, I believe I have had enough of this game for today."

"Come, now," one of the other guests protested, "you must give us a chance to win back a bit of the blunt you have lifted from us this afternoon, Angelstone."

"You don't seem to comprehend, Dodwell," Sebastian said. "I am bored with the play."

"Let him go," another man advised from the other side of the green baize table. "I expect Angelstone has more interesting entertainment in mind."

The men gathered around the table chuckled and exchanged knowing glances.

"Don't we all," one grumbled good-naturedly. "Unfortunately, it is a bit early in the day yet."

One of the players looked at Sebastian. "If you are anxious to see what your fiancée is up to at the moment, check the east gardens. I believe you will find her in the process of winning the ladies' archery contest."

"No doubt." Sebastian started toward the door of Curling's vast library. "She has already taken the honors in all the rest of the games that were arranged for the ladies today."

While Sebastian had spent the day with the other gentlemen who had been invited to Curling Castle, Prudence had been busily sampling the pleasures of a country house party with the ladies. In typical Prudence fashion, she had thrown herself wholeheartedly into the entertainments.

At noon, just as he was returning from a fishing expedition with the men, word reached Sebastian that Prudence had been first through the elaborate maze. At two o'clock, while he was touring his host's stables, he heard that the ladies had returned from their walk to the old Norman ruins. Prudence had apparently led the group in both directions and had done a detailed sketch of the view.

This afternoon she had won all the contests held on the wide sweep of lawn that fronted the castle and had signed up to participate in the amateur theatrics after dinner that evening.

Sebastian looked forward to watching her performance as an actress. He smiled, thinking of his mother.

He had a hunch that Prudence and his mother would have taken to each other on sight. They were both women of intelligence, passion, and integrity. His father had once told him that such women were rare and if a man was fortunate enough to find and keep one, no price was too high to pay.

Sebastian examined his surroundings as he made his way through the long hall to the terrace. Curling Castle was a cavernous pile of old stone that rose three stories above the land around it. It had been built during the previous century by a wealthy but rather eccentric merchant who had been determined to elevate himself to the level of a gentleman. In the attempt to achieve that goal, he had poured a fortune into his estate.

The result had been a monstrosity of a house. The hallways appeared endless. Curling had admitted at breakfast that he wasn't certain how many rooms the house contained. He had added that the top floor and the tower rooms were never used at all, even when the house was full, as it was that weekend.

That bit of information had intrigued Sebastian. According to all accounts, Ringcross had fallen from a tower room. Sebastian wondered what he had been doing in an unused portion of the house.

Tonight he and Prudence would do some investigating, he thought as he strolled out onto the terrace. Prudence would enjoy that enormously.

He saw the ladies lined up in front of the archery targets that had been placed in the east gardens. Each held a dainty bow and a tiny arrow that probably would not have felled a mouse at point-blank range.

There was a great deal of laughter from the contestants and good-natured cheering from the audience. Sebastian studied the crowd closely. He frowned when he saw that Underbrink was in the group.

Underbrink was evidently a new arrival. He certainly had not been around last night or this morning. Sebastian noted that there was no sign of Underbrink's ever-vigilant wife.

As Sebastian watched, Underbrink sauntered over to Prudence and apparently offered to help her with her bow. Prudence shook her head quite firmly. Underbrink shrugged and walked back to join the crowd.

Lady Pembroke also stood amid the onlookers. She glanced up, saw Sebastian on the terrace, and waved a violet hankie that matched her gown. Then she turned back to watch Prudence take her shot.

Prudence was last in line. She was the only contestant who was not giggling or coyly asking one of the gentlemen to show her how to cock the arrow. Her spectacles sparkled in the sunlight as she concentrated intently on the target. The seriousness of her expression made Sebastian smile.

The day was cloudy. A crisp breeze caused the skirts of Prudence's dull bronze afternoon dress to ripple enticingly about her legs. Sebastian admired her trim little ankles for a full minute before he became aware of the fact that he was not the only male doing so. He glanced to the side and saw that his host had come out of the house to join him.

"I must congratulate you, Angelstone. She's an oddly attractive little thing. Not at all in the usual style." Lord Curling's pale blue eyes were fixed on Prudence. "I'd heard your fiancée was an Original. But then, from all accounts that is the only sort of woman who would be likely to appeal to you. Is it true she investigates ghosts?"

Sebastian slanted Curling an assessing glance. In truth, the baron was probably no better or worse than most of the other gentlemen of the *ton*.

Sebastian knew there were many who would say his own reputation left more to be desired than did Curling's. The legitimacy of Curling's birth, for example, had never been questioned.

Sebastian had made a few inquiries before leaving London but had turned up little more than he already knew about Curling. In spite of his tendency toward lavish entertaining here at Curling Castle, there were no particularly unpleasant rumors about the man. No one had ever accused him of cheating at cards, for example. He had not fought any duels. There was no indication that he favored the same sort of brothels that Ringcross had.

But Sebastian could not bring himself to actually like the man. Studying him now, he thought he knew why. There was cold, sexual interest in Curling's eyes as he watched Prudence. Sebastian knew that if it weren't for the fact that he was committed to spending the weekend investigating Ringcross's death, he would have been tempted to take Prudence back to Town immediately.

But Sebastian also knew that if he even so much as suggested they leave, Prudence would be outraged. She was looking forward to tonight's investigations with such enthusiasm that he could not bring himself to disappoint her.

"My fiancée is extremely interested in spectral phenomena," Sebastian said without inflection.

"Fascinating." Curling turned his head to look at him. "And has she ever discovered a genuine ghost?"

"No."

"Pity." Curling's heavy features assumed a thoughtful expression. "I have occasionally wondered if ghosts actually exist."

"Have you?" Sebastian gripped the stone wall that surrounded the terrace and watched as Prudence shot her arrow. "What is it about the subject of ghosts that alarms you, Curling? Are you afraid of encountering one, or is it the possibility of returning as one yourself that makes you anxious?"

"You mistake me, Angelstone. The notion of ghosts does not alarm me in the least. It merely intrigues me. I frequently find myself consumed with ennui. Encountering a ghost would be a most amusing experience, would it not? Almost as amusing as some other experiences I can imagine."

Sebastian's hands tightened on the stone wall. "I would advise you to be extremely cautious about how you decide to relieve your boredom."

"Rest assured I am a very prudent man, Angelstone." Curling smiled with satisfaction as Prudence's arrow buried itself close to the heart of the target. "Excellent shot. I do believe your lady has won, sir."

"She usually does," Sebastian said. He noticed that Underbrink was applauding with a great deal of enthusiasm.

"I am delighted that you finally elected to accept one of my invitations," Curling said. His eyes were still on Prudence. "I wondered at first what had convinced you to come out into the country at last. But when I received your request for an invitation for your fiancée and her friend, Lady Pembroke, I understood your reasons."

"Did you?"

"But of course." Curling gave a knowing chuckle. "City

life can be quite restrictive in some ways for an engaged couple. Out here in the country things are far more casual. Enjoy yourself this weekend, Angelstone."

"I fully intend to do so."

. . .

Hark, my dearest Gerald, someone comes. Mayhap it is Lord Braxton. Flee. Flee at once. You must not be discovered here with me.

Seated on a chintz sofa in a small room that overlooked one of the castle terraces, Prudence frowned intently over the lines she was attempting to memorize.

She had secluded herself in the quiet room half an hour earlier and had worked very hard on her part. But she was coming to the conclusion that acting was rather more difficult than she had anticipated.

The short play was to be staged later in the evening. She was to act the role of Elisa, a young woman whose parents were about to announce her engagement to the mysterious Lord Braxton. Terrified of the match, Elisa was poised to run off with charming, handsome Gerald. Prudence personally thought Elisa had chosen the wrong man.

She tried the lines aloud. "Flee. Flee at once. You must not be discovered here with me."

"Have no fear, my darling," Edward, Lord Underbrink, said from the doorway. He glanced over his shoulder and then stepped quickly into the room. "It is quite safe."

"Edward." Prudence looked up in astonishment.

"Yes, it is I, my dearest." He closed the door behind him and gave her a conspiratorial smile. "The ladies are all upstairs resting before dinner and the gentlemen are with Curling in his library."

"What are you doing here? Do you have a role in the play?"

"No, my dearest Prudence, I am here because I must speak with you." Edward crossed the room swiftly and went down on his knee in front of her. He grasped one of her hands in both of his. "My darling, I have longed to see you alone."

Prudence tried unobtrusively to free her hand and failed. "Why?"

"Because there is so much to explain." Edward kissed the hand he had seized. "You must believe me when I say that I have never forgotten that magical summer in Dorset."

"Which summer? We have had several, you know. We get one every year, in fact."

"Such a charming wit, my dear. But there is only one summer that lives on in my heart, my dearest Prudence." Edward's eyes filled with emotion. "And that is the summer I met you. I cannot believe you have forgotten what we meant to each other."

"Edward, if you don't mind, I really must concentrate on learning my lines." Prudence tried to tug her hand out of his grasp once more.

Edward held on to his prize. "You cannot know how I felt when I saw you again in the park the other day. The sight of you brought back all of the memories. My life has been so empty without you, my dearest."

"Edward, you are married. You can hardly say that your life is empty."

"But it is. I am so lonely, my darling. You must know that my marriage is a loveless match. I was forced into it for the sake of my family and the title. But my wife does not understand my needs."

Prudence began to grow irritated. "Apparently I did not understand them, either, my lord. Had I done so, I would have realized sooner that you were merely amusing yourself with me that summer in Dorset."

"My dearest, nothing could be further from the truth. Only the most stringent sense of family duty forced me to leave you. I had no choice, my love."

"You could have told me at the start of the summer that

you were not free to love where you chose," Prudence said bluntly. "I did not appreciate being the last to know."

"Forgive me, I could not bear to tell you." Edward rained kisses on her palm. "I confess that the time I had with you was stolen time, my dearest. It was all I could give you. All I could give myself. And it was not enough for either of us, was it?"

"Actually, I believe it was quite enough for me," Prudence said.

Edward smiled sadly. "You cannot hide your true feelings from me, Prudence. I know that your love for me was too fine and too pure to ever be extinguished."

"I fear it was not quite that fine or that pure because it seems to have gone out like a candle."

"Then I shall devote myself to reigniting the embers which I know must be glowing somewhere inside you," Edward vowed.

Prudence wondered fleetingly how she could ever have taken Edward seriously that summer in Dorset. Of course, she reminded herself, she had been three years younger then. And she had not yet met Sebastian.

"I do not think that Angelstone will appreciate your efforts," Prudence said dryly.

"Angelstone. That *devil.*" Edward tightened his grip on her hand. "I cannot believe you are to marry the Fallen Angel himself. You are a woman of warmth and sunshine. It pains me to think of you trapped in the arms of such a cold man."

Prudence frowned. "Angelstone is not in the least cold."

"They say he has ice in his veins."

"Nonsense," Prudence said briskly. "He has acted as if he did for so long that I daresay he believes it himself. He has acting talent in his blood, you know. But he most assuredly does not have ice in his veins."

Edward gave her a pitying glance. "My dear, you are too kindhearted. You do not understand how dangerous Angelstone really is. For the sake of what we once shared, you must listen to me. You must not allow yourself to be carried off by the Lord of the Underworld."

"I am afraid that I have every intention of carrying her off, Underbrink," Sebastian said from the doorway. His voice was dangerously soft and very, very cold. "So I would advise you to release my fiancée's hand at once."

Edward dropped Prudence's hand as though it had singed him. He jumped to his feet. "Angelstone."

Prudence smiled at Sebastian. "Hello, Angelstone. I did not hear you come in."

"Obviously." Sebastian lounged in the doorway, arms folded across his chest. He kept his attention on Edward. "What is going on here?"

"Playacting, my lord," Prudence said gently. "Nothing more. Is that not right, Lord Underbrink?"

Edward flushed. "Yes," he stammered. "Playacting. I was helping Prudence—I mean, Miss Merryweather—practice her lines."

"Flee," Prudence murmured in her best dramatic accents. "Flee at once. I do not require your assistance, sir. Angelstone can help me memorize my lines."

"Yes, of course." Edward ran a finger underneath the edge of his snugly knotted cravat. "If you will excuse me, Miss Merryweather."

"Good-bye, Lord Underbrink."

Edward went toward the door with an uneasy expression. It was clear that he was not entirely certain Sebastian would move. At the last moment Sebastian stepped lazily aside. Edward sidled quickly past him and fled.

Sebastian arched a brow at Prudence. "Playacting?"

"Yes, and do you know, Angelstone, I have discovered that acting is very hard work."

"That's what my mother always said."

"I do not understand how those of us in the cast will ever manage to learn our lines by this evening."

"Most of the cast won't bother." Sebastian came toward her. "They will simply read them on stage."

"Oh, dear. Am I wasting my time, do you think?" Prudence smiled ruefully. "It is really a very silly play."

"Is it?"

"Yes, it is all about a lady who is engaged to a very interesting man named Lord Braxton. But she foolishly believes herself in love with an extremely weak-brained creature named Gerald. If I were her, I would say farewell to Gerald and then I would allow myself to be carried off by the mysterious Lord Braxton."

"Would you, indeed?" Sebastian drew her to her feet and framed her face in his hands.

"Definitely." She held her breath, wondering if he was going to kiss her. "That is exactly what I would do."

"I am delighted to hear it." He brushed his mouth lightly across hers. "Now, then, would you like some help learning your lines?"

"Would you mind?"

"Not at all. Acting is in my blood, you know."

Later that night Prudence dismissed the harried maid who had been assigned to her as well as several other ladies and began to pace the floor of her bedchamber. Silence had fallen over Curling Castle. The guests had all retired to their bedrooms after an evening of amateur theatrics, cards, and drinking.

Prudence had been rather proud of her first attempt at treading the boards. She was the only one who had memorized her lines and she was ridiculously pleased when Sebastian clapped loudly in response to her performance.

But now she was ready for the real adventure of the evening.

Prudence had removed her night rail as soon as the door closed behind the maid. She had quickly redressed in a sturdy woolen gown she had brought with her for the occasion and now she was impatiently waiting for Sebastian to fetch her so that they could begin their investigations.

It seemed forever before her door opened without any warning and Sebastian stepped quietly into the room. He glanced back over his shoulder as he beckoned her. "Are you ready?"

"Of course." Prudence picked up an unlit candle and hurried toward the door. "What kept you?"

"I was waiting for the traffic in the hall to fade somewhat." He smiled. "Did you know that young Dodwell is conducting a liaison with Lady Keegan?"

"Lady Keegan?" Prudence was startled. "But she must be twice his age. Furthermore, she is married."

"But her husband stayed behind in Town, if you will recall." Sebastian touched her lips with his finger. "Not a word, now, until we reach the stairs."

He took her hand and led her quickly along the silent hall. There was no need yet for the candle, Prudence realized. The light from a wall sconce provided just enough illumination to make out the doorways and stairs. Apparently Lord Curling was well aware of the late-night habits of his guests.

The staircase that led to the third floor was a different matter entirely. It was pitch-black and a cold draft made itself felt through the skirts of Prudence's warm gown.

Sebastian did not allow Prudence to light her candle until they reached the top of the stairs and were safely out of sight in the deep shadows of the upper hallway. When the taper flared to life, he took it from her and held it aloft.

"How will we know which room Ringcross was in when he died?"

"I had my valet make a few discreet inquiries among the servants earlier," Sebastian explained. "One of them told him it was the room in the south tower."

"It's quite chilly up here." Prudence rubbed her arms briskly as they walked toward the south wing of the sprawling castle.

"Curling said this floor was never used. No point wasting heat on it."

"If this floor is never occupied, what was Ringcross doing up here the night he died?" Prudence asked.

"A very good question, my dear." Sebastian paused in front of a closed door at the end of the hall. "This must be the chamber."

Prudence tried the doorknob. "It's locked."

"I'll take care of it. Here, hold the candle."

Prudence took the candle from him. She watched in admiration as Sebastian removed a short length of metal from his sleeve. He inserted it cautiously into the lock.

"Open for me, sweet," Sebastian whispered to the lock. "That's it, darling, let me inside. Give me what I want. Ah, yes. That's right. That's what I need. Beautiful."

There was a tiny click. Sebastian turned the doorknob and opened the door. The hinges squeaked eerily.

Prudence was impressed. "Very clever, my lord."

He smiled faintly as he moved into the room. "Thank you, my dear. It is always pleasant to have one's small accomplishments appreciated."

"You must teach me how to do that," Prudence said.

"I'm not certain that is a sound notion. If I teach you all my tricks, you might decide you no longer need me."

"Nonsense." Prudence started to follow him into the dark chamber. "We are a team, my lord. We must share our expertise with each— Good heavens." She gasped as a wave of deep, unrelenting cold swept through her.

"What's wrong?" Sebastian asked from the shadows.

"I don't know." Prudence glanced at the candle in her hand, fully expecting to see that it had gone out. But the flame still burned. "It's freezing cold in here."

"No colder than it is out in the hall."

"It feels much colder to me." She raised the candle and gazed around the chamber.

The furnishings were limited to a strange-looking bed

with iron posts, a massive wardrobe, a table, and heavy drapes covering the windows.

"Everything is in black," Prudence whispered in awe. "The drapes, the bedclothes, the carpet. Everything." She raised the candle higher and peered at two lengths of chain that dangled from the wall. "What on earth are those things?"

Sebastian walked across the room and examined the chains. "Manacles."

"Good heavens. How very odd. Do you suppose this was once a dungeon?"

"No. Dungeons are usually built at the bottom of the house, not the top."

"A most unusual decor."

"Yes." Sebastian took the candle from Prudence and began to move slowly around the room.

Prudence shivered as she watched him. It was definitely colder in here than out in the hall, she thought. She wondered why Sebastian didn't feel the difference. It was not just the chill in the chamber that bothered her. There was an unpleasant sensation of darkness and shadow that had nothing to do with the ordinary gloom of night.

"Sebastian, there is something very wrong about this chamber," she said urgently.

He glanced at her in concern. "Damnation. You're frightened. I should never have brought you up here. Come, I will take you back to your bedchamber."

"No." She managed a hasty smile of reassurance. "No, I am quite all right. Just a bit cold."

"Are you certain you don't want to go back to your room?"

"And miss the opportunity to observe your investigation techniques? Absolutely not," she said staunchly. "Carry on, my lord."

He gave her a last, speculative look. "Very well. But if you become any more alarmed, you must tell me at once. I won't have you terrified out of your wits by this business."

"I assure you I am not in the least bit terrified." Prudence sought for a way to change the subject. "Do you know, I cannot imagine using this as a guest room. It is far too bizarre."

"I agree." Sebastian stopped in front of the wardrobe and opened it. "There are not many houseguests who would be comfortable in such a chamber."

"Is there anything inside that wardrobe?" Prudence stepped closer, momentarily distracted by the expression of intense concentration she saw on Sebastian's face.

"No, it appears to be empty." Sebastian leaned into the shadowed wardrobe. "But there are a number of small drawers built into it."

"Let me see." Prudence glanced inside. Several rows of drawers occupied most of the space. "I wonder what one would keep in here?"

"I have no idea." Sebastian began systematically opening the little drawers.

They were all empty except for the very last one in the lower right-hand corner. Sebastian was about to close it as he had the others when he paused, frowning.

"What is it?" Prudence stood on tiptoe, trying to peer over his shoulder. She saw the gleam of gold in the corner of the small drawer. "A coin."

"No, a button." Sebastian plucked the little gold object out of the drawer and held it in front of the candle. "It's engraved." He studied it more closely. *"The Princes of Virtue."*

Prudence frowned. "Virtue? Do you suppose that button belongs to an Evangelical?"

"I doubt it." Sebastian looked thoughtful. "Members of some gentlemen's clubs often have their buttons engraved with the name of their particular clubs."

"Have you ever heard of a club called *The Princes of Virtue*?"

"No," Sebastian admitted. "I have not. But I might be able to learn something about it when we return to Town." He dropped the button into his pocket and closed the drawer.

"I suppose it's highly unlikely that button will provide any clues about the nature of Ringcross's death," Prudence said, disappointed. "I doubt if there is any connection. I suspect the button has been lying in that drawer for years."

"One never knows," Sebastian said cryptically. He made to close the wardrobe doors and paused. He leaned forward once again.

"What is it?"

"There is an unusual joining in the wood," Sebastian said.

Prudence looked closer. "It reminds me of the sort of joining I found in the section of the floor that concealed the Pembroke jewels."

"I believe there is a false back in this wardrobe." Sebastian pushed experimentally against the back of the wardrobe. Nothing happened. "There is probably a hidden spring around here somewhere."

Prudence went around the side of the wardrobe to take a look from the outside. "The wardrobe is directly against the wall, Sebastian. Even if you manage to open the back, you would find only stone behind it."

"Nevertheless, I would like to solve this small puzzle." Sebastian continued to examine the inside of the wardrobe.

Prudence understood the impulse that drove him. She, too, was curious to see if there was a hidden mechanism designed to open the back of the wardrobe.

She got down on her knees to see if there was any sign of a lever or spring beneath the cabinet. Out of the corner of her eye she glimpsed a small object beneath the bed.

"Sebastian, there is something over there."

"What is it?"

"It is under the bed. A little box, I believe." Prudence crawled toward the bed on her hands and knees. "Hold the candle lower."

"Let me get it." Sebastian reached down and hauled her upright. "We do not know what else may be under that damn bed."

She wrinkled her nose at his broad back as he went down on one knee. "Very well, my lord, but I want you to remember that it is I who spotted this particular bit of evidence, whatever it is."

"I would have gotten around to exploring beneath the bed in due course." Sebastian reached under the bed and picked up the little object.

"Well?" Prudence demanded eagerly. "What have you got?"

"A snuffbox."

"Is there anything else under there?" Prudence asked.

"Just a chamber pot." Sebastian got to his feet and turned the little snuffbox over in his hand. He opened it. "There is still some snuff inside." He held the box close to his nose and inhaled cautiously. "A very distinctive aroma."

"I am glad you do not use snuff," Prudence remarked. "It is a very nasty habit."

"But also a very common one. As is this snuffbox. It looks like dozens of others carried by gentlemen of the *ton.*" Sebastian got to his feet. "Nevertheless, this blend is quite unusual. It might be possible to discover which tobacconist created it and for whom it was created."

"Perhaps it belonged to Ringcross, which will tell us little."

"I'm not so certain about that." Sebastian swept the shadowed chamber with another intent glance. "One would have thought that if it had belonged to Ringcross, it would have gone out the window at the same time he did. Unless there was a struggle in this room before he died and the box somehow fell out of his pocket."

Prudence stared at him. "You think this might really be a case of murder?"

"It is too soon to say. But the investigation grows more interesting by the moment." He walked over to the window and swept the heavy black drapes aside.

Prudence studied the large window. "It would be awkward to fall from there unless one were standing on the ledge."

"Yes. But one could certainly push a man over the edge," Sebastian said.

Prudence shivered again as another wave of deep, endless cold assailed her. "Or one could jump."

She was abruptly swamped with emotions that seemed to emanate from some source other than herself. Rage and terror mingled within her for an instant, sending another shudder through her. Prudence staggered beneath the onslaught, yet she understood that she was not the one who had actually felt these horrifying sensations.

Someone else had experienced these dreadful feelings here in this chamber. Another woman. Prudence was certain of it.

"Prudence?" Sebastian held the candle high and gazed down into her face. "What's wrong?"

She looked up at him, willing him to understand. "I think I am encountering my first real ghost."

"Enough." He took her arm and started purposefully toward the door. "This has been too much for you. I am going to get you out of here at once."

"Sebastian, this is not my imagination. I vow, something terrible happened in here. I'm not at all certain it has to do with Ringcross. I can feel a woman's presence."

"Calm yourself, my sweet."

"But, Sebastian—"

He had her through the door. He paused long enough to

lock the chamber and then he urged her quickly down the black hallway toward the stairs.

Prudence was dismayed. "You think I am allowing my imagination to take control of my senses, don't you?"

"You are a very creative and intelligent woman, my dear. Such talents sometimes have their drawbacks."

"Fustian. Terrible events have occurred in that room, Sebastian. Perhaps they relate to Ringcross's death, perhaps not. But I swear to you that something awful happened there."

"I am not disputing you, Prue." Sebastian whisked her along the long hall toward the stairs.

"You don't believe me," she said.

"I admit I do not believe in ghosts. I also admit that I have a strong preference for solid evidence before I reach my conclusions."

"In other words, you think I am the victim of an overactive imagination."

"My dear, the fact that you have chosen to investigate spectral phenomena as a hobby would indicate that your imagination is very active, indeed. No offense, but you must understand that my own hobby requires a more stringent investigative approach."

"Hah. You think your approach is superior to mine?"

"Perhaps not in cases of spectral phenomena, but when it comes to investigating a crime, most definitely."

"That is an insufferably arrogant, high-handed thing to say," Prudence announced. "My methods are just as scientific as yours."

Without any warning the door they were passing on the right suddenly swung inward. There was a scratching noise and then a candle flared. An old man with a scraggly beard peered at them.

"What in bloody hell?" Sebastian jerked Prudence behind him and whirled to face the wizened figure in the doorway. "Who are you?"

The old man ignored him and gazed at Prudence with rheumy eyes. "You ain't her." His deeply lined face collapsed in obvious disappointment.

"I beg your pardon?" Prudence stood on tiptoe to look at him from her position directly behind Sebastian's right shoulder.

"I said, you ain't her." The old man squinted. "I been hiding up here ever since she done in the other one. I been watchin' for her to come. Figured she'd be back to get the others. I wanted to see her for meself."

"Who was it you were expecting to see?" Sebastian asked.

"The poor gel what jumped to her death from that cursed chamber." The man gave Sebastian a shrewd look. "I'm the one what found her, y'know."

"No, I didn't know," Sebastian said.

"Found her in the stream. They said she'd fallen in and drowned, but I seen her jump. They carried her body to the stream and dumped her in so folks would think she fell in and drowned. But I know better."

The man was half mad, Prudence realized, but he believed every word he was saying. "Who are you?"

"Higgins. Halfwit Higgins, they call me." Higgins laughed soundlessly, revealing a mouth that was virtually empty of teeth.

"When did the girl jump, Higgins?" Sebastian asked.

"A long time ago." Higgins spoke in a singsong voice now. His eyes seemed to be focused on something far away. "But I ain't forgot."

"Was Ringcross responsible for causing her to jump?" Sebastian demanded.

"They was all responsible." Higgins nodded wisely. "And they'll all pay. You'll see. They'll all pay. She cursed 'em afore she jumped, you see. Told 'em she'd be avenged. Now it's started."

"She came back for Ringcross?" Prudence gripped Sebastian's arm. "Is that what you mean, Mr. Higgins?"

"She'll come for the others, too." Higgins moved out of the doorway. He started down the hall.

"Wait. Who are the others?" Sebastian asked quickly. "When did the girl jump?"

But Higgins paid no attention. He hummed tunelessly and kept walking away down the hall. Sebastian made to go after him.

"Let him be," Prudence said. "The poor man is mad. If you try to question him further, you will only agitate him. There's no telling what he will do. He might cause a stir and alarm the household. It would ruin any chance we have of completing our investigation."

"Hell and damnation, he knows something about this affair." Sebastian watched in frustration as Higgins turned a corner in the dark hall and disappeared from sight.

"Perhaps less than you think," Prudence said thoughtfully. "He seemed to be suffering from some sort of delirium. The girl's death might be merely an old legend that he has somehow gotten confused with Ringcross's death."

"Who do you suppose he is?"

"I don't have any idea. An old family retainer long since pensioned off, perhaps." Prudence smiled. "Or mayhap he was a ghost."

Sebastian scowled at her as he took her arm and guided her toward the stairs. "That was no ghost."

"How do you know? You've never met one."

"I'll know one when I see one." Sebastian reached the stairs and extinguished the candle. There was a faint glow from the sconces on the floor below. "You, on the other hand, have seen one too many tonight."

"Nonsense. I won't allow you to make it sound as if I am in the habit of seeing apparitions. I assure you, I am not. Just because I felt something odd in that chamber does not mean I am weak-minded."

"Hush." Sebastian came to a halt midway down the staircase.

He flattened himself against the wall and pulled Prudence into his arms. He turned her so that her face was hidden against his chest.

"What are you doing?" Prudence mumbled into his shirt.

"Quiet," he whispered into her ear. "The traffic in the hall seems to have become somewhat brisk again."

"Oh."

Somewhere in the corridor a door closed. Sebastian waited a moment longer before releasing Prudence. "I think we are safe. It was Larkin. He tiptoed past the bottom of the stairs and never glanced up. Come, let's get you back to your bedchamber. We may not be so lucky the next time."

"This is really very exciting, isn't it, Sebastian?" Prudence allowed herself to be hauled swiftly to the bottom of the stairs. "I do believe I am going to enjoy our partnership immensely."

"I trust you will, my sweet," he muttered. "I, unfortunately, fear my nerves are going to suffer somewhat from the experience."

They reached the door of Prudence's bedchamber without further incident. Prudence could feel Sebastian's sigh of relief. He opened her door.

Prudence heard the squeak of another door down the hall. She hurried into her room and whirled about to make certain Sebastian was not seen by whoever was now traipsing down the busy corridor.

Sebastian was right behind her. He closed the door so softly that it did not make a sound.

"Damnation." He released the doorknob. "That was close."

"Yes, but we are quite safe now." Prudence lit a candle. The flaring flame revealed the determined expression on Sebastian's face. She looked at him in surprise. "Is something wrong? I am certain you will be able to return to your own room in a moment or two."

"As it happens," Sebastian said, "there is something I

wish to discuss with you." His gaze moved over her with unmistakable possessiveness. "Now seems as good a time as any."

She smiled, still bubbling with enthusiasm. "I expect you wish to analyze the results of our investigation tonight. We should make notes. Give me a moment and I'll fetch my journal."

"Later." Sebastian's eyes gleamed gold in the candlelight. "What I wish to discuss now is something of a much more personal nature."

"Personal?"

"Yes."

He took two steps toward her and pulled her into his arms. "Very personal."

The soft knock on the door came just as Sebastian covered Prudence's mouth with his own.

Nine

*B*loody hell." *Sebastian broke* off the kiss and turned his head toward the door. He had never looked more dangerous. "Who, in the name of the devil, thinks he can knock on your bedchamber door at this hour of the night?"

"I have no notion." She frowned in concern as she saw the cold rage that had flared to life in Sebastian's glittering gaze. "For heaven's sake, calm yourself. It's undoubtedly Lady Pembroke. Perhaps she is in need of assistance."

"Not likely." Sebastian swung around on his heel and started toward the door.

Alarmed by his menacing mood, Prudence grabbed for his arm and missed. "Sebastian, wait. You mustn't answer my door."

"You most certainly are not going to respond to that knock."

"Think about what you are doing, my lord." Prudence scurried after him. "This is not a logical, rational approach to the matter."

"You're wrong, Prue. It is a very logical tactic. My approach will be extremely effective in putting an end to future such late-night visits from whoever is out in the hall."

"May I remind you, sir, that it will be exceedingly difficult to break off our engagement if people believe we have been in the habit of sharing a bedchamber. The entire affair is going to be awkward enough as it is."

There was another soft, inquiring knock on the door.

Sebastian slanted Prudence a derisive glance. "My dear, you do not know the meaning of awkward."

Prudence had had enough. "This is nonsense. You are not thinking clearly. Obviously your masculine emotions are ruling your head."

"Is that so?" Sebastian had his hand on the doorknob. "And precisely what would you have me do under these circumstances, Miss Merryweather?"

"The practical thing. Get into the wardrobe and stay there while I deal with this."

He gave her a look of total disbelief. Then he jerked open the door.

Prudence was so annoyed with his high-handed behavior that the identity of her late-night visitor did not register for a few seconds. She gasped when she recognized Edward.

Lord Underbrink stood in the hall garbed in slippers and a dark blue dressing gown embroidered with his family crest. He did not immediately notice Sebastian because he was too busy checking the hall to the left to make certain it was still empty.

"Good evening, Underbrink," Sebastian said in a voice that could have frozen hellfire. "For the sake of efficiency, we may as well skip the formalities. Let us go straight to the point. I shall have my seconds call on yours as soon as we return to London."

"*What?*" Edward jumped a good three inches. His head snapped around and he stared at Sebastian with mounting horror. "Damnation. Angelstone, my apologies. I appear to have knocked on the wrong door."

"A brilliant observation. Definitely the wrong door."

"It was all a mistake, I assure you," Edward stuttered.

"A mistake for which you will pay dearly."

"Now, see here," Edward blustered, "you surely don't

intend to call me out simply because I knocked on your door."

"This is not my door," Sebastian said.

Edward affected blank confusion. "It's not? But you are standing right there in the doorway. I fear I do not comprehend."

"This is my fiancée's door, Underbrink, and you damn well know it. I do not intend to discuss the matter now, however. I prefer to do so over pistols."

Edward was stricken. "It was an honest mistake, I assure you. I was under the impression this was another lady's door. An older woman. Married for years. Under the circumstances, I'm sure you'll understand that I can hardly reveal her name, but it was definitely not Miss Merryweather."

"Good night, Underbrink."

Edward was clearly desperate. "Sir, you cannot mean to challenge me over this."

"That is precisely what I mean to do." Sebastian started to close the door.

Prudence put a restraining hand on Sebastian's arm. "My lord, do stop causing all this commotion." She smiled reassuringly at Edward. "I am certain Lord Underbrink intended no insult."

"None at all." Edward gave Prudence a grateful look. "Wrong door. That's the problem. They all look confoundedly alike in this damn hall."

"Yes, of course." Prudence wondered fleetingly why she had not noticed until now how soft and ineffectual Edward was. "I can see how it would happen. There is certainly a great deal of activity in the hallway this evening, is there not? One wonders how any of the guests will get to sleep."

Sebastian slanted her a warning glance. "Stay out of this, Prue."

"No, I will not," she said calmly. "Do stop trying to frighten Lord Underbrink. He made a mistake and he is very sorry."

"He will be even more sorry by the time I am through with him," Sebastian vowed.

Edward flinched. "My lord, I beg your pardon. I assure you this is all a grave misunderstanding."

"There, you see, Angelstone? Underbrink has apologized." Prudence smiled benignly at both men but fixed Sebastian with a determined look. "And you will kindly accept his apology before we attract undue attention."

Sebastian narrowed his eyes at Edward. "I shall deal with you later, Underbrink."

"Angelstone, you're being extremely unreasonable," Underbrink said frantically.

"Yes, you are, Angelstone." Prudence tugged futilely at his arm. "Now, do stop this nonsense at once." She turned to Edward. "Good night, my lord. You may rest assured that this matter is finished. Angelstone is not going to call you out."

Edward looked uncertain but hopeful. He stepped back and inclined his head with stiff formality. "Good night, Miss Merryweather. Again, I am very sorry to have disturbed you at this hour."

"Think nothing of it. I seem to be up and about at odd hours with amazing frequency of late." Prudence reached around Sebastian and gently closed the door.

Sebastian turned on her. He was still seething. "Do not ever dare to interfere like that again. I will not tolerate it."

She eyed him warily, but she did not back down. "You were being unreasonable, my lord. And entirely illogical. Underbrink made a simple mistake."

"The hell he did. He showed up at this particular door at this ungodly hour to see you."

Prudence brushed that aside. "Why on earth would he want to do that?"

"Because he wants you, you naive little ninny. He didn't take you three years ago and now he's wondering what he missed."

Prudence blushed. "Do not be an ass, my lord."

He loomed over her. "I am looking at the facts."

"You know nothing about the situation."

"Your brother told me the entire tale," Sebastian said.

"Did he?" That stopped Prudence for an instant. "Well, I assure you that whatever feeling Lord Underbrink may have had for me three years ago has long since vanished. He married another and that was the end of the matter."

"It would appear not." The glow of the candle cast the planes of Sebastian's face in demonic lines. "At least not on his part. What about you, Prue? How do you feel about him after all this time?"

"I am certainly not in love with him, if that is what concerns you, my lord." Prudence lifted her chin. "Although what business it is of yours, I cannot imagine."

"It is most definitely my business." Sebastian stalked across the room. "Furthermore, you needn't act as if my interest in the matter is unusual or odd. We're engaged, if you will recall."

His cavalier attitude toward their relationship outraged Prudence. "You seem to be the one suffering from memory lapses lately. Or have you forgotten that our engagement is a sham?"

He wrapped one hand around the bedpost and looked at her with hooded, unreadable eyes. "I wish to speak to you about this engagement of ours. I have had enough of this foolishness."

Dismay swept through her. "You wish to end it so soon, sir?" She floundered for a logical, rational reason that would forestall the inevitable. "What about our investigation?"

"Forget the damned investigation. I am beginning to think that if the matter were put to the test, I would finish a poor second to your interest in conducting investigations."

"I did not mean to imply that you are not also quite interesting, my lord," she said desperately. "Indeed, I have never met a more decidedly *interesting* man. I am quite persuaded your intellect is of the highest order. I have been deeply impressed by your inquiring nature. And by your cleverness with locks."

"*Enough.*" He released the bedpost and came toward her with an air of grim intent.

"Sebastian? What are you about?"

"Why don't you apply your intellect to that question, Miss Merryweather? I'm certain you will very quickly arrive at the answer."

He caught hold of her and swung her up into his arms before she realized what he intended.

"*Sebastian.*"

He tossed her lightly down onto the bed and sprawled on top of her, trapping her beneath his hard body. Prudence took a deep breath. The weight of him was indescribably exciting. She could feel the heat of him right through their combined layers of clothing.

She trembled a little as he carefully removed her spectacles and set them on the night table.

"Just once, Prue," Sebastian said against her throat, "do you think you might concentrate on me instead of on the bloody investigation?"

"I have been concentrating on little else except you for the past several minutes." She clutched at his shoulders and tried to focus on his implacable face. The jeweled fire in his eyes seared her. "What are you doing?"

"I am going to make love to you." He reached down and stripped her slippers off her feet.

"Now? Tonight?"

"Yes. Now. Tonight." He went to work on the buttons of her woolen gown.

A moment later she felt his fingers on the bare skin of her back. A tremor went through her as she realized how quickly he was working to undress her. In another minute or two he would have her bodice down to her waist. A deep, throbbing excitement awoke within her.

"Sebastian?"

"Hush, Prue." He stopped her faint, questioning words with a fierce kiss that effectively robbed her of breath. She moaned and instinctively tightened her grasp on his broad shoulders. Sebastian lifted his head to look down at her. "We will talk later."

He thrust his leg between hers, causing her skirts to tumble over his thigh. The startling intimacy of the action sent a wave of hot and cold chills through Prudence. Memories of the night in Mrs. Leacock's bedchamber crashed through her once more.

With quick, urgent motions, Sebastian finished unfastening her bodice and tugged it downward.

"My sweet, Prue." Sebastian's voice was little more than a ragged whisper. He looked down at her breasts for a moment and then he reverently lowered his head and took one nipple between his teeth.

Prudence swallowed and squeezed her eyes shut against the exquisite sensations that washed over her. She felt as if she were floating in a warm river, gliding along in a current that was quickly gathering force and speed. Because of what she had learned that night in Mrs. Leacock's bedchamber, Prudence knew that a magnificent waterfall lay ahead of her. She was suddenly impatient to reach it.

She arched herself against Sebastian's stroking hand. He groaned thickly in response.

"This time I am going to be deep inside you when you find your release." Sebastian looked down at her with blazing eyes. "I do not care if all the specters of hell put in an appearance around this bed."

He levered himself slightly away from her and yanked off his shirt, breeches, and boots. When he turned to face her, he was naked.

Prudence gazed at him in startled wonder. She had never seen a man in such a state in her life. The candlelight gleamed on his broad shoulders and highlighted the power-ful contours of his hard, lean body.

Even without her spectacles she could see that he was heavily aroused. The size of his jutting staff was disconcert-ing. She was inexperienced, but logic told her that a man was little different than the males of other species. She had lived in the country all her life and was well aware of how animals mated.

She knew Sebastian intended to thrust his manhood into her. The notion was strangely exciting, but common sense and logic made her hesitate. He appeared very large to her inexperienced eyes.

Prudence looked up at him. "I had not realized there would be such a disparity in terms of size between us, my lord."

Sebastian uttered a hoarse sound that was half laugh and half groan. "My sweet, logical Prudence. I have warned you that at times your intellect is something of a problem."

"There is no call to laugh at me," she said, hurt.

He came down onto the bed, pulled her close, and kissed the delicate skin behind her ear. "I am not laughing at you, Prue. And I assure you that in spite of appearances, we shall fit together with absolute perfection. Leave the logic of the situation in my hands."

She smiled tremulously, more than willing to trust him in that moment. "Very well, Sebastian. If you are certain that you know what you are doing, let us get on with it. I vow I cannot wait much longer to feel what I felt the last time you took me in your arms."

"You are the most incredible woman I have ever known," he whispered.

He drew her gown and chemise off entirely and tossed both over the side of the bed. The garments landed in a small heap on the carpet. Sebastian ignored them as he studied Prudence's nude body with an expression rendered stark by desire.

Prudence realized she was still wearing her stockings. For some reason the knowledge made her feel deliciously wicked. She felt her skin grow warm. "My stockings," she mumbled.

"I think we will leave your stockings in place," Sebastian said. "I find I rather like you in them."

"Sebastian, really."

"Yes, really." He slid his hand slowly down the length of her in an act of possession that made her shiver. "You are lovely, Prudence. With or without the stockings."

When his hand reached the triangle of soft hair between her thighs, Prudence cried out softly and turned her face into his chest. Shyness did battle with a growing sensual hunger deep within her. The hunger won. She curled closer against Sebastian, seeking more of his intimate touch.

"Silk and fire," Sebastian muttered against her breast. "That's what you are made of, my sweet. Silk and fire. And I cannot wait any longer to feel the flames."

Sebastian settled himself on top of her. He reached down and parted her thighs. His fingers dipped into her, gently testing. The touch made Prudence dig her nails into his back and lift herself against his hand.

"You like that, don't you?" Sebastian asked.

"You must know that I do." Prudence threaded her fingers into his hair and pulled his mouth down to hers. She was enthralled, she thought, caught up in a shimmering spell of love and passion that had swept over her like a summer storm.

And Sebastian wanted her just as intensely, she thought with growing certainty. He must love her just as much as she loved him. He could not make love to her like this unless his feelings for her matched her own for him.

Sebastian accepted the invitation of her mouth with an eagerness that spoke for itself. His tongue surged between her lips, claiming her with an intimacy that foreshadowed what was to follow.

He pressed her thighs more widely apart, making a place

for himself near her heat. Then he reached down between their bodies and fitted himself to the opening of her feminine passage.

The feel of his broad shaft poised to enter her brought Prudence briefly back to a vague sense of reality. "Sebastian?"

"Tell me that you want me, Prue."

She smiled dreamily. "I want you."

"Then all will be well," he whispered.

He thrust forward slowly.

Prudence gasped against his mouth. Her whole body stiffened in reaction to the invasion.

"Open for me," Sebastian urged. He withdrew slightly and then pushed forward again. "Let me inside, my sweet."

Prudence's fingers clenched in his hair as she bravely braced herself. But Sebastian did not force the entrance. Instead he again withdrew a short distance.

"You are like a lock that must be carefully opened," he said. There was perspiration on his forehead. His shoulders glistened in the candlelight.

"I told you this would not work."

"And I told you to trust me. I am very good with locks, if you will recall."

He moved his hand downward, dampened one finger in her moisture, and then found the firm little bud that seemed to be the center of her passions.

Prudence began to relax again as he caressed her with his wet finger. The delicious tension coiled within her. Her head tipped back over his arm as she arched herself upward.

"That's it." Sebastian's voice held satisfaction. "Now you will open for me, won't you, my clever little lock? Now you are ready to let me inside."

All Prudence could think about was the excitement his fingers were creating. Soon, she thought, soon she would feel that wonderful sensation again.

And then the thrilling release was upon her.

"Yes," Sebastian whispered. "The lock is open."

Prudence went wild beneath the onslaught. Her whole body convulsed with pleasure.

"Yes," she whispered. "Yes, Sebastian. Dear God, yes."

He guided himself into her once again and this time he did not hesitate or withdraw. He thrust deeply, relentlessly, into her snug channel.

"*Beautiful*," he said, his voice a dark, husky groan.

Prudence heard her own soft shriek of surprise muffled against his shoulder. Pain blended with the pleasure that was still rippling through her in tiny waves. She could not distinguish between the two sensations. She lightly bit Sebastian's shoulder.

"My clever, beautiful lock has teeth," Sebastian muttered.

But the small, passionate assault on his shoulder seemed to send him over some invisible edge. He gave a strangled shout and buried himself to the hilt. The muscles in his back were rigid beneath Prudence's fingers.

Prudence held him tightly as he shuddered heavily and poured himself into her.

The candle had burned very low before Sebastian finally stirred on top of Prudence. He raised his head and looked down at her. His mouth curved faintly with lazy satisfaction. He leaned down to brush his lips across hers. Then he eased himself out of her and rolled to one side.

"Bloody hell. I've never felt anything that good before in my life." He fell back against the pillows and pulled her down on top of him. "I told you I could open that particular lock."

Prudence blushed. "So you did."

He grinned and touched his finger to the tip of her nose. "It'll get better with practice."

"Are we going to practice a lot, my lord?"

"You may depend upon it." He buried his fingers in her tousled hair and brought her mouth down to his for a quick, hard kiss. "We shall practice at every opportunity. Which brings me to the topic I was attempting to discuss earlier."

"Our false engagement?" A sudden sense of wariness drove out some of Prudence's contentment.

"Precisely. I wish to end it."

Prudence was vastly more shaken than she would have believed possible. Surely he had some feeling for her, she thought. After experiencing the intensity of his lovemaking, she could not believe he felt nothing. *He loved her. He had to love her.* She tried to keep her voice calm. "I see."

"No, I don't believe you do." Sebastian smiled slightly, but his eyes were watchful. "I want us to be married immediately."

"*Married.*" Prudence was speechless.

Sebastian frowned. He appeared annoyed at her failure to grasp a concept that was apparently quite clear to him.

"Come, now, my dear," he said persuasively. "How else are we to practice our lovemaking? I assure you, it would be extremely difficult to conduct an affair in Town. The other option is to accept every country house party invitation that comes along, and that would be a decided nuisance. We shall be forever on the road."

"Yes, but marriage?" She had not expected this. She stared at him in shock, trying frantically to focus without the aid of her spectacles. "Sebastian, are you serious?"

"I assure you, I have never been more serious in my life."

Joy leaped to life within her. It was instantly tempered with caution. She was well aware that she amused Sebastian. He found her interesting and obviously he felt some degree of passion for her. But thus far he had said nothing about being in love with her. He had not even said the words while in the act of making love to her.

"Do you truly believe we would suit, Sebastian?"

"I can think of no one who would suit me better," he said.

"Yes, well." She cast about for a way of eliciting the answer she wanted. "I am, of course, extremely honored, my lord."

"Good. Then the matter is settled," Sebastian said brusquely. "I shall see about securing a special license in the morning. Lady Pembroke can be a witness."

Panic seized Prudence. "As I said, I am deeply honored. And I can quite understand that it would be more efficient to conduct an affair within a marriage. But I am not certain that efficiency is a valid reason for such a permanent entanglement."

"There are a number of other logical reasons for a marriage between us," Sebastian said very coolly.

"There are?"

"Naturally. I would not have proposed the notion otherwise."

Prudence reached for her spectacles and adjusted them on her nose. "Perhaps you would care to name a few of them?"

He gave her his most arrogant, most superior sort of smile. "As you wish, although I would have thought them obvious. You are a very passionate female, Prue. That is important to me, as I have certain physical desires which need to be addressed from time to time—"

Prudence could not bear to hear their mutual passion described in such a casual manner. "Go on with your list."

"Yes, of course. In addition to a, uh, healthy approach to such matters, we have several mutual intellectual interests."

"That is very true," she admitted.

"In short, you will not bore me, my sweet." He brushed his mouth lightly across hers. "And I shall endeavor not to bore you."

"You could never do that," she said quickly.

"I should also like to point out that living together as man and wife will greatly facilitate our investigations. We shall be able to advise each other and to study each other's methods much more efficiently if we are under the same roof."

"Yes, I can see that." But her sense of uneasiness grew stronger. She sought carefully for the right words. "Nevertheless, do you think mutual interests and a . . . a certain degree of warmth between us will form a sufficient foundation for marriage?"

He looked surprised at the question. "I cannot think of a better foundation."

"Some might say that love would be a nice addition to the list," she whispered tentatively.

"Love?" His eyes narrowed in disapproval, as if she had not only startled him but also disappointed him. "Come, now, Prue, surely you are not the victim of a romantic nature. I refuse to credit the notion that an intelligent, perceptive, very clever female such as yourself is foolish enough to believe in something as vague and illusory as love."

She swallowed uneasily. "Well—"

"You and I rely on our intellects, not our emotions," he continued ruthlessly. "We unravel mysteries and search for evidence. Our logical brains are not prey to the fevered fancies that excite the likes of Byron and his crowd."

"Granted. Nevertheless—"

"Rest assured, my dear, I have far too much respect for you to allow myself to believe that you actually seek to fall in love before you marry. Love is for silly young girls fresh out of the schoolroom. A mature, responsible, intelligent woman such as yourself does not indulge in such fancies."

Prudence nearly choked. "Yes, I know, but the thing is, Sebastian—"

"After all, there is much less evidence for the existence of love than there is for the existence of spectral phenomena."

"I wouldn't say that, my lord," she argued earnestly. "Love has been the motivating force behind a great many historical occurrences. People commit crimes for love. They are sometimes made ill by it. Surely there is ample evidence to suggest it exists."

"Nonsense. The motivating force you refer to is passion. Or, to be perfectly blunt, lust." He traced the outline of her lips with his finger.

Prudence's spirits sank. "Do you feel some affection for me, Sebastian?"

"Naturally," he said roughly. "That goes without saying."

"It does?" Affection wasn't love, but one might be able to turn it into love, she told herself optimistically.

"What about you?" he asked casually. "Do you feel some degree of affection for me? As distinct from that which you feel toward my hobby, that is?"

"Oh, yes," she said. "Yes, definitely. I am really quite fond of you, Sebastian."

"And I am rather fond of you. What more could either of us ask? We are two like-minded people who share mutual intellectual interests and mutual passion. We shall do very well together. Now, then, say that you will marry me as soon as I can make the arrangements."

"Why must we hurry the thing along? Could we not wait and give our mutual affection a chance to mature?" Prudence asked weakly.

"I think that would not only be a waste of time, but also potentially awkward."

"Awkward? How?"

"Surely you know the answer to that. Use your considerable intelligence, Prue. You might very well turn up pregnant after what just transpired between us."

Prudence stared at him as the reality of what he had just said struck her. "Good heavens. I had not thought of that."

"You may be certain I have," Sebastian said flatly. "Having been called a bastard often enough myself, I am not about to have my son or daughter labeled as such."

"No, of course not. I quite understand." And she did, Prudence thought.

Sebastian's cold pride and arrogance had caused him to fling the question of his own legitimacy into the very teeth of his family and of society. But that same arrogant pride would make him equally determined that no child of his carried the stigma.

Sebastian looked at her from beneath half-lowered lashes. "Well, then, Prue? Do we have another bargain? Will you marry me?"

Prudence took a deep breath and thrust aside her doubts and hesitations. The risk she was about to take was worth it, she assured herself. She was going to marry the man she loved.

"I will marry you, Sebastian."

Something that might have been relief flared in his eyes. But his voice remained cool and even slightly amused, as usual. "An eminently logical, rational decision, my sweet. I expected no less from you, of course."

"Of course," Prudence muttered. But inside she shivered with hope and dread.

A frightening sense of foreboding wrapped itself around her. She knew that if she was wrong about Sebastian's feelings for her, she had just bargained away her entire future and perhaps her very soul to the Fallen Angel.

Ten

Four days later Garrick confronted Sebastian in his favorite club. "So, Angelstone, how is married life?"

Sebastian glanced up from the copy of the *Morning Post* that he was perusing. He fixed Garrick with a baleful look.

"I have learned a great deal about wives during the past few days," Sebastian said. "You may be interested to know, for instance, that even the most intelligent among them is not always logical in her thinking."

Garrick put down his cup of coffee and grinned. "Squabbling with your lady already? For shame, Angelstone. One would think that at this stage you would still be making an effort to present your best side to Lady Angelstone. Time enough to let her see the real you later."

Sebastian swore softly as he recalled the small but lively scene that had ensued that morning when he had announced over breakfast that he intended to spend the day visiting tobacconists. Flowers had just finished pouring their tea and had left them alone.

Prudence's lovely eyes had shone with enthusiasm behind her spectacles. "You are going to try to identify the person for whom that special mixture of snuff is blended?"

"Yes." Sebastian sliced into a plump sausage. "Now that the business of our wedding is settled and we have got you moved in here with me, I believe we can at last get on with our investigation."

Her gaze turned curiously opaque. "Poor Sebastian," she murmured. "You had no notion of the commotion our wedding would cause, did you? I expect you thought you could simply put an announcement in the papers and that would be the end of it."

"There is a great deal of unnecessary nonsense associated with weddings which I had not anticipated," he said, "but I am hopeful that the worst is behind us."

In truth, they had not had any peace since their return to London, Sebastian thought, vastly annoyed. He had fully intended to spend the majority of his free time during the past four days in bed with his new wife. The polite world deemed otherwise. To his disgust, he had discovered that weddings— even quiet, uncomplicated ones—generated a great deal of fuss and attention.

On the morning of the wedding Hester had cheerfully reminded him that the marriage was bound to create a sensation among the *ton*. She had been accurate in her prediction. There had been a steady stream of visitors to Sebastian's town house. A new mountain of cards and invitations arrived every morning. The presence of Lord and Lady Angelstone was requested at every soiree and ball in Town.

Sebastian had been strongly inclined to ignore every visitor and all the invitations. But Prudence had put her dainty foot down on that notion. His reputation for ill-mannered behavior was bad enough, she had explained. She was not going to see it savaged any further simply because he could not be bothered with a few social niceties.

"Do you regret our marriage, then?" Prudence had inquired in a suspiciously neutral voice from the far end of the breakfast table.

"What an idiotic question. Of course not. We are perfectly suited, as I have gone to great lengths to explain." He eyed her warily, wondering what had made her ask such a question. The possibility that she, herself, had a few regrets made him once more aware of the cold place inside himself.

He did not see how she could doubt for a moment that she belonged with him. She looked right at home sitting there at the other end of the breakfast table. The morning sun streamed through the window behind her. It turned her hair the color of the warm honey that was in the little pot next to the toast. A shaft of lazy desire went through Sebastian as he remembered how Prudence's hair had looked earlier when it was fanned out across the white pillows of his bed.

"I shall accompany you to interview the tobacconists," Prudence announced.

"No, you will not." He forked up another bite of sausage. "I intend to make as much progress as possible today. There is no way of knowing how many shops I shall be required to visit."

"Are you saying I will hinder your investigations?" Prudence's brows snapped together in a straight line across the rim of her spectacles. "I would remind you that we are supposed to be a team, sir."

Sebastian knew it was time to tread warily. He was rapidly learning the business of being a husband, he thought wryly.

"You misunderstand me, my dear." He smiled benignly. "The fact of the matter is that if the pair of us are seen visiting a series of tobacconists, someone might notice and think it odd. Questions might be asked."

"Perhaps I could disguise myself as a footman or a groom. No one would question my presence if I looked like a member of your household staff, would they?"

"My entire household staff would certainly wonder about it," Sebastian said brusquely. "Not to mention anyone else who might chance to recognize you." The thought of Prudence traipsing about in men's attire sent a wave of outrage through him.

Prudence frowned in thought. "I think it would work very well, my lord. I believe that after breakfast I shall just nip downstairs and see what I can find in the way of livery."

At that point Sebastian abandoned strategy and diplomacy and fell back on ruthless threats.

"If you try that trick, madam, I promise you I will find myself unable to accompany you to the Arlington ball tonight."

"Sebastian, you wouldn't." Acute dismay filled her eyes. "You must put in an appearance tonight. I am told that several members of your family will be there, including your aunt and your cousin Jeremy."

"As far as I'm concerned, that is an excellent reason for not putting in an appearance. In any event, I wouldn't be surprised to learn that Lady Arlington has deliberately planned her damned ball with the express purpose of producing a scene for the *ton*."

"Come, now, Sebastian, that is highly unlikely. She is trying to be polite."

"My dear, you may be very intelligent, but you are amazingly naive at times."

"Lady Arlington's ball will be the first occasion on which the members of your family will all be gathered together in public. If you don't turn up, the Fleetwoods will be humiliated in front of the *ton*."

He was thoroughly amused. "Do you think that matters to me?"

"You are being deliberately difficult, my lord. You know perfectly well that if you fail to show up tonight it will add fuel to the notion that there is a feud within your family."

"The feud is very real, Prue." Sebastian put down his knife and folded his arms on the table. "And you would be well advised to remember just which side you are on. Furthermore, it would be most unwise of you to try to play peacemaker. I want no part of the Fleetwoods, and that's final."

"Really, Sebastian."

"Yes, really." Having taken his stand, Sebastian knew better than to back down. Prudence would spot any weakness in his defenses in an instant. "Now, then, if you wish me to put in an appearance at the Arlington ball, you had best forget any notion of dressing up in a footman's livery."

"Now, see here, Angelstone, just because we happen to be married, you must not get the idea that you can start giving orders and making threats in the manner of ordinary husbands."

He gave her a cool, quizzical smile. "You do not consider me an ordinary husband?"

"Certainly not." She refolded her napkin and set it beside her plate with an air of grave precision. "Our alliance is supposed to be a partnership. Two like-minded individuals joined together by the bonds of mutual interests, if you will recall."

"I recall the terms of our bargain very well." Sebastian got to his feet.

Prudence watched warily as he walked toward her. "Sebastian?"

Sebastian said nothing. When he reached the far end of the table he leaned down and kissed Prudence full on her surprised mouth. She tasted delicious. He had a sudden urge to make love to her right there on the breakfast table. The only thing that stopped him was the realization that Flowers could enter the room at any moment.

"As you said, ours is an alliance based on mutual interests." He brushed his mouth across hers again and felt her tremble in response. "And some of our mutual interests were particularly stimulating last night. I look forward to more of the same tonight."

She glowered at him suspiciously through her spectacles. "Do not think that you can manipulate me with . . . with that sort of thing, Angelstone."

"What sort of thing would that be? This, perhaps?" He

nibbled her earlobe and let his hand drift down over the modest fichu that filled in the bodice of her brown and white striped morning gown.

"You know precisely what I mean, sir."

"Do I?" He palmed her breast and was well satisfied by the response he got. Prudence's cheeks turned pink and a delightfully flustered look replaced the wifely chastisement in her eyes.

"Be off with you," she muttered. "And do not forget the Arlington ball tonight or I shall never forgive you."

Sebastian now smiled faintly at the memory of the morning and poured himself another cup of coffee from the pot he and Garrick were sharing.

As he sipped his coffee, he contemplated the thought of Prudence seated opposite him at breakfast every morning for the rest of their lives and wondered how he had ever gotten along without her there.

Garrick scanned the advertisements in the paper he was reading. "Thought I'd take myself off to Tattersall's after a bit and see what they're offering. I could use a good hunter." He looked up. "What will you be about today?"

"I have some business to attend to."

"Ah, I recognize that tone in your voice." Garrick grinned briefly. "It is the one you use when you are in the process of conducting one of your little investigations. Pray do not tell me that you are so bored with married life already that you must seek out your old amusements."

"I assure you, married life is anything but dull. But I have not given up my hobby."

"I see." Garrick eyed him curiously. "Does your lady know what you do to entertain yourself?"

"She knows."

"And approves?"

"She has no complaints," Sebastian said.

Garrick chuckled. "I congratulate you, Angelstone. I do

believe you have married the one woman in all of England who is capable of understanding you."

"I am certain of it."

The only thing that worried Sebastian was that Prudence might not be as well satisfied with married life as he was.

He told himself that the matter was settled. Prudence belonged to him now. He had claimed her under the law and in the privacy of the marriage bed. And she had given herself to him with a willing passion that should have reassured him.

But sometimes he would catch her watching him with a strange wistfulness that made him uneasy. He could not forget her words that night at Curling Castle. *Some might say that love would be a nice addition to the list.*

For all her intellect and her admirable powers of logic, Prudence was a woman. Sebastian suspected that she had a woman's romantic attitude toward marriage. She had wanted to marry for love.

He was well aware that he had deliberately coerced Prudence into a hasty wedding. He had done so using all the weapons at his command. He had justified the ruthless tactics by telling himself that she would be happy with him.

She was old enough and intelligent enough to realize that whatever emotion she had felt for Underbrink was fleeting and insubstantial. In any event, the pompous ass had betrayed her affections. She could never trust Underbrink again. Surely she knew that.

At four o'clock that afternoon a portion of Sebastian's brain was still pondering the unexpected dilemmas posed by marriage. But a good deal of his attention was now focused on a more immediate problem.

Thus far he had visited nearly half a dozen tobacconists in a fruitless search to find one who could identify the blend of snuff in the small snuffbox Prudence had discovered in the black chamber.

It had seemed a relatively simple task when he had set out on his mission. But thus far no one recognized the blend.

He went up the steps of one R. H. Goodwright, tobacconist, without much hope. Goodwright was number six on Sebastian's list.

Sebastian glanced at the life-size wooden carving of a Highlander that guarded the shop entrance. The statue's dress was painted in the colors of a famous regiment. The popular symbol of the snuff dealer's trade was similar to the five other wooden Highlanders Sebastian had already seen that afternoon.

If he did not have any luck here, Sebastian decided, he would have to seek out less successful establishments in less fashionable streets. He had been working on the assumption that whoever had lost the snuffbox had been a member of the *ton* and therefore shopped in the better establishments. Sebastian could not envision Curling inviting anyone to Curling Castle who did not move in fashionable circles.

Sebastian opened the door and walked into the small shop. The aroma of the well-aged tobacco stored in glass cases and in wooden barrels engulfed him. Clay pipes were prominently displayed on one counter. On another counter a selection of small snuffboxes was arranged. Sebastian took a closer look at them but saw none as fine as the one he was investigating.

"How may I serve you, sir?" inquired a raspy voice.

Sebastian looked around and saw a plump, white-haired, heavily whiskered man wearing a green apron and a pair of gold spectacles. The shopkeeper's pudgy fingers were stained yellow from years of handling tobacco.

"I'm trying to discover the name of this particular blend of snuff." Sebastian plucked the snuffbox out of the pocket of his greatcoat and held it out to the shopkeeper. "An acquaintance gave me enough to fill this box, but I shall soon run out and would like to order more. It's quite distinctive. Do you happen to recognize it?"

The shopkeeper examined Sebastian's gleaming boots and elegantly tailored clothes as he opened the box. He sniffed cautiously at the snuff, careful not to inhale it. "I certainly do recognize it, my lord. I created this blend myself."

The familiar thrill of discovery flashed through Sebastian. Until Prudence had entered his life, he reflected, he had been forced to rely on these rare moments of fleeting excitement to keep the cold at bay.

Sebastian schooled his features to a mask of polite interest. "It seems I am in luck, then. I suppose it is a popular blend?"

"Might be if I sold it to all and sundry, but the gentleman I make it up for has stipulated that he be the only one who gets it. He makes it worth my while to keep the blend special for him."

"It's not for sale to the general public, then?" Sebastian frowned with what he hoped passed for disappointment. His luck was holding, he thought. He would not have to investigate a long list of snuff purchasers. All he needed was the name of the one who had commissioned this special mixture for himself.

"Afraid not." The snuff dealer eyed him with a shopkeeper's assessing look. He was obviously reluctant to lose the trade. "Mayhap I can blend a special batch for you, m'lord. Something with a bit of Turkish in it, perhaps? Just got a nice shipment of fine tobacco from America. Very mild, it is. I can do you a most distinctive blend that will be the envy of your friends."

"That's very kind of you, but I very much wanted a supply of this particular blend. I am prepared to pay well for it."

The snuff dealer sighed with regret. "I cannot risk offending my client, sir. I'm sure you understand."

"Your client?" Sebastian prompted carefully.

"Mr. Fleetwood would be only too likely to take his patronage elsewhere if I didn't honor my agreement with him."

Sebastian stared at the dealer, hoping his mouth wasn't hanging open in astonishment. "Fleetwood?"

"Yes, sir. Mr. Jeremy Fleetwood." The snuff dealer frowned. "You must know him, sir, if he gave you a sample of his snuff."

"We met in passing at a boxing match," Sebastian said, thinking swiftly. "Afraid I didn't catch his name. You know how the crowd is at a mill."

"Right you are, sir. Attended an interesting match just last week. Crowd nearly rioted when Iron Jones lost. He was the favorite, you know. Lost a packet on him, m'self."

"I heard the outcome of the match was extremely disappointing," Sebastian said as he walked toward the door. "Thank you for Mr. Fleetwood's name. I shall look him up at once. Perhaps I can prevail upon him to allow you to make up a supply of this blend for me."

"But, sir, if I might suggest another blend—"

Sebastian closed the shop door and walked the short distance to where his groom waited with the phaeton.

What in the name of hell did Jeremy have to do with any of this? Sebastian wondered as he vaulted up onto the seat and took the reins.

Prudence was going to be as startled by this bit of information as he was. He was suddenly impatient to discuss the new twist in the case with her.

"What do you mean, she's not here, Flowers? Where the devil is she?" Sebastian had hurried straight home in order to share with Prudence the details of the singular new development in the investigation. It was extremely irritating to learn that she was not waiting eagerly to applaud his brilliance.

"I believe Lady Angelstone has gone out, my lord."

Sebastian made a bid for his fraying patience. "Where did she go, Flowers?"

Flowers gave a small, discreet cough. "To the home of the Misses Singleton in Wellwood Street, sir."

"Who the devil are the Misses Singleton?"

"Lady Angelstone described them as clients." Flowers looked deeply pained. "A message arrived from them shortly after you left. They apparently wished to consult with her ladyship about a matter of spectral phenomena. Her ladyship set out almost immediately."

"So she's pursuing an investigation, is she?"

Flowers gave him a woeful look. "Something was said about an electricity machine, my lord."

Sebastian frowned. "Electricity machine?"

"I have reason to believe her ladyship has borrowed one from a Mr. Matthew Hornsby and intends to use it in the course of her investigation today."

Sebastian was momentarily distracted from his own case. "That might prove interesting."

Flowers drew himself up. "I would like to inquire, my lord, whether staff should accustom itself to this sort of behavior on the part of her ladyship?"

"Yes, Flowers, I think you had all better get used to the notion that this will never be a completely normal household."

"You say the strange moaning sounds seem to come from this section of the garret?" Prudence pushed the electricity machine into place in the center of the small dark room directly beneath the roof of the narrow house.

"I think that is about right." Evangeline Singleton, a stout, forthright woman of indeterminate years, frowned thoughtfully. She turned to her sister for confirmation. "Don't you think that is about right, Iphigenia?"

"I suppose so," Iphigenia, small, frail, and fluttery, eyed the electricity machine with deep dread. "I hear the sounds downstairs in my bedchamber, so they must be coming from somewhere around here. But I really do not know if we should be attempting to find the ghost, Evangeline."

"We cannot allow the thing to continue moaning at all hours of the night," Evangeline said. "You need your rest." She turned back to Prudence. "Now, then, Lady Angelstone, how is this machine going to force our ghost to appear?"

"According to my new theory," Prudence said, "spectral phenomena utilize electricity in the atmosphere in order to render themselves visible. I believe that the chief reason they are only rarely seen is because it is uncommon for them to have access to sufficient electricity."

Iphigenia's eyes widened in alarm. "You intend to provide our ghost with the electricity it needs to make itself visible?"

"Precisely." Prudence straightened and surveyed the machine she had borrowed from Trevor's friend, Matthew Hornsby.

It was a simple arrangement involving a glass cylinder, a hand crank, a leather pad, and a jar. Matthew had assured her there was no danger involved in the operation of the machine.

"I beg your pardon, Lady Angelstone, but does your husband approve of you carrying out these investigations?" Iphigenia asked cautiously.

"Oh, yes." Prudence bustled around the machine, making certain everything was ready. "Angelstone has a very intellectual nature. He is quite interested in my work."

"I see." Iphigenia gave her a strange glance. "One hears that Angelstone is a rather unusual man."

"I suppose he is." Prudence tested the hand crank. It turned easily. The glass cylinder started to rotate beneath the leather pad. "I certainly do not know any other man quite like him."

Iphigenia traded a silent glance with her sister. "One hears that he is somewhat dangerous."

"Not in the least." The cylinder began to rotate faster as

Prudence worked the crank. "Would one of you put out the lamp? I doubt we shall be able to see anything if there is too much light."

"Lady Angelstone," Iphigenia began uneasily, "I really do not think this is such a good idea. There are no windows up here and it will be quite dark if we put out the lamp."

"Really, Iphigenia, you must not be so timid." Evangeline went briskly over to the lamp and turned it off.

The room was plunged into complete darkness.

"Excellent," Prudence said. "If there is a ghost up here we shall make him visible in no time." She cranked the handle of the electricity machine as rapidly as possible.

"But I do not actually want to see the thing," Iphigenia whimpered. "I just want you to get rid of it."

"Get hold of yourself," Evangeline ordered crisply. "Lady Angelstone knows what she is about, don't you, madam?"

"Certainly," Prudence called above the noise of the whirling cylinder. "I have great confidence in my latest theory. We should produce sufficient electricity for a ghost very soon now."

"Oh, dear," Iphigenia said forlornly. "I really do wish we had consulted another sort of expert, Evangeline. This whole experience is unsettling my nerves."

"You can take a dose of laudanum when it is over," Evangeline said. "Now do stop fussing. You might scare off the ghost."

Prudence turned the crank faster and faster. "Creating electricity is a bit more difficult than I had thought it would be," she said breathlessly.

Light flashed suddenly in a white-hot arc that illuminated the room for a few brief seconds. Prudence heard Iphigenia's horrified gasp.

"Dear heavens, Evangeline, we've raised the devil himself."

"What in the world?" Prudence looked around just in time to see Sebastian's face rendered in harsh, demonic relief by the brilliant spark of electricity. His golden eyes burned in the glare of the unnatural light.

An instant later he was gone.

Iphigenia moaned weakly as the room was once more enveloped in complete darkness.

"My goodness." Evangeline's voice shook. "What on earth was that, Lady Angelstone?"

Prudence scowled into the gloom. "Angelstone? Is that you?"

"Sorry, my dear." There was a scratching noise and then a candle flared. Sebastian smiled faintly. "Didn't mean to interrupt your investigation. The housekeeper said you were all up here, so I decided to join you."

"Good lord," Evangeline said, sounding extremely relieved. "You gave me quite a start, sir. I do believe my sister has fainted."

"Oh, dear." Prudence glanced down and saw Iphigenia lying on the floor. "So she has. Angelstone, next time you decide to observe my investigation techniques, kindly announce yourself in the proper fashion."

"Forgive me, my dear," he said humbly. "I was trying to be unobtrusive."

"You are not the unobtrusive sort, my lord. Look what you did to my client. You have quite terrified her out of her wits." Prudence sighed. "I suppose we shall have to start all over again now."

"It was Lucifer himself. I saw him." Iphigenia's eyelashes fluttered but did not open. "No more. I beg of you, Lady Angelstone. Please stop the investigation."

Prudence frowned. "But we were just getting started."

"Quite right," Evangeline said as she held a vinaigrette bottle under her sister's nose. "We cannot stop now. But perhaps it would be best if Angelstone did not participate in the investigation. No offense, your lordship. It's just that my sister's nerves are easily overset."

"I'm afraid she's right." Prudence looked at Sebastian. "I

think you had better leave, sir. I cannot have you alarming my clients."

Sebastian frowned. "I wished to speak with you, Prue."

"Later, my lord." She shooed him out of the garret with a sweeping movement of her hands. "As you can see, I am quite busy at the moment. Run along, if you please."

Sebastian's jaw tightened. "Very well, madam. I shall see you later."

"Yes, yes, of course." Prudence turned back to the electricity machine and started to work the crank. "Good-bye, my lord."

Sebastian disappeared through the door by which he had entered a few minutes earlier.

Evangeline stared after him. "I do not believe it."

"What don't you believe, Miss Singleton?" Prudence took a deep breath and bore down on her task. She could feel perspiration gathering between her shoulder blades.

"That you just told Angelstone to *run along*. And he did so."

"Serves him right." Prudence cranked harder. "He did not allow me to assist him today."

"I see." Evangeline gave her an odd look. "It would seem that you do, indeed, have a talent for dealing with spectral phenomena, madam. You appear to be able to banish the devil himself."

By the time Sebastian stalked into Lady Arlington's ballroom in search of Prudence, he was not in a good mood. He heard the ripple of anticipation that went through the crowded room as he walked through it and his temper did not improve. The *ton* was hoping for a scene tonight. He was in just the right frame of mind to provide one.

He located Prudence from halfway across the glittering room. She was the center of a cluster of people and she glanced up as he forged a path in her direction. The lenses of her spectacles glittered cheerfully in the light of the chandeliers. Her smile was more brilliant than all the massed candles overhead.

She was wearing a demure muslin gown that was a weak shade of blue. The neckline was cut far higher than that of any other lady's in the room. Sebastian heartily approved of the modest style. As far as he was concerned, Prudence's unfashionable clothes served very nicely to veil her from the eyes of other men. Only he knew how soft and graceful her breasts were. Only he knew how her nipples responded to his touch. Only he knew how she arched beneath his mouth, how she clung to him.

Sebastian stifled a groan as he realized he was growing hard and heavy right there in the middle of the ballroom.

He wondered ruefully what had happened to the well-honed self-control that he had taken for granted for years. He realized that he had begun to lose his iron grip on his passions the night that Prudence had leaped from the wardrobe to save him from Thornbridge's pistol. Sebastian knew of no one else who would have gone out of his or her way to save his neck.

He had almost reached Prudence's side when he glimpsed Jeremy out of the corner of his eye. He paused and watched as his cousin left the crowded room to go out onto the terrace. Jeremy was alone. Now was as good a time as any to confront him.

Sebastian abruptly changed direction to pursue Jeremy. When he reached the open doors he glanced outside and saw his cousin standing near a low stone wall. As Sebastian watched, Jeremy withdrew a small snuffbox and flipped open the lid with an elegant flick of his finger. He had obviously been practicing the gesture.

Sebastian took the snuffbox he had found at Curling Castle out of his pocket and started forward.

"Allow me to offer you a special blend, cousin." Sebastian held the box out to Jeremy.

"What? Oh, it's you, Angelstone." Jeremy did not immediately look at the snuffbox in Sebastian's gloved hand. Instead he surveyed him without any enthusiasm. "Surprised to see you here tonight, though Mother said she thought you would show. Said you would seize the opportunity to demonstrate your contempt for the rest of us."

"Seizing such opportunities requires more energy than I wish to exert this evening. Do you recognize this snuffbox?"

Jeremy glanced at the box and frowned. "Since when did you take up the habit?"

"I have not taken it up." Sebastian flipped open the lid. "I am told this mixture is unique. Blended expressly for one particular person."

"What the devil are you on about?" Jeremy took a closer look at the box. "Damnation, Angelstone, that's my snuffbox. Where did you get it?"

"It came my way not long ago. When and where did you lose it?"

Jeremy picked up the snuffbox. "I do not recall precisely. I noticed it was missing after I returned from a house party at Curling Castle. Why do you ask?"

"I found it at Curling Castle."

Jeremy shrugged. "That explains it, then. But how did you know it was mine?"

"I made inquiries."

"I see." Jeremy stared at him, perplexed. "But why did you go to the effort of tracking down the owner? The box is rather nice, but it's not all that valuable."

"I was very curious about the owner of that box," Sebastian said softly, "because I found it in a most unusual chamber on the top floor of Curling Castle. A room done entirely in black."

"Black?"

"A month ago a man named Ringcross fell to his death from that particular chamber. You may recall hearing of the incident?"

Jeremy gazed at him, dumbfounded. "Ringcross's fall occurred the weekend I attended one of Curling's house parties. What is this about, Angelstone?"

"Nothing, at the moment." Sebastian studied him intently. "I merely find the coincidence interesting."

"What coincidence?" Jeremy demanded. "The fact that you found my snuffbox in the chamber where Ringcross died? Well, I find it interesting that I only have your word that you discovered the snuffbox there."

"Do you think I am lying about the matter?"

"I think you are quite capable of it if it suited your own ends." Jeremy pocketed the snuffbox. "But I vow I cannot conceive of why you would want to invent such a tale. For your information, I never visited the top floor of the castle. I never saw this black chamber you describe."

"Are you certain of that?"

"Yes, damn it, I am very certain." Jeremy's face was tight with anger. "Why in blazes are you trying to connect me to that chamber?"

"I am not trying to connect you to it. The snuffbox does that all by itself." Sebastian turned on his heel and started back into the ballroom.

"Hold on a moment, Angelstone," Jeremy called after him. "What devil's game are you playing now? I demand to know what you think you are doing."

Sebastian paused on the threshold of the French doors and glanced back at Jeremy. "As it happens, I am about to ask my wife to dance the waltz with me."

Prudence appeared in the doorway before Jeremy could react. Her smile was as bright as it had been earlier, but her eyes held speculation and concern. "I see you are getting some fresh air, Mr. Fleetwood. Lovely night, is it not?"

"A fine night, madam," Jeremy said stiffly.

"Yes, it is. A bit chilly, however. And I believe we shall have more fog before morning." She turned to Sebastian. "They are playing a waltz, Angelstone. I have been searching all over for you. No less than a dozen people informed me that you had arrived, but when you did not seek me out, I thought perhaps you were unable to locate me in the crowd."

Sebastian smiled slightly as he took her arm and led her out onto the floor. "Never fear, Prue. I will always find you, regardless of where you go or how well hidden you may be."

She wrinkled her nose at him as he swung her into the dance. "That sounds more like a threat than a promise."

"Yes, I suppose it does."

"Honestly, Sebastian, sometimes you are impossible."

"I know, my dear, but you seem to be able to deal with me. How did your investigation conclude this afternoon?"

"It was very disappointing, if you must know," Prudence said. "I could not produce a single ghost with the electricity machine. I am beginning to wonder if there is a flaw in my new theory."

"Perhaps there was no ghost to be found in that particular garret."

"Probably not. I discovered a scarf in the room that belonged to one of the housemaids. When I interviewed her she admitted that she has been meeting one of the footmen up in the garret late at night. I believe they are the source of the moaning sounds Miss Singleton heard."

"Another blow for logic and reason."

"I suppose so, but hardly an interesting solution to the puzzle." She eyed him closely. "What was going on out there on the terrace between you and your cousin? I do hope you were not causing trouble."

"I am crushed by your lack of faith in my social tact."

"Hah."

"I have been wanting to speak to you for the past several hours," Sebastian said.

"Have you?"

"I tracked down the owner of the snuffbox."

Prudence brightened. "That is wonderful, my lord. How very clever of you."

"Thank you." Sebastian could not keep the trace of smugness out of his voice.

"I am delighted to hear the news and I cannot wait to learn the details, but what has that got to do with Mr. Fleetwood?"

"The snuffbox belongs to Jeremy."

Prudence stared at him. "Sebastian, are you serious?"

"Very." Sebastian watched his cousin reenter the ballroom and move quickly through the throng. Jeremy's face was grim as he headed toward the door. His stride was that of a tense, angry man.

"Good heavens," Prudence whispered in dismay as she followed his gaze. "Jeremy looks upset."

"Yes."

"Oh, dear. The word will be all over Town tomorrow that you and he have quarreled."

Sebastian shrugged. "A quarrel between Jeremy and me will not be news, Prue. The only thing that would interest the gossips would be rumors that he and I had engaged in a friendly conversation."

"Did you?" she asked, looking extremely hopeful.

"No," Sebastian said. "We did not."

Eleven

Prudence awoke abruptly, aware that something was wrong. This was the first night she and Sebastian had gotten to sleep before dawn. The combination of the demands of their busy social life and Sebastian's lovemaking had somehow combined to keep her awake all night every night since her marriage. She got the feeling that Sebastian was accustomed to staying up all night. He seemed in the habit of not going to bed until after dawn.

Prudence had begun to wonder if she would ever be able to return to a normal schedule, one that involved going to bed at a decent hour and getting up early in the mornings. Perhaps now that she had married Sebastian she would be obliged to adapt to Town ways. The thought of being up all night for the rest of her life was daunting.

She lay still for a moment. Ghostly remnants of a dream drifted through her mind. She concentrated, but could not quite catch them. She thought she recalled black drapes blowing in front of a window that opened out onto an endless night. But the image vanished almost at once.

Then she realized that she was alone in the big bed. She turned on the pillow.

"Sebastian?"

"I'm here, Prue."

She glanced toward the window and saw the large but rather fuzzy shape of him standing there. He had his back to her, one hand braced against the sill. Prudence sat up against the pillows and reached for her spectacles.

When she fumbled them into place on her nose she saw that Sebastian had put on his black dressing gown. He looked more like a Fallen Angel than ever as he stood there gazing out into the night-darkened gardens. Lucifer was sitting on the windowsill next to Sebastian. The cat was as intent on the night as Sebastian was.

"Are you having difficulty sleeping?" she asked softly as she lit the candle by the bed.

"I never sleep before dawn."

"Oh. Then there is nothing wrong?"

"No." His voice was dark and brooding. "Go back to sleep, Prue."

Prudence ignored the instruction. She drew her knees up under the bedclothes and wrapped her arms around them. "You may as well tell me what you are thinking about. I am unlikely to go back to sleep with you standing there staring out the window like that. It makes me uneasy."

Sebastian stroked Lucifer. "I'm sorry that I'm keeping you from your sleep."

She smiled. "Well, you are, so you had best tell me what it is that you are contemplating so intently. Otherwise I shall never get back to sleep."

He glanced at her, momentarily amused. "I believe you mean that."

"I do mean it." Prudence rested her chin on her knees. "You are contemplating the investigation, are you not?"

"Yes."

"I thought that might be it." Prudence hesitated. "I suspect you are thinking about Jeremy's snuffbox. You are no doubt trying to figure out why it was in that chamber."

"I have begun to wonder lately if you have developed a talent for reading my mind."

"As you once observed, my lord, we are very much alike in our thinking processes."

"Yes." Sebastian stroked Lucifer in silence for a moment. "It puzzles me," he said at last.

Prudence knew without being told that he had leaped back to the original topic. "Jeremy's connection to the investigation? I agree with you. It is very puzzling."

She and Sebastian had discussed the matter at length after the ball. Sebastian had told her about his confrontation with Jeremy and of how Jeremy had denied any knowledge of the black chamber.

"I made some inquiries earlier this evening. It seems my cousin is not one of Curling's close friends. That weekend that Jeremy spent at the castle was the only time he had ever been there."

"Who told you that?" Prudence asked. "Jeremy?"

"No, a man named Durham who is in the habit of regularly attending Curling's house parties. He's a professional hanger-on who maintains a presence in Society by making himself amusing and agreeable. You know the sort."

Prudence smiled ruefully at Sebastian's obvious contempt. "I suppose poor Mr. Durham's role in the polite world is rather like that of an Original such as myself. People tolerate us as long as we are amusing."

Sebastian turned his head swiftly. His eyes gleamed fiercely in the shadows. "You, madam, are now the Countess of Angelstone. Do not ever forget it. You do not exist to amuse and entertain Society. Quite the contrary. Society exists to amuse and entertain you."

Prudence blinked at the controlled violence of his response to what she had intended only as a small jest. "An interesting concept, my lord. I shall consider it more closely some other time. For now, let us return to the matter of your cousin Jeremy."

"The problem," Sebastian said slowly, "is that there is nothing to which one may return. We know nothing else yet except that Jeremy was at the castle when Ringcross died and that it was his snuffbox that we found in that damn chamber."

"Along with the gold button."

Sebastian tapped one finger slowly on the windowsill. "Yes. I have not yet started my inquiries in that direction. It might prove interesting to see what we learn about the button."

Prudence studied him for a moment. "Do you think your cousin lied to you when he claimed he had never been in that black chamber?"

"I don't know."

"Are you concerned that he may actually be involved in Ringcross's death?" Prudence asked.

"I think the coincidence of that snuffbox being in that black chamber is a bit hard to dismiss out of hand. My instincts tell me there is some connection."

"Coincidences do happen, Sebastian."

"I'm aware of that, but they don't happen often and it has been my experience that they rarely occur at all in an investigation of this sort."

Prudence considered the matter for a minute. "I do not know him well, but from what I have seen of your cousin, I would have a hard time envisioning him as a murderer. He seems to be very much a gentleman."

Sebastian stared out into the fog-bound night. "Any man can be driven to murder if there is sufficient motivation. A gentleman may kill as easily as the next man."

"But what on earth could the motivation be in this case? Why would Jeremy want to kill Ringcross?"

"I don't know. There are a number of questions to be answered. Among other things we must learn if there was any connection between Jeremy and Ringcross."

"You seem hesitant, Sebastian. What is wrong?"

He glanced back over his shoulder. "The question I am

asking myself tonight is whether or not I wish to continue this investigation."

"I thought that might be it," Prudence said sympathetically. "I can certainly comprehend your reluctance to investigate a member of your own family."

Sebastian's mouth curved humorlessly. "Do not mistake me, madam. It is no concern of mine if Jeremy gets himself arrested for murder."

Prudence was shocked. "How can you say that? He is your cousin."

"So? Do you think that the scandal involved in having a Fleetwood arrested would bother me? Not bloody likely. It might be rather amusing."

"Sebastian, we're talking about murder here."

"Yes, we are, are we not?" Sebastian's smile could only be described as feral. "It would be interesting to watch that bitch Drucilla and the rest of my charming relatives get a taste of Society's brutal tongues."

"Sebastian, that kind of gossip would devastate that side of the family."

"Quite possibly. If Jeremy is arrested for murder, his mother would no doubt be banished from the *ton*. Society would turn its back on her just as it turned its back on my parents. It would be a most appropriate sort of justice."

Prudence shivered. "You cannot mean that."

"You think not?" The gold band on Sebastian's finger glinted in the candlelight as he continued to pet Lucifer.

"You are the head of the family, Sebastian," Prudence said very steadily. "You will do whatever is necessary to protect it."

He reached for her without any warning. He caught hold of her shoulders and held her still in front of him. "This family," he said through set teeth, "consists of you and me and whatever children we may be fortunate enough to have. I do not give a damn if all of the rest of those incredibly boring Fleetwoods hang."

"You cannot mean that. One cannot dismiss one's relatives simply because they are unpleasant or insufficiently amusing."

"I assure you that the Fleetwoods had no difficulty at all dismissing my parents out of hand."

Prudence framed his hard face between her palms. "Is it revenge you seek, then, my lord? If that is the case, why have you not already taken it?"

Sebastian's hands tightened on her. "You think I have not dreamed of doing so?"

"I don't understand. Your friend Mr. Sutton explained to me that you have it within your power to cut off funds to the rest of the family or even to get them all banished from Society. If you feel so strongly about punishing the rest of the Fleetwoods, why did you not exercise your power over them when you first came into the title?"

Sebastian's eyes gleamed. "Do not doubt for one instant that I will exercise all of the power I hold over my relatives if they ever push me too far. But until then they are safe, although they do not know it."

"Why are they safe?"

"Because I am bound by a promise. A promise I made to my mother as she lay dying."

Prudence was stricken. "I thought your parents and brother were killed in that fall of rock you told me about."

"I received word early in the evening of what had happened up in the mountains." Sebastian's voice was very distant. "I took a group of men from the village and went in search of my family. We reached the pass at midnight. We set up lanterns and started to dig through the fallen rocks and debris."

"Dear God, Sebastian."

"It was so cold, Prue. And there was a heavy fog. I will never forget the damned fog. We found them just before dawn. My brother first. Then my father. They were both dead. My mother was still barely alive. She lived until sunrise."

"I am so sorry," Prudence whispered. "I did not mean to resurrect such tragic memories."

"You may as well hear it all now. I have told no other living soul that the Fleetwoods are safe from me because with her dying breath my mother pleaded their cause."

"Your mother asked you not to take revenge against them?"

"She knew that someday I would inherit the title. And she guessed that when I did, I would use the power it would give me to punish the rest of the family for what they had done to my father and to her. She did not want that to happen. She said the family had been torn apart long enough."

"Your mother sounds as if she was a very kind and compassionate woman."

"She was. But I am neither kind nor compassionate and I confess there have been times when the temptation to ruin the Fleetwoods in a variety of interesting ways has been almost irresistible."

Prudence searched his grim face. "I can imagine."

"Unfortunately, the oath I gave my mother has restrained me as effectively as an iron chain. 'Give me your word of honor that you will not cause the Fleetwoods any harm for what they did to us,' she said. She was dying. So I gave her my word. At the time it did not seem such a great thing. I had other, more important vengeance on my mind."

"What other vengeance?"

Sebastian's face was set in stark, inscrutable lines. "My only goal that day was to find the bandits who had been responsible for the rockfall. I was not thinking about Fleetwoods when I buried my family in those damn mountains. I was thinking about slitting the throats of those who had killed them."

Prudence stared at him. "You went after the bandits yourself?"

"I took some of the men from the village with me. They were willing to help. They had suffered enough from the bandits, themselves. What they had lacked was a leader who could provide a plan of action."

"You provided the leadership and the plan?"

"Yes." Sebastian moved away from her. He went back to the window and stared out into the darkness. "It took me less than a week to come up with a way to lure the bandits into the trap. They all perished in it, every last one of them. I killed their leader myself."

"Oh, Sebastian."

His hand clenched the edge of the windowsill. "I told him precisely why he was dying as he lay bleeding to death at my feet."

Prudence went over to Sebastian and wrapped her arms around him from behind. She leaned her head against his shoulder. "It was not your fault. Your father was an explorer. Journeys in wild lands involve great risks."

Sebastian said nothing.

"It is not your fault that he took that mountain pass, Sebastian. Your father was an experienced traveler. He chose to cross those mountains. He obviously assumed it was safe to do so. It was your father who made the tragic mistake, not you."

Sebastian still did not respond.

Prudence pressed herself closer to him. It seemed to her that he felt very cold. She had no more words. All she could do was share her warmth with him.

She held him tightly for a long time.

After a while she was aware that some of the tension had left Sebastian. He touched one of her hands that was clasped around his waist.

"Now you know the reason why I have never taken real vengeance against the Fleetwoods," he said quietly.

"I see. But Sebastian, what will you do about the investigation? Surely you will not walk away from it."

"No," he said. "I admit that I am curious now. I want to learn the answers."

"I knew it," Prudence said with satisfaction. "I knew you could not just abandon the case."

"But I have not yet decided what I will do with the answers that I discover," he added softly.

"*Sebastian.*"

"Calm yourself, Prue. I will not turn the evidence against Jeremy over to Bow Street. That would be a violation of my oath to my mother. But neither am I under any obligation to protect Jeremy if Bow Street discovers its own evidence."

Prudence eyed him uneasily. "This sounds like another of your cat-and-mouse games that everyone says you enjoy playing with the Fleetwoods."

"I only play such games when I am excessively bored," Sebastian said. "Believe it or not, most of the time I have more interesting things to do than to go about baiting Fleetwoods."

Prudence shook her head. "Sebastian, you should be ashamed of yourself."

"No lectures, madam." He turned around and touched her lips with a warning finger. "I am in no mood to listen to any of your sermons on responsibility and mature behavior."

"What if I am inclined to give you such a sermon?"

"Then I shall simply have to find a way to silence you." He drew her hand to his mouth and kissed the inside of her wrist. His eyes did not leave hers. "I'm certain I'll think of some suitable method."

"Sebastian, I am trying to have a serious discussion here." Prudence could already feel the liquid warmth coiling inside her. She snatched her hand out of his grasp. "Do you intend to spend the rest of your life tormenting the Fleetwoods whenever you have nothing better to do?"

"As I said, I generally have better things to do. Fleet-woods are, by and large, a dull lot."

"How fortunate for them."

"Furthermore, now that I am a married man I have a duty to establish my nursery and set about the business of getting myself an heir. I expect I shall be well occupied in the foreseeable future."

"You are incorrigible, my lord."

"I work at the task." His expression hardened again. "There is something you must understand, Prue."

"What is that?"

"It is true enough that the Fleetwoods are safe from me. But only to a point."

"A point?"

Sebastian smiled his coldest smile. "If one of them steps too far over the line, the promise I made to my mother will not protect them."

"What do you consider stepping too far over the line?" Prudence asked cautiously.

"If my aunt or any of the others goes after you in any way, I want to know about it. I will crush whoever is responsible."

"*Sebastian.*"

"I vowed to my mother that I would not punish the Fleetwoods for turning their backs on her and my father. But nothing was said about what I could do to them if they insulted or offended my wife."

"But Sebastian—"

"No, Prue. You bargained with me once on that score after my aunt insulted you during our engagement. I would have taken action against her then, but I allowed you to talk me out of it."

"I do not believe you let me talk you out of it," Prudence said. "You listened to reason and decided to behave in the noble manner one expects of a man of your status and power."

Sebastian's brows rose. "I gave in to your pleas, my sweet, naive little Prue, because we were merely engaged then, not married."

"I beg your pardon?"

"At the time I was in a somewhat precarious position. I did not wish to anger my future bride to such an extent that she might call off the engagement. So I indulged her."

"I do not believe you."

"No doubt because you have convinced yourself that I am still Lucifer before the fall."

"This is intolerable." Prudence glowered at him. "Are you saying that now that you have married me, you are no longer concerned with the prospect of making me angry?"

"I much prefer you when you are in a charming, cooperative mood, my dear. But the fact of the matter is we are legally bound now." Sebastian stroked his finger along the curve of her shoulder. He smiled when she shivered. "And we are bound in other ways as well, are we not? No matter how angry you become, you cannot walk out on me."

"And if I did?"

"I would follow you and bring you home," he promised. "Then I would make love to you until you shuddered in my arms, until you pleaded with me to take you. Until you could no longer even recall why you had been angry with me."

"*Sebastian.*"

"Until you realized that what you and I have together is all that matters."

Prudence looked into his candlelit eyes and caught her breath. "I warned you once not to think you could manipulate me with your lovemaking."

He smiled slowly. "So you did. But I have always liked a challenge."

"Sebastian, do not tease me, I beg you. This is a very serious matter."

"I assure you I am taking it very seriously." He caught her chin on the edge of his hand. "Attend me well, madam.

The vow my mother extracted from me will not keep me from punishing the Fleetwoods if they insult you or offend you in any way."

Prudence tapped one bare foot. "I have the impression that you rather hope one of them does manage to step over this invisible line you have drawn."

The devil's own laughter danced in Sebastian's gaze. "You are very perceptive, my sweet. And quite right. I would not mind in the least if one of them, preferably my aunt, crosses that line. But you needn't worry. I give you my solemn oath that it will only happen once."

"Because that is all the excuse you will need for taking retribution?"

"Just one offense," he said softly. "One insult to you and I will see them banished from Society. I will cut their considerable incomes down to tiny allowances."

Prudence was stunned by the implacable intent in his words. Her palms were suddenly damp. "Is that the real reason you chose to marry an unfashionable Original, then, my lord? Because you knew that only someone as odd as myself could manage to draw the insults you wanted from your relatives?"

Sebastian frowned. "Now, Prue—"

"Did you marry me just so that you would finally have cause to exact the vengeance you crave?"

"Don't be a fool." Sebastian's lashes veiled his eyes. "Do you think I would tie myself for life to a woman whose only recommendation was that she was bound to annoy the Fleetwoods?"

"The thought crossed my mind, yes."

Sebastian swore. "If that had been the only thing I required of a wife, I would have married long ago. I assure you that there are any number of females here in London who would have offended the Fleetwoods."

"No doubt."

"Use your admirable intellect, madam. I'll admit I would

very much like to punish the Fleetwoods, but not at the price of marriage to a female who would have made me a totally unsuitable wife."

"Of course, my lord." Prudence fought back tears. "I should have considered the matter more closely. Now that I do, I can see that you needed a most unusual combination of characteristics in your countess."

"I most certainly did." He smiled.

"You needed a female who was both odd enough to draw the condemnation of your relatives and yet clever enough to amuse you."

Sebastian scowled. "You are being deliberately difficult, Prue. I have told you why I married you."

"Mutual interests and mutual passion." Prudence drew the back of her hand across her eyes. "I understand those reasons for our marriage. But I feel I was grossly misled on this other requirement you have mentioned, my lord."

"Prue, stop this nonsense. You are getting it all mixed up."

"Am I?" She took a step back. "You never explained that I was to be a convenient tool you could use to bait the Fleetwoods. I do not like being used in such a fashion."

Sebastian's expression turned dangerous as she moved away from him. "You are twisting my words, Prue."

She blinked away more tears. "You ask too much of a wife, my lord. My list of duties grows longer every time I turn around. I am to amuse you. I am to be an intellectual companion so that you will have someone on hand to admire your brilliance when you are conducting an investigation. I am to warm your bed. And now you expect to use me as an excuse to punish the Fleetwoods for what they did to your parents."

Sebastian took a gliding step toward her. "I have had enough of this nonsense."

"So have I. It is time for me to draw a line of my own and I am going to do so."

"What line would that be?" He took another step toward her.

"You will not use me as an excuse to avenge yourself on your relatives. I do not care what insult is offered. *You will not use me.* Is that clear?"

"You are my wife, Prue. I will not tolerate any insult to you. On that score there will be no bargaining."

"Then I demand the right to decide whether or not I have been insulted," she said defiantly.

"Damnation, Prue, are you crying?"

"Yes, I am."

"I warn you, I will not be manipulated with tears," he growled.

"And I will not be manipulated with lovemaking."

Sebastian gave her an ironic look. "Where does that leave us?"

Prudence wiped her tears away with the sleeve of her night rail. "I have no notion, sir. If you will excuse me, I believe I am going to go back to bed."

He watched her intently. "I shall join you shortly."

"No, you will not. I am going back to my own bedchamber, my lord. I find I cannot sleep well here in your room."

Prudence walked to the connecting door, opened it, and went through to her own room. She shut the door behind her and held her breath.

She was not certain what Sebastian would do next. She half expected him to follow her and give her a lecture on her wifely duties.

But the door to her bedchamber remained closed.

Twelve

I rather like the neckline on this gown," Hester mused.

Prudence tried to rally her flagging interest as she obediently contemplated the fashion plate. This shopping trip had been her idea, she reminded herself. She had certainly had the best of intentions when she started out this morning.

But after an enthusiastic beginning at the fabulous shopping bazaars which featured everything from clever little toys to delicious ices, she had long since grown bored.

Prudence pushed her spectacles into place and studied the gown closely. "It looks as though one would pop right out of the bodice if one took a deep breath."

"That is the whole point," the unctuous modiste hastily assured her in a false French accent. "A lady's ball gown should give the illusion of being made of nothing but gossamer spider webs spun while the dew is still fresh upon the strands."

"Quite right," Hester declared. "And to be the very glass of fashion, the gown should be in a lavender hue."

Prudence eyed the plate dubiously. "Well, if you think it's what I want, Hester, then I shall order it at once."

Hester smiled with satisfaction and turned to the modiste. "We will need it made up immediately. We are prepared to pay extra if you can promise that it will be delivered by eight this evening."

The modiste hesitated and then smiled blandly. "It can be arranged, madam. I shall have all of my seamstresses work on it this afternoon."

"Excellent," Hester said. "Now, then, we shall also want the riding habit, the morning gowns, and the carriage dresses as soon as possible. Remember, they are all to be done up in violet- and lavender-colored materials. You may use a bit of purple for the trims."

"I understand, madam. You shall have everything within a few days." The modiste turned to Prudence, who was examining a display of buttons. "If her ladyship will step this way, we can take her ladyship's measurements."

"What's that?" Prudence looked up from the buttons. "Oh, yes, of course."

She allowed herself to be led into the fitting room, where she stood obediently still as a plump woman bustled about with a tape. The modiste supervised with a critical eye.

Prudence smiled at the modiste. "I have heard that it is the fashion to have the buttons of one's riding habits and pelisses engraved with one's family motto or a crest. Is that true?"

"Ladies rarely concern themselves with such." The modiste kept her attention on the seamstress. "It is gentlemen who are more likely to order engraved buttons."

"What sort of things do they have engraved on them?" Prudence inquired with what she hoped sounded like nothing more than mild curiosity.

"A variety of things. Military insignia. Symbols of their regiments, perhaps. Family crests. Some of the members of certain gentlemen's clubs have the names or mottoes of their clubs engraved." The modiste looked at her politely. "Did madam wish to order special engraving on her buttons?"

"Not unless it is a requirement of fashion. I was merely curious. Where would one go to order such buttons?"

"There are a number of shops that can supply them." The modiste scowled at the seamstress. "I think you had better measure her ladyship's bosom again, Nanette. We do not want any mistakes. There will not be time to make adjustments. Madam has a very . . . ah . . . slender, refined form. We would not want the bodice to be too large."

"Could you give me a list?" Prudence asked as Nanette tightened the tape around her breasts.

The modiste glanced at her again. "A list of what, madam?"

"A list of shops that deal in specially engraved buttons. It occurs to me that if there is not already a fashion for such items among ladies, I might start one."

"But of course. Very clever of madam to think of that." It was clear the modiste was merely humoring her patron. "I shall make a note of some of the better shops that specialize in trims and buttons and the like before you leave."

"Thank you," Prudence murmured. For the first time in several hours her interest in shopping returned. "I would appreciate that."

Twenty minutes later Prudence and Hester were handed back up into the Angelstone carriage by a footman dressed in the black and gold Angelstone livery.

"I must say, my dear," Hester remarked as she seated herself, "I am extremely pleased to see that you are finally taking an interest in fashion. Now that you are a countess, you must give more attention to such matters. It is expected of you. Drucilla Fleetwood and the rest of Angelstone's clan will be watching you quite closely."

"Hoping, no doubt, that I will humiliate myself by doing something totally unsuitable, such as wearing a riding habit and a pair of half boots to a ball."

Hester gave her a searching glance. "Is that the reason

behind your newfound interest in gowns and furbelows? Are you afraid of offending the Fleetwoods?"

"Let's just say I'd rather Angelstone's aunt did not issue any more insults to me in public," Prudence said dryly. "The Fleetwoods have already decided I am not going to make a very suitable countess. I would just as soon not give them any ammunition to support their assumptions."

"Well, well, well." Hester chuckled. "No offense, my dear, but I am rather amazed to learn that you are so concerned with pleasing Angelstone's relatives. He certainly has never worried about pleasing them."

"Perhaps becoming a countess has given me a more informed view of the social world," Prudence muttered. She gazed out at the busy streets and wondered if her efforts to turn herself into a fashion plate would be of any use.

She did not dare explain to Hester the real reason she was going through the trouble of redoing her wardrobe. The sole goal of the task was to save the hapless Fleetwoods from Sebastian's vengeance.

The best approach to the problem, she had decided, was to take a preventive course of action. She had wakened this morning determined not to provide her new relatives with grounds for any grave insults.

It had been obvious to Prudence that the first step she needed to take was to become more fashionable.

The note she had sent to Hester late in the morning inviting her on the shopping expedition had brought an immediate response. Hester had been delighted at being given a free hand and a virtually unlimited budget.

Thus far she had seen to it that Prudence replaced her spectacles, at least for evening wear, with a fashionable little glass that hung from a purple velvet ribbon. It could be attached to any of her gowns. Prudence had complained that it was awkward to have to raise the glass to her eyes whenever she wished to see clearly, but Hester had ruthlessly brushed aside that petty complaint.

They had purchased dancing slippers in every shade of lavender and violet, and several pairs of matching gloves. Parcels containing a variety of hats and fans were piled high on the roof of the carriage.

"All in all, this has been an extremely successful day," Hester said with great satisfaction. "Shall we stop for an ice?"

Prudence perked up at that. "Yes, I should enjoy that. And afterward, I would like to visit one or two shops on this list that the modiste gave me."

Hester glanced at the piece of paper in Prudence's hand. "What sort of shopping do you intend to do?"

"I am interested in inquiring about having some buttons especially engraved."

Hester was delighted. "That would certainly make an interesting touch for your riding habits and perhaps your pelisses. What a clever notion."

"I thought so," Prudence said, feeling a trifle smug. "I am looking for someone who does this sort of work. Very fine quality, don't you think?" She reached into her reticule and pulled out the gold button she and Sebastian had found at Curling Castle.

"That looks like the sort of button that would suit a gentleman's waistcoat," Hester said. "What on earth is that, engraved on it?"

"I have no idea. The name of a gentleman's club, perhaps. Or it might have some significance to an Evangelical." Prudence casually dropped the button back into her reticule.

"Where did you get it?"

"I found it lying about somewhere," Prudence said easily. "I cannot recall precisely. But I noticed the workmanship and decided I should like to find the merchant who supplied it to the original owner. If I do, I shall put in a special order for myself."

"I imagine any number of merchants can supply you with engraved buttons. Why bother to search for the one who did that particular button?" Hester asked curiously.

"Because I wish to be assured of getting this quality of workmanship," Prudence explained smoothly. "Angelstone prefers that his wife wear only the best."

"Very well, my dear. If you wish to spend the rest of the day shopping for buttons, who am I to stop you?"

Shortly after two o'clock Sebastian walked out of the establishment of Milway and Gordon, a Bond Street shop that specialized in gentleman's gloves, cravats, and other assorted accoutrements required by men of fashion. He paused to consult the list of merchants his valet had drawn up for him.

Thus far he had visited four shops which claimed to take orders for specially engraved buttons. No one had recognized the button he described to them.

"Gold, with the phrase *The Princes of Virtue* engraved on it," he had explained to the shopkeepers. "Suitable for a waistcoat. I should like to duplicate it for a waistcoat of my own."

"Perhaps if his lordship had brought along the button he is attempting to duplicate I could say for certain whether or not I have seen its like previously," one shopkeeper suggested. "I am quite positive we could reproduce it. But it would be helpful to see the original button."

Unfortunately a verbal description was all Sebastian could offer the merchants because Prudence had made off with the original button. He'd had one brief glimpse of it gleaming between her gloved fingers before she dropped it into her reticule.

"My turn to investigate, my lord," she had murmured for his ears alone. "This marriage is a partnership, if you will recall, and so is this investigation. I would feel guilty if I did not endeavor to perform my share of the labor."

"Damnation," Sebastian growled. "You know very well that I am going to visit certain shops today. It will not do for both of us to inquire about the same confounded button at the same damn shop."

"You are quite right, my lord." Prudence's eyes flashed with determination. "We must be clever about this, mustn't we? I have it. I shall make my inquiries in the neighborhood of Oxford Street. You may make your inquiries elsewhere. That way we will not be likely to stumble across each other at the same establishment."

"Bloody hell, Prue, I will not allow you—"

"Forgive me, my lord. I must be off. My aunt will be waiting for me."

Aware that the presence of the servants in the hall severely limited Sebastian's reaction, Prudence had sailed on past him through the open door to the waiting carriage.

Sebastian had been sorely tempted to go after her and haul her out of the carriage right in front of the servants. It would serve her right. She knew full well he had intended to conduct his own investigation on the button that day.

But something held him back and he knew it wasn't simply the possibility of creating a small domestic scene in front of the household staff. It was something much more fundamental.

He did not wish to rekindle the emotions that had blazed in her last night. Sebastian admitted to himself that he was not certain how to handle Prudence when she was in tears. He had been stunned when she had walked back to her own bedchamber and closed the door in his face.

Sebastian frowned as he refolded the list of merchants. Prudence had overreacted last night, he thought as he started toward his phaeton. That was the problem. There had been no logic to her emotion.

It was not as if he had married her for the sole purpose of using her as bait to lure the Fleetwoods to their doom.

He was merely going to capitalize on the circumstances of the marriage to achieve a goal that had long been denied him. Where was the harm in that? he wondered. Prudence's overly emotional reaction had taken him by surprise. It was not like her.

Sebastian now came to a halt on the sidewalk as a thought struck him. He had heard that women were subject to strange emotions when they were breeding. Prudence might very well be pregnant. *Pregnant with his babe.*

He started to smile in spite of his foul mood. He could see her now, round and ripe with his seed growing inside her. A strange sensation of tenderness swept through him.

He had told himself that once he had bound Prudence to him with the legal ties of marriage and the physical claims of passion, she would be his. He had been right in some ways. But last night he had realized for the first time that the bonds of marriage and passion and even mutual interests might not be enough.

A child would tie Prudence to him in a way that nothing else could, Sebastian thought as a carriage drew to a halt in front of him.

The door of the carriage opened and Curling got out. He nodded at Sebastian and paused on the sidewalk.

"I hesitate to inquire into what is amusing you at the moment, Angelstone. Given your reputation, one can be certain that the source of your entertainment will no doubt be rather unusual. Nevertheless, I am curious."

"It's a private matter. Nothing that would interest you, Curling." Sebastian glanced at the door of the shop where he had just made inquiries. "Do you patronize this establishment?"

"Milway and Gordon have made my gloves for years." Curling examined him with a look of bland curiosity. "I did not know you used them."

"They were recently recommended to me," Sebastian said easily. "Thought I'd give them a try."

"I'm sure you'll be satisfied with their work." Curling started toward the door and paused again. "By the way,

Angelstone, I played a few hands of cards with your cousin last night."

"Did you?"

"Mr. Fleetwood was in his cups and he did not play well. I won a rather large packet off him. But that is neither here nor there. The thing is, I could not help but notice that he appeared to be in a rather volatile mood. Quite irate, in fact. You, I believe, were the cause."

"That bit of information is not of much interest to me."

"I understand," Curling said quietly. "I know you have never been on the best of terms with your relatives."

"The feeling is mutual," Sebastian said. "What are you getting at, Curling?"

Curling studied an arrangement of gloves and accessories displayed in the rounded shop window behind Sebastian. "I hesitate to offer advice to you, of all people, Angelstone. The devil knows you can take care of yourself. Nevertheless, I strongly recommend that you watch your back around Mr. Fleetwood."

Sebastian inclined his head aloofly and stepped off the sidewalk. "As you say, Curling, I can take care of myself."

"A very fortunate circumstance," Curling murmured. "You might begin by taking precautions when you cross the street. I gained the distinct impression from Mr. Fleetwood that he would not mind in the least if a serious accident befell you."

"I'm sure you mistook my cousin's meaning, Curling. I feel certain Fleetwood would never pray that I fall victim to a serious accident. He would much prefer that the accident proved fatal."

Curling smiled. "I see that you do not require any advice from me, sir. You obviously know your cousin very well. Good day to you. Perhaps I shall encounter you and your charming lady this evening at the Hollington ball."

"Perhaps."

Sebastian walked off toward the waiting phaeton. He still

had two more establishments to visit before he went home to see if Prudence had had any luck in her inquiries.

Thus far he had learned only one thing of interest. Of the four shops he had visited, three had been eager to secure an order for engraved buttons from him. Only Milway and Gordon had shown no interest in his trade.

Shortly before five o'clock Sebastian handed his wife up into the phaeton and vaulted onto the seat beside her. He slanted her a sidelong glance and decided he did not like the expression of barely suppressed irritation on her face. It did not bode well. His worst fears were confirmed. She had obviously spent a good portion of the day fretting over last night's argument.

He decided to test the waters. "You are looking very charming in that gown, my dear."

"This old thing?" She glanced disdainfully down at her modestly cut brown muslin gown and dark brown pelisse. "I am surprised you find it attractive on me, my lord. It is hardly in the first stare of fashion."

Sebastian smiled as he turned the horses toward the park. "Since when have you concerned yourself with being fashionable?"

"I feel I have a duty to become more conscious of such matters. Hester is helping me to achieve my goal." She shot him a speculative glance. "We spent a goodly portion of your fortune on my new wardrobe today, sir."

"I hope you enjoyed the process."

Sebastian wondered if Prudence thought a shopping spree constituted sufficient retaliation for what had taken place between them last night. If so, he would consider himself fortunate to have escaped so easily.

He had sent word to her earlier that he expected her to accompany him on a drive in the park this afternoon, but he'd wondered if she would find some excuse to avoid him. Several hours ago when she had made off with the button there had been challenge and cool, feminine resolve in her lovely eyes.

On his way home from Bond Street he had vowed he would not allow her to avoid him. It was very easy for husbands and wives to go their own way here in Town. It was considered fashionable to do so. A man and a woman could live together in the same house and rarely even see each other if they so chose.

Prudence must be made to understand that he did not intend his marriage to turn into such a cold alliance, Sebastian thought. He had married her for her warmth.

He was ruefully aware of the relief he had experienced when Prudence had arrived downstairs dressed for the drive. She might be sulking, but she was apparently not going to defy him openly.

But it was equally obvious she was not happy. He decided to try a safe topic.

"Well, madam," he said as he drove into the park, "you have had your opportunity to involve yourself in my investigation today. What did you learn?"

"Not a blasted thing." Prudence seemed to explode with what was obviously pent-up exasperation. "I must say it was extremely discouraging. Not a single shopkeeper could identify the button. Oh, Sebastian, I was so disappointed. My whole day was ruined. Absolutely *ruined*."

Sebastian stared at her. It finally dawned on him that the reason for her sullen expression had nothing at all to do with last night's scene. Prudence was not angry with him. She was frustrated and annoyed because her inquiries had led nowhere.

Sebastian knew the feeling all too well.

His spirits soared. He started to smile.

"I am glad you are pleased, my lord," Prudence snapped. "I expect you will gloat for ages. It is really very bad of you."

Sebastian was caught off guard by the manner in which his own mood had become so unexpectedly buoyant. His smile changed into a grin and then he succumbed to laughter.

The occupants of a passing carriage, a couple Sebastian had known for more than a year, stared at him as if they had never seen him before. They were not the only ones who turned their heads at the sight of the Fallen Angel overcome with laughter.

"You needn't laugh at me, sir," Prudence muttered.

"I assure you, my sweet . . ." Sebastian struggled to swallow the rest of his jubilant response, "I assure you that I am not laughing at you. How could I? I had no more success than you did."

She scowled at him. "You made inquiries, too?"

"Certainly. Of course, I was greatly hampered by the fact that I could not produce the original button. I was forced to rely on a detailed description due to the fact that you had absconded with the real thing."

"I did not steal it," Prudence grumbled. "I simply got to it first before you could make off with it."

"An interesting point of view. Nevertheless, I did my best to discover what I could about it. But I came up empty-handed." He hesitated, remembering the strange behavior of the shopkeeper at Milway and Gordon, the last establishment on the list. "Although there was one merchant whose reaction interested me."

"Which one was that?" Prudence's frustration vanished in a flash. It was instantly replaced with intense curiosity. "What did he say?"

"It wasn't what he said." Sebastian frowned. "It was the way he brushed aside my questions. Almost as if they made him uneasy. He was the only merchant I interviewed who did not try to persuade me that he could duplicate the button from my description."

"He did not act as if he wanted your trade? How very strange."

"It is, isn't it? I think it might be worth my while to

return to his shop later this evening. I'd like to have a look at his records."

"Sebastian, are you actually going to sneak into his shop? How exciting. I will come with you."

Sebastian braced himself for the argument. "No, you will not, Prue. There is entirely too much risk involved."

"You allowed me to accompany you when you explored the black chamber at Curling Castle," she reminded him in a persuasive tone. "I was very helpful to you on that occasion."

"I know, but that was different."

"How was it different?" she demanded.

"For one thing, we were not doing anything for which we could have been arrested and transported or hung," Sebastian said. "Enough, Prue. You will not accompany me on tonight's investigation, but I promise that I will give you a detailed report when I return."

"Sebastian, I will not allow you to exclude me from this." The cajolery and persuasion vanished from Prudence's voice. She switched to her lecturing tone. "We are a team. I demand equal participation and—" She broke off abruptly and glanced to the side of the carriage. "Oh, hello, Trevor. I didn't know you were going to be riding in the park today."

"Good afternoon, Prue." Trevor guided his bay gelding into step alongside the phaeton. He nodded almost shyly at Sebastian. He looked both expectant and uncertain. "Angelstone."

Sebastian was amused to find himself actually feeling a certain gratitude toward Prudence's brother. For once Trevor had timed his appearance rather well. "I see you have changed tailors, Merryweather. My congratulations."

Trevor turned a dull red. "I've been to see your tailor, Nightingale, sir. I thank you for the introduction."

"I thought I recognized the cut of that coat," Sebastian said mildly. "It is exactly like my own."

"Yes, sir, it is. I specifically requested Nightingale to copy yours." Trevor watched him anxiously. "I hope you don't mind."

"No," Sebastian said, hiding a smile. "I don't mind in the least."

Trevor was a model of restrained masculine elegance today. His neckcloth was tied in a simple style that actually permitted him to turn his head comfortably to the side. The collar of his shirt no longer brushed his earlobes. His waistcoat did not blind onlookers. Sebastian counted only one fob hanging from his watch pocket.

"Trevor, you look wonderful," Prudence said, her face alight with genuine admiration. Then she smiled with complacent anticipation. "And I am going to appear just as fashionable myself tonight. Wait until you see the first of my new gowns. Hester assures me the style and color are all the crack."

"I shall look forward to it, Prue," Trevor said gallantly. He promptly spoiled the effect by adding, "About time you took an interest in fashion." He turned back to Sebastian. "By the by, Angelstone, I have received an invitation to one of Curling's house parties, just as you and Prue did."

"Have you, indeed," Sebastian said.

"Yes, sir. It's for next weekend. I'm told it will be just a small crowd this time. Gentlemen only." Trevor grinned, obviously pleased at the evidence of his elevated status in the social world. "A very select group. We'll no doubt do a bit of hunting and fishing."

Sebastian thought about the black chamber that he suspected was not used for any wholesome purpose.

"Just how small and select is this group?" he asked quietly.

"Don't know precisely. Curling says he only does this type of party on rare occasions. Very exclusive."

"I'd think twice about accepting the invitation, if I were you," Sebastian said. "I will certainly not be accepting any more invitations from Curling. His parties are not amusing."

Trevor was startled. He looked momentarily confused and then he gave Sebastian a knowing glance. "Not amusing, eh?"

"A dead bore."

"Say no more, sir. I understand," Trevor said with a man-to-man air. "Appreciate the tip, Angelstone. Don't think I'll waste my time traipsing out to Curling Castle next weekend, after all."

"A wise decision," Sebastian said softly.

"Well, then, I'll be off." Trevor tipped his hat to his sister. "See you later this evening, Prue. I'll look forward to your new gown. Good day, Angelstone."

Sebastian nodded. "Good afternoon, Merryweather."

Trevor swung his horse around in the other direction and cantered off down the path.

Prudence frowned at Sebastian. "What on earth was that all about? Since when is an invitation to Curling Castle considered a dead bore?"

"Since I declared that it was two minutes ago," Sebastian said. He eased the horses into a stylish trot. "I don't want your brother tied up in this investigation in any way. I doubt if you do, either."

"No, of course not. But how could an invitation to one of Curling's house parties present a problem?"

"I don't know," Sebastian said. "I'm following my instincts. I feel it would be best if Trevor did not get mixed up with Curling."

"Very well. You are the expert at this sort of thing, Sebastian. I agree that we should be guided by your inclinations."

"I am pleased to hear you say that, my dear. Because it is also my instincts that tell me it would be best if you did not accompany me tonight when I pay a visit to the premises of Milway and Gordon."

"A clever wife knows when to listen to her lord's advice," Prudence said with charming grace.

Sebastian was so stunned by the easy victory that he almost dropped the reins.

"And she also knows when to ignore him," Prudence added in a very dry tone. There was bright challenge in her eyes.

"Bloody hell," Sebastian said.

Thirteen

Prudence made another attempt to reason with Sebastian later that night when he rendezvoused with her at the Hollington mansion. She got nowhere. In fact, she could have sworn that his stubborn, high-handed attitude actually worsened as soon as he caught sight of her in the crowd.

He had barely arrived before he took her arm and drew her forcefully toward the door.

She cast him a disgusted sidelong glance through her fashionable new glass as they stood on the steps waiting for the carriage to appear out of the fog.

"What on earth has gotten into you tonight, my lord?" she asked as she fumbled with the glass. Having to deal with a fan, a dangling glass, and a tiny reticule was really too much to ask of a woman, she thought irritably. Being fashionable was no easy task. "I vow, you are in a devilish mood."

"Am I, indeed?" Sebastian's jaw was rigid. He watched impatiently as his coachman maneuvered the Angelstone carriage out of the long line of gilded coaches that waited on the street in front of the mansion.

"Yes, you are. Sebastian, don't you think you're carrying this surly attitude a step too far? I know I nagged you for the better part of the afternoon, but that is no reason to turn downright rude in front of my friends this evening."

"Was I rude? You wound me, my dear. I had no notion that my behavior was in any way objectionable."

"Rubbish. You know perfectly well it was most objectionable." Prudence dropped the dangling glass and clutched at her feather-light embroidered cashmere shawl. The delicate wrap was in the first stare of fashion, but unfortunately it provided very little protection against the damp, foggy night. "You were most unpleasant to Lord Selenby and Mr. Reed."

"You noticed, did you?" The carriage had arrived at the bottom of the steps. Sebastian took Prudence's arm and half dragged her toward it. "I'm astounded and, I must say, deeply flattered that you even saw your poor husband standing in the crowd of gentlemen that was gathered around your bare bosom."

Prudence squinted at him as one of the Hollington footmen hurried to open the carriage door. "My bare bosom?" she yelped. "My lord, are you implying that you do not care for my new gown?"

"What gown?" Sebastian tossed her into the darkened carriage and crowded in behind her. "I did not notice any gown on you tonight, madam. I thought perhaps you had forgotten to put it on before you left home."

Prudence was outraged at the affront to her new lavender silk ball gown. "I will have you know that this gown is in the very forefront of fashion."

"How can it be in the forefront when it has no front at all?"

Prudence gave a small, choked exclamation. She gave up trying to wield the eyeglass and fished her spectacles out of her little beaded reticule. "You are being unreasonable, my lord, as I am certain you are well aware." She pushed her spectacles onto her nose and glowered at him. "I thought you would approve of this gown."

"I prefer you in your usual style."

"I have been assured by a great many people, including Hester and my own brother, that my usual style is no style at all."

Sebastian lit the carriage lamp and lounged back against the cushions. He folded his arms and let his brooding eyes drift over her filmy, low-cut gown. "Why this sudden taste for fashion, madam?"

Prudence pulled the airy shawl more snugly across her chest. It was quite chilly in the carriage. She wished she had her cloak with her.

"You are the one who keeps reminding me that I have a duty to remember my new position."

Sebastian's expression turned stark. "Your new position gives you the privilege of wearing anything you like. As the Countess of Angelstone you may set the fashion, not be a slave to it."

Prudence raised her chin. "What if I happen to like wearing gowns such as this?"

"Damnation, Prue, you're about to fall out of that thing. Every man in the room was leering at you tonight. Is that the effect you wished to create? Were you deliberately attempting to make me jealous?"

Prudence was horrified. "Of course not, Sebastian. Why on earth would I wish to make you jealous?"

"A good question." His gaze was bleak and dangerous. "But if that was your goal, I assure you it worked."

She blinked at him in amazement. "You were jealous of me, my lord?"

His mouth twisted grimly. "How did you expect me to react when I walked into that room tonight and found half a dozen men hovering over you?"

"I was not trying to incite your jealousy, my lord." Prudence was appalled that he had so completely misunderstood her intentions. "To be perfectly truthful, I would not have guessed that I could do so."

"Is that so? You would not be the first to play such

games." Sebastian leaned his head back against the seat and studied her through half-lowered lashes. "Other women more accomplished in such skills have tried those tactics."

She smoothed her lavender skirts, remembering what Hester had once said about the notorious Lady Charlesworthy's ill-fated attempt to make Sebastian jealous.

"I am certain they have," Prudence said quietly. "I am also aware of my own limitations. It never occurred to me that I could make you jealous." She searched his cold, unreadable expression. "I did not think I had that sort of power over you."

"As my wife, you have a great deal of power, madam," Sebastian said far too quietly. "We are bound together, you and I. In the past when other women have tried to inspire jealousy in me, I have been free to walk away. But I cannot walk away from a wife, can I?"

"No, I suppose not." Prudence felt oddly deflated. She should have known that any jealousy Sebastian felt would be based on pride and possessiveness, not love.

"Jealousy does not amuse me, madam."

"Sebastian, you have got it all wrong."

"Have I?"

"Yes." Prudence sighed. "I did not choose this gown in an attempt to attract the attention of other men."

He slid her a suspiciously bland look of inquiry. "Why, then, did you select it?"

"So that I would no longer invite cómment," Prudence muttered, exasperated.

Sebastian did not move, but there was a sudden aura of alertness about him that made Prudence wary.

"Comment from whom?" Sebastian asked in a silky voice.

Prudence belatedly realized she was on treacherous ground. She wondered if she had been lured onto it with all that nonsense about jealousy. Sebastian was nothing if not clever. "Why, from the social world, my lord."

"You mean from my dear aunt, don't you?"

Prudence drummed her fingers on the carriage seat. There were distinct disadvantages to finding oneself married to a shrewd man. "Now, Sebastian, you must not leap to conclusions."

"Bloody hell." Sebastian uncoiled with the lethal grace of a predator pouncing on its prey. He reached out and closed the curtains on the windows over the doors in two swift movements.

"Why are you doing that?" Prudence asked sharply.

Instead of giving her an answer, he caught hold of her upper arms and hauled her up off the cushions. "I knew there was something behind this sudden interest in fashion."

"Really, my lord." Prudence's diaphanous skirts billowed out as he sat her down across his legs. Her shawl fell off her shoulders, once more exposing the upper curves of her breasts. "Just because I have taken an interest in fashion, there is no need to react quite so energetically."

"You're trying to forestall insults from that old witch Drucilla, aren't you?" Sebastian's eyes gleamed gold in the lamplight. All traces of icy anger as well as any emotion that might have even remotely resembled jealousy had vanished.

"Sebastian, it really is not proper to go about calling your aunt an old witch."

"Why not? That is exactly what she is. You're hoping that if you turn yourself into a diamond of the first water, she won't have cause to insult you."

Prudence stifled an oath. The familiar unholy amusement was back in Sebastian's eyes now. She was certain that he had tricked her into a confession. "I am merely trying to dress in the sort of style that the polite world considers appropriate for your wife, Angelstone."

"I will decide what is appropriate for my wife."

Prudence was very conscious of the muscled contours of his thighs beneath her soft derriere. The thin skirts of a fashionable ball gown left very little to the imagination. "Your arrogance leaves one breathless, my lord."

His long-fingered hand tightened around her waist. His gold signet ring gleamed dully in the lamplight. "You think that if you can keep my aunt from insulting you in public, you can prevent me from punishing the Fleetwoods, don't you?"

"I am not going to dignify that silly conclusion with an answer."

He smiled faintly. "It was a clever notion, but I've got news for you, my dear: It will never work. Drucilla is looking for excuses to find fault with you. It is useless to try to placate her, because she will never be placated. If your dress gives her no cause for comment, she will find something else to criticize. It is the nature of the beast."

"Your aunt could hardly say anything more insulting about my gown than you have already said." Prudence tried to straighten the lavender plume in her hair.

"My status as your husband does give me some privileges, my dear."

"That is open to debate." She glanced at him uncertainly. "Tell me the truth. Do you really think this gown is cut too low?"

"It is far too low to wear in public." Sebastian studied the gentle curves of her breasts with grave consideration. "However, I can see that the cut of the bodice does have a practical use."

"Practical?"

"It affords easy access to a charming view." He slipped his finger just under the edge of the low neckline.

Prudence felt a tremor of wicked excitement go through her. "Sebastian, stop that. You mustn't do that sort of thing here in the carriage."

"Why not? It will take the coachman nearly half an hour to work his way home through the traffic. The fog is getting thicker. That may delay him even longer." Sebastian gently eased the edge of the gown downward, freeing one of Prudence's breasts.

Heat rushed through her. She batted ineffectually at his hand. "Sebastian, this is too bad of you. I cannot allow you to make love to me in a carriage."

"This is what comes of wearing the latest fashions, my sweet." Sebastian started to lower his head to the rosy tip of her breast.

Prudence sank her fingers into his hair, closed her eyes, and tried to concentrate on her main objective. "Now that we have finished discussing my gown, I want to talk to you about your plans to return to that shop in Bond Street tonight."

"I promise to give you a full report when I get home." Sebastian's breath was warm on her skin.

"It is most unfair of you to leave me behind. I'm your partner." Prudence gasped as he grazed his thumb across the firm bud that crowned her breast. Her eyes opened and she saw a scrap of paper that was lying on the seat where she had been sitting. "What is that?"

"A nipple, I believe." He touched it with the tip of his tongue. "Yes, definitely a nipple. And an extraordinarily lovely one, at that."

"No, not that." Prudence peered over his lowered head. "That piece of paper on the seat. I must have sat down on it when I got into the carriage a few minutes ago. It looks like a note."

Sebastian raised his head slightly and glanced at the folded piece of paper. "What the devil?"

He reached out and picked up the note. Then he straightened and held it so that the light from the carriage lamp fell across it. He examined it closely and then he unfolded it. There was a short message scrawled inside.

"I thought so—a note. Someone left it here in the carriage while we were at the ball." Prudence tugged her bodice back into place and straightened her spectacles. She gazed at the unfamiliar writing as Sebastian read the message aloud.

> *"The names of The Princes of Virtue are Ringcross, Oxenham, Bloomfield, and Curling. I have provided their addresses at the bottom of this note in hopes that you will not ask for any more information. I assure you I have no more to give. I implore you to leave me in peace."*

Sebastian frowned. "There's no signature. It was most likely written by one of the shopkeepers we interviewed to-day."

"How can you be sure?"

"It's obviously from someone who does not want us troubling him with further inquiries. The only people we have been questioning are the shopkeepers."

"Lord Curling's name is on the list," Prudence said. "That makes sense, I suppose. We found the button in his wardrobe, after all."

"Ringcross is dead. Curling wants his death investigated. Both belonged to The Princes of Virtue club." Sebastian tapped the note absently against his thigh, his expression intent. "I think the next step is to talk to Bloomfield and Oxenham."

"Do you know them?"

"I have met Oxenham. He's involved in shipping. Some-where along the line he managed to marry two heiresses. I heard that both young women died soon after their wed-dings. One in a carriage accident. One from an overdose of laudanum. That was several years ago."

Prudence shuddered. She reached for her shawl and wrapped it around herself. "That sounds rather ominous."

"Yes, it does, doesn't it?" Sebastian leaned back into the corner of the carriage and eyed Prudence with a thoughtful expression. "I believe I will talk to him first."

"What about Bloomfield?" Prudence asked.

"I don't know much about him. Rumor has it he's a bit mad. He does not frequent the clubs and I have never encountered him in Society."

"And Curling?"

"We must take this investigation one step at a time," Sebastian said. "It is not yet obvious what Curling's role is in all this. Nor do we know the role my cousin is playing."

Prudence mulled that over for a moment. "According to that note, Oxenham lives on Rowland Street."

"Yes." Sebastian paused. "I think I would prefer to visit their homes while they are absent before I talk to them."

"It occurs to me, my lord," Prudence said softly, "that as you no longer need to pay a late-night visit to that establishment in Bond Street, you are quite free for the rest of the evening."

"If one assumes that this list of names is complete, which is a dangerous assumption." Sebastian regarded her with a hooded gaze. "What are you getting at, my dear?"

Prudence smiled expectantly. "We shall pass near Rowland Street on our way home tonight."

"No," Sebastian said immediately. "Don't think for one moment that I am going to take you on a late-night visit to Oxenham's home."

"We could at least drive past his house and see if he is out for the evening," Prudence said persuasively. "Surely there would be no risk in that, Sebastian."

"Absolutely not. I am not going to allow you anywhere near his house."

"We would not need to stop," Prudence argued. "We could simply determine whether or not he is at home this evening. Then, if you wished to return later we would know if it was safe to do so."

Sebastian hesitated, obviously torn. "I suppose it would do no harm to drive past his house."

Prudence hid her smile of satisfaction. "None at all. We

would be merely one more carriage traveling home from a ball. No one would take any notice."

"Very well." Sebastian stood up and raised the trapdoor in the top of the carriage.

"Aye, m'lord?" the coachman called down.

"I wish to go home by way of Rowland Street," Sebastian instructed.

"It's a bit of a side trip, m'lord."

"Yes, I know, but I think it will be faster. Less traffic."

"Aye, m'lord. Whatever you say, sir."

Sebastian lowered the trapdoor and sat down slowly across from Prudence. "Why do I have the feeling that I am going to regret letting you talk me into this little excursion?"

"I have no notion," Prudence said lightly. "There is certainly no risk involved."

"Hmm."

Prudence chuckled. "You may as well face the truth, Sebastian. You want to do this as much as I do. In some ways we are very much alike, as you keep pointing out to me."

"A prospect which I find increasingly alarming." Sebastian extinguished the interior lamps. Then he tugged aside the curtains that concealed the windows and lowered the glass.

Prudence watched curiously. "What are you doing?"

"Making certain of our anonymity while in the neighborhood. The fog is quite heavy now, so there is probably no need to worry that someone will recognize the carriage. Nevertheless, one cannot be too careful."

Sebastian reached under the seat and pulled out a flat piece of wood that had been painted black. He attached it to two small hooks on the inside of the door and suspended it over the side.

Prudence realized the painted board would cover up the distinctive Angelstone crest. "Very clever, Sebastian."

"A reasonable precaution." He sat back in the seat.

Prudence smiled. "And one you have taken before, I collect."

"Yes."

She could not see his expression in the deep shadows, but she could hear the current of anticipation in his voice. He was caught up in the excitement of the adventure now, just as she was.

Rowland Street proved to be a remarkably quiet neighborhood. As Sebastian had predicted, there was very little traffic. Prudence gazed out the open window. Through the drifting tendrils of fog she saw that most of the houses were dark.

Sebastian leaned forward. "If the direction given on that note is correct, that will be Oxenham's house."

"There are no lights on at all." Prudence glanced at Sebastian. "I'll wager no one is home. This would be a perfect opportunity to take a quick look around."

"The servants are probably at home." Sebastian was staring at the darkened house with keen interest.

"If so, they are asleep below stairs. They might even have gone out for the evening," Prudence suggested. "It is not unknown for house staff to take the night off if they are certain their master will not be home until quite late."

"True."

"We could instruct the coachman to wait at the corner while we take a short walk down the alley behind Oxenham's house."

"Damnation, Prue, I told you I was not going to take you with me when I paid my visit to Oxenham."

"But who knows when you'll get another opportunity like this? By the time you take me home and return, Oxenham might very well have come back. You would have to wait until another night."

Sebastian hesitated. "I suppose I could leave you here in the carriage while I take a quick look at the back of the house."

"I want to come with you."

"No. I forbid it." Sebastian raised the trapdoor and spoke softly to the coachman. "Drive to the end of the street and turn the corner. I shall get out briefly. If anything unusual occurs while I am gone, you are to drive Lady Angelstone home at once. I shall find my own way home."

"Aye, yer lordship." The man spoke with the resigned voice of a servant who was accustomed to odd late-night forays and even odder instructions from a very odd master.

Prudence made one last attempt to change Sebastian's mind. "This is most unfair of you, my lord."

"It was your idea," he reminded her. He removed his greatcoat. "Here, you had better take this. I might be gone for some time and I don't want you taking a chill."

"But I fully intended to accompany you," Prudence said as she struggled into the greatcoat.

"I told you at the start that I would not allow it," he said.

"You wouldn't even be here now if I hadn't thought of driving down Rowland Street."

"You are quite right," he said as the carriage came to a halt. "Nevertheless, this is as far as you go on this investigation." He caught her face between his gloved hands and kissed her fiercely.

When he raised his head Prudence straightened her spectacles. She could hardly make out his face in the darkness, but she could definitely feel the controlled excitement in him.

"Sebastian, listen to me."

"Be reasonable, Prue, you cannot possibly go running about in this fog dressed like that."

"Do not dare use my gown as an excuse. The truth is, you don't want me to have any fun. Admit it."

His teeth flashed briefly in the shadows. "I shall return presently, my dear. Don't leave the carriage."

He opened the door, jumped down onto the pavement, and vanished almost instantly into the fog-shrouded night.

"Bloody hell," Prudence muttered.

A moment later she opened the carriage door.

"Beggin' yer pardon, ma'am, but where are ye goin'?" the coachman hissed in alarm. "I was instructed to keep an eye on ye. His lordship will have me head if ye don't stay in the coach."

"Do not concern yourself," Prudence whispered reassuringly. "I shall speak to his lordship. He won't blame you for this."

"The hell he won't. Please, ma'am, I beg ye on bended knee. Get back in the coach."

"Try not to worry. I shall return soon."

"I'm a dead man," the coachman said sadly. "Always knew that when he married, his lordship would pick a female as bloody-minded as himself. Serves him right, suppose. But what's goin' to happen to me, I ask ye?"

"I shall see to it that your post is secure," Prudence said softly. "Now I must be off."

Prudence was grateful for Sebastian's heavily caped coat as she made her way down the lane behind the row of town houses. She counted garden gates until she found the one that belonged to the house Sebastian had pointed out earlier.

She was not surprised to find the gate unlatched. Sebastian was only a few minutes ahead of her, after all. He had already come this way. What sent a chill of alarm through her was the realization that there was a light in one of the windows on the ground floor at the back of Oxenham's house.

Someone was home.

Prudence hesitated, wondering why Sebastian had gone on into the garden knowing that the house was occupied. Then she reminded herself that he was perfectly capable of investigating a lady's bedchamber while the lady herself was downstairs playing hostess to half the *ton*. Nor had he hesitated to explore the upper floor of Curling Castle while Curling's guests traipsed about from bedchamber to bedchamber one floor below.

She ought not to be surprised that Sebastian had decided to take a closer look at Oxenham's house in spite of the light in one window.

Emboldened by the realization that he had already gone ahead, Prudence opened the gate and stepped into the garden. She winced when she found the graveled path. She could feel every tiny pebble through the soles of her soft satin evening slippers.

Midway through the garden Prudence was forced to alter her course slightly due to a high hedge. She stepped around the corner of the prickly foliage and collided with a large, solid masculine chest. Strong arms tightened around her, crushing her face against a familiar shirt.

"Umph."

"Damn it to hell." Sebastian's voice was very soft and very annoyed. "I had a hunch you wouldn't follow orders. Don't make a sound, do you understand?"

Prudence nodded her head frantically.

He released her cautiously. Prudence raised her face. She could just barely make out Sebastian's irritated expression. "What are we going to do?" she asked in a voice that was even softer than his had been.

"You are going to stand right here while I take a closer look. Then we're going to leave as quickly as possible."

Sebastian moved away from her. Prudence watched anxiously as he made his way past the darkened windows of the ground floor. She saw his hand move once or twice and realized he was testing the windows to see if any were open.

She held her breath when he approached the one window through which light could be seen. Sebastian flattened himself against the wall and looked into the room from an angle.

He did not move for a long moment. Then he edged closer and studied the room from a slightly different angle.

Something was wrong, Prudence realized. She could

sense it in the way Sebastian was standing. He was staring through the glass now, studying the scene inside very closely. Prudence took a cautious step forward. Sebastian did not notice. He was concentrating on whatever was inside the room.

Prudence watched in amazement as he reached out and opened the window. She darted toward him.

"Stay back," Sebastian ordered softly as she approached him. "I mean it, Prue. Don't follow me."

"What are you doing? You can't go inside. Someone is obviously home."

"I know," Sebastian said quietly. "Oxenham. But I do not believe he will notice that he has a visitor."

Sebastian swung his leg over the windowsill and dropped lightly into the room.

Shocked in spite of herself at this fresh evidence of Sebastian's outrageous boldness, Prudence hastened over to the window. She peered inside.

For an instant she could not comprehend what she was seeing. Then the sight registered. Prudence took an instinctive step back in horror.

A man lay sprawled facedown on the carpet. There was blood all over his head and more blood on the carpet beside him.

xenham had committed suicide. Either that or someone had gone to a great deal of trouble to make it appear that he had.

The pistol lay inches from the dead man's hand. There was no evidence of a struggle.

Sebastian glanced quickly around the library. He could not stay long. He had to get Prudence out of the vicinity. But he wanted to find something that would convince him Oxenham had put the pistol to his own head and pulled the trigger.

Or something that would prove that he had not.

Gold gleamed on the carpet near Oxenham's outflung hand. Sebastian edged closer, careful to stay clear of the blood. He glanced toward the window and saw Prudence watching him anxiously.

The gold object on the rug was a ring. He crouched down to get a closer look at it, wondering why it seemed familiar. Then he saw the elaborate letter *F* worked on the top. A Fleetwood ring, much like his own.

"Damnation." Without stopping to think about it, he scooped up the ring and rose quickly to his feet.

He turned toward the window and hesitated once more. He needed to be certain it was Oxenham that lay in the pool of blood. It was impossible to see the man's face from this angle. He steeled himself and stepped back toward the body.

"Don't touch him," Prudence whispered urgently. "Sebastian, we must get out of here."

"I know." But he could not leave until he was certain. Sebastian reached down, grasped the body by the shoulder, and turned the dead man over far enough to see what was left of his face.

It was definitely Oxenham.

Sebastian started to lower the limp corpse back into position. Gold gleamed once more, this time from the buttons of Oxenham's waistcoat. Sebastian leaned down and saw the words *The Princes of Virtue* engraved on them.

He let Oxenham's body fall back onto the carpet.

"For heaven's sake, Sebastian, hurry," Prudence whispered.

"I just want to take a quick look at his desk."

He walked carefully across the carpet to the desk. There were a handful of papers scattered about on top. Sebastian glanced through them quickly, searching to see if the dead man had left a note.

There was no letter explaining the suicide, but someone had, indeed, left a message. Sebastian read it by the light of the dying lamp. It was short and to the point.

Lillian will be avenged.

Sebastian heard the voices from the front of the house at the same instant that Prudence did. The servants had returned.

"Sebastian, for God's sake, get out of there."

He picked up the note, shoved it into his pocket along with the Fleetwood ring, and ran for the window.

He vaulted over the sill, caught Prudence's hand, and drew her swiftly toward the garden gate.

They reached the lane without incident. Sebastian

glanced back over his shoulder and saw no signs of pursuit. He hurried Prudence toward the waiting carriage.

The coachman eyed his passengers with doleful resignation as they emerged out of the fog. "It weren't my fault she took after ye, m'lord. I did me best."

"Home," Sebastian ordered. "We'll discuss your duties later."

"Aye, m'lord. Does this mean I've still got me job?"

"Your position is secure until you get us safely home." Sebastian opened the carriage door and tossed Prudence inside. "After that, the matter is questionable." He got into the cab behind Prudence and closed the door.

"You must not chastise the poor coachman. He did his best to follow your instructions," Prudence said breathlessly.

"He has been with me long enough to know that when I give an order I expect it to be obeyed," Sebastian said. "I pay the best wages in London and in return I demand that every member of my staff carry out my instructions to the letter. You could have been seen."

"Do stop worrying, Sebastian. I am certain we were safe." She struggled to extricate herself from the voluminous folds of the greatcoat. "It will most likely be quite some time before someone checks the library and finds Oxenham's body."

"Or no time at all." Sebastian closed the curtains over the windows as the carriage rumbled forward. "Madam, in the future you will not disobey me."

"You may lecture me later, my lord. Tell me what you found."

He had only himself to blame for marrying a woman who shared his enthusiasm for investigation, Sebastian thought. He fumbled with one of the interior lamps until it flared to life. Then he lounged back in the seat and studied Prudence's expressive face. Her eyes were bright with the excitement of the adventure they had just shared. It was difficult to scold her when he was still feeling the same thrill course through his own veins.

He removed the ring and the note from his pocket. Without a word he handed both to her. "I'm not sure yet what I found. By the by, Oxenham's waistcoat was trimmed with buttons that had *The Princes of Virtue* engraved on them."

"Fascinating." Prudence studied the ring intently for a moment. "This ring is just like yours, my lord."

"Yes."

"What was it doing lying on the floor near Oxenham's body?"

"An excellent question," Sebastian said softly.

"And who is Lillian?"

Sebastian realized she was looking closely at the inside of the ring, not the note. "What do you mean?"

"The ring is inscribed on the inside." Prudence held it closer to the lamp. *"To Lillian with love."*

"Let me see that." Sebastian plucked the ring out of her fingers and examined the inscription. "Who the devil is Lillian?"

"You have heard the name before?"

"Read the note," he said.

Prudence glanced down at the sheet of foolscap on her lap. *"Lillian will be avenged.* Good grief, Sebastian, what on earth is going on?"

"I don't know, but I am starting to wonder if Lillian is the name of the woman that mad old man at Curling Castle mentioned. The one he said had jumped from the tower room."

"The ghost he thought had come back to carry out her curse?" Prudence nibbled thoughtfully on her lower lip. "Do you think the deaths of Ringcross and Oxenham have anything to do with the tale that he told us?"

"Perhaps." Sebastian gazed at the ring on his palm. "It's possible that someone who cared about the mysterious Lillian has decided that The Princes of Virtue were responsible for her death."

Prudence stared at him. "Do you think her avenger is going after them one by one?"

"It looks that way."

Prudence's eyes rested on the ring. "Sebastian, you said that your ring is a family ring."

"Rings such as this one have been worn by the Fleetwood men for five generations." Sebastian thought of the day he had received his from his father. He had been told to wear it with pride. His father had explained that it was a symbol of his personal honor.

The opinion of the world does not matter, my son. All that matters is that you know in your heart that you have not stained your honor. Honor is a sacred trust and must be treated as such. A man can survive scandal and ruin and worse if he knows that his honor is safe.

Sebastian tightened his fingers around the ring.

"Do you think it possible that a Fleetwood gave that ring to Lillian?" Prudence asked.

"Yes, it's possible." More than possible, Sebastian thought. It was highly probable.

Prudence looked at him. "You're thinking that it was Jeremy's snuffbox we found at Curling Castle, aren't you? You're wondering if that ring also belongs to him."

"Yes."

"But Sebastian, I saw Jeremy earlier this evening. He was not wearing gloves and I seem to recall that he had a ring like that one on his finger."

Sebastian looked at her. "It would not be difficult to have a ring such as this duplicated. Assuming one could afford the cost, it would be a simple matter for a good jeweler to create a copy."

Prudence was silent for a long moment. "What do we do next? Are you going to start interviewing jewelers?"

"No." Sebastian made his decision. "I think that I had

better have another talk with my cousin. Jeremy's name has come up once too often in the course of this investigation."

"I agree," Prudence said. "I shall help you conduct the interview."

"I'm not so certain that would be a sound notion, madam."

"It will be very useful to have two opinions of his reactions, don't you agree?"

Sebastian hesitated. He would not mind having her observations on Jeremy. There was no denying Prudence was extremely perceptive. But it was equally true that she tended to be unpredictable, not to mention softhearted where family was concerned.

"Very well, Prue. You may listen while I talk to Jeremy. But you are not to interfere in any way, is that understood?"

Prudence smiled cheerfully. "Perfectly, my lord."

Jeremy was shown into the library at eleven-thirty the next morning. Prudence's heart went out to him the moment he appeared. His resentment at being summarily summoned by the head of the family was obvious.

"What the devil is this all about, Angelstone? I've got better things to do than respond to messages from you."

Sebastian was seated behind the desk near the window. He had Lucifer draped over one arm. He did not bother to rise. "The pleasure is mutual. Perhaps you would care to greet my wife in a civil fashion before you finish telling me what you think of me?"

Jeremy glanced across the room and saw Prudence standing near the tea tray. He turned a dull red. "Lady Angelstone." He inclined his head stiffly. "Your pardon. Didn't see you there. Good morning to you, madam."

"Good morning, Mr. Fleetwood." Prudence smiled. "Would you care for tea?"

Jeremy looked uncomfortable. He glanced at Sebastian. "I don't know if I'll have time."

"You'll have plenty of time to drink a cup of tea," Sebastian assured him coldly. "Sit down, cousin."

Jeremy took the teacup from Prudence. "Thank you, madam." He stood waiting until Prudence had seated herself and then he lowered himself uneasily into a chair across from Sebastian.

"Well?" Jeremy inquired brusquely. "Let us get on with it, then. Why did you send for me, sir?"

Sebastian studied him for a long moment. Prudence suspected the silence was a deliberate act of intimidation. She was about to speak up when Sebastian moved. Without a word, he opened the desk drawer, took out the ring he had found in Oxenham's library, and tossed it at Jeremy.

"What in blazes?" Jeremy caught the ring with an angry reflexive action. He glanced down at it.

Prudence could not miss the jolt of surprise that went through Jeremy when he realized what he held in his hand. She glanced at Sebastian and saw that he was watching his cousin very intently. There was no hint of cold amusement in Sebastian's eyes this morning, only an unnervingly alert intelligence that gleamed like fire-heated gold.

"Damnation." Jeremy looked up with an expression of wary confusion. "Where the devil did you get this?"

Sebastian stroked Lucifer very slowly. "Do you recognize it?"

"Yes, of course. It's mine." There was a strange edge in Jeremy's voice. "I lost it about three years ago. I never mentioned it because I knew Mother would kick up a fuss. You know how she is about family traditions."

"Yes." Sebastian's hand stilled on Lucifer. "I know."

"Didn't want to overset her by telling her I'd lost the heirloom ring my father had given me. So I had another one made to replace it."

"Who is Lillian?" Sebastian asked softly.

"I have no notion." The teacup rattled in its saucer as Jeremy picked it up.

"Who is Lillian?" Sebastian repeated, his voice lethally soft. Lucifer twitched his tail.

"I don't know who you're talking about, I tell you," Jeremy said loudly. "I don't know any Lillian." He set the cup down with a crash.

"I think you do," Sebastian said. "You are not leaving here until you tell me who she is."

"Damn you, Angelstone. Who the hell do you think you are?"

"He is the head of the family," Prudence said quickly. She shot a quelling glance at Sebastian, who ignored it. "And he is only trying to help. Isn't that right, Angelstone?"

"The only thing I am attempting to do at the moment," Sebastian said evenly, "is ascertain who Lillian is."

Prudence glared at him. "There is no need to sound so threatening, my lord. We are trying to establish some facts. We don't wish to alarm your cousin."

Sebastian did not take his eyes off Jeremy. Nor did he respond to Prudence's appeal. She gave up trying to control his manners and turned to Jeremy.

"Please understand, Mr. Fleetwood," she said gently. "We are merely seeking to determine why your ring was found in some very unusual circumstances last night."

Jeremy looked at her. "What circumstances?"

"It was found lying next to the body of Lord Oxenham," Sebastian said bluntly. "You wouldn't happen to know how it got there, would you?"

"Body?" Jeremy frowned in confusion. "Oxenham is dead?"

"Very," Sebastian said.

Jeremy's eyes widened slightly. "My ring was nearby?"

"Yes."

"You think I killed him, is that it?" Jeremy's outrage overwhelmed his confusion. "Because someone found my ring near the body?"

"That question did arise." Sebastian's smile was laconic. Lucifer blinked his golden eyes.

Prudence scowled at Sebastian. "Do stop trying to intimidate him, my lord."

"Stay out of this, madam." Sebastian did not glance at her.

She ignored the warning and turned back to Jeremy with a reassuring smile. "Mr. Fleetwood, at this point the authorities do not know that your ring was found near Oxenham's body. And we certainly do not intend to tell them, do we, Sebastian?"

"That remains to be seen," Sebastian said coolly.

"But I didn't kill him." Jeremy's desperate glance swung back and forth between Prudence and Sebastian. "I swear it. Why would I kill Oxenham?"

Sebastian rubbed Lucifer's ears. "Perhaps because you think he might have had something to do with Lillian's death?"

"But Lillian's death was an accident. She drowned, for God's sake." Jeremy broke off abruptly as he obviously realized he had just admitted to knowing who Lillian was. He gave Prudence a pleading look. "I was told that she drowned."

Prudence reacted instinctively to Jeremy's pain and bewilderment. She leaned forward and touched his hand in a gesture of comfort. She was aware of the brief anger that flashed in Sebastian's eyes, but he said nothing.

"Who was Lillian, Mr. Fleetwood?" Prudence asked quietly.

Jeremy closed his eyes for a few seconds. When he opened them again, his expression was one of bleak resignation.

"I suppose you may as well know the whole story, although why it has surfaced after all this time defeats me." Jeremy took a steadying sip of tea. When he put down the cup he kept his gaze focused on Prudence. "I loved her."

"Did you?"

"She was the daughter of a prosperous merchant. His only child and the light of his life after his wife died. He saw to it that she was gently reared. She was well educated and her manners were above reproach. She was a lady in every way but for the circumstances of her birth."

"I understand," Prudence whispered.

"I met her sometime after her father had died. She had been left in the care of an aging uncle who consumed her inheritance and forced her to work in his tavern."

Out of the corner of her eye Prudence saw Sebastian open his mouth to ask a question. She silenced him with a tiny motion of her hand. Somewhat to her surprise, he subsided.

"How did you meet Lillian?" Prudence asked.

"At a fair here in town three years ago." Jeremy's mouth curved in a reminiscent smile. "She was eating an ice. I accidentally bumped into her and the ice went all over my coat. It was love at first sight."

"Then what happened?" Prudence asked.

"I started seeing her whenever I could. I knew Mother would never approve, of course. In her eyes Lillian would have been a mere tavern wench, without even a merchant's fortune to make up for her lack of background." Jeremy's mouth hardened. "You must remember that at the time Mother thought I would become the next Earl of Angelstone."

"I think it's safe to say that my aunt would have found a tavern wench totally unacceptable as the next Countess of Angelstone," Sebastian said dryly. "Almost as unacceptable as an actress."

Jeremy flushed. "If it's any consolation to you, Angelstone, I have often thought that I understood your father's decision to marry the woman he loved. I had made plans to do the same. Regardless of the consequences."

Sebastian narrowed his eyes. "Did you?"

"Yes. I truly loved Lillian. She was a beautiful creature. Gentle and pure." Jeremy sighed. "But she died before we could be wed."

"How tragic," Prudence said.

"I never mentioned her name to Mother or anyone else in the family," Jeremy said. "With Lillian in her grave, there did not seem any reason to do so."

"Who told you she had drowned?" Sebastian asked.

"Her uncle. He said she had gone to stay with a friend in the country for a few days. While she was there she fell into a stream that was in flood after a recent storm. She was swept away and drowned."

"I am so sorry, Mr. Fleetwood," Prudence said quietly. "It must have been terrible for you."

Jeremy looked down at the ring. "The worst part was that I could tell no one of my grief. There was no one who would have understood or approved." He glanced up again. "I have recovered. One does eventually. Lillian is in the past. But I shall never forget her."

Sebastian eyed his cousin. "You gave her that ring?"

Jeremy nodded. "The one I wear is a duplicate. I had it made when I gave Lillian this one. I did not want to have to explain to Mother or the rest of the family why I was no longer wearing the Fleetwood ring. Not until I was ready to announce my marriage."

"You may not have found it necessary to explain the missing ring to the rest of the Fleetwoods," Sebastian said, "but I think you are going to have to explain to me how it wound up in Oxenham's study."

"But I don't know how it got there," Jeremy said quickly. "I swear it. As far as I knew, the ring was lost when Lillian drowned. It occurred to me that someone—one of the villagers, perhaps—might have stolen it after finding her body. The ring was, after all, rather valuable. But I knew I had very little chance of recovering it, so I let the matter rest."

Prudence turned to Sebastian. "Perhaps we should talk to her uncle, the tavern keeper."

"You cannot do that," Jeremy said quietly. "He was taken off by the fever over a year ago. I learned of his death when I happened past the tavern one day and discovered it was being operated by new owners."

"So much for that notion," Prudence said, frustrated.

"I do not understand any of this." Jeremy glared at Sebastian. "First you return my snuffbox to me and now my ring. You have practically accused me of murder in both instances. What game are you playing now, Angelstone?"

Sebastian stroked Lucifer in silence for a moment. "Two men have died recently: Ringcross and Oxenham."

"I am aware of that."

"Personal items belonging to you were found in the vicinity of the deaths. This note was also found near Oxenham's body." Sebastian handed Jeremy the note he had discovered.

Jeremy read it quickly. When he glanced up again he appeared more baffled than ever. "What is this about avenging Lillian? What the bloody hell is going on?"

"There would appear to be two possibilities," Sebastian said. "Either you have decided to avenge Lillian because you believe her death was not an accident, or . . ."

"Or what?" Prudence demanded before Jeremy could ask the same question.

"Or someone wishes to make it appear that such is the case," Sebastian concluded softly.

"But who would wish to do that?" Prudence asked swiftly.

Sebastian contemplated Lucifer. "The real murderer, perhaps."

Jeremy was clearly staggered. "How do you come to know all this, Angelstone?"

Sebastian gave him a derisive smile. "Rumors have reached me."

"Rumors from where?" Jeremy demanded.

"Bow Street."

"Bow Street." Jeremy was horrified. "Do you mean to tell me that Bow Street is investigating the deaths of Ringcross and Oxenham?"

"Yes," Sebastian said. "Very discreetly, of course."

"But how did you get hold of my snuffbox and ring if they were found at the scenes of the deaths?"

"Let us just say that I have connections both high and low. Some of them are in Bow Street."

"I suppose that does not surprise me," Jeremy muttered. "God knows you have your tentacles everywhere."

"That is certainly one way of putting it," Sebastian agreed. "In any event, one of my tentacles—I mean, one of my *connections*—is involved in the investigation. A certain individual saw fit to let me know that evidence linking you to the deaths has come to light. At the moment this person is content to let me deal with the matter."

"You must pay him very well to keep you informed," Jeremy said bitterly.

"I like to be kept informed," Sebastian said in a neutral tone.

Prudence glanced at Sebastian in brief admiration. He had finessed that issue very nicely, she thought. It was entirely believable that a man in Sebastian's powerful position could have picked up rumors from Bow Street, especially rumors that affected his own family. It was also reasonable to assume that he could have used his influence to convince someone in authority to turn evidence over to him rather than use it against his cousin.

"The problem," Sebastian continued softly, "is that there may be more deaths. I do not know if I will be able to keep your name out of the matter if that happens."

"Good God." Jeremy stared at Sebastian. "What am I to do? I know nothing about the deaths of Ringcross and Oxenham. If someone is trying to implicate me, I might eventually be arrested for murder. How would I prove my innocence?"

"You must not fret, Mr. Fleetwood." Prudence patted Jeremy's arm. "Angelstone is going to help you, aren't you, Angelstone?"

Sebastian shrugged. "Perhaps."

"Angelstone, what are you saying?" Prudence shot to her feet. "It is grossly unkind of you to torment Mr. Fleetwood in this fashion. I will not have it."

Jeremy stood up abruptly. His hand clenched into a fist. "I suspect your husband is enjoying himself, Lady Angelstone. It occurs to me that if I am taken up for murder, he will have a rather nasty sort of revenge against the family. There is no telling what the shock and scandal would do to my mother."

"Do not say such things, Mr. Fleetwood," Prudence begged. "It is not Angelstone's intent to hurt the family by seeing you arrested for murder."

"No?" Jeremy looked down at her, his eyes a little wild. "In case you do not fully comprehend the sort of man you have married, madam, allow me to tell you that Angelstone hates the rest of us. He would not mind seeing all Fleetwoods ruined."

"That's not true," Prudence said.

"It is true." Jeremy cast a scathing glance at Sebastian. "In fact, now that I consider the matter, I find it more than likely that he is the one behind all this."

"No," Prudence gasped.

Jeremy stared at Sebastian. "Is it you who is doing this to me, Angelstone? Are you trying to get me arrested for murder?"

Sebastian smiled coldly. "If that was my goal I would not have given you the snuffbox and the ring. I would have let Bow Street have them."

"How do I know that?" Jeremy shot back. "Perhaps this is all part of a larger plot. You are like a cat with a mouse, are you not? You intend to amuse yourself for a time by tormenting the rest of us until you grow bored. Then you will end the entertainment once and for all by seeing me hung and the rest of the family disgraced."

Sebastian's mouth curved in cynical amusement. "I congratulate you on your vivid imagination, cousin."

"Stop it, both of you," Prudence ordered. She stepped in front of the desk, placing herself between Jeremy and Sebastian. "That is quite enough theatrics for the morning. Mr. Fleetwood, perhaps it would be best if you took your leave. Try not to worry about being taken up for murder. Angelstone will not permit that to happen."

"Angelstone may not be able to prevent it," Sebastian said very softly.

Prudence rounded on him. "As for you, Angelstone, I demand that you cease trying to terrify your cousin."

Sebastian's eyes glittered. "Why are you always trying to spoil my fun, madam?"

"Not another word," Prudence said through set teeth. She glanced at Jeremy over her shoulder. "Good day, Mr. Fleetwood. I shall see that you are kept informed of events. Please try not to worry. All will be well."

"Not if Angelstone has decided upon some fiendish amusement." Jeremy inclined his head in a rigid gesture of farewell. "Good day, madam. You have my deepest condolences. It cannot be easy being wed to the Fallen Angel."

He walked out of the library without a backward glance.

Fifteen

Sebastian knew *Prudence was* going to scold him as soon as the door closed behind Jeremy. He was not in the mood for it.

She whirled around to confront him the instant Jeremy had left the room. Behind the lenses of her spectacles, her eyes sparkled with outrage. "How could you be so unkind to poor Jeremy?"

"I assure you, it was not in the least difficult." Sebastian set Lucifer on the desk and got to his feet. He was going to be forced to help Jeremy. He knew it, but he did not have to like it.

The prospect of helping out a Fleetwood made Sebastian feel short-tempered and henpecked. At a time like this a man needed his club. Unfortunately, he could not avail himself of the traditional masculine refuge because he had an appointment to keep. But at least he had an excuse to escape the house, he thought.

"It was most uncivil of you, sir. Surely you could see that your cousin is under a dreadful strain. He needs help and reassurance. I insist that you do not play any more games with him, Sebastian."

"And I insist that you cease interfering in my affairs, madam." Sebastian stalked around the edge of the desk.

"Furthermore, I am in no mood to be lectured on the manner in which I choose to treat my bloody relatives."

Prudence folded her arms beneath her breasts and tapped one slippered toe. "You know perfectly well that you are going to help your cousin. Why did you make him think otherwise?"

Sebastian lounged against the edge of his desk. "What makes you think I'm going to help him?"

She gave him a fulminating look. "There cannot be any question of it."

"On the contrary, madam." Sebastian smiled blandly. "As far as I am concerned, there is most definitely a question. I have already done a great deal for my ungrateful cousin. Or have you forgotten that on two very recent occasions I have concealed evidence that implicated him in the deaths of two men?"

Prudence bit her lip. "You didn't actually conceal it, my lord. You simply returned it to the rightful owner."

"Who may very well be the killer."

"Mr. Fleetwood did not kill Oxenham or Ringcross. I am certain of it."

"I'm glad you are so certain, because I am not."

"How can you say that?" Prudence demanded.

"Let me put it this way." Sebastian straightened and started for the door. "If I thought I knew the names of four men who had been involved in my lady's death, I would not hesitate to murder each and every one of them."

Prudence unfolded her arms and gaped at him in astonishment. "Sebastian? What are you saying? That you understand why your cousin may have killed those men?"

"I understand perfectly well why he may have done so." Sebastian had his hand on the doorknob.

Prudence brightened. "Then surely you want to help him, even if you do think he's guilty."

"Not necessarily. I still have my own objectives to consider." Sebastian opened the door and glanced back over his shoulder. "And I assure you that helping Fleetwoods has never been one of them. As far as I am concerned, I have done more than enough for Jeremy. He has been warned. I owe him nothing else in the way of assistance."

"But Sebastian—"

Sebastian went through the door and closed it quickly. He heard the soft patter of Prudence's slippered feet running across the carpet and knew he had only seconds to get safely out the front door.

"Tell her ladyship I will not be back until this afternoon, Flowers."

Flowers gave him a reproachful look as he handed Sebastian his hat and his gloves. "Yes, my lord."

The library door was flung wide just as Flowers opened the front door for Sebastian.

"My lord, wait," Prudence called urgently. "Damn it, Angelstone, come back here."

"Sorry, I must be off, my dear. I fear I am late for an appointment." Sebastian went swiftly down the steps to the sidewalk.

Prudence stood in the doorway behind him. "I'm not through talking to you."

"I'm aware of that," Sebastian muttered under his breath as he reached the safety of the sidewalk. She could not follow him out into the street, he assured himself.

"Coward," Prudence shouted from the top of the steps.

Sebastian saw several people stop and turn to stare in shock at the sight of the Countess of Angelstone yelling after her husband like a fishwife.

Sebastian could not resist turning around, too. Prudence was standing in the doorway, glaring furiously. Even as he watched, she stamped one small foot in exasperation.

Directly behind her loomed Flowers with an unholy grin on his normally dour face. It occurred to Sebastian that he had never seen Flowers smile like that.

Sebastian's spirits lightened abruptly. He found himself

grinning, too, in spite of his bedeviled mood. In addition to a host of other endearing wifely virtues, Prudence could play the shrew. Fresh confirmation of what he already knew, Sebastian decided. Life with her would never be dull.

He hailed a hackney coach and gave the coachman the familiar direction of the coffeehouse near the docks. He vaulted up into the cab, sat down, and pulled Whistlecroft's latest message out of his pocket. It had arrived an hour and a half earlier.

> *Must see yr lordship as soon as possible. Very urgent.*
> *I'll be at the usual place shortly after noon.*
>
> > *Yrs.*
> >
> > *W.*

He had not been lying when he had told Prudence that he was late for an appointment, Sebastian thought. He pulled his watch out of his pocket and saw that it was already twenty after twelve. It would not hurt Whistlecroft to wait. Sebastian settled back to contemplate the interview with Jeremy.

Half an hour later the hackney drew up in front of the coffeehouse. Sebastian alighted and walked inside. Whistlecroft had commandeered their usual booth.

"Glad ye could make it on such short notice, m'lord." Whistlecroft wiped his nose on his well-used handkerchief. "I feared ye might not show. We've got a problem with the client."

"What sort of problem?" Sebastian signaled for a mug of coffee.

"He's gettin' anxious, he is. Seems Lord Oxenham was found dead in his study last night. Curling's very agitated. He seems to think there's a connection." Whistlecroft eyed Sebastian closely. "He wants to know why I ain't makin' any progress on the investigation, m'lord."

"Does he, indeed?" Sebastian looked at his mug of coffee

as it was set down in front of him. "Just how anxious would you say your client is?"

Whistlecroft snorted and sniffed a few times. Then he leaned forward and lowered his voice. "If I didn't know better, I'd say he's afraid he might be next."

"Interesting." Sebastian considered that briefly. So Curling was getting anxious. Probably because he knew there were only two Princes of Virtue left: himself and Bloomfield. "You may tell your client that you are making progress and expect to solve the case very shortly."

Whistlecroft slitted his eyes. "Yer sure of that, are ye? Because my client says if I can't find out who's behind the deaths of Ringcross and Oxenham very soon, he's going to hire another Runner."

"Do not concern yourself, Whistlecroft. I have every hope that you will be able to collect your reward for another successful investigation."

"Trust so." Whistlecroft looked glum. "Now that we're living in a house of our own, me wife wants to put in one of them water closets like the fancies got. Told her the privy in the garden worked just fine, but she's got her heart set on havin' one indoors. You know how women are when they make up their minds."

"I'm learning."

At three o'clock that afternoon Prudence returned from a trip to a bookshop. She was still fuming over Sebastian's cowardly retreat earlier in the day. The fact that she had found several interesting volumes on spectral phenomena had done nothing to sweeten her temper.

She was in the library examining her purchases when Flowers announced that she had a visitor.

"Mrs. Fleetwood to see you, madam." Flowers paused respectfully and then added smoothly, "I shall, of course, be happy to inform her that you are not at home."

"No, no, that's all right." Prudence glanced critically

down at her attire. Thank heavens she was wearing one of her new gowns, she thought. It was a pale lavender muslin trimmed with matching ribbon and several rows of flounces around the hem. It seemed a bit fussy and frilly to Prudence, but according to Hester the gown was very à la mode. Drucilla Fleetwood would not be able to fault it. "Show her in, Flowers."

Alarm lit Flowers's houndlike features. "Perhaps you misunderstood, madam. It's Mrs. Fleetwood who is calling. His lordship's aunt."

"I heard you, Flowers. Show her in here, please. And have tea sent in, will you?"

Flowers cleared his throat with a small cough. "If I might make a suggestion, madam. It would perhaps be best to wait until his lordship returns home in order to seek his opinion on whether or not he wishes his aunt to be received."

"This happens to be my home now as well as Angelstone's," Prudence said coolly. Nothing could have been more calculated to annoy her at this particular moment than the notion of asking Sebastian's opinion on who she should and should not receive. "Show Mrs. Fleetwood in, Flowers, or I shall show her in myself."

"Yes, madam. But I would be most humbly grateful if you would give me your word that you will inform his lordship that receiving Mrs. Fleetwood was your idea," Flowers said dolefully.

"Of course." Prudence wrinkled her nose in exasperation. "For heaven's sake, Flowers, there is no need to go about in fear of his lordship. He is a perfectly reasonable man."

"Allow me to tell you, madam, that you are probably the only person on earth who sees his lordship in quite that light."

Prudence smiled wryly. "Do not concern yourself, Flowers. I shall deal with his lordship."

"Yes, madam." Flowers gave her an odd look. "I am beginning to believe you might very well do just that." He backed respectfully out of the library.

A moment later Drucilla was ushered into the room. She made a grand entrance in a beautifully cut green gown. Her velvet pelisse was done in a slightly darker hue. It matched the elegant little hat perched at a clever angle on her head. Prudence noticed that there was only one small row of flounces around the hem of the gown.

"Good day, madam." Prudence rose politely. "What an unexpected surprise. Please be seated. I have sent for tea. I do hope you will join me in a cup?"

"Thank you." Drucilla scanned Prudence's heavily trimmed gown with a shuttered gaze, but she said nothing. She lowered herself gracefully into a chair. Her spine did not touch the back.

The housekeeper appeared with the tea tray. She wore a look of impending doom as she dutifully set the tray down near Prudence.

"Thank you, Mrs. Banks," Prudence said. "I shall pour."

"Yes, madam. Expect his lordship will have something to say about this," Mrs. Banks muttered.

Prudence pretended that she had not heard the comment. She handed a cup of tea to Drucilla as the library door closed behind Mrs. Banks.

"How kind of you to pay me a visit, Mrs. Fleetwood."

"You needn't act as if this were a social call." Drucilla set her cup and saucer down on a nearby table. "I am here on extremely urgent business. Lord knows that only the most dire necessity would bring me to this house."

"I see. What sort of business would that be?" Prudence asked cautiously.

"Family business."

"Ah, yes. Family business."

Drucilla straightened her already extremely straight shoulders. "I have had a long talk with my son. He tells me he is the victim of a most malicious set of circumstances."

Prudence stifled a small groan. She had hoped Jeremy would not feel compelled to drag his mother into the situation. Prudence's intuition had told her it would be easier to keep Sebastian working on the investigation if Drucilla were not involved.

"What has Jeremy told you, madam?"

"That someone, very probably Angelstone, is playing a cruel game. Angelstone apparently claims to have found evidence that implicates my son in the deaths of two men. That is utter rubbish, of course. Angelstone is obviously lying."

Prudence frowned. "I assure you Angelstone is not lying."

"He certainly is. There is no other explanation. It is clear to me that he has concocted some devious scheme to avenge himself on the rest of us."

"Angelstone did not invent the evidence against Jeremy," Prudence said.

"Do not contradict me, madam. I have given the matter a great deal of thought. There is only one explanation for what is happening. Angelstone intends to use my son as a pawn in order to bring scandal and ruin down on the family. I will not have it."

Prudence's sympathy for the woman vanished beneath a wave of hot outrage. "I assure you, Angelstone is not responsible for the situation in which Jeremy finds himself. In fact, Angelstone has gone out of his way to keep the evidence from falling into the hands of the authorities."

"Bah."

"It's true." Prudence slammed her teacup down on its saucer. "Allow me to inform you, madam, that if Angelstone had not acted to prevent it, Jeremy might already have been arrested."

"My son had nothing to do with the deaths of those two men. He does not even know them."

"He may very well have to prove that, madam. Because

the way things are going, Jeremy is in danger of becoming entangled in a very sticky web."

"A web woven by your husband." Drucilla's voice was rising.

"That is a lie. Why would my husband want to see Jeremy arrested for murder?"

"For the sake of vengeance." Drucilla's mouth formed a thin, bitter line. "He hates all of us. He knows what the scandal of a murder charge would do to the family."

"I happen to know for a fact that Angelstone has no intention of avenging himself on the Fleetwoods because of what happened in the past. You are safe enough on that score, madam."

"So you say." Drucilla gave her a scornful look. "But you never knew his side of the family. You never met Angelstone's father." A strange expression flashed briefly in her eyes. "As it happens, I knew him rather well."

Prudence sat very still. It occurred to her that the look she had glimpsed a moment ago in Drucilla's eyes might have been pain. "Did you?"

"Oh, yes. Yes, indeed." Drucilla made a small, oddly savage gesture with her elegantly gloved hand. "The man had no respect for family tradition. No sense of his responsibilities. He was cruel and callous and his son takes after him."

Prudence was shocked in spite of herself at the deep bitterness that blazed in the older woman. There was something more here than the disapproval of a domineering matriarch.

"That is a very sweeping statement, Mrs. Fleetwood. How did you come to know Angelstone's father well enough to make such a judgment?"

"At one time," Drucilla said coldly, "there was talk of marriage between myself and Angelstone's father. It came to naught, of course. He ran off with his common little actress and I married his brother."

Prudence was thunderstruck. "You were engaged to Angelstone's father?"

Drucilla's mouth pursed angrily. "We were never engaged. Matters did not get that far. As I said, there was talk of marriage between us, but that was all. Both of our families were convinced it would be an excellent alliance. But, as I said, Jonathan Fleetwood was not concerned with what was best for the families. He believed himself in love with his little actress. He would have her, and that was that."

"From all accounts he did love her."

"Rubbish." Drucilla gave a soft exclamation of disgust. "A man of his station does not marry for love. Even if he was fond of the girl, there was no necessity to run off with her. He could have done his duty by his family and kept his doxy on the side. No one would have thought twice about it."

"Not even you?"

Drucilla flinched. "That is certainly none of your business, is it?"

"Perhaps not," Prudence said. She was beginning to see the Fleetwood family feud in a whole new light. "Nevertheless, I cannot allow you to insult my husband's side of the family simply because his father chose to marry his mother."

"She was an *actress*," Drucilla said in anguished fury. "He could have married me, but he chose someone who was no better than a professional courtesan. It was intolerable. He probably did it just to spite his family."

"You go too far, Mrs. Fleetwood. If you cannot keep a civil tongue in your head, I will have to ask you to leave."

Before Drucilla could respond, the library door slammed open.

Prudence nearly dropped her teacup. She spun around in her chair and stared as Sebastian, looking very much like Lucifer after the Fall, stormed into the room with an air of barely controlled violence.

"What the devil is going on here?" he asked in a deadly soft tone.

Prudence leaped to her feet and summoned up a smile. "Your aunt has very kindly come to visit."

Sebastian gave Prudence a frozen glance. "Has she, indeed? How fortunate I arrived home early." He inclined his head to Drucilla. "Good afternoon, madam. You should have sent word around that you intended to call." His smile was as cold as his eyes. "I very nearly missed seeing you."

"I wished to speak with your wife, Angelstone," Drucilla said. "I did not particularly desire to see you."

"I am devastated." Sebastian stalked over to a table that held the crystal decanter of claret. "Did you think it might be easier to intimidate Prue without me around?"

Prudence raised her eyes to the ceiling and prayed for patience. "Angelstone, there is no need to be rude. Mrs. Fleetwood is very concerned about Jeremy's predicament."

"So he went straight to his mama, did he? I wondered if he would." Sebastian sipped his claret and smiled his Fallen Angel smile. "I am deeply affected by this evidence of maternal concern. What's the matter, Aunt? Afraid that if Jeremy is arrested for murder you will no longer be welcome in the best drawing rooms?"

"Angelstone," Prudence began in a warning tone. She was cut off by Drucilla, who was watching Sebastian as if he were a demon from the Pit that had been set loose in the library.

"Do not think to amuse yourself by playing your devil's games with my son," Drucilla said. "I vow I do not know what you hope to accomplish by frightening Jeremy into thinking he will be arrested at any moment, but I insist you stop it at once."

Sebastian swirled the claret in his glass. "What makes you think I'm playing a game?"

Drucilla glowered at him. "Surely even you would not let an innocent man hang for murder."

Sebastian looked thoughtful. "I'm not certain about that. He is a Fleetwood, after all."

"Good God, sir," Drucilla whispered. "Have you no shame?"

Prudence tried to regain control of the situation. "Mrs. Fleetwood, I assure you Sebastian is not trying to terrify Jeremy. Nor does he intend to allow Jeremy to be arrested." She frowned severely at Sebastian. "Do you, my lord?"

Sebastian took a sip of claret and pondered that carefully. "Well . . ."

Prudence smiled reassuringly at Mrs. Fleetwood. "Do not concern yourself, madam. He will take care of Jeremy."

"You expect me to take your word for it?" Drucilla snapped.

Sebastian gave Prudence a dangerously amused look. "Mrs. Fleetwood is quite right to be skeptical, my dear. Why should I go out of my way to help a Fleetwood?"

"Stop it, Angelstone," Prudence said. "Stop it right now. You are not to torment your aunt like this. She is deeply concerned."

"And with good reason," Sebastian said.

Mrs. Fleetwood's nostrils were pinched with the strain of her rage. "I knew there was very little point trying to deal with you, Angelstone. That is why I made an effort to speak to Lady Angelstone in private."

"An effort which has failed." Sebastian sauntered across the room, sat down behind his desk, and propped his booted feet on the mahogany surface. "Tell me, Aunt, what did you expect to accomplish by pleading your case to my wife?"

"I did not come here today to plead with anyone. I came here to insist that your cat-and-mouse game be stopped immediately. I thought it just barely possible that Lady Angelstone might have some small influence on you."

"Really?" Sebastian's brows rose. "Whatever gave you the notion that she would take your side in all this? She is my wife, after all. Her loyalty lies with me."

"Angelstone, behave yourself." Prudence looked at Drucilla. "Rest assured, madam, that Angelstone is not plotting against your family. The evidence that he kept out of the hands of the authorities is quite damning, however. I must tell you that it is necessary to find out why it was left at the scene of the deaths."

"I have heard that Ringcross was killed in an accidental fall and that Oxenham was the victim of suicide," Drucilla said. "There is no talk of murder. Except by Angelstone."

"There has been no talk of murder because the evidence implicating Jeremy was concealed by Angelstone," Prudence said. "He took a great risk for the sake of the family, madam."

Sebastian smiled his most wicked smile and sipped his claret. "My devotion to my family knows no bounds."

Drucilla slanted him a narrow glance. "Bah. I do not believe there ever was any evidence implicating Jeremy at the scene of the deaths. Angelstone has fabricated the entire business."

"No, he did not." Prudence was beginning to get angry again.

"Yes, he did," Drucilla said. "I can see it all quite clearly. He obviously heard that those two unfortunate souls had departed this earth. He then created his own evidence implicating my son, claimed it was found at the scene, and presented it to Jeremy as proof. He intends to hold the so-called evidence over our heads as a threat."

"A very logical conclusion," Sebastian said approvingly. "You surprise me, Aunt. I would not have expected such clever reasoning from you. There is just one tiny flaw in it. I did not create the evidence. It was very real and it was indeed found at the scenes of the deaths. And there may be more evidence if there are more of these odd deaths."

"Nonsense. This whole thing is some sort of scheme designed solely to torment your family." Drucilla rose to her feet. "Even I, who know what sort of behavior to expect from your side of the family, cannot bring myself to believe that you would actually present your false evidence to the authorities."

"You think not?" Sebastian smiled. "But it would be so

very amusing, would it not? Just imagine what the papers would say if a Fleetwood went on trial for murder. Just imagine what the *ton* would say."

"*Sebastian.*" Prudence wanted to strangle him.

Drucilla looked at Sebastian. "I do not think you would allow an innocent young man to die simply in order to amuse yourself, sir. Not even you would stoop so low for the sake of revenge."

"What if he is not so innocent?" Sebastian asked softly.

Drucilla started for the door. "Do not be a complete ass, Angelstone. My son had no reason to kill those two men."

Prudence realized that Sebastian was about to argue. She sent him a warning look as she frantically yanked the bell rope to summon Flowers. "Good day to you, Mrs. Fleetwood. I know this has been an unpleasant experience. I want to assure you once again that Angelstone will take care of the situation."

"See to it." Drucilla peered at Prudence's gown as Flowers opened the door. "By the way, lavender is utterly atrocious on you, madam. It makes you look quite drab."

Prudence saw Sebastian take his booted feet down off the desk. "Thank you for your opinion, Mrs. Fleetwood," she said hurriedly. "I shall keep it in mind when I shop."

"And you had best get a new modiste." Drucilla swept toward the open door. "That gown you wore to the Hollington ball last night was positively indecent. Not at all suitable to your station. You were hanging out of it like a demirep dressed for the opera."

Sebastian was on his feet now. "Goddamn it, my wife can wear what she bloody well wants to wear."

"Angelstone, please," Prudence said, "last night you held the same opinion of my gown, if you will but recall."

"That's different." He strode swiftly across the room, his expression lethal as he bore down on his aunt. "Have you anything else to say about my wife's clothes, madam?"

"I do not know why you have taken offense, Angelstone."

Drucilla glanced back from the doorway. "That dress was a disgrace. One could almost see your wife's nipples. It was the sort of gown an actress would wear."

Sebastian's eyes gleamed like hellfire.

Prudence threw herself into his path. "Perhaps you had better take your leave, Mrs. Fleetwood," she called over her shoulder.

"I certainly have no reason to stay here." Drucilla went past Flowers and out into the hall. She seemed oblivious of the danger.

Flowers took one look at his master's face and discreetly pulled the door closed with a quick jerk.

"That damned bitch." Sebastian shook off Prudence's clinging hands. "I'll see her and her whole brood in hell. Jeremy can swing, for all I care. They can all swing."

"Sebastian, no, wait, you don't mean that. Stop." Prudence dashed ahead of him and flung herself in front of the door. She stood with her back to it, arms stretched out to form a barricade.

"Get out of my way, Prue."

"Listen to me. The reason she resents you so much is because she was in love with your father."

"Have you lost your wits? She hated my father."

"Because he married another. Don't you understand? She was in love with him and he ran off with another woman. Then you come along and claim the title. No wonder she has never forgiven him. Or you."

Sixteen

"*Be reasonable, Sebastian,*" *Prudence* panted as she braced herself in front of the door. "What would you do to her if you went after her? She's a woman and she's at least twenty years your senior. You cannot touch her and you know it."

"I am not going to put a hand on her." Sebastian was seething with anger. "I am merely going to inform the old bitch that I intend to cut off most of her income from the Angelstone fortune. I may also cut off the allowances of the rest of the family while I'm at it, for good measure."

"Because of her comments on my clothes?" Prudence looked at him in disbelief.

"She insulted you."

"She did not insult me. She was kind enough to offer her expert advice."

"*Advice?*"

"She is considered highly fashionable. Hester told me so. She knows what she's talking about," Prudence said.

"She insulted you to your face. In front of me, no less."

"Yes, well, as it happens, I agree with her about this particular gown." Prudence shook out the skirts of her dress. "I have never particularly cared for lavender. I only ordered this shade because I was told it was all the rage. And I did wonder about all these flounces. Your aunt is quite right. I shall have to change my modiste."

"Bloody hell." Sebastian heard the sound of Drucilla's carriage wheels in the street outside the front door. It was too late to go after her, even if he managed to peel Prudence out of the doorway. He turned on his heel and stalked back to his desk. "The woman is a bitch."

"I will not allow you to use a few petty remarks about my attire as an excuse to take your revenge, Sebastian."

"No?" He dropped into his chair and put his feet back on the desk.

"No." Prudence moved slowly away from the door. She pushed her spectacles higher on her nose, blinked several times, and swallowed hard. She focused intently on the fireplace. "I told you that I do not want to be used in that fashion. It is unworthy of you, my lord."

Sebastian eyed her with a sense of savage frustration. Then he frowned as she took a hankie out of her pocket and dabbed at the corner of her eye.

"Devil take it, Prue, are you crying again?"

"No, of course not." She shoved the hankie back into her pocket. "I just had something in my eye. I believe it's gone now."

Sebastian knew she was lying. "You don't understand," he said roughly. He did not look at her. He was afraid he would see more tears.

Prudence sniffed. "What don't I understand?"

Sebastian struggled to find a way to explain what he was only now just beginning to comprehend himself. "It was not revenge for the past that was on my mind a few minutes ago when I tried to go after my aunt."

"If you were not looking for an excuse to punish her because of what happened in the past, why were you so upset by her comments on my gowns?" Prudence's voice sounded steadier now.

Sebastian decided it was safe to look at her again. He did

so cautiously, hoping against hope that he would find her dry-eyed.

She was. She stood watching him solemnly, her hands clasped in front of her. Her eyes were clear and intent behind the lenses of her spectacles.

Sebastian was vastly relieved. "I was angry simply because of the insult to you."

"To me?" She looked surprised. "That's all there was to it?"

"She had no right to talk to you the way she did." Sebastian looked down as Lucifer vaulted lightly onto his lap. He started to stroke the cat.

Prudence smiled, looking vastly relieved herself. "It was nothing, Sebastian. Her small offense was certainly not worth the sort of retaliation you had in mind."

"I'm not so certain of that." Sebastian paused. "What was all that nonsense about her being in love with my father?"

"My intuition together with some of the things she said before you arrived lead me to believe that to be the case." Prudence sat down across from him. "It is very sad, is it not?"

"I cannot imagine my aunt being in love with anyone."

"I can." Prudence leaned back in her chair. "Now, then, let us resolve this issue of what to do about Jeremy once and for all. I don't want you keeping everyone, including me, on tenterhooks just because it amuses you to do so."

Sebastian toyed with the silver-plated wax jack that he used to melt sealing wax. "I'm still making inquiries."

"I rather suspected you were. You are going to help Jeremy, aren't you?"

"I suppose so."

"Do you mind if I ask why?"

"Does it matter?" Sebastian was thoroughly irritated by the question.

Prudence smiled apologetically. "I cannot help being curious. It is my nature, you know. Are you going to continue your investigation because you feel it is your responsibility to your family?"

"Hell and damnation. No."

Disappointment dampened her smile of expectation. "I see. Then is it because your own curiosity is aroused to such a degree that you cannot resist learning the answers?"

Sebastian shrugged. "That is no doubt part of it." He scratched Lucifer's ears. "But not the whole of it."

"Are you doing it because it amuses you to continue the investigation?"

"Goddamn it, Prue, I'm doing it because of you." Sebastian shoved aside the wax jack. "There. Does that satisfy you?"

She stared at him. "You're going to help Jeremy because I want you to do so?"

"Yes," he said. "I am in a mood to indulge my new bride. What is so unusual about that?"

She frowned. "I see. You're doing this because it amuses you to indulge me."

"As everyone knows, I am inclined to take pleasure in some very odd forms of amusement."

"But Sebastian—"

There was a discreet knock on the library door. Sebastian was profoundly relieved by the interruption. "Enter."

Flowers cautiously opened the door. He was carrying a small silver salver that held a folded note. His dour face relaxed somewhat when he saw that the lord and lady of the house had not come to blows.

"Your pardon, madam, m'lord. A message has arrived for Lady Angelstone."

"For me? I wonder who could have sent it." Prudence leaped to her feet and hurried across the room before Flowers could get to her.

Her impulsiveness caused Flowers to heave a long-suffering sigh. He handed over the note and backed out of the library.

Sebastian watched as Prudence tore open the seal. She charmed him, he thought. Or perhaps *enthralled* was the right word. Everything about her worked on him like a magic spell, driving out the cold. Her animated face, her feminine vitality, her passionate sincerity, all warmed him from the inside out.

"Good heavens, Sebastian." Prudence looked up from the note. Her face was tense with excitement. "It's from Lord Bloomfield."

"Bloomfield? What the devil does he want?" Sebastian put Lucifer aside. He got to his feet and swiftly crossed the room to snap the note out of Prudence's hand. He scanned the spidery handwriting.

> My Dear Lady Angelstone,
>
> *I desire to consult with you in your professional capacity. The matter is of an extremely urgent nature. It concerns recent occurrences involving spectral phenomena. I would call upon you but I suffer from nervous sickness and find it difficult to travel even short distances. Would it therefore be possible for you to call on me tomorrow morning at eleven? I shall be extremely grateful.*
>
> Yrs.
> C. H. Bloomfield.

"He refers to recent occurrences of spectral phenomena." Prudence's eyes narrowed with speculation. "Do you suppose he is referring to the deaths of the other two Princes of Virtue?"

"Bloomfield is said to be extremely odd, perhaps quite mad. It's possible that after learning of the deaths of Ring-cross and Oxenham he might have convinced himself that Lillian's ghost has come back."

"He wouldn't be the only one who believes that," Prudence reminded him. "That is exactly what that poor old man who called himself Halfwit Higgins believed."

Sebastian studied the note. "Either Bloomfield is as mad as rumor claims he is, or else this is a ruse to lure you to his house."

"A ruse? Why on earth would he want to lure me to his home?"

"I don't know. One thing is for certain: You are not going to go there alone."

"Of course I won't go alone. I shall take my maid."

"No," Sebastian said. "You will take me."

"I am not at all certain I wish to take you with me, my lord. This is my area of expertise, after all."

"God knows you have meddled enough in my end of the investigation." Sebastian refolded Bloomfield's note. "The least you can do is allow me to meddle a bit in your area of expertise. Now you must excuse me, my dear. I am off to my club."

"But we were in the middle of a very interesting conversation before Flowers brought in that note. I wish to continue it."

"Sorry, Prue. Told Sutton I'd meet him." Sebastian kissed her lightly on the mouth and then headed toward the door. "I also want to observe Curling to see if he appears as anxious as Whistlecroft says he is."

"Whistlecroft said he was anxious?" Prudence followed Sebastian out into the hall. "You never told me that."

"I have not had the opportunity. If you will recall, you were busy entertaining my aunt when I returned." Sebastian collected his hat and gloves from Flowers. "Do not wait up for me, madam. I shall be late getting home tonight."

"Angelstone, wait." Prudence cast a quick glance at Flowers, who looked as if he had gone deaf. She took a few quick steps forward and lowered her voice. "My lord, we

were in the midst of a rather important conversation a few
minutes ago. I should very much like to continue it."

"Later, perhaps."

"Angelstone, are you trying to avoid me?"

"Of course not, madam. Why would I wish to avoid
you?"

For the second time that day, Sebastian escaped through
the front door of his home. He breathed a sigh of relief when
he heard Flowers close it behind him.

The last thing he wanted to do was finish the conversation he and Prue had been involved in before Bloomfield's
note had arrived, he reflected. He was not entirely certain
why he was afraid to pursue it. He only knew that he did not
want Prudence asking any more pointed questions about
why he was continuing the investigation.

He had allowed her to think it amused him to indulge
her in the matter, but he knew that was not the whole truth.
The reality was that she had become so important to him
that she had acquired an incredible amount of power over
him. He would do almost anything to please her. That
knowledge worried him.

No one had wielded any real emotional power over him
since that cold, fog-shrouded dawn in the mountains of
Saragstan. He had built a barrier of ice against any possible
threat. The cold place he had constructed had protected him
until now, but he knew that somewhere inside him the thaw
had begun. The sunlight Prudence had brought into his life
was having an insidious effect.

Sebastian craved her warmth, yet he feared it. He knew
there was a very real possibility that if the ice inside him was
completely destroyed he might discover that there was nothing at all left to fill up the empty space.

Yet even as he feared the dark nothingness that might be
waiting where the cold was now, he ached to know what
Prudence was feeling for him. He needed to know if she was

drawn to him by anything deeper than mutual interests and shared passion.

He wondered if she would ever be able to love him.

Shortly before midnight Sebastian walked out of the card room of his club. He had spent the past three hours playing whist with several inebriated members in hopes of learning something useful about Ringcross and Oxenham. There had been gossip aplenty about the deaths, but no one spoke the word *murder*. No one mentioned The Princes of Virtue, either. All in all, it had been a wasted three hours.

"Ah, there you are, Angelstone." Garrick strolled across the room to join him in front of the hearth. "I was wondering if you were still about. Any luck in there?" He nodded in the direction of the card room.

"A bit." Sebastian shrugged. "I won a thousand pounds off Evans and probably could have won a great deal more, but I was too bored to continue the play. No challenge to the sport. The man was so cup-shot he could barely hold his cards."

It occurred to Sebastian that he had not told Garrick about his latest case. He realized that there were two reasons why he had not confided in his friend. The first was that the investigation involved a Fleetwood and he knew without asking that Prudence would not want him discussing it with outsiders. In truth he had no wish to do so. Like it or not, it was a family matter.

The second reason he had not talked to Garrick about the investigation was that he no longer needed a confidant. He had Prudence.

"Speaking of cup-shot," Garrick said quietly, "there comes Curling. He looks like he can barely stand upright."

Sebastian watched Curling walk through the door of the club with the overly careful stride of a very drunk man. "One does not often see him in that condition."

Garrick held out his hands to the fire. "The last time I

saw him in such a condition was about three months ago. We both wound up at a card table together after a long night of drinking. I cannot remember much about it, but I seem to recall that he was as drunk as I."

"I believe I remember the evening in question." Sebastian watched Curling lower himself gingerly into a chair. "It was the following morning that you informed me you intended to give up drinking for a while."

Garrick's mouth tightened. "I swear to you, Angelstone, I never again want to get into the condition I was in that night. I don't like the feeling of not being able to recall what I said or did. And I definitely do not want to ever again feel as ill as I did the next day."

"You say Curling was just as deep into his cups that night?"

"Yes. His coachman is responsible for getting us both home," Garrick said in a tone of self-disgust.

"If you will excuse me, I believe I will have a word with him."

"As you wish. I will see you later."

Sebastian walked to where Curling was sitting by himself. There was a fresh bottle of port on the table beside him. Curling had already poured himself a glass. He glanced up at Sebastian with bleary eyes.

"Oh, it's you, Angelstone. Join me?"

"Thank you." Sebastian sat down and poured a small measure of port into a glass. He stretched out his legs and made a pretense of settling in for a long session of companionable drinking. He took only a small swallow of the rich, sweet port.

"Here's to wedded bliss," Curling said in a slurred voice. He raised his glass and downed half the contents. "I trust your lady is still managing to amuse you?"

"Very much." Sebastian turned the glass between his hands.

"Tell me, is she still pursuing her little hobby?" Curling

held his own glass so tightly his knuckles were white. He stared down into the contents as if peering into bottomless depths.

"She is still interested in spectral phenomena. The hobby amuses her and I have no objection to it."

"Do you remember our conversation about ghosts at the castle?"

"Vaguely," Sebastian said.

"I believe I told you that I thought it might be rather entertaining to actually encounter one."

"I seem to recall you felt the experience would be an excellent tonic for the ennui you say plagues you."

"I was a fool." Curling rubbed the bridge of his nose. "You might be interested in knowing that I have since changed my mind."

"Why?" Sebastian smiled without any humor. "Have you actually encountered one?"

Curling slumped farther into his chair and gazed into the middle distance. "What would you say if I told you that I am beginning to wonder if ghosts truly do exist?"

"I would say you have consumed too many bottles of port tonight."

Curling nodded. "And you would no doubt be correct." He closed his eyes and leaned his head against the back of the armchair. "I cannot recall how many bottles I have had this evening."

"I'm sure they will all be accounted for on your bill."

Curling's mouth twisted. "No doubt."

There was silence for a moment. Sebastian made no attempt to end it. His instincts told him that Curling would do so soon enough. Unless the baron fell asleep first.

"Did you hear of Oxenham's death, by any chance, Angelstone?" Curling asked after a moment. He did not open his eyes.

"Yes."

"I knew him rather well," Curling said.

"Did you?"

"He and I were friends." Curling opened his eyes.

"I understand."

"Never thought he'd be the type to put a pistol to his head."

Sebastian examined his wine. "Perhaps he had suffered recent financial reverses. It is a common enough reason for suicide."

"No. I would have known if he had lost a great deal of money."

"Was he a gamester?"

"Only in a small way. He did not lose his fortune in a card game, if that's what you're implying." Curling took another large swallow of port. "Nor was he prone to fits of melancholia. I don't understand it."

"Is it important to you that you find a reason for his suicide?" Sebastian asked carefully.

"I think so." Curling's hand bunched into a fist. "Bloody hell, yes. I have to know what really happened."

"Why?" Sebastian asked gently.

"Because if it can happen to him and Ringcross, it can happen to all of us." Curling finished his port and tried to put the glass down on the table. He missed. Abandoning the effort, he kept the glass in his hand.

"I don't quite take your meaning, Curling. Perhaps you could explain."

But Curling was beyond making coherent explanations, even if he had been so inclined. His head sagged into the corner of the wing chair. "Hard to credit that after all this time . . ." The words trailed off. He closed his eyes once more. "God help us. Perhaps we deserve it."

Sebastian sat quietly for a few minutes, watching as Curling slid deep into a drunken slumber. He caught the glass just before it fell from the baron's hand.

·   ·   ·

Sebastian did not get back to his town house until after one o'clock in the morning. There was plenty of time for reflection as his coachman made his way home through the streets. The cold fog had once again slowed the normally brisk late-night traffic to a crawl.

Through the window Sebastian watched the lamps of other vehicles appear and disappear in the gray mist like so many lost ghosts trying to find their way to a final resting place.

When his carriage eventually drew to a halt in front of his door, Sebastian got out and went up the steps with an odd sense of foreboding. Flowers opened the door promptly.

"A bitter night, m'lord." Flowers held out his hand for Sebastian's hat, coat, and gloves.

"An interesting night. Is her ladyship home yet?"

"Lady Angelstone arrived home over an hour ago."

Prudence would be in bed by now, Sebastian thought. He did not know whether to be relieved or not. At least this way he would be able to avoid having to continue the uncomfortable conversation she had wanted to conclude earlier. On the other hand, if she was sound asleep he would not be able to tell her about Curling's unusual behavior.

"Put out the lamps and go to bed, Flowers." Sebastian untied his cravat as he started toward the stairs.

"I beg your pardon, sir." Flowers cleared his throat portentously. "Madam has not yet retired for the evening."

Sebastian paused, one foot on the bottom step. "I thought you said she was home."

"She is, sir. I believe she is waiting up for you in the library."

Sebastian smiled faintly. "I should have known."

Prudence was not the sort of female who would be easily deflected from her course. She had been attempting to lecture him all day. There was no reason to think she would give up simply because it was after one o'clock in the morning.

Sebastian took his boot off the bottom step and walked back across the hall. Flowers opened the library door without a word.

For a moment Sebastian did not see Prudence. The library was dimly lit by a small blaze on the hearth. Much of the room was in shadow.

A soft, welcoming meow greeted him. Sebastian glanced first at his desk and then at the sofa that faced the hearth. Lucifer was curled on the back. Beneath his august perch a pool of lavender silk spilled over the edge of the sofa and fell to the carpet.

Sebastian went forward until he could look down over the back of the sofa. Prudence had kicked off her lavender satin slippers. She lay curled up, sound asleep in front of the fire. Her spectacles were on the end table next to a book she had evidently been reading.

For a long while Sebastian simply stood there gazing down at her. The warm light of the flames turned her honey-colored hair to dark gold and created a tantalizing shadow between her graceful breasts.

She was wearing another of her new ridiculously low-cut gowns. He decided that lavender was no better a shade on her than violet had been. But he could not deny that the deep neckline was an erotic frame for her gently curved breasts.

Sebastian felt himself growing hard as he contemplated the woman he had married. Everything about her was just right, he thought. Her intelligence, her passion, her amusing taste in clothes, even her annoying tendency to lecture him on his responsibilities. All those factors went together to make up Prudence. He would not change a single thing.

He had lived with her such a short time, yet he could not imagine being married to anyone else. He wondered if Prudence ever imagined herself being married to another man. Underbrink, for example.

Sebastian's gut twisted at the thought. He knew he need

not fear that Prudence would be unfaithful. He was certain she would never betray him. Her bone-deep integrity would make it impossible for her to dishonor him in that way.

But he could not help wondering how deeply she cared for him.

Mutual interests and mutual passion were all very well as far as they went, he thought, but they were no longer enough. He needed more from Prudence. He wanted her to love him.

The extent of his need for her love made him uneasy, but he could no longer deny it.

As he watched, she stirred on the sofa, snuggling into a more comfortable position. The ornately ruffled skirts of her new gown rode higher on her legs, revealing her silk stockings.

Sebastian peeled off his coat and tossed it onto a chair. He removed his dangling cravat and threw it aside. As he walked around the sofa he started to unfasten his shirt.

He was unable to take his eyes off Prudence. His body was already taut with desire. When he had finished undoing his shirt, he went down on one knee and slid his hand beneath the skirts of her gown. He closed his fingers around her soft thigh. He leaned forward and kissed her slightly parted lips.

"Sebastian?" Prudence's lashes fluttered and then opened partway. She looked up at him with drowsy welcome. "Good evening, my lord. It's about time you got home."

"I'm glad you waited up for me."

"I wanted to talk to you."

"Later." He covered her mouth again with his own, deliberately deepening the kiss to cut off her sleepy protest. After a second or two, she did not try to argue. Instead she sighed softly and wrapped her arms around his neck.

Sebastian slid his hand up higher under the lavender skirts and found the lush, firm curves of her derriere. With his finger he lightly traced the cleft that separated the two soft mounds.

Prudence trembled at the unexpected caress, but she did not pull away. Sebastian drew his questing finger lower, down between her thighs. When he found her snug feminine passage he gently penetrated it and discovered that she was already becoming moist for him.

"Sebastian."

There was a sleepy passion in her voice that sent another surge of pulsating desire through Sebastian. He thrust his tongue into her mouth and reached down to unfasten his breeches.

God, how he wanted her, he thought. All he had to do was look at her and his blood began to heat. The craving deep within him seemed insatiable. He had to have her. To-night and forever.

The embers of the questions that had been burning within him all afternoon flared into fresh flames. *Do you love me, Prue? Can you love me in spite of the cold?*

He would not ask the questions, he promised himself. The answers did not matter. After all, she wanted him. There was no question of that. He could feel it. She did not even attempt to hide her physical reaction to him.

It was enough. It had to be enough.

Sebastian scooped Prudence lightly off the sofa. He lowered himself back onto the carpet and tumbled her down on top of him.

Her gossamer gown had not been designed to withstand such activity. Her graceful breasts sprang free. Sebastian caught them in his palms.

He looked up at Prudence, who was watching him through heavy-lidded eyes. He could feel his manhood throbbing beneath the tantalizing weight of her body.

Without a word, he reached down and opened his breeches. Lavender silk cascaded over his rigid shaft. He grabbed a fistful of Prudence's ruffled skirts and dragged them up to her waist.

"Sebastian?"

"Take me inside you," he said urgently. "Hurry, sweet. I cannot wait."

She fumbled briefly, then her fingers closed tightly around him. Sebastian sucked in his breath. She began to guide him into her, growing bolder as she gained confidence.

"That's it. Open for me," he whispered. "Let me inside. All the way inside."

Sebastian groaned when he felt the slick, damp heat of her. When her tight body slowly began to accommodate him, he sighed. She was so warm and he had been cold for so long.

He was just barely inside her now and he could not stand the torment any longer.

"Now, love. I have to have you now." Sebastian tightened his hands on her thighs and pulled her legs more securely around his hips.

Then he clasped her waist and pushed her downward as he thrust upward.

Prudence cried out softly as he forged into her tight, moist passage. She closed around him. Sebastian felt his whole body start to clench in response. He found the small, swollen bud between her legs and began to tease it with his fingers.

He felt Prudence hold herself still for a moment as she adjusted to the deep penetration. He closed his eyes as he felt the warmth of her body seeping into him.

Then she began to move slowly. She lifted herself again and again, gliding up and down his heavy shaft. Sebastian lifted his lashes and was enchanted by the sight of her in the firelight. Her head was tipped back. Her hair was heated gold by the flames of the fire. The line formed by her throat and breasts was the most elegantly sensual sight Sebastian had ever seen.

When she gently convulsed in her release Sebastian shuddered heavily and surrendered to the raging torrent that roared through him.

A long while later he finally stirred. Prudence was still lying on top of him. He opened his eyes and saw that she was drifting off to sleep.

The questions came back with such force that he could no longer push them aside.

"Prue?"

"Ummm?" Her voice was husky. She did not open her eyes.

"Why did you marry me?"

"Because I love you."

Sebastian went utterly still. His clever mind was, for once, in a complete muddle. He could not even think for a moment.

"Prue?"

There was no response. He realized that she had fallen sound asleep.

After a while, Sebastian eased himself out from under her, lifted her up off the carpet, and carried her upstairs.

He tucked her carefully under the covers and then he got in beside her. He lay against the pillows, his arm around Prudence, until the fog outside the window had turned a paler shade of gray.

The cold dawn had arrived. It was barely visible through the dark mist, but it was there.

Sebastian went to sleep.

$\mathcal{P}$rudence had difficulty concealing her astonishment the next morning when she and Sebastian were ushered into the hall of Lord Bloomfield's town house.

There was barely room to move. Crates and boxes were stacked everywhere. Old newspapers were piled high in the corners. A strange mix of items cluttered the hall. Books, globes, small statues, walking sticks, and hats filled all the available space.

The chaos continued up the staircase. Only half of each step was visible. The other half was taken up with a trunk, a crate, or a pile of old clothes.

There was a dank, airless feeling in the town house, Prudence thought, as if no one ever opened the windows. It was also quite dark. An oppressive sense of gloom pervaded the atmosphere of the dank hall.

She slanted a sidelong glance at Sebastian from beneath the large, sweeping brim of her new violet straw bonnet. She had to hold the trailing ends of a huge purple bow out of the way in order to see him clearly. He was examining the surroundings with carefully veiled curiosity.

"His lordship never throws nothin' away," the slatternly housekeeper announced with a touch of pride.

"I can see that," Sebastian said. "How long has Bloomfield lived here?"

"Oh, some time now. But he only started accumulatin' stuff about three years ago." The housekeeper chuckled hoarsely. "His old housekeeper quit about that time and I took the job. Far as I'm concerned the master can store anything he pleases so long as he pays me my wages."

The door to what once must have been the drawing room stood open. Prudence took a quick look inside and saw that the room was filled to overflowing with more crates, papers, and other assorted items. She noticed the drapes were pulled.

"Watch yer step." The housekeeper led the way along a narrow path through the hall. "We don't get many visitors here. His lordship likes his privacy." She chortled again. Her broad back heaved with the force of her mirth.

Prudence glanced again at Sebastian. She was uncertain of his mood today. He had talked of little else except this visit to Bloomfield since he had gotten up this morning. He had not said one word about last night.

For the life of her, Prudence still could not tell if her small confession of love had had any effect on him.

He had taken her by surprise last night. She had been half asleep when he had asked his startling question. She had been caught off guard, warm and relaxed from his lovemaking. She had responded without thinking.

Why did you marry me?

Because I love you.

Her first conscious thought upon awakening this morning was that she had made a serious error. All along she had been uneasy about how Sebastian would react to a declaration of love from her. His failure to mention it today had only made her all the more anxious.

She would have given a fortune to know what he was thinking. She could not tell if he was irritated or merely bored with the notion that his wife was in love with him.

It occurred to Prudence that she might not have said the words aloud. Relief went through her at the thought. Perhaps she had only dreamed that she had told Sebastian she loved him.

But surely if she had been dreaming, she would have also dreamed his answer. The sad reality was that either way, aloud or in her dreams, there had been no response from Sebastian. If he knew now that she loved him, he had apparently decided to politely overlook the fact.

Perhaps it did not amuse him.

"The master'll see ye in here." The housekeeper paused beside a flowerpot that contained the remains of a long-dead plant. She opened a door.

Prudence felt Sebastian's hand tighten briefly on her arm as if he instinctively wanted to draw her back. She peered into Bloomfield's library, wondering why it was filled with the gloom of night at this hour of the day.

Prudence glanced around and realized that all the drapes had been drawn. Only one lamp burned on the desk in the corner.

Behind the desk sat a massively obese man with bulging eyes, wild, unkempt hair, and a beard that reached halfway down his chest. There was enough gray in the beard to indicate that he was probably in his late forties. He was clasping his hands very tightly together on the desk. He did not rise.

"So you were good enough to come, Lady Angelstone. Wasn't sure if you would. Not many people come here anymore. Not like the old days."

"You're Bloomfield, I assume?" Sebastian asked.

"Aye, I'm Bloomfield." Shaggy brows snapped together above Bloomfield's pale eyes. "Expect you're Angelstone."

"Yes."

"Humph. I wanted to consult Lady Angelstone alone. Professional matter, y'know." Bloomfield appeared to be shivering although the room was very warm.

"I do not allow my wife to have private consultations

with her male clients. I'm certain you understand my position. If you wish to speak to her, you must do so in my presence."

"Bah. As if I'd try to take advantage of her," Bloomfield rasped. "I've no interest in women."

"What was it you wished to consult with me about, Lord Bloomfield?" Prudence picked her way around a pile of aging copies of the *Morning Post* and the *Gazette*. She found a chair in front of the desk and sat down. There was no point waiting to be asked, she thought. Bloomfield obviously did not concern himself with social niceties.

This morning she and Sebastian had discussed their strategy over breakfast. They had agreed that she would keep Bloomfield's attention focused on her as much as possible so that Sebastian would be free to observe the man and his surroundings. Now that she had seen the monumental clutter that filled the room, however, Prudence did not think Sebastian would be able to observe very much at all.

Bloomfield turned his staring eyes toward Prudence. "I hear you are an authority on spectral phenomena, Lady Angelstone."

"I have studied the subject at some length," she allowed modestly.

Bloomfield's expression turned crafty. "Have you ever actually encountered a ghost?"

For some reason the memory of the presence she thought she had detected in the black chamber at Curling Castle flashed into Prudence's mind. "There was one instance where I believed I might have discovered a genuine example of spectral phenomena," she said slowly. "But I was unable to find any evidence to support my conclusion."

Out of the corner of her eye she saw Sebastian glance at her in surprise.

"At least you're honest about it, not like some of the charlatans I've talked to. Claim to talk to ghosts regularly, they do. Tell me what they think I want to hear, just to get their fee."

"I do not charge a fee for my services," Prudence said.

"I heard. It's one of the reasons I sent you that message." A soft rustling noise interrupted Bloomfield. Instead of glancing about casually to see what had caused it, he jerked wildly around in his chair.

"What was that?" he demanded shrilly. "What made that sound?"

"A pile of papers slid to the floor." Sebastian smiled his cold smile and walked across the room to where several copies of the *Morning Post* were scattered on the carpet. "I'll restack them for you."

Bloomfield stared at the papers as if he had never seen them before. He shuddered. "Leave them."

"I don't mind putting them back." Sebastian bent down to scoop up the papers.

Bloomfield turned urgently to Prudence. "I shall make no bones about it, madam. I have reason to believe I am being pursued by a ghost. I demand to know if you can rid me of this thing before it murders me the way it has the others."

Prudence looked into Bloomfield's strange eyes and knew that he believed every word he was saying. She pushed the trailing end of the purple bow out the way again. "Do you know the identity of this ghost?"

"Oh, yes. Yes, I know her." Bloomfield removed a handkerchief from his pocket and mopped his sweating brow. "She said she would have her vengeance. Thus far she has killed two of us. Sooner or later she will come for me."

"What is the name of this ghost?" Prudence asked.

"Lillian." Bloomfield stared at the handkerchief in his hand. "She was a pretty little thing. But she wouldn't stop screaming. They finally had to close her mouth with a gag."

Prudence felt her palms dampen inside her gloves. She exchanged a brief look with Sebastian. He had finished restacking the newspapers and was standing quietly in the shadows. She was suddenly very glad that he had insisted upon accompanying her today.

She braced herself and turned back to Bloomfield.

"What did they do to Lillian?" Prudence asked. She did not really want to hear the answer, but she knew she had to lead Bloomfield through the tale step by step if anything was to be accomplished.

Bloomfield gazed into the flaring lamp, lost in his own private world. "Just wanted to have some sport with the wench. She was nothing but a tavern girl. It wasn't as if we hadn't paid for our fun. But she made such a fuss. Wouldn't stop screaming."

Prudence closed her gloved fingers into small fists. "Why did she scream?"

"Don't know. None of the other girls ever did." Bloomfield's hands were shaking. "You'd have thought she was gently bred, the way she carried on. I suggested we get another, more cooperative little cyprian. But Curling wanted this one. We finally got her into the carriage. Finally got the gag on her." Bloomfield's face relaxed. "That stopped the screams."

Prudence set her teeth against the rage that poured through her. "Where did you take her?"

"To Curling Castle. Curling has a room for that sort of sport. Created it especially for The Princes of Virtue." Bloomfield glanced at her as if he'd momentarily forgotten she was there. He scowled. "That was the name of our club. We liked the irony of it, you see."

"I see." Prudence wanted to go for his throat.

Sebastian must have sensed the fury that was boiling like a sickness in her stomach. He moved to stand directly behind her. She felt his hand settle on her shoulder.

"Do The Princes of Virtue still use that room for their private entertainment?" Sebastian asked matter-of-factly, as if such lechery were the norm for high-ranking gentlemen.

"What?" Bloomfield appeared briefly confused. "No, no. That's all over now. We never met again after that night. She ruined everything. *Everything,* damn her soul."

"How did she ruin things?" Prudence managed to ask in a relatively calm tone.

"Killed herself." Bloomfield shuddered. Then he went back to staring into the heart of the lamp.

Prudence fought for her self-control. Her task was to pry the answers from Bloomfield, not tell him what she thought of him. "Did she kill herself because of what you did to her?"

"Curling had her first." Bloomfield spoke very softly. "There was blood. Didn't expect that, you know. Curling was pleased. Said he'd gotten his money's worth. Then Ringcross and Oxenham got on top of her."

"What about you?" Prudence asked.

"By the time it was my turn, the ropes had loosened. She got free of them and ran to the window. Curling tried to grab her, but he slipped and fell. The robes, you see. We all wore black robes. The others were too drunk to catch her in time."

Prudence remembered a vague dream of black drapes blowing in front of a window that opened onto darkness. "Lillian jumped out the window?"

"She stood on the sill for a second. Then she tore the gag out of her mouth and looked back at us. I will never forget her eyes as she cursed us. Never, as long as I live." Bloomfield slammed his fist onto the desk. "Her eyes have haunted me for three damned years."

Prudence choked on her rage. For a few seconds she literally could not speak. It was Sebastian who quietly took over the questioning.

"What did she say when she cursed you?" he asked without any sign of emotion in his tone. "What were Lillian's exact words, Bloomfield?"

"You will pay. As God is my witness, I swear you will pay. There will be justice." Bloomfield looked down at his shaking

hands. "Then she leaped to the stones below. Broke her neck."

"What did you do then?" Sebastian asked.

"Curling said we had to get rid of the body. Make it appear that she had drowned. He had us wrap her up in a blanket and take her to a stream." Bloomfield frowned. "She was so light. Didn't weigh much at all."

Prudence straightened her shoulders and told herself that she had to hold up her end of the investigation no matter how unpleasant it was. "And now you believe that Lillian has come back to claim her vengeance."

Bloomfield's eyes burned with a barely controlled terror. "It's not fair. She was just a tavern wench. We just wanted a bit of sport."

"Tavern wenches have feelings just like other women," Prudence said tightly. "What right did you have to force her into that carriage and carry her away like that?" She broke off with a small gasp as Sebastian's fingers bit into her shoulder.

But she saw at once that there was no need to worry about having interrupted Bloomfield's story. He was staring into the lamp again, pondering some vision that only he could see.

"It's all so unfair," he muttered. "The wench has already had her vengeance on me. Why does she want to kill me? Hasn't she done enough?"

Prudence leaned forward. "What do you mean? What vengeance has Lillian taken against you?"

"I have not had a woman since that night," Bloomfield howled. Despair was carved on his face. He did not appear to see Prudence at all now. He was still looking into the vision that he saw in the lamplight. "I can no longer even have a woman. *She destroyed my manhood that night.*"

Prudence started to tell him it served him right if he had indeed been impotent for the past three years. But Sebastian's hand tightened again on her shoulder, silencing her.

"And now you think she is going to kill you?" Sebastian prodded quietly.

"She has already killed Oxenham and Ringcross." Bloomfield clasped his shaking hands together. "I know they say that Ringcross's death was an accident and that Oxenham committed suicide, but it's not true. I got this note, you see."

He picked up a small piece of foolscap and handed it to Prudence. She read the brief message.

Lillian will be avenged.

"Where did you get this?" Prudence asked.

"I found it lying on my desk yesterday. *She* must have put it there. I want you to make her go away and leave me alone," Bloomfield said.

"How, precisely, do you expect me to do that?" Prudence asked.

"Contact her. Tell her I have paid for my part in what happened."

Prudence looked at him. "It might be difficult to convince her that she should be satisfied. After all, you are still alive and she is dead."

"It's not fair," Bloomfield said again. "I have paid for what happened. I never even took the girl."

"But you watched while the others did," Prudence said. "And you would have taken your turn if Lillian had not leaped to her death."

"I do not deserve to be hounded to my death by her ghost. I have paid, I tell you."

"I think," Sebastian said very coolly, "that you would be wise to leave Town for a while."

"What good would that do?" Bloomfield swung his frightened eyes toward Sebastian. "She is a ghost. She has already found Ringcross and Oxenham. She will find me regardless of where I go."

Prudence glanced at Sebastian. Apparently he wanted

Bloomfield to leave London. She pursed her lips in a considering manner. "It is my professional opinion that there is an excellent chance you will escape her notice for a while if you leave Town today."

"Tell no one where you are going," Sebastian said. "Absolutely no one. Not even your housekeeper."

Bloomfield shook his head in a helpless gesture. "You don't understand. I want Lady Angelstone to deal with Lillian's ghost. Tell her she has already had her vengeance."

"I shall need time to reflect upon the proper way to contact her," Prudence said. "These things require investigation and planning. Angelstone is right. It would be best if you left Town for a while."

"But I don't care to travel," Bloomfield whined. "I rarely leave the house. It makes me very uneasy. I suffer from the nervous sickness, you know."

"I have the distinct impression that if you do not leave this house as soon as possible," Sebastian said, "you will find yourself suffering from something far more debilitating than the nervous sickness."

Bloomfield's eyes widened. "She will come for me next, won't she?"

"Very likely," Sebastian said easily.

"I believe that Angelstone is probably quite right," Prudence said briskly. "I cannot positively guarantee your safety anywhere, of course. After all, we're talking about a ghost. But I am persuaded that if you leave Town at once and tell absolutely no one where you're going, I may be able to accomplish something useful."

"At the very least we shall purchase a little time for you, Bloomfield," Sebastian said. "And I have the impression that time is of the essence."

Bloomfield looked at Prudence. "You'll find a way to contact Lillian's ghost while I'm gone? You'll talk to her?"

"If I encounter her, I shall definitely talk to her about the matter," Prudence said.

"Very well." Bloomfield heaved himself wearily to his feet. "I shall make arrangements to leave at once. I am grateful to you, Lady Angelstone. I did not know where else to turn. I began to worry after Ringcross fell from the tower room. But when I learned that Oxenham had died, too, I truly began to fear for my life."

"It was very wise of you to call upon my wife for advice," Sebastian said. "She is quite expert at this sort of thing."

"Nothing has been the same since that terrible night," Bloomfield whispered. "Nothing at all."

Sebastian took Prudence's arm. "I think we had best be off, my dear. You have work to do and I'm certain Bloomfield wants to be on his way as quickly as possible."

Prudence did not say a word as Sebastian led her through the maze of clutter that filled the shadowed library. She glanced back once when they reached the door.

Bloomfield was standing behind his desk, his inner terrors easily visible in his staring eyes. He was gazing down into the lamp.

Sebastian and Prudence went swiftly along the hall to the door. Neither was inclined to wait for the housekeeper. Sebastian opened the door and swept Prudence out into the cold sunshine.

"Tell me, my dear," Sebastian asked softly as he handed her up into the waiting carriage, "just what will you say to Lillian's ghost if you do manage to speak with her?"

Prudence gripped her reticule fiercely in her lap. "I shall tell her that I think she has every right to wreak vengeance on The Princes of Virtue. I shall wish her luck in the endeavor. And I shall tell her that Jeremy loved her very much and that he, too, intends that she be avenged."

"Yes." Sebastian smiled his most chilling smile as he sat down across from her. "I think that would be a very suitable message to give her. But somehow I do not think that Lillian's ghost is behind the deaths of Ringcross and Oxenham."

Prudence took a deep, calming breath. "I gathered that when you suggested Bloomfield leave Town. Was that for his own protection, Sebastian? Did you want him to disappear for a time so that he will not fall prey to the person who killed Ringcross and Oxenham? Why do you not warn Curling, also?"

"I do not particularly care if either Bloomfield or Curling gets himself killed. From the sound of things, all The Princes of Virtue deserve to die under Lillian's curse. But I wanted Bloomfield out of the way so that I could search that mausoleum of his at my leisure."

That statement wrenched Prudence's attention away from her anger and focused it back on the investigation. "You're going to search his house?"

"The library, at any rate." Sebastian lounged back against the cushions. "Bloomfield has apparently thrown almost nothing away for the past three years since Lillian's death. It should prove interesting to go through the contents of his desk."

"I shall accompany you."

"Now, Prue—"

"In my professional capacity, of course." She pushed the dangling purple ribbon aside and gave him a determined look. "I must insist, Sebastian. After all, I have given my word to Lord Bloomfield that I will attempt to contact Lillian's ghost."

"I don't think it wise."

"It will be perfectly safe, my lord. If we are caught I shall merely explain that I am carrying out an investigation of spectral phenomena for my client."

Sebastian's eyes gleamed. "Very well, my dear. If we are apprehended, I shall let you handle all the explanations. But bear in mind that the last time you did so, you wound up engaged to me."

"I am hardly likely to forget that, my lord."

Prudence wished very badly that she knew whether or not he had heard her confession of love last night.

At one o'clock that morning Sebastian lit the lamp on Bloomfield's desk, removed the length of wire he had tucked into his sleeve, and inserted it into the lock.

"Do you always carry that with you?" Prudence asked.

"Always."

Getting into the house had proved relatively simple. Bloomfield's locks were large and forbidding in appearance but not particularly complicated. Sebastian had opened them effortlessly and Prudence had been suitably admiring of his talents.

"This place is even worse at night than it is during the day," Prudence whispered. She stood nearby, peering over Sebastian's shoulder as he worked on the desk lock. "I don't know how Bloomfield can stand to live in such a dark, cluttered house. It would drive me mad."

Sebastian did not look up from his work. "He already is mad, in case you failed to notice."

"Hardly. He is a very strange man."

"At least we have the house to ourselves. Bloomfield certainly did not delay leaving Town today. He actually is afraid of Lillian's ghost." Sebastian felt something give inside the lock. Satisfaction coursed through him. "Ah, yes, love. That's it. Open for me. Easy, now. Let me inside. Beautiful."

Prudence gave a soft, annoyed exclamation. "Are you aware that you tend to talk to locks the same way you talk to me when we are making love?"

"Naturally. You and a fine, clever lock have much in common. You are both endlessly amusing."

"Sebastian, sometimes you are impossible."

"Thank you. I do try." Sebastian opened the first drawer and surveyed the crammed interior. "Damnation. This is going to take some time."

Prudence's new purple cloak drifted against Sebastian's

boots as she leaned closer. "Bloomfield appears to have filed his business papers in a somewhat haphazard fashion."

"Only to be expected, I suppose. Here, you take this batch." Sebastian handed her a fistful of papers. "I'll go through these." He removed three journals from the drawer.

"What am I to look for?"

"I'm not certain. Anything that makes reference to Ringcross, Oxenham, or Curling would definitely be of interest. Also anything that mentions a large sum of money. Preferably both."

Prudence glanced up curiously. "I don't understand."

"It is very simple, my dear. There are only a handful of motives for murder. Revenge, greed, and madness. I do not believe we are dealing with a madman."

"We have already decided revenge is a definite possibility."

"Yes, but the only one around who appears to have a reason for vengeance, aside from our ghost, is Jeremy. If you are right in thinking that he knew nothing about the deaths of Ringcross and Oxenham, then we must examine the third possible motive."

Lamplight glittered on the lenses of Prudence's spectacles. "Greed?"

"Precisely."

"What if we find nothing to indicate that there is such a motive?"

Sebastian opened the first journal. "Then we must reconsider the possibilities of revenge or madness."

Prudence chewed gently on her lower lip. "What are you going to do if you discover that Jeremy is behind the murders?"

Sebastian ran his finger down a list of figures. "I shall take him aside and give him a very stern lecture."

Prudence blinked in astonishment. "A lecture on the evils of committing murder?"

"No. A lecture on the evils of leaving behind evidence

that can identify him as the killer. If Jeremy is bent on vengeance, he will need to become a bit more efficient and a little less melodramatic about the business."

Prudence smiled warmly. "Does this mean you have decided you do not wish to see him arrested?"

"I have concluded that it would not be particularly amusing."

It was after two before Sebastian finally discovered what he had begun to suspect he might find. The familiar surge of satisfaction flashed through his veins. His instincts told him that he had found the key to the puzzle.

"Ah, yes," he said. "This must be it."

"What is it?" Prudence put down the pile of old receipts she had been perusing.

Sebastian smiled as he scanned the business agreement he had turned up in the back of the bottom drawer. "A motive that accounts quite nicely for the deaths of Ringcross and Oxenham. It would also account for Bloomfield's demise, should that occur."

"Not madness or revenge?"

"No, the simplest of all." Sebastian refolded the document. "Greed."

Eighteen

en minutes later Sebastian got into the carriage behind Prudence. He closed the curtains as the vehicle rolled forward. Then he lit the lamp and unfolded the document he had discovered in Bloomfield's desk.

Prudence sat across from him, huddled deep into her cloak. She watched with keen anticipation as he studied the papers. "Explain it to me at once, Sebastian. I am consumed with curiosity."

He looked up briefly, frowning in concentration. Then he saw the look in Prudence's eyes and he smiled. She was enjoying this as much as he was. It struck him again that he had been incredibly fortunate in his choice of brides. No one else except his unusual Prudence would be able to understand how he felt at this moment, let alone share that moment with him.

And she loved him.

"Well, Sebastian? Do not keep me in suspense."

He returned his attention to the document. "This is a business agreement formed for purposes of making investments in shipping ventures." He smiled. "The principals of the firm are Ringcross, Oxenham, Bloomfield, and Curling."

Prudence gave him a quizzical look. "The Princes of Virtue were in business together?"

"Precisely. This agreement is dated three and a half years ago. They sold stock in the company and invested the money in a series of ventures."

"What has that got to do with the deaths of Oxenham and Ringcross?"

Sebastian scanned the fine legal handwriting, searching for details. "According to this agreement, if any one of the principals dies, the others would assume his portion of the company." He looked up. "Following that logic, if three out of the four were to perish, then the last of the four would inherit the company."

Prudence understood at once. Her eyes widened as she leaped to the obvious conclusion. "Curling."

"Yes." Sebastian smiled with cold satisfaction. "Conceivably it could be Bloomfield, but I rather think it has to be Curling. Bloomfield is obviously too disordered in his mind to concoct, let alone carry out, this elaborate scheme."

"You believe Lord Curling has already killed two of his friends?"

"I think it highly likely. Bloomfield was no doubt next on his list."

Prudence tapped one gloved finger thoughtfully on the seat beside her. "The first two deaths have raised no questions. Everyone assumed Ringcross's fall was an accident and that Oxenham's death was a suicide. It would have been easy to make Bloomfield appear a suicide also. Everyone already considers him mad. Why go to the trouble of trying to implicate Jeremy as the murderer?"

"Because someone might have eventually questioned the convenient deaths of three men who were in business with a fourth," Sebastian said. "Especially when the fourth became extremely wealthy by taking complete control of the company."

"So Curling, if he is the one behind the murders, decided to take precautions?"

"That's the logical assumption. He protected himself by

trying to arrange for someone else to appear guilty. He needed to produce a motive for that other person, however."

"Curling must have discovered that Jeremy was in love with Lillian at one time," Prudence said. "He realized your cousin had the perfect motive for murdering The Princes of Virtue."

"He set Bow Street to investigate so that he would appear entirely innocent when it all came to light. Who would suspect the man who had commissioned the investigation?" Sebastian thought about Curling's behavior the previous night. "Especially when that man has made it increasingly clear that he fears for his own life."

Prudence tugged her cloak more closely around herself. Her face was shadowed by the hood. "If we're right in assuming Curling is the killer, then there is another interesting aspect of this investigation to be considered."

"What is that?"

"We cannot overlook the fact that you were the one who made the inquiries for Whistlecroft. Do you not find it is a rather extraordinary coincidence that the person who conducted the investigation happened upon evidence at the scene of the deaths that implicates a member of his own family?"

Sebastian smiled with slow appreciation. "My dear, there are occasions when I do not know quite which it is that I admire most about you: your cleverness or your passionate response to me in bed."

"*Sebastian.*"

"I know, it is a difficult choice. Fortunately for me, I do not have to decide between the two. I am able to enjoy both. Now, then, you are quite correct. We cannot assume that my involvement in this particular investigation was entirely a coincidence."

"How do you suppose Curling knew about your hobby?"

"If he was able to learn of Jeremy's affection for Lillian, then he must have excellent sources of information."

Prudence frowned. "But who could have informed him?"

Sebastian shrugged. "Whistlecroft, no doubt. Although why he gave Curling the information defeats me. Whistlecroft has always been even more eager than I to keep my hobby a secret. He prefers to take full credit for the investigations so that he can collect the rewards."

"Well, I suppose it does not matter how Curling learned of your interest in conducting investigations. The point is he did." Prudence shook her head in disgust. "He left evidence implicating poor Jeremy at the scenes of the deaths, trusting that you would find it and identify it."

"Which I did."

"I cannot imagine what made Curling believe that you would be eager to see Jeremy arrested for murder."

"Everyone knows I have no love for my relatives," Sebastian said.

"Yes, but Curling should have realized that when all is said and done, family is family. He should have understood that you would protect Jeremy."

Sebastian arched a brow. "My dear, your naïveté alarms me at times. Curling was far more pragmatic than you in his logic. He knew my opinion of the rest of the Fleetwoods and he had every reason to suspect I would not lift a finger to protect any of them."

Prudence glowered at him. "Do not tease me anymore about this matter, my lord. You know very well that you would never have let Jeremy hang."

Sebastian smiled at her. "Your boundless faith in my character never fails to amuse me, my dear."

Prudence gave him a quelling frown. "What are we going to do now? We cannot prove that Curling is behind the murders. So far all we have accomplished is to remove the evidence against Jeremy before it fell into the hands of the authorities. Next time we might not be so fortunate."

"I think it is time I had another talk with my cousin," Sebastian said.

"Right now?"

"I cannot envision a better time," Sebastian said. "It is nearly three. He will no doubt be at his favorite club."

"I shall come with you," Prudence said eagerly.

"You will not come with me," Sebastian said evenly. "You know damn well that you cannot enter a gentlemen's club."

"I am aware of that." Prudence smiled serenely. "I shall wait in the carriage with you until Jeremy leaves the club."

"Bloody hell," Sebastian muttered. But there was no real heat in the words. He was learning to recognize a losing battle when he saw one.

They did not have to wait very long in the fog outside the St. James Street club before Jeremy emerged. Sebastian watched his cousin descend the steps and start toward a waiting hackney. He noted with satisfaction that Jeremy did not appear unsteady in his walk.

Sebastian opened the carriage door just as Jeremy went past. "A word with you, Cousin."

"What the devil?" Startled, Jeremy looked into the darkened carriage. His glance went from Sebastian to Prudence. "What are you doing here, Lady Angelstone?"

She smiled reassuringly at him. "We wanted to speak with you about a very urgent matter, Mr. Fleetwood. Would you mind joining us?"

Jeremy hesitated, clearly torn between good manners and a distinct distaste for Sebastian's presence. Good manners won.

"Very well." He got into the carriage and sat down. "I trust this will not take long. I am on my way home. It's been a long night and I plan to attend a boxing match in the morning."

"It concerns Lillian," Sebastian said quietly. He closed the carriage door.

"Lillian?" Jeremy stared at him as the carriage rumbled forward. "Haven't you already said enough on that subject?"

"I have recently learned how she died," Sebastian said. "I thought you should know the truth."

"I don't understand. I told you that Lillian drowned."

Prudence touched Jeremy's arm. "Listen to Angelstone, Mr. Fleetwood. Your beloved Lillian did not drown. She was driven to her death by four terrible men."

Jeremy gazed at her in astonishment. "I don't understand," he said again.

"Neither did we until tonight." Sebastian relit the carriage lamp. He leaned back into the corner of the seat and quietly told Jeremy the entire tale, including his own involvement in the investigation.

It was just as well he had brought Prudence along, he reflected when he was finished. Jeremy might not have believed him otherwise. But Prudence's presence and her air of genuine concern lent credibility to the story. Jeremy looked at her several times for confirmation. Each time Prudence nodded soberly.

"It's true, Mr. Fleetwood," she said at last. "All of it. I myself helped question Bloomfield."

"And Curling is the one who is trying to implicate you in the deaths of Ringcross and Oxenham," Sebastian added. "He deliberately made certain that I would find the evidence that pointed to you."

Jeremy's mouth tightened. "Because he thought that you would seize the opportunity of seeing me arrested for murder."

"Yes."

"You say you occasionally involve yourself in investigations such as this?" Jeremy looked at Sebastian.

"Yes."

"But why in God's name would you choose to do so?" Sebastian shrugged. "It amuses me."

Prudence pushed the hood of her cloak back slightly.

"Curling miscalculated badly, of course. He apparently did not realize that as the head of the family, Sebastian would not hesitate to protect you."

"I beg your pardon, Lady Angelstone," Jeremy said tightly, "but I find that as difficult to believe as Curling obviously does."

"Nonsense," Prudence said. "I told you the other day that there is no question of where Sebastian's ultimate loyalty lies."

Sebastian regarded her with a hooded gaze. "There is no necessity to go into that right now, madam."

Jeremy glanced at him and then looked back at Prudence. "Did those four men really abuse my poor Lillian and drive her to her death?"

Prudence nodded sadly. "I do not think there is any question about it. But we will never be able to prove it."

Jeremy's eyes narrowed. "I do not care whether or not you can prove it, Lady Angelstone, as long as you are certain of the facts."

"As certain as we can be." Prudence looked at Sebastian. "Is that not right, sir?"

"I believe Bloomfield's tale." Sebastian watched as Jeremy's gloved hand curled into a fist. "But I think it will be possible to get confirmation."

Jeremy's head turned swiftly toward him. "From whom?"

"From Curling himself," Sebastian said slowly. He met Jeremy's eyes. "I suggest that you and I talk to him."

Jeremy hesitated, searching Sebastian's face. Then he jerked his chin up abruptly. "By God, yes."

"It is obviously time to make our plans." Prudence glanced expectantly at Sebastian. "What shall we do first?"

"First, my dear, Jeremy and I are going to take you home."

"Oh, no, my lord, you cannot leave me out of this."

Jeremy frowned. "You cannot possibly come with us,

Lady Angelstone. This is men's business. Isn't that right, Angelstone?"

"Yes," Sebastian said, surprised by the vehemence in Jeremy's voice. "Quite right."

He braced himself as Prudence opened her mouth to argue. This time he would stand his ground, he told himself.

But to his astonishment, she closed her mouth again without saying a word.

It was nearly four in the morning before Sebastian finally found himself alone in the carriage with Jeremy. They were headed for Curling's house. Prudence had maintained her unaccustomed silence all the way home, where Sebastian had quickly escorted her inside and sent her upstairs to bed. He knew she would be waiting up for explanations when he got home.

"I shall challenge Curling, of course," Jeremy burst out as soon as the carriage was in motion.

"Will you?"

"It is all I can do to avenge poor Lillian. When I think of what she must have gone through that night, my blood boils."

"Risking your neck in a duel will not bring her back," Sebastian said softly.

Jeremy's eyes glittered. "I intend to kill him."

"Are you a creditable shot?"

"I have practiced for some time at Manton's gallery."

Sebastian smiled faintly. "Is your mama aware of your interest in the sport?"

Jeremy shifted uncomfortably. "No, 'course not. She wouldn't approve."

Sebastian listened to the clatter of the horses' hooves on the paving stones. "Tell me, Cousin, have you ever actually engaged in a duel?"

"Well, no, but I'm certain I can hit my target."

"Putting a bullet in a man who is aiming a pistol at your

heart is not quite the same as putting a bullet in a target at Manton's," Sebastian said quietly. "It requires ice, not fire, in one's veins. You are too hot-blooded for dueling."

Jeremy scowled at him. "There are rumors that you have fought one or two duels in your time."

Sebastian gave him a bland look. "Dueling is illegal."

Jeremy's eyes slid awkwardly away from Sebastian's face. "Yes, sir, I know." He cleared his throat. "You are accounted something of a legend, sir, as I'm certain you are well aware. You are a man of the world. I would greatly appreciate it if you would give me some hints on the subject of conducting a duel."

"Your mama would not approve."

"Hang my mama." Jeremy's eyes were suddenly fierce. "It's none of her affair. I have to do this for Lillian. Don't you understand? I loved her."

Jeremy meant every word, Sebastian thought. He made his own decision. "Very well. If it comes to a duel, I shall act as one of your seconds."

Jeremy was taken aback. "You will?"

"Yes."

"I say, Angelstone." Jeremy stared at him in astonishment. "That's very good of you, sir. I appreciate it."

"You do realize that if you get yourself killed your mama will blame me. And so will my wife." Sebastian smiled faintly. "I can deal with your mama, but I do not like to contemplate my future if Lady Angelstone concludes that I did nothing to prevent you from getting yourself shot."

"I do not intend to get myself shot," Jeremy said. "The goal is to put a bullet in Curling."

"No, Cousin," Sebastian said softly. "The goal is to destroy Curling. Challenging him to a duel is a tactic of last resort."

"Why?"

"The results would be far too uncertain. He might very well survive, for example, even if you do lodge a bullet in him. Many men do. Trust me when I tell you that there are other, more reliable methods for accomplishing your goal."

Jeremy watched him as the carriage rumbled down the street. "How do you suggest I go about destroying Curling?"

Sebastian explained the plan he had been formulating since the moment he had discovered the business agreement that bound The Princes of Virtue.

They arrived at Curling's town house an hour before dawn. The fog was thickening rapidly.

Curling's butler, disheveled and angry at having been summoned from his bed at such an early hour, answered the door. He sighed at the sight of two gentlemen standing on the doorstep.

"Inform your master that Angelstone wishes to see him at once," Sebastian said.

"His lordship only got in an hour ago," the butler said. "He won't like being awakened."

Sebastian smiled. "I do not particularly care if he likes it or not."

The butler eyed Sebastian's smile. "Very well, m'lord. If you and your gentleman friend will step inside, I'll see that his lordship is informed of your presence." He stalked away.

Sebastian looked at Jeremy, who was rigid with anger and tension. "Calm yourself, Jeremy. Or at any rate, try to give the appearance of being calm. Nothing does more to unsettle the nerves of one's foe than to appear unutterably amused or even bored."

"You should know," Jeremy said dryly. "You're a master at the art. I'd give a fortune to know how you manage to act so damnably amused or excruciatingly bored in a situation such as this."

"There is acting talent on my side of the family, if you will recall."

Jeremy slid him an assessing glance. "There are many who say you are cold-blooded by nature."

Sebastian thought of Prudence waiting at home. "And one who says I am not."

The sound of voices at the top of the stairs caught Jeremy's attention. "Here comes Curling."

"You will allow me to conduct this interview," Sebastian said quietly.

"Yes, sir."

Curling, garbed in a silver gray dressing gown, ran a hand through his hair as he descended the staircase. He had a vaguely irritated expression on his face, suitable to a man who has been rudely awakened, but his eyes were alert and watchful.

"What the devil do you want at this ungodly hour, Angelstone?" He gave Jeremy an unreadable glance. "I do hope this won't take long."

"Not long at all," Sebastian assured him. "Shall we go into the library?"

Curling shrugged and led the way into the small library that opened off the hall. He casually motioned toward two chairs as he went to the brandy table. "Will you join me in a glass?"

"No," Sebastian said. He sat down in an armchair and hooked one booted foot over his knee in a casual manner.

"No," Jeremy said in the same cold tone. He stole a quick glance at Sebastian and then he, too, sat down. He was unable to achieve the same degree of ennui in his manner, but it was obvious he was making the effort.

"As you wish." Curling poured himself a glass of brandy and turned to face them with a shuttered gaze. "Well? What is so important that you felt you must call upon me at this hour?"

"We are here to discuss the recent deaths of two of your business associates," Sebastian said.

"Business associates?"

"Ringcross and Oxenham."

Curling swallowed brandy. "What makes you think they're business associates of mine?"

Sebastian smiled. "A document I found in Bloomfield's desk. It is obvious by the terms of the agreement that you are now a great deal more wealthy than you were a few days ago. And if you succeed in finding and murdering Bloomfield, you will be even richer."

Curling went very still. "Good lord, man. Are you accusing me of murdering my business partners?"

"Yes," Sebastian said. "I am."

"That's nonsense." Curling shot a narrow glance at Jeremy. "Ringcross died in a fall and Oxenham committed suicide."

"Give it up," Sebastian said. "I know everything, including how you attempted to implicate my cousin. I would be interested to learn how you came to know that I occasionally conduct investigations for Bow Street, but that is neither here nor there."

"You are mad," Curling snapped.

"No. And neither is Bloomfield. At least not entirely. He told me about what The Princes of Virtue did to Lillian."

Jeremy's hands tightened around the arms of his chair. "You kidnapped her. Raped her. Drove her to her death."

Curling turned on him with glittering eyes. "She was nothing but a tavern whore. Her uncle sold her to us for the night. We paid quite well for her services."

"She was not a prostitute," Jeremy shouted. "She would never have agreed to go with you. You kidnapped her, you bastard."

"Rubbish." Curling's mouth curved in contempt. "She was nothing but a cheap little doxy with rather pretty legs."

"You do not even deny it?" Jeremy asked in disbelief.

"Why should I?" Curling asked. "I know a nice bit o' muslin when I see one. And as I said, I paid well for her."

"Damn you." Jeremy was half out of his chair.

"Sit down," Sebastian said softly.

Jeremy hesitated and then dropped reluctantly back into the chair. "You raped her," he accused Curling.

Curling lifted one shoulder in casual dismissal. "I'll admit that I took a turn on her. She wasn't very skilled, if you want to know the truth. The old man assured us she was a virgin and I do believe he was right."

Jeremy stared at him with hatred. "You son of a bitch."

Curling was amused. "You actually thought yourself in love with her, didn't you?"

"Yes, I loved her, damn you."

"And that's why you killed Ringcross and Oxenham, isn't it?" Curling concluded coolly. "You thought you were avenging your little tavern doxy."

"I did not kill them," Jeremy whispered. "Because I did not know about their guilt. But I fully intend to see you destroyed for what you did to Lillian."

"Destroyed?" Curling chuckled. "How do you intend to destroy me?"

Sebastian decided he had better take charge again. He had known it would be difficult to rein in Jeremy's hotheaded nature. "Curling, there is no sense dragging this out. Suffice it to say that I believe you killed Ringcross and Oxenham."

"You cannot know that for certain."

"You are the only one who had a motive," Sebastian countered softly.

"Your cousin had a motive," Curling retorted. "Avenging his tavern wench."

"No, he did not, because he did not know about what The Princes of Virtue had done to Lillian until I told him."

Curling's nostrils flared. "How can you be sure of that?"

"Let's just say I am trusting my instincts." Sebastian rested one hand negligently on his boot. "Not that it matters. If I thought Jeremy had killed Ringcross and Oxenham to avenge Lillian, I would not concern myself with the business."

"We're talking about murder," Curling said swiftly.

"So? They deserved to be murdered. If Jeremy had been responsible, my main concern would be to see that he did not leave any evidence around the next time."

Jeremy flashed him a startled glance.

Rage glittered in Curling's eyes. "Damnation, Angelstone. Are you saying that you would protect a Fleetwood from the authorities even if he was guilty of murder?"

"I prefer not to make sweeping statements," Sebastian said. "I can assure you, however, that I am not going to turn my cousin over to Bow Street because of these particular murders."

"I cannot believe you would shield a Fleetwood," Curling rasped. "Everyone knows you hate the lot of them."

"I will admit I am not overly fond of certain members of my family. But I do not despise them nearly as much as I despise men who kidnap and rape helpless young women."

Curling slammed his hand down on a table with such force that the vase on top trembled. "She was a tavern wench. Why in the name of hell do you keep bringing her into this?"

"You don't seem to understand," Sebastian said. "Lillian is all that matters in this."

"I don't believe it," Curling snarled.

Jeremy's hands clenched into fists. "I will have justice for her."

Sebastian realized he was beginning to develop some grudging respect for Jeremy.

"Goddamn it, you can prove nothing, Angelstone." Curling finished the brandy and flung the glass aside. "Absolutely nothing."

Sebastian twisted his mouth into another humorless smile. "We do not have to prove anything. You have admitted you bought Lillian from her uncle. You have admitted that you raped her, That is enough."

"Enough for what?" Curling asked derisively. "No court

would convict me of rape. It all happened three years ago and she was nothing but a whore."

"It is enough for me to insist that you leave London this afternoon. You have another two days to make arrangements to leave England. You are not to return."

Curling stared at him, stunned. "You are as mad as Bloomfield. Why should I leave England?"

Sebastian met his eyes. "Because if you do not I shall take it upon myself to inform your creditors that the company you have formed with the other Princes of Virtue is insolvent and that the shares are worthless."

"But it's not insolvent. The shares are not worthless, damn you, they're worth a bloody fortune."

"They will be worth less than the paper on which they are written by the time I'm finished," Sebastian said. "I have the power and the connections to do it. We both know it."

Curling shook his head, dazed. "This makes no sense. I don't understand any of it. You're trying to banish me from the country because I once tumbled a tavern wench?"

"I believe that at long last, you're beginning to grasp the situation." Sebastian got to his feet. "If you will excuse us, my cousin and I must be on our way."

Jeremy leaped to his feet. He faced Curling. "Make no mistake, Curling. If you do not leave London today, I shall challenge you to a duel. Angelstone has agreed to act as one of my seconds."

Curling's eyes instantly narrowed in fresh speculation. He looked at Sebastian. "Ah, now this makes a bit more sense. It would no doubt amuse you no end if I were to kill a Fleetwood for you, would it not, Angelstone? Is that the little drama you are trying to stage?"

"On the contrary, I would find it extremely tiresome if you managed to put a bullet into my cousin." Sebastian walked toward the door. "Because I would then be obliged to issue a challenge to you."

"Goddamn you, Angelstone. Why in hell would you

challenge me in order to avenge a Fleetwood?" Curling shouted.

"I'm not precisely certain why," Sebastian admitted. "Something to do with my responsibilities to the family or some such nonsense. I expect my wife could explain it."

Nineteen

Sebastian *got home shortly* before dawn. He heard the distant clatter of pans from the kitchens as he went up the stairs. Even as the day was ending for the high-ranking members of the *ton*, it was just beginning for their servants.

He slowly untied his cravat as he walked down the hall to his bedchamber. He could feel the familiar tension deep inside. This was the hour he hated the most. It was the time when the new day did battle with the night and neither light nor darkness promised hope.

It seemed to Sebastian that he was most aware of the cold place deep inside himself at this hour. The feeling of being forever trapped in an icy gray fog always seemed strongest at dawn.

But it wasn't quite as bad as it had been in the past, he realized. He knew it was because he had Prudence waiting for him. After dawn he would be able to lose himself in her warmth. How had he survived all these years without her?

He opened the door of his bedchamber and saw that the room was not empty. Prudence was asleep in his bed instead of her own. Lucifer was curled up beside her. The cat opened his golden eyes and stared unblinkingly at Sebastian.

Sebastian walked over to the bed and stood looking down at Prudence for a moment. Her hair was loose and her night rail had slipped down over one shoulder. She looked soft and warm and forever innocent. Because of her he was no longer completely alone.

He turned away from the bed and went across the room to the small table that held the brandy decanter. He poured himself a glass and sat down in front of the window to wait for the dawn.

Lucifer appeared beside the chair. He leaped effortlessly onto Sebastian's thigh and settled down to watch the silent conflict through the window.

Sebastian stroked the cat and took a sip of brandy.

"Sebastian?"

"I'm home, Prue."

He heard her get out of bed and cross the room to stand behind him. She put her hand on his shoulder.

"Is everything all right?" she asked softly. "Did your meeting with Curling go as you had planned?"

"Yes." Sebastian stopped stroking Lucifer and reached up to clasp her hand. "I believe that he will leave England very soon."

Prudence squeezed his fingers gently. "I knew you would take care of matters, my lord."

"Did you?"

"Yes. You are a fine man, Sebastian. I am very proud to be your wife."

The simple words touched him deep inside, melting more of the ice. "I did it for you, Prue."

"I believe you would have done what you did for Jeremy, even if you had never met me."

He did not want to argue with her, so he said nothing. He took another sip of brandy.

Prudence was silent for a moment. "Do you think you will ever be able to sleep at this hour?"

"Never. I hate the dawn. No matter how bright the day, the cold fog is still out there, waiting."

"It is waiting for everyone, Sebastian. The secret is not to try to face it alone."

He tightened his grip on her hand. Together they watched the light wrestle with the darkness. After a time Sebastian saw that the fog had turned a much paler shade of gray. The morning had arrived.

Sebastian put Lucifer on the floor. Then he rose from the chair, picked Prudence up in his arms, and carried her to the bed. He drew her close, savoring her welcoming warmth.

The news of Curling's departure from London did not cause so much as a ripple of interest among the guests at the Brandon soiree that evening. Prudence remarked upon that fact to Sebastian as they stood together near the window.

Sebastian smiled. "There is no reason anyone else should be particularly concerned with the fact that Curling has left Town suddenly. There is nothing unusual about it."

"Will they show an interest when they hear that he has left the country?"

"Yes," Sebastian said with cool satisfaction. "That will no doubt draw attention." He glanced across the room. "I see Lady Pembroke has arrived."

Prudence lifted her dangling glass to her eyes and spotted Hester. "Yes, so she has." She waved her fan enthusiastically at her friend. "I wonder if she has lined up any new clients for me. Now that your investigation is finished, it is time I turned up an interesting project for us."

"I can do with some peace and quiet for a while." Sebastian narrowed his gaze. "Damnation. Here comes Jeremy."

"Where? This silly glass is such a nuisance." Prudence held the fashionable glass up to her eyes again and peered through it. Jeremy was making his way toward them through the throng. He looked eager to reach Sebastian's side. "I do believe you have become something of a hero in your cousin's eyes, my lord, just as you have in Trevor's."

"I can think of other, far more interesting ways in which to amuse myself than playing hero to young men." Sebastian downed the champagne in his glass as Jeremy arrived.

"'Evening, Lady Angelstone." Jeremy bowed gracefully over Prudence's hand.

"Good evening, Jeremy." Prudence smiled at him.

Jeremy gave Sebastian a man-to-man look. "Expect you've heard that Curling left Town this afternoon."

"I heard."

"He'll no doubt be on his way to the Continent before long." Jeremy snatched a glass of champagne off a passing tray. "I suppose that I should be content with seeing him forced out of the country, but I still think the man should be made to pay more dearly for what he did."

"Believe me, Curling will find it hell to be banished from England," Sebastian said. "Especially when he realizes that his newfound fortune will evaporate very quickly."

Prudence looked at him in surprise. "Why will it evaporate? I thought you allowed him to keep the investment company intact on condition that he left the country."

"I did." Sebastian smiled his coldest smile. "For all the good it will do him. When word gets about that he has left England and that the only other principal in the firm is mad Bloomfield, the value of the shares will fall swiftly. Within a few months they will be worthless. The company will be forced into bankruptcy."

Jeremy stared at him. "I had not realized that, sir. You mean Curling will not be able to hold on to his fortune?"

"Not for long. The rumors that Bloomfield is in charge will surely destroy the confidence of the creditors."

"Excellent." Jeremy smiled with satisfaction. "So that is what you meant by destroying him. Very clever, if I may say so, Angelstone."

Prudence grinned proudly. "Angelstone is a very clever man."

Sebastian quirked a brow at her. "Thank you, my dear."

Jeremy frowned. "I wonder if Curling is aware of his ultimate fate."

"I imagine he will comprehend the extent of his punishment soon enough," Sebastian said. "His bankers will no doubt keep him informed of his falling fortunes."

Jeremy looked at him in alarm. "Do you think he will attempt to return to England, then?"

"To face a host of furious creditors and the distinct possibility of being thrown into debtors' prison?" Sebastian asked. "I sincerely doubt it. But if he does, we will deal with the problem."

"So it's finished."

"I believe so," Sebastian said.

Prudence chuckled. "I do hope the two of you are aware of the stares you are drawing."

Jeremy grinned. "I know. People are not accustomed to seeing Angelstone chatting in a friendly manner with the members of his family. Oh, by the by, that reminds me, sir. I told Mama that you saved me from being arrested for murder."

Sebastian choked on a mouthful of champagne. "Bloody hell. I trust you did not tell her the entire tale."

"Of course not," Jeremy said seriously. "I knew she would have fits if I told her everything. I explained that everyone knew about the feud between you and the rest of us and that a murderer had attempted to capitalize on that information in order to cover his own tracks."

"What else did you tell her?" Sebastian asked ominously.

"Only that you had used your power to make certain Bow Street would take no interest in me."

"Hmm."

Prudence saw the blurry outline of a familiar figure forging through the crowd. She raised her glass to her eye again. "Speaking of Mrs. Fleetwood, here she comes now."

"Good lord," Sebastian said. "Am I going to be obliged to spend the entire evening in the company of my relatives?"

"I'm certain Mama only wishes to apologize to you, sir," Jeremy assured him.

"No doubt that is exactly what she intends." Prudence fixed Sebastian with a warning look. "The least you can do is be gracious, Angelstone."

Sebastian smiled grimly. "If Aunt Drucilla actually undertakes an apology, I will eat my cravat."

Drucilla came to a halt in front of Sebastian. "There you are, Angelstone."

"Yes, madam, here I am. What of it?"

"Behave yourself," Prudence hissed under her breath.

Drucilla ignored the byplay. She glowered at Sebastian. "My son tells me that you have done your duty by the family regarding a certain matter that might have become potentially embarrassing."

A familiar unholy amusement sprang to life in Sebastian's eyes. "You may rest assured, madam, that Jeremy is in no immediate danger of hanging."

"I should hope not. He's a Fleetwood, after all. No Fleetwood has been hung since Cromwell." Drucilla snapped her fan closed in a crisp, elegant gesture. "Jeremy also tells me that you were not the one who was attempting to implicate him in the deaths of those two men."

"Jeremy explained that to you?" Sebastian asked.

"Yes, he did."

"And you believed him, madam?"

Prudence drove her elbow into his ribs and smiled at Drucilla. "Angelstone is teasing you, madam. As you know, he has a very unusual sense of humor."

"Ouch." Sebastian gingerly fingered his ribs. "I am not laughing now, madam," he said through his teeth.

Drucilla gave Prudence a quelling glance. "Really, my

dear, that sort of foolish play is hardly suitable to the ball-room."

"I wasn't playing," Prudence murmured. She was aware that more and more heads were starting to turn.

Prudence could feel the anticipation rise like a surging wave all around her. She could also feel Sebastian readying his next taunting remark to his aunt. She prayed for deliverance and it arrived in the shape of Hester.

Having apparently decided, along with everyone else in the room, that social disaster was looming, Hester made a bold bid to forestall it. She gave Prudence an anxious glance and then turned to Drucilla with an affected start of surprise.

"Oh, hello, Drucilla," Hester said. "Didn't see you standing there. How are you this evening?"

"I am fine, thank you, Hester. I was just about to speak to Prudence about her gown."

"Lovely, isn't it?" Hester said, delighted with what seemed to be a safe topic. "That particular shade of lavender is all the rage at the moment, you know."

"It makes her look like a washed-out dishrag," Drucilla said. "And all those ruffles are perfectly ridiculous on her." She frowned at Prudence. "I see you have not yet found a new modiste."

Prudence felt herself start to turn pink. She glanced helplessly at Sebastian, but he showed no signs of offering assistance. "No, madam, I have not had time. But I intend to do so at the earliest opportunity."

"There is no help for it, I shall have to introduce you to mine," Drucilla said grandly. "I do believe she might be able to do something with you. You have possibilities."

Prudence's heart sank. She was acutely aware of the gleam in Sebastian's eyes. She managed a polite smile. "That is very kind of you, madam."

"Someone's got to take you in hand. You are the Countess of Angelstone, after all. It seems I shall have to take it upon myself to educate you. Certain things are expected from the wife of the head of the family."

"Yes, of course," Prudence said weakly.

"I shall arrange to go shopping with you at the earliest opportunity." Drucilla turned on her heel and sailed off through the crowd.

Hester fluttered her fan with an air of excitement. "Dear me, Prudence, she may have a point. Now that I consider the matter, I'm not at all certain lavender and violet are particularly flattering on you."

"You're the one who chose these colors," Prudence said, thoroughly disgruntled.

"Yes, I know, and they are extremely fashionable. Nevertheless, I feel we should bow to Drucilla's expertise." Hester examined Sebastian's austerely elegant black and white attire. Then she glanced at Jeremy, who was equally striking. "The Fleetwoods do have a certain natural instinct for style. You may as well take advantage of it."

Sebastian smiled blandly at Prudence. "Quite right, my dear. Put yourself in my aunt's hands and do not concern yourself with the cost. No price is too high to pay to see how you fare on a shopping expedition with her."

Prudence scowled at him. He knew very well she was already dreading the experience. "Don't you dare laugh at me, Angelstone, or I shall do something drastic, I swear I will."

"You must forgive me, my dear." Sebastian's eyes held the devil's own mirth. "But it would appear that a whole new world of entertainment is about to open up for me."

"Really, Sebastian."

"You were the one who wanted peace in the family, madam wife. Well, you've got your fondest wish. It will be vastly amusing to see you deal with the old witch. I beg your pardon, I mean with Aunt Drucilla."

Jeremy grimaced. "Mama means well, Lady Angelstone.

But I fear she has a very strong notion of family responsibility."

"I'm sure she does," Prudence said dolefully.

"As do you, my dear," Sebastian said smoothly. "The two of you should get along famously." He started to laugh.

Prudence glared at him. Sebastian merely laughed harder. He did not even have the decency to stop when everyone in the room turned to stare.

Prudence looked pointedly at Jeremy. "Would you mind very much dancing with me, Jeremy? If I remain here with Angelstone I shall no doubt disgrace myself by kicking him in the shin."

Sebastian gave another shout of laughter.

Jeremy glanced curiously at Sebastian. Then he grinned and held out his arm to Prudence. "It will be my pleasure, madam."

"Thank you."

It was only after she had taken the floor with him that Prudence realized she had inadvertently given the *ton* something else at which to marvel. Every eye in the room was now on her.

"People are staring at us."

"Can you blame them?" Jeremy chuckled as he swung her into a waltz. "The Fallen Angel's lady is dancing with a member of the Fleetwood clan. Furthermore, there is no indication that the devil is about to unleash his wrath against me in retaliation. He is too busy laughing his head off at a joke no one else can comprehend."

"They will think Angelstone has lost his wits," Prudence said. "And they may be correct."

"It will be all over Town by morning that the Fleetwood feud is finished," Jeremy mused.

"I suppose being taken in hand by your mother is not too high a price to pay for ending the feud," Prudence said, trying to be optimistic.

"Don't be too certain of that."

* * *

Prudence was still grumbling about the forthcoming shopping trip an hour later when Sebastian escorted her out into the cold, foggy night.

"It is most annoying, Sebastian. Back home no one ever remarked upon my clothes. Here in Town I do not seem to be able to please anyone. And what am I to do with the wardrobe I ordered when Hester took me in hand, I ask you?"

"Give it away, I suppose." Sebastian signaled for his carriage. The Angelstone coach was nowhere to be seen amid the crowd of vehicles that filled the street in front of the large house.

"To whom?"

Sebastian's mouth tilted. "To someone who looks good in shades of violet and lavender." He took her arm and started impatiently down the steps. "Come along. It will take another twenty minutes for the carriage to make its way through this press. We may as well walk to it."

"Very well. I certainly don't care to stand out here for long. It's quite chilly tonight." At least she had worn a cloak this evening, Prudence thought. Sebastian had insisted upon it.

It was difficult to tell one coach from another in the heavy fog. The black Angelstone carriage was waiting at the end of a long line of vehicles. A footman in the familiar black and gold Angelstone livery appeared to open the door for Prudence.

Something about him seemed different. She glanced up and realized she did not recognize him. Before she could raise her glass to her eyes for a closer look, she heard Sebastian swear softly.

"Who the devil—"

A soft, sickening thud cut off his words. Sebastian groaned. Prudence whirled around as she felt him release her arm.

"*Sebastian.*" Instinctively she reached out to him as he crumpled to the pavement. But he was too heavy for her. She went down on her knees beside him. "Dear God, Sebastian, what's wrong?"

A man loomed up out of the fog. His face was a blur, but Prudence had no difficulty seeing the large blunt object in his hand.

"Don't you worry yerself none, ma'am. He'll be all right. I knows me job. Get on with ye, now. Into the coach. I'll put his nibs in there with ye."

Prudence rose swiftly, her mouth already open to scream for help. A rude male hand was instantly clamped across her lips, silencing her.

"Shut yer bloody mouth, yer ladyship," the strange footman hissed in her ear.

Prudence started to struggle. She kicked out wildly, but her movements were severely hampered by the heavy folds of her cloak. The other villain grabbed her ankles. She realized there were three men in all, including the coachman.

"Behave yerself or it'll be the worse for yer man," the false footman muttered. "We're in a hurry, ye know. Ain't got all night. Me and me two mates promised to deliver ye on time. Don't get paid unless we do."

Prudence glanced desperately up at the box as she was bundled into the carriage.

"Get 'em inside," the man on the box said in a voice that definitely did not belong to Sebastian's regular coachman. "We ain't got all night."

Prudence's captors tossed her onto the floor of the carriage. There was a small, sharp crack that she recognized at once as the sound of her dangling eyeglass shattering beneath her cloak.

She floundered about, trapped in the folds of the garment.

"No sense wearin' yerself out," one of the men said

gruffly. He reached into the carriage and hoisted Prudence onto one of the seats. "Best save yer energy. Expect me client's got plans for a pretty little thing like you."

The man wearing the Angelstone livery stuffed Sebastian's limp body into the vehicle. Sebastian sprawled facedown on the floor. He did not move.

Prudence gazed at him in horror, trying desperately to see if there was blood on his head or if his eyes were open. It was impossible to tell. Even if she had been able to get to her spectacles in her reticule, she knew she would not have been able to see how badly Sebastian was injured. The interior of the carriage was very dark.

The villain in the Angelstone livery jumped into the carriage and sat down across from Prudence. There was just enough light for Prudence to see the pistol in his hand.

"Well, now, reckon you and me will have to find somethin' to talk about for the next hour or so, ma'am. Yer man ain't goin' to be in the mood fer conversation for a while." He nudged Sebastian's still body with the toe of his boot.

"Don't touch him," Prudence said.

"Don't worry, he'll be in reasonably good shape when I deliver him to Curling Castle. That was the deal I made with his lordship, y'see. Both packages to be delivered in good shape."

Prudence could hardly breathe. "You're taking us to Curling Castle?"

"That's where we're headed, right enough. This damn bloody fog will slow us down somewhat but not much. Jack up there on the box is real good with the reins. I reckon we'll get there in no time."

The black chamber was every bit as cold as Prudence had remembered. The dark, heavy chill seemed to have a life of its own. It emanated from the stones themselves, not from the night air outside the castle walls. Like the fog, it shrouded everything in the room.

Prudence turned her head. The men who had brought her and Sebastian here a few minutes ago had left a single candle burning on the table. The flame was of little use against the oppressive shadows that filled the chamber.

She lay very still on the bed, listening to the sound of retreating boots in the hall. A small sense of relief washed over her. The kidnappers had departed.

She sat up stiffly. Her hands and feet were still bound, but at least the villains had not gagged her. Not that she intended to start screaming now, she thought. The last thing she wanted to do was summon one of her captors.

Chains clanked against stone.

Prudence raised her head swiftly and peered into the shadows. "Sebastian? Are you awake?"

"Bloody hell."

The surly sound of his voice revived her spirits as nothing else could have done. "They put you in those awful manacles on the wall."

"I noticed." Chains scraped lightly on stone again, as if Sebastian was quietly testing them. "Are you all right?"

"Yes." Prudence managed to sit up on the edge of the bed. "What about you?"

"I feel as if I've gone a hundred rounds with Witt himself, but other than that I seem to be in one piece."

"You've been unconscious for a very long time. I was terribly worried about you."

"I wasn't unconscious, just dazed." Sebastian sounded coldly furious now. "I couldn't seem to move for a while, at least not quickly enough to take that pistol away from the man in the carriage. I decided to bide my time."

"We're at Curling Castle," Prudence offered.

"Believe it or not, I figured that out all by myself."

Prudence frowned. "There's no need to get sarcastic. I was just trying to help you orient yourself."

"I beg your pardon, madam. I am not in the best of moods." Chains rattled again. "Damnation."

"What's wrong?" Prudence asked.

"What isn't wrong? This entire investigation has been wrong right from the beginning. Bloody hell."

"I mean what's wrong right now?" Prudence said patiently. "Why are you swearing?"

"Because I can't get quite the right angle on the locks of these manacles. I need to be a few inches higher."

Prudence brightened. "You're trying to pick the locks?"

"Yes." Chains rattled softly. "Damn it to hell."

"Is there anything I can do?"

"See if that chamber pot I saw under the bed last time is still there," Sebastian said.

"A chamber pot? Don't you think you can restrain yourself for a little while? We're in something of a hurry here, Sebastian."

"I need the damned pot to stand on so that I can get the wire into these locks," Sebastian said through his teeth. "If you find it, try to kick it over here."

"Oh. Yes, of course."

Chagrined, Prudence scooted off the bed. Unable to use her bound hands or legs to control her descent, she landed with a thud on her knees. "Ow."

"Hurry."

She bent down and looked beneath the bed. The fuzzy outline of the chamber pot was just barely visible in the deep shadows. "It's there."

"Get it over here," Sebastian ordered.

That was going to be easier said than done, Prudence thought. But there was no point complaining about the difficulty of the task. She had the uneasy feeling that their lives might very well depend on her getting the chamber pot out from under the bed.

She lay on her side and wriggled partway under the iron bed. It took three attempts before she successfully hooked her bound ankles around the pot.

"Got it," she whispered.

"Push it over here."

"I'm trying."

Prudence tried three different positions before she finally rolled onto her back and used her feet to guide the pot.

"I feel like a worm." She inched the pot along the cold stone floor.

The process seemed to take forever. She was perspiring in spite of the terrible chill. She heard her delicate silk skirts shredding against the stone.

"A little closer, Prue," Sebastian said softly. "You're almost here."

She wriggled forward and pushed the pot ahead a few more inches.

"I have it," Sebastian said with soft triumph. He caught the chamber pot with the toe of his boot and dragged it closer.

Prudence sat up and watched as Sebastian stood on the overturned pot. She squinted, trying to see what he was doing.

"That's it, love," Sebastian crooned softly. "Give me what I want. Open for me, sweet. Let me inside. All the way inside." There was a small snick of sound. "Yes. Ah, yes. Beautiful."

"Did you get it open?" Prudence asked.

"One of them. One more to go."

The second lock went much faster. Sebastian was free a moment later.

He stepped down from the pot and went to work on the ropes that bound Prudence's hands and feet. She realized she could feel nothing at all in her upper arms.

Then the feeling began to come back.

Prudence bit back a scream as a painful tingling sensation swept through her arms. She stuffed a handful of the cloak into her mouth and bit down hard.

"Christ. I should have realized." Sebastian began to rub her arms swiftly. "Hold on, Prue. You'll be all right in a minute. Can you feel my hands?"

She nodded, not yet daring to spit the fabric out of her mouth. She was still hovering on the edge of a scream.

"Good." Sebastian sounded relieved. "That means they didn't bind you too tightly. You'll be fine."

Prudence was not so certain of that. But after a short while she was no longer afraid she would cry out if she moved her arms. She let Sebastian pull her to her feet.

"My God," she whispered.

"We've got to get out of here," Sebastian said. "We can't wait any longer."

"I know." Prudence took a deep breath. She looked down at the broken lens of her glass dangling on the end of the fashionable velvet ribbon. It was useless. Her tiny beaded reticule was still attached to her wrist, however. She opened it and discovered her spectacles safe inside. The wire frames were bent, but the glass was undamaged. She pushed them quickly into place on her nose.

"I'm ready," she announced.

"You are an amazing female, my dear." Sebastian grabbed her hand and hauled her toward the door.

Prudence heard the footsteps in the hall at the same instant that Sebastian heard them.

"Hell and damnation." He stopped. "Is nothing going to go right tonight?"

Prudence felt his fingers tighten again around her wrist. He jerked her over to the wall on the far side of the door.

"Don't move," he whispered.

She pressed herself against the stones. Sebastian strode swiftly across the room and scooped up the chamber pot. Then he flattened himself to the wall alongside her.

The door opened. A man with his hands tied behind his back stumbled into the chamber. He was given a push from behind that sent him reeling. He lost his footing and fell.

The candlelight flickered on Garrick Sutton's face. His eyes met Prudence's in the shadows.

Before she could react, one of the men who had kidnapped her and Sebastian stepped into the room. He was holding his pistol in one hand.

"Well, now, that's that, then," he announced in tones of satisfaction. "A job well done, if I may say so."

Then his gaze fell on the empty bed. Prudence saw his eyes start to widen as he glanced at the dangling manacles. "What's this? They've escaped."

He opened his mouth to yell for assistance.

Sebastian took one step away from the wall and brought the chamber pot crashing down on the villain's head. The pistol fell and skittered under the bed.

The man sank to the floor with no more than a groan. He did not move.

Sebastian looked down at Garrick. "This certainly complicates matters."

"Sorry about this," Garrick said ruefully. "They were waiting for me when I left my club."

"Untie him," Sebastian said to Prudence. "I'll get the pistol. At the rate we're going, we shall undoubtedly need it."

But before Prudence could move, the door of the massive black wardrobe swung wide. Lord Curling stood there, a pistol in his hand. Behind him yawned the black opening of a hidden staircase. Prudence belatedly recalled the false back Sebastian had discovered in the wardrobe. Now she knew what had been concealed behind it.

"Pray do not move so much as an inch, Angelstone." Curling stepped down from the wardrobe. "Or I shall put a bullet into your lady."

Sebastian froze. "This has gone far enough, Curling."

"Not quite." Curling beckoned to Prudence. "Come here, my dear."

Prudence did not move.

Curling's eyes narrowed. "I said, come here. If you do

not, I may change my mind and put the first bullet into your precious Fallen Angel."

Prudence walked forward reluctantly. As soon as she was within reach, Curling put an arm around her throat and pulled her against him to use as a shield.

"There, now," Curling said. "This is much better."

Twenty

*S*ebastian *fought for his* self-control. The urge to throw himself at Curling in a mindless rage was almost overpowering. The sight of Prudence being held hostage sent a shock of wild anguish through him. He knew such ungoverned emotion would be lethal if he did not master it.

"What do you hope to accomplish, Curling?" Sebastian forced himself to use the bored tone of voice he had perfected so well.

Curling's smile was thin with menace. "You know what I intend to accomplish. Did you really think I would allow you to banish me from England and destroy my fortune?"

"Your fortune?"

"Do not pretend ignorance. You know very well what I'm talking about." Curling's arm tightened around Prudence's throat. "I'm not a fool. I know what will happen to my business affairs if I leave England. The investors will assume that madman, Bloomfield, is in charge. There will be panic. The company will go bankrupt in no time if I am not here to take command."

Sebastian shrugged. "A possibility, I suppose."

"Goddamn it to hell. You know that is exactly what you intended," Curling snarled. "Did you really think I'd let you get away with it? I had everything carefully planned and I am not about to let you ruin those plans."

Garrick stirred on the floor. "This is all my fault, isn't it?"

Curling did not bother to glance at him. He kept his gaze on Sebastian. "You can take some of the credit, if you like. I needed information on Angelstone, you see. Everyone talked about how much he hated the rest of the Fleetwoods, but I was not so certain how deep his hatred went."

"You mean you didn't know if I would use my position to protect my cousin if he were implicated in murder?" Sebastian asked.

"Precisely," Curling said. "I could never figure out why, if you hated your relatives so much, you had not already used your power to crush them."

"You did not comprehend," Prudence said in her most admonishing tones, "because you knew that if you had been in Angelstone's position, you would have long since crushed the family."

"Exactly." Curling's eyes were still on Sebastian. "I needed to know more about Angelstone's motives and how he would react if I proceeded to use Jeremy Fleetwood in my scheme."

"So you got me drunk and pried the information out of me," Garrick said in a tone of savage self-disgust.

"It was an easy enough task," Curling said. "And extremely rewarding. You assured me that Angelstone would be quite happy to see any one of his relatives rot and that he would probably find it vastly amusing to see one actually taken up for murder. Then you let slip a most fascinating tidbit."

Garrick swore in despair. "I told you about his hobby, didn't I?"

"Yes, you did." Curling smiled slowly. "You told me all about Angelstone's very interesting little hobby, including the name of his Bow Street contact."

"Damnation." Garrick glanced at Sebastian. "I don't remember any of it, Angelstone. I swear to God, I don't. I was drinking so heavily in those days. There's so much I cannot recall from that time."

"I know." Sebastian did not take his attention off Curling. "It makes no matter now."

"I altered my plans accordingly," Curling said. "I decided it would be ideal to have Angelstone actually conduct the investigation. He would be certain to recognize the evidence I intended to use to implicate his cousin."

"An interesting precaution," Sebastian said softly. "Bow Street might have overlooked the items found at the scenes of the crimes, or failed to properly identify them. I assume you were also the one responsible for leaving the message in my carriage the night of Oxenham's death?"

"Of course." Curling frowned. "I wanted you to be the first on the scene so that you could find the evidence against your cousin. I needed young Fleetwood rather badly, you know."

"Because you knew you could not murder your three partners and assume complete control of the company without drawing attention to yourself as a suspect," Sebastian said. "One death, perhaps even two, might have been accepted as accidents. But three deaths would have been hard to explain, especially when you so clearly profited from them. You needed to be able to produce someone else who had a motive to kill those three men."

"Your cousin was perfect," Curling said. "He had a motive which only I knew about but which he would be unable to deny in a court of law. I had planned to reveal everything about Lillian's death, you see. After all, I had nothing to hide. The stupid wench jumped out of a window while I and my friends were having a bit of sport with her."

"You would have testified that my cousin, who was in love with her, discovered the facts surrounding her death years later, blamed The Princes of Virtue, and set out for revenge," Sebastian said.

"Precisely." Curling shrugged. "It would have appeared that I was fated to be his last victim, but fortunately he was caught in time."

"And just to make certain he would look guilty, you provided evidence at the scenes of the murders that incriminated him," Prudence concluded, scorn dripping from her words. "Lord Curling, you were very stupid, indeed. You actually thought you could use Angelstone to help you carry out your scheme?"

"It seemed a reasonable assumption."

"Hah." Prudence gave a disdainful sniff. "You know nothing about my husband."

Curling's jaw tightened. "From what I was told and from the gossip that has always followed him, I assumed Angelstone would be only too happy to use the evidence against his cousin."

Prudence's eyebrows came together in a fierce line above her spectacles. "You were much mistaken in my husband's character, weren't you?"

Sebastian saw Curling's arm tighten a little around Prudence's throat. "Uh, Prue—"

"Angelstone knew his duty to his family and he did it," Prudence continued, undaunted.

"Silence," Curling ordered. "You are beginning to annoy me, Lady Angelstone." He used his grip on her throat to give her a warning squeeze.

Sebastian winced.

"You were wrong about Angelstone," Prudence squeaked. "Everyone was wrong about Angelstone."

Sebastian started to worry that Curling would lose his temper and casually choke Prudence to death. "That's enough, Prue."

She blinked at him. Something she saw in his face made her fall silent.

Sebastian arched a brow. "I have been curious about one thing, Curling. How did you come to find out that my cousin cared for Lillian?"

"I have known from the beginning." Curling chuckled. "Lillian's uncle told me that the Fleetwood boy fancied himself in love with the girl. But the old man was pragmatic. He knew damn well the Fleetwoods would never allow the precious heir to marry a tavern wench, so he sold her to me instead."

"What did you do after the girl died?" Sebastian asked.

Curling shrugged. "I told her uncle that she had drowned and compensated him for his loss, of course. I gave him enough money to ensure that he would keep any questions he might have had to himself."

Sebastian folded his arms and leaned against the iron bedpost. "You won't be able to get rid of the three of us tonight without raising a few questions."

"On the contrary," Curling said softly. "This will all work out very nicely, I think. I shall tell everyone that during the course of a small weekend house party here you discovered your new bride in the arms of your best friend."

"How dare you," Prudence gasped, outraged. "I would never betray Angelstone."

"I believe I understand, Curling," Sebastian said coolly.

"It's simple enough." Curling looked amused. "You will use a pistol on both your wife and your best friend. When I arrive, pistol in hand, to see what is happening, you come at me. I am forced to shoot you dead in order to save my own life. A suitable ending for the Fallen Angel."

"It will never work," Garrick said quickly.

"It will work." Curling leveled the pistol at Sebastian. "Now, then, I am afraid you must be the first to die, Angelstone, because you are the most dangerous. Sutton will go next."

Sebastian readied himself. He would have to launch himself straight at Curling and hope that the first shot went slightly wide. If his luck held, the bullet would not bring him down immediately. All he needed to do, Sebastian thought, was stay on his feet long enough to reach Curling.

"Bastard," Prudence yelped. She clutched the remains of her shattered eyeglass. "Don't you dare shoot Sebastian."

Curling smiled. "You might be interested to know that I shall delay your passing until dawn, Lady Angelstone. You see, I have been very curious to know just what sort of female could keep the Fallen Angel amused in bed. Tonight I shall find out."

Sebastian saw Prudence raise her hand upward toward the arm that Curling had wrapped around her throat. He realized what she intended to do.

Prudence raked Curling's arm with the jagged bits of glass that had once been her fashionable eyeglass.

Curling yelled. He instinctively released his grip on Prudence and grabbed at his arm. Blood spurted between his fingers. "*You little bitch.*"

Prudence darted out of reach.

Curling swung back to confront Sebastian, but it was too late.

Sebastian was already moving.

Curling tried to bring the pistol back in line, but there was no chance. Sebastian lashed out with his foot and knocked the weapon from Curling's hand.

He went in quickly. He smashed his fist into Curling's jaw. The blow sent Curling staggering back toward the tower windows. They must have been unlatched, because they banged open under the impact.

Wind howled into the chamber. The candle flared and went out, plunging the room into almost total darkness. The windows shuddered heavily on their hinges.

Sebastian started forward. There was just enough light to discern the outline of Curling's figure as he crouched in front of the window. The wind screamed into the room.

"No," Prudence shouted above the roar of the wind. "Sebastian, wait. Stay away from him."

It was the shattering sense of urgency in her voice that stopped Sebastian. He glanced back over his shoulder. He could just barely see the pale shape of her face. He realized she was staring past him.

Curling screamed. It was a keening, mind-numbing sound of fear.

"My God," Garrick whispered.

Sebastian whirled around. Curling was still screaming.

"Stay away from me," Curling yelled. But he was not talking to Sebastian. He was looking toward the bed, his hands held out in front of him as if he would ward off whatever he saw there. "No, stay away from me. *Stay away from me.*"

Fascinated dread gripped Sebastian. He watched the dark shape that was Curling edge backward in a crablike fashion until he was pressed against the window ledge.

"It's you," Curling gasped. He climbed up onto the windowsill and stood in the opening. "It's you, isn't it? No, don't touch me. I never intended for you to die. Don't you see? You were the one who chose to jump. You didn't have to do it. I only wanted to have some sport. You were just a tavern wench. . . . *Don't touch me.*"

Curling shrieked and recoiled from something only he could see. He toppled backward through the window and fell into the blackness that was waiting for him.

His scream pierced the night for what seemed an endless time.

Then there was silence. Absolute silence. Even the strange wind that had sprung up out of nowhere suddenly ceased. Outside the window the fog resettled itself like a shroud around Curling Castle.

Sebastian realized that no one, including himself, was moving. He took a deep breath and shook off the paralysis that had held him in thrall. He turned and went swiftly across the chamber. He groped for the candle. It took him two tries before he managed to light it.

When the flame finally flickered into life it was strong and steady. Sebastian turned toward Prudence, expecting to see stunned shock in her eyes.

She was standing in the middle of the room, her brows drawn together in a thoughtful expression. She did not look like a woman who had just seen a ghost.

"Does it strike you, Sebastian, that it is not nearly as cold in here now as it was earlier?" she asked.

He stared at her. "Yes," he heard himself say very softly. "It is much warmer in here now."

Garrick struggled to a sitting position and grimaced with pain. He glanced at the man lying on the floor. "There were three of these villains. All hired from the stews for the night. This one sent the other two back to London after they were paid."

Sebastian hefted the pistol. "Then they will not be a problem for us tonight." He went to the window and looked down. The fog swirled, providing a brief glimpse of Curling's boots on the stones below the tower.

"We'll have to rouse the magistrate," Garrick said.

"Who's going to tell him about Lillian's ghost?" Prudence asked.

"I think we'll leave the ghost out of it," Sebastian said. "I, for one, never actually saw her. And neither did either of you."

"No," Garrick said, sounding relieved. "I never saw anything resembling a ghost."

"I'm not so certain of that," Prudence said. A look of speculation appeared in her eyes. "I believe I may have witnessed some significant evidence of spectral phenomena."

"I believe you are mistaken, my dear," Sebastian said. "This is my investigation and I am the one who will discuss it with the magistrate. And I saw no ghost."

Prudence's brows rose. "As you wish, my lord. I cannot

help but notice, however, that the curse Lillian placed on The
Princes of Virtue has come true. All four of them have been
destroyed, one way or another. Even Bloomfield has paid a
price for what he did to her."

Sebastian started to argue and then thought better about
it. There was no denying that for all intents and purposes,
Lillian had been avenged.

It was nearly three in the morning before the explanations had been made to the local magistrate. Mr. Lewell was
a large, bluff man who took his duties seriously. He seemed
deeply awed at finding himself dealing with an earl. He asked
very few questions, which was just as well because Sebastian
had decided to alter a few facts to suit his own purposes.

As he had explained to Prudence and Garrick, there was
no reason to drag Jeremy into the matter at this juncture.
And no way to prove that the deaths of Ringcross and Oxenham had been anything other than what they had appeared, an accident and a suicide.

"So Curling committed suicide." Lewell shook his head
when Sebastian had concluded the tale. "Well, he was an odd
one. There have been rumors of some strange doings up at
the castle from time to time."

"Is that so?" Sebastian said politely.

"Aye. Servant gossip, you know; nevertheless, one wondered. There was a young girl who went missing a few years
ago. Some said that Curling and his friends had . . ." Lewell
let the sentence trail off into thin air. "Well, that's neither
here nor there now. The man is dead."

"Quite dead," Sebastian said.

Lewell nodded sagely. "I regret to tell you that he will not
be missed around these parts."

"Because of the strange doings up at the castle?" Sebastian asked.

"Not exactly," Lewell admitted. "Curling, I fear, was in
the habit of bringing his fancy friends up from London at

every opportunity. Unfortunately for the local shops, he brought his supplies along with him. Claimed he couldn't get good quality in the village. Never spent so much as a penny here."

"I see." Sebastian smiled.

When the interview was over, Garrick opted to spend what remained of the night at a nearby inn. "My head hurts too much to even contemplate a carriage ride. I'll make arrangements to return to Town tomorrow. What about you two?"

Prudence patted away a wide yawn. "I could fall asleep right where I stand."

Sebastian looked at her. He wanted to take her home, where he knew she would be safe. He wanted to put her into his bed, where he could hold her so close that nothing, not even a ghost, could take her away from him. He wanted to protect her, shield her, keep her next to his heart for the rest of his life.

"You can sleep in the carriage on the way home," he said quietly.

"Of course, my lord," she said equably.

It did not take Sebastian long to make the arrangements. Half an hour later he and Prudence set off for London in a hired post chaise.

"I do believe the fog is beginning to lift." Prudence yawned delicately once more and adjusted the carriage rug over her knees. "We should make good time, Sebastian."

Sebastian put his arm around her and drew her against him. He gazed out into the night. "We shall be home by dawn."

"Very likely. It has all been terribly exciting, but I vow I cannot keep my eyes open another minute." Prudence nestled into the curve of his arm.

"Prue?"

"Umm?" Her voice was thick with impending sleep.

"I wish I could have introduced you to my parents. They would have liked you very much."

"I wish you could have met mine," she whispered. "They would have been most pleased to have you for a son-in-law."

Sebastian struggled to find words for what he wanted to say. He probed warily inside himself, testing the deep, hidden place that had been frozen for so long.

The ice was definitely gone, he realized, but he was still uneasy about looking too closely at the place where it had been. It was like trying to peer through the fog outside the carriage. He was not certain what he would discover. The fear of finding nothing at all where the cold had been made him hesitate.

"I did not take very good care of you tonight, Prue," he said finally. "Things will be different in the future."

She did not respond. Sebastian looked down and saw that her lashes were closed. She was sound asleep. He was left to wonder if she had even heard him.

They made excellent time. When the carriage halted in front of the town house, Sebastian lifted Prudence out and carried her straight upstairs. He put her carefully into the bed. She did not awaken when he got in beside her.

Sebastian gathered her close, and for the first time in four years he fell sound asleep before the first gray light of dawn had appeared.

A month later Sebastian pushed aside a journal of accounts that he had been perusing, stretched out his legs, and leaned back in his chair. Lucifer rose from the back of the sofa, bounded onto the desk, and strolled across a pile of papers. He jumped down into Sebastian's lap.

Sebastian glanced at the ormolu clock as he stroked the cat. "She'll be home any minute now and we shall see what my aunt has done to her."

Lucifer curled his tail around himself and rumbled in response.

"I hope my poor Prudence has survived the experience." Sebastian smiled. "She was certainly dreading it. Put it off as long as she could, you know. But in the end Aunt Drucilla got her."

Lucifer twitched his ears and gave another rumbling purr in response.

A few minutes later the loud commotion in the hall announced Prudence's return from the shopping expedition.

"Ah, here we are." Sebastian watched the door expectantly. "I'll wager my aunt has done her over in emerald greens and deep yellows."

The library door opened abruptly and Prudence rushed into the room. She was still wearing the heavily flounced lavender gown she had left in earlier. Her bonnet, a ridiculously oversized concoction decorated with massive lavender flowers, flopped wildly. Behind the lenses of her spectacles, her eyes were alight with excitement.

"Sebastian, you will never guess what has happened."

Sebastian dumped Lucifer on the floor and rose to greet his wife. "Please be seated, my dear. I am curious to hear all the details of your shopping trip."

"My shopping trip?" She gave him a puzzled look as she perched on a chair.

"Perhaps you will recall it if you try very hard. I believe you left a little more than three hours ago in the company of my aunt." Sebastian sat down again. "You were going to be redone from head to toe."

"Oh, yes. The shopping trip." Prudence took off her bonnet and tossed it to one side. "I believe it was quite successful. Your aunt seemed very pleased, at any rate. I hope you like green and yellow because I fear I shall be wearing a great deal of it."

Sebastian smiled.

"But that is not what I wanted to tell you about." Prudence smiled with satisfaction. "I have got us another client, my lord."

Sebastian stopped smiling. "Bloody hell."

"Now, Sebastian, you must not take that attitude. Perhaps I should make it clear that this will be one of my investigations. I shall be looking into a matter involving spectral phenomena. I thought you would enjoy assisting me this time."

Sebastian eyed her warily. "I do not want you taking any risks, madam, and that is final."

"If you are worrying about your heir, you may relax." Prudence patted her still-flat stomach. "I am certain he is made of sturdy stuff. He will take no notice of a ghost or two."

"Now, Prue—"

"Calm yourself, my lord." She smiled serenely. "There will not be any risks at all. This is a matter involving a very old family ghost. Apparently it has been seen of late at the Cranshaws' country house. They would like me to verify whether or not it actually exists."

"And if it does?"

"Why, then, they would like me to find a way to get rid of it. Apparently it is terrifying the staff. The Cranshaws have been forced to hire three new maids and a new cook in the past two months. That sort of turnover among one's staff is very annoying, Mrs. Cranshaw tells me."

Sebastian heard the anticipation in her voice. He saw it sparkling in her eyes. He was also ruefully aware of the familiar sense of controlled excitement bubbling to life deep inside himself. "I suppose there would not be much harm in conducting a small investigation."

"None at all," Prudence agreed cheerfully.

Sebastian got to his feet again and stalked over to the window. "You are quite certain this is merely a matter of spectral phenomena?"

"Absolutely certain."

"There is no question of murder, mayhem, or criminal schemes here?"

"Of course not."

"There is absolutely nothing of a dangerous nature involved?" he persisted.

Prudence chuckled indulgently. "Really, Sebastian. It's perfectly ridiculous to even think that this investigation could involve any dangerous criminal activity. We are talking about a very old ghost."

"Well," Sebastian said cautiously, "I suppose it will be all right for you to look into the matter. I shall, of course, accompany you. It will give me an opportunity to observe your methods."

"Of course."

He smiled. "It might be somewhat amusing."

"I hoped you might find it so, my lord," Prudence said demurely.

She was laughing at him, he thought. The little baggage had known that he would be as intrigued as she was by the opportunity to investigate another interesting puzzle. She knew him too well. Hardly surprising, he reflected. She was, after all, the other half of himself.

Sebastian gazed out into the sunlit garden. "I have only one stipulation to make before I agree to pursue this investigation with you."

"Yes, my lord?"

"I want you to tell me again that you love me," Sebastian said very quietly.

One could have heard a feather drop in the silence that ensued. Sebastian held his breath. He steeled himself and turned slowly around to face Prudence.

She was on her feet, her hands clasped in front of her. Her eyes were very bright and a little wary. "So you did hear me that night."

"I heard you. But I have not heard you say those words again. Have you changed your mind?"

"No, my lord. I have loved you since the moment I met you. I shall love you all the days of my life." She smiled wistfully. "I did not say the words again because I thought perhaps you found them at best merely amusing."

"Knowing that you love me is not a source of amusement." Sebastian realized that his hands were shaking with the force of the emotion that was pouring through him. "It is my salvation."

"Oh, *Sebastian.*" Prudence flew into his arms.

"I love you, Prue." He crushed her close. "Always. Forever."

It was safe, after all, to look into the dark place inside himself that had once been so very cold, Sebastian thought. It was not empty, as he had feared. Love filled the part of him that had been locked in ice for so long.

He held Prudence very close for a long time. Her warmth poured into him, filling him completely.

"There are a few small details about our next investigation that I should perhaps mention," Prudence mumbled at last into his shirt.

"Details?" Sebastian raised his head.

Prudence smiled her most winning smile. "Well, according to my client, there is some question of a diamond necklace that has recently gone missing."

"Diamonds? We're talking about missing diamonds? Now, hold on just one minute, here. It has been my experience that where there is a question of missing jewelry, there is likely to be a question of foul play."

Prudence cleared her throat with a discreet little cough. "Well, apparently there have been one or two indications— small ones, mind you—that someone may have attempted to search the Cranshaws' house."

"Damnation, Prue, I said nothing dangerous this time."

"I'm sure there is nothing in the least bit dangerous about this investigation, my lord. Just some rather intriguing elements that I know will amuse you. I would not wish you to become bored."

Sebastian smiled wryly. "You think you can wrap me around your little finger, don't you, my sweet?"

"Just as you can wrap me around yours." She stood on tiptoe and put her arms about his neck. "I think, my dearest Sebastian, that you and I were meant for each other."

He looked into her glowing eyes and felt the warm fires of love burning inside himself. "There is no question about that."

He threaded his fingers through her hair and covered her mouth with his own. He knew he would never again be cold.

All Orion/Phoenix titles are available at your local bookshop or from the following address:

Littlehampton Book Services
Cash Sales Department L
14 Eldon Way, Lineside Industrial Estate
Littlehampton
West Sussex BN17 7HE

telephone 01903 721596, *facsimile* 01903 730914

Payment can either be made by credit card (Visa and Mastercard accepted) or by sending a cheque or postal order made payable to *Littlehampton Book Services*.
DO NOT SEND CASH OR CURRENCY.

Please add the following to cover postage and packing

UK and BFPO:
£1.50 for the first book, and 50P for each additional book to a maximum of £3.50

Overseas and Eire:
£2.50 for the first book plus £1.00 for the second book and 50p for each additional book ordered

----

BLOCK CAPITALS PLEASE

name of cardholder ....

address of cardholder ....

....

....

....

postcode ....

delivery address
(if different from cardholder)

....

....

....

postcode ....

☐ I enclose my remittance for £.............................

☐ please debit my Mastercard/Visa (delete as appropriate)

card number ☐☐☐☐☐☐☐☐☐☐☐☐☐☐☐☐

expiry date ☐☐☐☐

signature ....

prices and availability are subject to change without notice